REBOUND
MANHATTAN RUTHLESS ,

SADIE KINCAID

RED HOUSE PRESS LTD

CONTENT WARNING

This book deals with mature themes including parental death, fertility issues, and discussion of past sexual assault. It also contains scenes of a sexual nature.

To Mr. Kincaid, for always seeing me, even when I was invisible.

With all my love. x

PROLOGUE

ELIJAH—AGE 28, NEW YEAR'S EVE

I look out the window and watch the fireworks explode over the city. New York at night is always stunning, but the explosion of color flashing over the skyline takes the view up a notch. All the way to awe-inspiring.

I've loved fireworks for as long as I can remember, but tonight they only make me feel sad. They remind me of when we were kids. Of when she was still with us.

This now deathly quiet house was always so full of laughter and music, the happy sound of family and friends celebrating New Year's together. My younger brothers and I would drive our mom crazy, five overexcited miscreants tugging at her party dress, demanding it was time for the fireworks—now, now, now!

Inevitably, she gave in. She loved us too much to say no, and we would end up setting them off before midnight. We'd whoop and holler as they shot up into the night sky, the grown-ups all laughing at our enthusiasm. That's what I'm seeing out there tonight. Every bang and sparkle is being watched by young, excited eyes.

I rub my hand over my jaw and sigh. I need to shave, but I can't be bothered to care. Hell, maybe I'll grow a damn beard and be done with it. I'm only twenty-eight, but tonight I feel like an old man.

Remembering us as kids sucks. Remembering my mom sucks. Remembering being happy sucks. None of those things feel real anymore. She's gone, and we're a mess without her.

We're all back here again tonight, along with our dad. Well, technically together. We're all lost in our own thoughts. Nathan is staring out the window as intensely as I am. I have no idea what's going on in his mind. The same is true for all my brothers. Then again, I don't suppose they can tell from looking at me that my whole world is falling apart.

Dad pours generous measures of his precious fifty-year-old Macallan into tumblers. The sound of the ice clinking and fizzing is way too festive for the current mood. He hands them out to each of us, his face set in grim lines. Maddox, the baby at only sixteen, does a piss-poor impression of being surprised—as though he's never touched alcohol before. I don't know who he thinks he's fooling.

"Does anyone else feel like it's weird that it's just us?" says Mason, breaking the silence. He's right, of course. I see how much it cost him to put it into words, how much it cost all of us to hear them. I am the oldest, and although I have my own troubles, I try to think of a way to lift their spirits. Or at least fill in some goddamn time before this torture is over.

"We could put the TV on," I suggest half-heartedly. "Watch the ball drop?"

"Nah." Drake immediately objects. "She used to hate that, remember? Was always convinced the time was off by a few seconds." He smiles to take the sting out of the comment, but it doesn't reach his eyes. No surprise there—I don't think I've seen a real smile on Drake's face since she died two months ago.

Laughing, Mason grabs onto the memory. "Remember how she'd always insist on using Great-Grandad's old Navy diving watch to determine when it was midnight instead?"

It was one of her little quirks. One of a thousand little details about her that once seemed mundane but now feels precious.

"Where the hell is that thing?" Nathan asks, and Maddox pulls the watch out of his pocket. The tears in his eyes threaten to set me off.

Mason finishes his Scotch and gets up. "Jesus, it feels so weird without her here. Like this house has no fucking soul anymore. Let's get the fuck out of here and go somewhere."

Go somewhere? Like home, back to Amber? The woman I love and have committed my whole life to. The woman who lately feels like she's closing herself off from me more every single day? I should go to her and fix whatever it is that's going wrong. But I can't. Not right now. Not when my dad and my brothers need me. There'll be time to work on my marriage as soon as they're all taken care of. Amber and I promised each other forever.

"Like where, jerkwad?" Ever the careful planner, Drake doesn't bother hiding his disdain at Mason's spontaneous suggestion.

"I dunno. A club or something. A place where there's life."

I try to imagine us all in a club right now. The mighty James brothers, weighed down by their loss, hitting the dance floor. More like hitting the bottle and blacking out in public. Drake's right on this one. It's a terrible idea.

"And what about me, dickface?" Maddox says. He's built like an SUV, but he's still very clearly under twenty-one.

As Mason opens his mouth to issue a retort, most likely a foul-mouthed one, Dad holds up his hand, and we all shut up. Diminished he may be by the loss of the wife he adored, our father is still not a man you mess with. He has the natural authority of a born leader and a rock-solid confidence that is based on a lifetime of achievement. He made his first billion by the time he was thirty-five, and although he is a loving father, he demands just as much respect from his sons as he does at work. When Dalton James has something to say, you'd better listen.

"Nobody is going anywhere," he informs us firmly. "So quit your whining and drink your Scotch."

"Sorry, Pop," Mason says, returning to his seat.

Dad stands in front of the window and downs his Scotch, his gray eyes on us, but they seem to be staring at something beyond the physical. His pain is so thick, so heavy, you could almost reach out and touch it. It breaks me in two to see him like this.

"I have a piece of advice for all you boys," he says, his deep voice grim. We all look at him, waiting. "You live by this, and I promise that you'll never know a day's heartache in your life."

"And what's that, Dad?" I ask.

He pauses and clears his throat. For the briefest moment, he squeezes his eyelids shut, and I know he's clenching back tears. He composes himself and answers me. "Never fall in love."

Well, fuck. That ship has well and truly sailed, Pop.

CHAPTER

ONE

AMBER

T check my teeth for rogue lipstick and smooth down a maverick hair. Heaven forbid I should have even one out of place—what would people say? I'd be the talk of Manhattan. I can imagine the headline: Shock in the City: Scandal as Amber James Looks Less than Perfect.

I allow myself a small smile at the idea. Maybe I should turn up in jeans and Birkenstocks just for fun. Maybe even Elijah's old Ramones T-shirt. No, that won't work. Can't risk him thinking I've cherished it all these years. Wouldn't want him to know that I sleep in it every night when he's away. He might start thinking I have fond feelings about our early days together, and that would never do. I've worked too hard to convince him and the rest of the world that I have no feelings at all to blow it with a twenty-year-old scrap of cotton.

I scoop the T-shirt up from my bed, where I left it this morning, and hold it under my nose. Obviously it's been washed in the last two decades, but some trick of the brain allows it to retain a lingering scent of that time in my life: hint of Love Spell, a trace of Elijah's shower gel, and base notes of pancakes, coffee, cheap beer, and the occasional cigarette. Carefree times when the world looked like a very different place. I allow myself one last inhale before I stash the shirt in its rightful place at the bottom of my underwear drawer. That's where I keep all evidence of my one guilty secret—that I am actually human.

That taken care of, I pose in front of the full-length mirror and carefully examine myself from all possible angles. Dressing for a wedding is always a challenge, at least partly because I hate weddings. They're too full of hope and promise. Still, I can't get out of this one, so I need to tough it out. It could be worse—at least my in-laws won't be there.

My dress falls to right below the knee and is fitted but not full-on bodycon. It's a deep shade of red that communicates restrained class. I add some earrings, tastefully small diamonds, and a spritz of my favorite perfume. I've moved on from Love Spell to something French and unfathomably expensive, as is befitting a woman of my station. I slip on my heels and do a final inspection. Yes, that'll do nicely.

Thanks to years of practice, I know how to find the proper balance for a wide variety of social occasions. For a wedding, one mustn't try too hard and risk accusations of attempting to upstage the mother of the bride. However, one must always look perfectly put together or risk whispers and titters behind her back about how she's letting herself go.

In the mirror, I practice my repertoire of wedding smiles —a wide-eyed, excited to see you; a soft, doesn't-the-bride-look-gorgeous bit; and my personal favorite, the simpering oh-my-goodness-how-long-has-it-been routine. As I check the time, I'm unable to help a small laugh at my cynicism. I remember when this life seemed so glamorous. How long has it been since I felt that way?

Is it too early for a glass of wine? Maybe a quick glass of pinot would help me through the day. Tempting, but no. It's not quite noon, and although I've never known what a yardarm is, I'm pretty sure the sun isn't past it yet. Vivid memories of my own mother still haunt me—raising her glass at breakfast, laughing as she said, "It's definitely gin o'clock somewhere in the world, darling." I have no desire to stagger in her footsteps and continue that family tradition, even if I can now understand its appeal.

Of course, I could get away with it if I wanted to most days. I could drink a whole bottle and nobody would notice. I am alone in this vast, beautiful townhouse of ours. A Beaux-Arts building constructed in 1908, it comes complete with four stories, six en suite bedrooms, and a roof garden that offers stunning views of the city. How many women have lived here over the decades, and have any of them ever felt as lonely as I do right now?

Despite the size of the place, we don't have any live-in staff because that's how Elijah and his brothers grew up. His mom liked it that way, but there was always noise and energy in their home. This place feels more like a mausoleum. A memorial to all our broken dreams. When Elijah isn't here, I rattle around it alone. Actually, I pretty much rattle around it alone even when he is. It's so big we can both easily live here without ever seeing each other. Perhaps that's half the problem. Perhaps we should sell it and buy a trailer instead. That would force us to confront the reality that is the state of our marriage. And what then?

Would we choose to fix it or to walk away? Hold 'em or fold 'em? I have no idea.

We have people who clean and fix and drive and keep everything running perfectly so we can get on with our Very Important Business. In Elijah's case, that would be making more money. In my case, it would be giving it away. I'm under no illusions—I live a blessed life, at least financially. The only work I do is for charity, and in all fairness, I'm good at it. It's another role I play well, like Loving Wife and Delighted Wedding Guest. I plan an epic party, I've raised funds for at least a hundred different causes, and I'm an asset to Elijah and the company he runs. On the surface, I have everything a woman could want.

Beneath the surface is a completely different story, of course. Beneath the surface, it's a total shitshow.

Damn. That glass of pinot is really starting to call my name.

ELIJAH'S TEXT COMES THROUGH, telling me he'll pick me up in "ten minutes sharp." Obviously, I'm ready, but I'll make a point of keeping him waiting anyway. He'll be expecting it, I suppose. I don't think I've left the house on time in years. Something always stops me from walking out the door when he arrives. Even now, knowing he's on his way, I feel nerves begin to flutter in the pit of my stomach. I check my appearance once more in the full-length mirror. Everything looks perfect.

Perfect.

Before long, I hear the sound of the Bentley's horn

tooting outside. But I stay where I am, as though my feet have taken root to the floor. The thought of a whole day of pretending, of being the perfect wife ... My blood runs cold. I perch on the edge of the bed and take a series of deep breaths. A few hours and it will all be over. I just need to get through today in one piece, and then I have no social events to attend for another three nights. Three whole nights when I can watch TV alone or plan my next triumphant gala. Three whole nights when I don't have to see Elijah and be reminded of how much of a failure I am.

Another beep of the horn, and I glance at my phone. How have fifteen minutes already passed with me sitting here, trying to find enough oxygen to fill my lungs? He will only become more irate when he sees that I've read the increasingly irritated messages he's sent. I really must go down there. I sneak a quick glance through the window, hidden by the drapes. There he is, my husband, leaning against the car and looking mad. Mad and far too sexy for my own good.

When I do emerge from the house, Elijah's nostrils are flaring, his gray eyes flashing. Both signs of extreme annoyance, which I very much deserve. I see him take in my outfit, his gaze lingering on my legs, and can practically feel him making the effort to calm down. There remains a physical attraction between us that neither of us can ignore, no matter how hard we try. And I do try, but my husband is effortlessly sexy and impossible to ignore. He feels that pull too, I see it in his eyes, but he fights it as much as I do—which is no doubt why he left our marital bed.

"You look beautiful," he says quietly, catching me unaware. It's a simple statement, the words sincere, and my breath catches in my throat. After all these years, all the coldness between us, this man can still unravel me so easily. I was expecting him to snap, and instead, he chose to soothe. It's much more difficult to handle. My sudden vulnerability has my legs shaking and my heart pounding. I'm emotional, and emotions are the enemy.

I simply nod in thanks, and he opens the car door for me. It's such a small gesture of chivalry, but he's never once failed to do it. Even in the midst of a fight that will leave us not speaking for days, Elijah always opens the car door for me. Sometimes I think it's sweet, and often I want to tell him I'm a grown woman who can open her own damn doors. Today? Today, I simply accept it and gratefully climb into the darkened interior of the Bentley. Once inside, I feel far less exposed than I did standing in the unforgiving autumn sunlight.

"Hi, Gretchen," I say to our driver. "Sorry I kept you waiting."

She meets my gaze in the mirror, her dark eyes sparkling with amusement. Gretchen insists on wearing a driver's cap even though we don't ask her to, and her curls spill out from underneath it in a black tumble. "Are you really, Mrs. J?" she replies. "Are you really?"

I wink at her but don't answer. Elijah settles himself next to me, and Gretchen activates the privacy screen.

"How was your night?" he asks, smoothing down his pant legs and removing a piece of invisible lint. He smells divine—almost as good as that Ramones top, but a lot more sophisticated.

"Oh, the usual high-octane thrill of event-planning drama. As you know, I'm joint hosting at the Met next month, and I had a few fires to put out."

"Yeah? Were you kicking down doors and taking names?"

"Absolutely. I mean, who on earth seats Rowena Fitz-patrick next to Olivia Samson at a charity function?"

He squints his eyes for a moment before responding. "I can't quite remember what their beef was. Did Rowena steal Olivia's husband?"

"It was much worse than that. She stole her housekeeper."

One half of his mouth quirks up in amusement. I love Elijah's lopsided grin. It's one of the few things about him that hasn't changed over the years, and it reminds me of earlier incarnations of our relationship. Maybe that's why I soften a little and make a mistake. "And how was your night with your family? Is everyone well?"

As soon as the words are out, I regret them. Elijah and I are not what you would call happily married, but we have, in our own way, made this work. Admittedly, it's more like a business arrangement than a love match these days, but we function as a couple. One of the ways we achieve that harmony is our unspoken agreement to avoid difficult subjects. The biggest and baddest of those taboos is his family. We both pretend they don't exist for the purpose of our marriage, because talking about them never ends well. For some unknown reason, I opened that particular can of worms, and now they're crawling all over me. I mentally slap myself and issue a silent Homer Simpson–style "Doh!"

His eyebrow arches as he looks at me, and I get my compact out of my purse and apply fresh lipstick, not because I need to, but because it provides some cover.

"Ah, they were great, thanks for asking," he says, his tone neutral. "Melanie was there with baby Luke and her little sister, Ashley, who's working on her MBA at Harvard. She's a lot like Mel, only bubblier. And Amelia joined us later."

I snap my compact shut and nod. Drake's girlfriend is safer ground. I've spent quite a bit of time with Amelia, and she really is quite a marvelous human. He was lucky to find the love of his life in his secretary. He is truly happier than I've ever seen him. Nathan's wife, Melanie, I've only met once, and our interaction was brief and tense. At least it was tense from my end, as I assumed my darling brother-in-law had told her what a poisonous bitch I am. I didn't pick up any hostility from her, but I know better than anyone how well women can hide what they really feel.

I'm doing it right now, nodding and smiling in all the right places as he speaks. He tells me about Dalton's health and Mason's love life and rambles on about how much Luke resembles Nathan while I give the impression that none of it upsets me at all. I hide the fact that I actually spent last night alone and sad with only my laptop and a bottle of red for company. I pretend it doesn't bother me that he spends so much time with people who can't stand me—that he chooses them over me, every time.

It wasn't always like this, of course.

"That sounds nice," I reply curtly, hoping he senses how hard this is for me. Praying that we can possibly move on to something less controversial, like politics or religion or whether *Die Hard* is a Christmas movie.

He absentmindedly tugs at his tie the way he does when he's feeling nervous. I reach out and straighten it for him. My fingers brush the skin of his neck, and we both look shocked at the unexpected contact. "There," I say. "You're all good. Wouldn't want you showing me up in public."

"Heaven forbid," he says, rolling his eyes. "Anyway, I was wondering ..."

Oh god. Here it comes. I don't know what exactly, but it will be something unwelcome, I can feel it.

"I was wondering if you'd like to see a picture of Luke?"

Jesus. Is that all? Why did he make it sound like he was going to tell me something terrible? I may not be involved with his family, but I'm not a complete monster.

I nod cautiously, and he pulls out his phone and flicks through the pictures, and I soon realize that it's not only Luke on there. It's all of them. The James family en masse, all together in a house I haven't set foot in for years. It's strange, seeing the small changes—different color paint on the walls, a new couch, a whole corner full of toys and kid things. Elijah reaches a series of shots of Luke, who's approaching ten months old. He's sitting on Nathan's lap wearing a jack-o-lantern outfit, looking cute as a button. Even the presence of Nathan in the background can't stop my smile. Elijah scrolls through three or four, each one featuring the baby with a family member. I concentrate on Luke—he can't help who he's related to. Eventually, he reaches a picture of him in the arms of a pretty young woman I don't recognize.

"This is Mel's sister, Ashley," he explains. "She's the one at Harvard. Bright girl."

Hmmm. Bright and bubbly. And young and gorgeous and more at home with the James family after knowing them for five minutes than I am after two decades.

Good old Ashley. And good old Melanie and good old Dalton and good old Nathan. How lovely for them all.

I know I'm overreacting. That I'm being petty and stupidly jealous. I can't object to being left out of something

I've made clear I want no part of. This is what I hate about emotions—they make no sense and they're impossible to control. I feel sad and angry and also resentful that Elijah hasn't noticed any of that.

I'm aware that I'm being irrational—I've shown zero sign of what I'm feeling on the outside. I'm way too good at hiding what's going on inside me. It's like my superpower.

Still, it's getting more and more difficult to keep calm with every passing moment. With every sweet photo and each adoring comment that comes out of my husband's mouth. It's hard for Elijah, managing the two halves of his world, but it's also hard for me. I wanted so much to be a part of that world too—until I couldn't any longer. Listening to him now, sounding so happy as he talks about them, only emphasizes how far apart we are. He might be stuck in the middle, but I'm stranded all by myself on the other side, and it's lonely over here. I want to scream and yell and cry. I want to shout at him: If they're all so fucking perfect, why don't you go and live with them instead? Why don't you find someone new? Why don't you do what your brothers think you should do and leave? Why not put us both out of our misery and accept that you'd be happier without me?

It's not like he's short of offers. He is, after all, disgustingly handsome. Not to mention rich, charming, kind, and in his own way, hilarious. I don't see that side of him much anymore, but another woman probably would. Amelia and Melanie and Melanie's precious little sister undoubtedly see more of that side of him than I do. Hell, I'm guessing even the woman who runs the bagel shop on the corner gets to see more of that side of him.

"Look at this one," he says. "It's Luke actually walking."

He's oblivious to the conflict going on inside me even though I'm literally inches away from him. Yes, I am that good. I stare at the phone, falling to pieces even as I make all the right noises. Luke is adorable, and I'm sure he will have a little brother or sister on the way before long. And Drake and Amelia are so in love that I wouldn't be shocked if they join the parent club before long. Everyone is playing happy families, it seems.

The way Elijah talks about Luke, the way he talks about them all … that's what he wants too. What he expected to have when we first got together. An affectionate wife, beautiful babies, a home life filled with love and laughter.

Unfortunately for Elijah, he married me. And I haven't given him any of those things.

"Maybe we could, I don't know, get together for a drink sometime?" he asks, finally putting the damn phone away. "Me and you, Drake and Amelia. Maybe Maddox. You haven't seen him since he moved back to the States. Possibly even Mel and Nathan?"

Fuck. Is he for real? Can he hear himself? Does he really think that showing me a few snapshots of a cute baby is going to change anything? How the hell does he think Nathan would react to the idea of a fun night out with me? I suspect he'd rather have his balls tasered.

It's my own fault. I was weak. I showed an ounce of interest and opened the door to this. Now I need to slam it firmly shut again.

He wants us all to be friends. He sees their happiness and thinks it might still be possible for us. Hell, he wants us all to hold hands and put the past behind us and be besties forever. Deep down, Elijah is a good man who simply wants the important people in his life to get along. Unfortunately, he has no clue how impossible that is for the rest of us. He's stuck in that no man's land between the trenches, calling for a ceasefire that will never happen.

"I'm busy that night," I say immediately. "Charity dinner. Sorry."

"Really?" he asks, lifting his eyebrows. "What charity?"

"Save the Red-Footed Corn Warbler," I answer quickly. "It's an endangered species. Very rare." Even more than rare, actually—it's a creature that only exists in my mind.

Nodding, he appears to accept my excuse as he looks out at the streets of Manhattan passing us by. When he looks back at me, he speaks ever so casually. "Funny how you already knew you were busy without me suggesting a specific date. Remind me to make a donation to the poor corn warbler, won't you?"

"Of course, darling," I assure him, maintaining the lie. "You can count on me." Deliberately, I avert my eyes, making it clear that our brief détente is over. I can't wait to get out of this car and away from him, at least for a few minutes so I can compose myself. So I can remember that I am Amber James, and while no man is an island, this woman is pretty damn close to it.

I don't need the James brothers. I don't need them to like me or approve of me or to know how much I miss the days when I would have been at those family gatherings too.

I don't need any of them—including Elijah.

CHAPTER
TWO

ELIJAH

I sneak a glance to the right, risking a look at my wife. She cut me dead in the car because I pushed too hard. It was too much, too soon, and she's now firmly locked back into full ice-queen mode.

I know from bitter experience that there will be no salvaging the day now. She'll share space with me out of a sense of social obligation, but there will be no real warmth. No real pleasure. No real anything, in fact, apart from her contempt and her very cold shoulder.

It was probably the baby pictures. No, it was suggesting drinks with Nathan. Or maybe it was ... Fuck, all of it.

She never voluntarily talks about my family, and I was both surprised and pleased. So much so that I got carried away—one photo of Luke would have been enough. She didn't need to see my whole damn camera roll.

Now, I'm paying the price. I would have preferred it if she yelled at me, even slapped me for being an insensitive asshole. Which I kind of was—I know she doesn't like me going on about them. If she told me to shut the fuck up, I would've apologized and we would have had a chance at enjoying ourselves. No such luck—she went straight for the big freeze instead.

She hasn't spoken a word to me since we arrived. I'm dead to her, at least for now.

Despite my frustration, despite the chill, I still can't take my eyes off her. I'm trying to play the game and stay cool, but I'm nowhere near as good at it as she is. My gaze just keeps getting drawn back to her, sucked into the black hole of her beauty. Amber is breathtaking, even more stunning now at forty than she was when I met her at nineteen.

Her caramel-blond hair is sleek and shining, her makeup perfectly accentuating her high cheekbones and delicate features. The lines of her dress hug her toned figure in that Amber-trademarked blend of class and sass. She crosses her legs, and my eyes wander down her shapely calves all the way to the sky-high heels. Nobody should be able to walk in those shoes, but she manages it with complete elegance.

Without wanting to, I vividly imagine those long legs wrapped around my ass, my wife naked apart from the glossy nude pumps, moaning in ecstasy as I slide myself inside her. Fuck! Why does this always happen? What the hell is wrong with me? For both our sakes, I need to keep my distance—that would definitely be the wise choice. And in all other aspects of life, I'm a man who makes wise choices.

When it comes to Amber, though, my dick has a habit of jumping in and making its feelings known, no matter how wise the rest of me is attempting to be. My dick is a fucking idiot. My dick needs to get with the program and treat her with the caution she warrants. Amber might look graceful and serene on the surface right now, but she has battery acid running through her veins instead of blood.

Right on cue, she slowly swivels her head to face me. Her expression leaves me in no doubt that she's read my mind and has no interest whatsoever in engaging in any of the things I've spent the last few minutes thinking about. I want to look away, but that's simply not possible with her. I'm trapped, pinned by her whiskey-brown eyes, bewitched by the dark swoop and flutter of her insanely long lashes. She puts a perfect smile on her lips, just in case anyone's watching, and leans toward me. Her breath is deliciously warm on my neck as she whispers, "You need to stop looking at me like that, Elijah. We don't do that anymore, remember? Not since you moved into your own bedroom."

She purrs the words, and although their content is less than encouraging, the sound goes straight to my cock. Her mere presence makes me hot, but her message is like a bucket of ice water dumped over my head. The stark contrast between the two leaves me reeling. I hate the fact that I want her. Even more, I hate that she knows it.

Jesus fuck. I hate it all. I wish she didn't still have so much of a hold on me. She sits there completely unaffected while I feel like I'm going crazy. I'm intoxicated by her nearness, by that simple touch of her breath, by her thigh only inches from mine. It's not even merely physical—it would be easier to handle if it were.

It's Amber, the whole of her. Body, mind, and tortured soul. I don't understand how I can still love a woman who seems to hate me. Who can't bear to be around my family and punishes me every time I make a mistake. Nathan is forever telling me to end it, to find someone else, but none of my brothers get it. If I wanted someone else, this would be easy—but she's the one. She has always been the one.

Now that she's said her piece, my wife looks away and clasps her hands together, sighing with apparent delight as we stand and turn to look at the bride positioned at the head of the aisle. She's doing a terrific impression of being transfixed by the whole magical scene, and I follow her lead. We are at a wedding, after all, and we should behave appropriately. Once we're alone, we can go back to our real relationship—one that can make the gladiator pits of Rome look like a day at the spa.

I ignore my own turmoil and focus instead on the young woman in white. Elodie Perkins practically floats toward the altar to the sound of a string quartet playing Wagner's "Bridal Chorus." She glows with happiness as she holds onto the arm of her father, my company's head of finance, Harper Perkins. Her waiting groom looks speechless with wonder, his joy-filled eyes fixed firmly on his beautiful bride-to-be.

It's a genuinely moving sight, and I feel a rush of affection for the happy couple. Affection and maybe a touch of yearning. They're at the beginning of everything, and they have no idea how lucky they are.

Is it possible that the romantic moment has also melted the block of ice Amber keeps where her heart should be? She certainly looks swept away by the sweet scene playing out in front of us, but I know her too well to be fooled. As she's reminded me today, the woman could win an Oscar for her ability to perform. She could just as easily be planning mass murder as admiring the bride's dress—her expression would stay exactly the same.

I regain a little of my self-control and clasp my fingers

over Amber's. She might be the queen of faking it, but I've learned from the master. I lift her hand to my mouth and, ignoring her subtle resistance, place a soft kiss on her palm. From the outside, it will look as though I'm moved by the tender moment of Elodie approaching her tearful fiancé. Fuck this bullshit. I'm not some helpless sap she gets to kick whenever she feels like lashing out.

"I wouldn't share a bed with you if we were in the middle of the Arctic and I was butt-ass naked," I whisper, leaning in close. "I've learned not to want things that are bad for me, darling."

Nobody else would be able to see that I hurt her. Nobody else would see anything other than what she lets them see—the ultra-stylish society wife, happily married to the CEO of a multibillion-dollar corporation. Only I see the slight flare of her nostrils, the tiny twitch at the corner of one eye. By Amber's standards, that's a full-on meltdown.

She tries to pull her hand from mine, but I tighten my grip, making it impossible for her to break free. My dick is still doing the thinking, and he's enjoying this—the physical contact, the power play, the way her chest rises and falls as she breathes more heavily. If we were alone, she'd walk out —but here? Here, she's stuck. Here, I have a little power, and I decide to use it. I want to confuse her, to surprise her. Hell, let's be honest—I want to play with her.

I slide my free arm around her shoulder. "That being said, darling wife, this dress could persuade me otherwise. I love this color on you," I murmur. "But I'd probably love this dress even more off you. It'd look great on the men's room floor."

Her breath catches, and the skin of her décolletage turns

the faintest shade of pink. She wants to tell me to go to hell, but we both keep up our smiles, both putting on the show the world expects of us.

"I'd rather die than share a bed with you again too," she murmurs. "Go find one of your little whores—one of your little playthings—if that's what you want. I'll even lend them the dress if it helps get you off."

Furious, I drop her hand like it's a dead animal. Where the fuck did that come from? I don't have little whores, and I don't play with other women. In the twenty-one years since we started dating, I have never once cheated on Amber. She knows that … Doesn't she? Amber and I may not have made love for over six months, but I would never cheat.

No, I think bitterly, scratch that—we haven't "made love" in well over a decade. There's been angry sex, screwing each other into silence after fights, and we're occasionally overcome by the physical attraction that never seems to fade between us. But our furious, fantastic fucking is always followed by one of us—usually Amber—retreating, leaving us both full of regret and self-loathing. I imagine she scrubs herself clean in the shower while chastising herself for being weak. Maybe she writes "I Must Not Sleep with My Husband" a hundred times in one of the notebooks she keeps with her at all times.

Whatever she does, it's been working, because even that accidental contact hasn't happened recently. We have stuck to our own rooms, our own sections of the too-big town-house we share. Stuck to our own lives. None of this is new, though, so why would she think I'd cheat on her now? Or is she screwing with me? Fuck. It's so hard to tell with her. I course correct my frown back into a smile.

"Oh my!" Amber shuffles slightly farther away from me. She's talking more loudly now, happy to be overheard gushing. "Look at the way Mitchell is gazing at her. Right there, that's what a recipe for love looks like."

An older woman sitting in the row in front of us turns and smiles, as tearfully emotional about the scene playing out before us as Amber pretends to be.

And this right here, I think as I try not to be provoked by her giving me the cold shoulder, is what a recipe for love looks like when you add one more ingredient: a sprinkle of hate.

THREE

AMBER

My husband is, to use a technical term, hotter than a solar flare. He's tall and broad-shouldered and in terrific shape, his dark hair and beard perfectly well-groomed. He dresses impeccably and has a big smile that can melt a woman's heart at twenty paces and her underwear at ten. He is smooth, sophisticated, and stylishly put together—the very definition of high-society sex appeal.

Despite all that surface charm, it's actually his eyes that do it for me. They always have, ever since the first day we met. An unusual shade of deep gray, Elijah's eyes have a touch of the wild to them that is a world away from business meetings and boardrooms. When he's annoyed or just plain pissed, they shine with a hint of ferocity that never fails to make my heart beat faster. And as he is usually annoyed or just plain pissed when I'm nearby, that tends to happen way too often for comfort. My poor heart becomes quite exhausted by it all.

I'm avoiding meeting his gaze for exactly that reason. I've pushed and prodded and provoked, and I've gotten a sick thrill out of unbalancing him. Was it worth it? I glance at him from beneath my lashes and decide that it wasn't. He doesn't even look angry anymore. His whole face lit up with his smile when he watched Elodie walk down the aisle, genuine warmth infused in his expression. Against all odds, he remains a romantic. Now, though, he looks tense and drained, and that's all thanks to yours truly. I really am the gift that keeps on giving.

He doesn't deserve this. I don't deserve this. Yet neither of us seems to know how to fix it nor has the guts to walk away. It's like we're locked in this endless cycle of hell.

We are sitting together at the reception, although "together" might be a stretch. We are in close physical proximity, but as ever, the distance between us is vast and bleak. I can't even remember the last time either of us tried to cross that void. Him moving into his own bedroom six months ago was the final nail in that coffin, taking away the last scrap of intimacy between us. Not that a lot happened in our shared bed—but at least we were in the same space. At least some form of intimacy was possible. Now, we lead increasingly separate lives, and it's only at events like this that we're forced to share the same air.

A waiter approaches, smiling nervously over his big silver tray. "Wine, madam?" he asks. The poor kid looks terrified.

"Yes, please," I reply, and his hand shakes as he passes me the glass. "First day?"

"Um, yeah." He offers a sheepish grin. "That obvious?"

"Not at all. Lucky guess. You're doing great—and don't worry, it'll get easier. Plus, before long everyone will be so drunk they won't care anyway."

A flicker of surprise dances across Elijah's face as the boy leaves.

"What? I can't be nice?"

"Not in my experience, no," he says, before going back to his phone. He's been glued to the damn thing since the reception started, and I can't say that I blame him. Maybe he's messaging one of those mistresses I accused him of having earlier—and again, if he were, I couldn't blame him. The unrestrained glee and optimism inherent to weddings coupled with the conversation in the car have caused me to be an even bigger bitch than usual. Yet again, his family has caused a rift between us—this time without even being present. I wish I could feel as neutral on the inside as I look on the outside, but I can't. Pain and rejection are like a plague of locusts, landing on my exposed nerves and devouring me whole.

I sip my wine and tap my toes along to the music. The swing band version of "No Diggity" is working oddly well. We used to jam to this song at parties in college, singing along with our friends as we danced around in a big drunken circle. That was a million years ago, but I wonder if he remembers too. If he does, there's no sign of it on his face. No sign of much on his face at all. He has gone to ground, switched off. Left the field of play.

With my expression carefully schooled in my practiced wedding smile, I wave to people I know and have brief conversations with anyone who stops by our table. I'm playing my role to perfection. That is what is expected, and on this occasion, it's also what is right—it wouldn't be fair to drag poor Elodie down with my bitterness on the happiest day of her life. At least the happiest day of her life until a few years down the line when her pals organize the traditional male stripper–strewn divorce party. Ha. Thoughts like that are exactly why I have to pretend.

Elijah has barely touched his drink and hasn't eaten. I notice these things because I notice everything about him, but I don't comment. He's a grown man, and I am very much not his mother. His tie is tugged down a little and his long fingers are flying over the phone keyboard. Crap, what if he actually *is* messaging another woman? I didn't mean it when I told him to go play with someone else. The thought of it alone is enough to break me, even if I would never let him see that.

I briefly wonder what would happen if I leaned over and took that phone from his grip. If I tangled my hands in his thick hair, looked up into his eyes, and invited him in. Would he welcome it? Would he pull me onto his lap and kiss me the way he used to, all possessive tongue and hot lips and big hands roaming my body? Or would he be horrified and push me away before returning to his phone?

It doesn't matter. I'll never do any such thing. The whole idea is ludicrous. I'm not a child anymore, and I gave up on silly dreams a long time ago.

"I'm just messaging Mason about work," he says, as though sensing my scrutiny. "They've landed in London."

Ah, Mason. Of course it's not another woman. It's his little brother, who is admittedly a lot more fun than Nathan. Too bad he hates me just as much.

I let out a laugh, the kind that anyone who overheard would find pleasant and lighthearted and perfectly suited to the occasion. "Darling, you could be talking to Margot Robbie about playing strip poker in a hot tub for all I care.

Surely you know by now that I don't care one single iota?" I say all of this in a gentle and amused tone, and his shoulders stiffen in response. Why do I poke so hard? Ah, that's why, I think as fury flashes in those gorgeous gray eyes once more. For a mere moment, I feel alive at the proof that there's still something between us—even if that something is only anger.

"Right. Message received and understood," he says, returning my oh-so-fake beam. "Feel free to plan your own poker night with George Clooney."

"George is a very happily married man, honey. Don't you remember the wedding? I suppose I could give Channing a call, though."

I slowly stroke the stem of my wine glass as I speak, and his eyes go to my fingers, his Adam's apple bobbing as he swallows. A little thrill runs through me. He might hate my guts, but he still wants me. That's got to count for something.

He drags his gaze away from the glass, away from my fingers, and back to his phone. "Go for it, babe. Whatever floats your boat." He shrugs, Mr. Nonchalant. "I'm sure one of us has his number somewhere."

I'm about to respond when Elodie, the blushing bride herself, joins us at the table. Her cheeks are carrying a pretty flush, and her updo is charmingly disheveled after a round of "No Diggity" on the dance floor.

Both Elijah and I smile, for once genuinely. We've known Elodie since she was ten, and it really is nice to see her so joyful. I feel guilty for even imagining her divorce party.

"Has anybody mentioned how beautiful you look today, Elodie?" Elijah says warmly.

"Oh, a few people, which is really nice," she replies giddily. "I just wanted to come over and thank you both for being here, and for the generous gift. I ... We ... We're both very grateful!"

Elijah doesn't let on, but he has no clue what we got them. That falls firmly within my wifely remit—I leave him to run his intergalactic business affairs, and I deal with the charity lunches, the social calendar, the parties, the house, and of course, the wedding gifts. I could torture him a little here, and normally I'd enjoy that, but it would be unkind to Elodie. Plus, I think I've hit my quota of Elijah-baiting for the day.

"You're very welcome, darling," I say, patting her hand. "And I hope you have a wonderful time. Every marriage should start with a grand adventure."

"Well, I think a private jet flying us to our very own Caribbean island for a week definitely counts as that. It's an amazing honeymoon, and Mitch and I are very much looking forward to it." She blushes and giggles, and it is beyond sweet. So young. So naive. I may be bitter and cynical about my own life, but I truly do wish them all the best. There are happy couples in the world, and while I don't personally know many of them, I sincerely hope that Elodie and Mitch remain one of the few.

I watched Elijah's face as she mentioned our gift, and his eyebrows raised maybe a millimeter. His poker face is nearly as good as mine. Not that he minds—I know better than that. He is many things, my darling husband, but tight-fisted he is not. He grew up surrounded by tremendous wealth and privilege, but he's aware of that and doesn't take it for granted. My whole life, I have mixed with the one percent, and many of them are god-awful assholes about their cash. Elijah? He'd happily hand over his last dime if he felt it was the right thing to do. Luckily, it's unlikely to ever come to that considering he's built Jamestech into even more of a behemoth than it was before he took over from Dalton. If money really could buy happiness, he'd be permanently swinging from a rainbow while singing show tunes.

"Have a fabulous time, Elodie," he says, smiling at her, his gray eyes shining. Her blush deepens, and I realize she has a crush on him—or at least she did at some stage in her life. And why wouldn't she? He's an older man with model good looks. She probably fell in love with him when she was twelve. "I think you and Mitch are going to be very happy together. I can feel it in my bones," he adds. "And my bones are never wrong."

"Gosh, I hope so," she gushes, looking at the two of us. "If we're even a fraction as happy as you guys, that'll do for me. How long have you been together?"

I briefly wonder if he might accidentally bark out "too fucking long," but he's nearly as good at this performance as I am. "We've been a couple for twenty-one years, and married for eighteen," he says. "And every single day with Amber has been incredibly ... special."

I bite back a laugh. *Special*—what a fantastically ambiguous word. It could accurately be used to describe anything from eternal love through to a nuclear holocaust, taking in Labrador puppies and serial killers who dress up as clowns along the way. Special!

"What's your secret?" Elodie apparently missed the pause and caught no double-meaning in the word.

My gaze meets Elijah's, and we give our well-rehearsed

answer. "Give and take," we both say, for once perfectly in sync.

I don't let the sorrow that floods me show on my face. We were in love once, this man and I. We shared everything, keeping no secrets from one another, our lives woven together like the threads of a tapestry. He was my soulmate, my best friend, my lover. Our passion lit up my heart and made me shine from the inside out.

Now, there's only one thing that Elijah and I seem to do well together.

Lie.

CHAPTER
FOUR
AMBER

I wait for a respectable amount of time before I consider making a run for it. Or, in these heels, making a brisk walk for it. Elijah won't even notice—he's deeply embedded in conversation with his assistant, Luisa, and Harper. They have their heads bent together over a table, probably sketching out their next takeover on a napkin. They're cut from the same cloth, and for all three of them, work is paramount—the rest is filler.

Harper has enjoyed his big day as the doting father, but if I know him—and I do know him quite well—he is now relieved to be discussing Jamestech. Elijah bluffed the devoted-husband routine for hours before he gave in to the siren call, and Luisa has—no, actually, Luisa never tries to be anything she isn't. She wore a tailored business suit to the wedding and has had earbuds in all day.

The small group looks engaged and focused, Luisa gesticulating as she speaks. It's clear from watching her that she's one of those people who talks with her hands. Other guests are dancing and drinking, but these three are getting their kicks in a different way. Nothing sets their pulses racing quite like the thrill of the big deal—the lunge, cut, and parry of the ruthless world they inhabit.

My father was exactly the same. Perhaps it should come as no surprise that I found myself married to a man who would choose the Dow Jones over date night. I barely saw my dad as a child, and he remains a distant figure. That's partly because I was whisked away to boarding school pretty much as soon as I was on solids and partly because he literally lived in the office. He actually had a bed in there. My mom coped the best way she knew how—by losing herself in a bottle of gin a day and, ever the cliché, by fucking the pool boy. In comparison, I'm a roaring success—I only drink wine, and we don't have a pool boy.

From my spot at the bar, I continue watching Elijah, letting my mind wander as I pretend to be interested in the orthopedic specialist sitting next to me. At the start, I thought he might entertain me with juicy stories of A-listers given his reputation as "surgeon to the stars," but all I've gotten so far is a fifteen-minute lecture about hip-replacement procedures. As I nod and smile at all the right places, I'm far more interested in my husband. My eyes are constantly drawn to him no matter how much I fight it. It's the same kind of feeling I get after eating that second slice of chocolate cake—knowing I'll regret it later but eating it anyway.

He wasn't always like this. When we met in college, Elijah was hardworking and ambitious but also a huge amount of fun. The kind of guy who'd be the first to do a keg stand at a party, but only after he attended all his lectures and a daily study session at the library. After we got married, he remained attentive and loving, and being the apple of his eye made me feel like the luckiest woman on earth. I felt like I was his number one priority in life despite the demands that were placed on him from an early age. Coming from money doesn't equal an easy life, and with Dalton as his dad, he knew from the start that he had big boots to fill. He was the oldest son—the heir—and he carried a lot of expectation on those wide shoulders.

He also always took his job as big brother to his four siblings seriously, especially after their mom Verona died. He tried to soak up their pain, even while he was drowning in his own.

"Oh, really? How amazing," I say, responding to some brain-numbing detail about titanium rods.

Elijah points at something on Luisa's tablet, and the conversation between the three of them grows more animated. His work is everything to him now, that and his family. His blood family. Because slowly, as the years slipped past like thieves in the night, robbing us of so much time, I was edged out of my position as the number one priority in his life. Or more accurately, I saved him the trouble and removed myself from his list altogether.

What we have now is a social contract, not a marriage, and the gravity of that arrangement is dragging me under tonight. I'm sinking in a sea of pain and trying to swim, but I'm weighed down with chains of regret. Even as I sit here, calmly chatting and being sociable, doing everything I'm supposed to do, I'm screaming on the inside. Inside, I am panicking, horrified at being trapped inside what my life has become. I'm not sure I can stand even one more minute of this. Unsure I can fake one more smile, make one more empty comment, or have one more meaningless exchange with people I barely know and have no interest in knowing. I need to leave before something terrible happens—like I burst into tears in public. Heaven forbid the world—or even worse, my husband—should witness such weakness.

It's barely nine p.m. Leaving this early will be noticeable, so I may need to start faking the signs of a socially acceptable ailment. Migraines are always good. I let my hand flutter up to my forehead and wait for my companion to ask me if I'm feeling okay. He's a doctor—he might come in handy after all. Sadly, he's too engrossed in the sound of his own voice to notice. My eyes narrow slightly, and I consider collapsing at his feet to test exactly how bad his powers of observation are.

"Amber," says someone from behind me. "Can I steal you for a moment?"

I turn around to see Martha Kemp, one of my alleged friends and co-chair of several charity committees. No, she is a friend—the alleged part is me being cynical. We are as close as our lives and personalities allow, which is to say that we're never any closer than an air kiss on the cheek. I apologize graciously to Dr. Dud and accompany Martha to a nearby table.

"I was worried you might fall asleep," she whispers, sliding her too-thin body into a chair. Her husband Freddie is a well-known hound dog, and she is on an eternal quest to keep his interest. She hasn't eaten a carb in over a decade and has a face that is more filler than flesh. None of it has worked; Freddie is as badly behaved as ever—because the problem obviously lies with him and not with her. There are rumors that he has a cocaine problem, which likely only adds to his manic ways. I'd advise her to leave him, but frankly I'm not in a position to counsel anybody about the state of their relationship.

Whatever goes on in her personal life, though, Martha possesses a deeply bitchy sense of humor that I find scandalously amusing. It makes the endless round of charity events and prissy lunch parties a lot more fun.

"I got stuck with him earlier," she continues, topping up my glass. "He lost me at titanium rods."

"He talked to you about titanium rods too? Damn. Now I feel so cheap. Thanks for the rescue. He is one dull mother*fucker*." I wink at her, and she giggles.

"An absolute ball bag, but with less hair."

I laugh at that one, because the ball bag in question is indeed bald as a coot. "I was about to have a migraine," I say, sipping a little more wine in the hope that I finally start to feel drunk. "In fact, I think I still might."

"Are you sure?" Martha asks. "I mean, of course you could have a migraine—I will attest to the fact that you were looking peaky to anyone who asks—*but* ... You could also stay. We could dance and flirt with the cute waiters who look like Abercrombie & Fitch models and complain about our tediously privileged lives."

There's a flash of something desperate in her eyes, and I consider saying yes. Maybe I can stick this out for another couple of hours. What else have I got to do, anyway? If I go home, I'll just sit and drink more while I watch TV and feel sorry for myself. Then I'll go to my perfectly lovely bedroom and lie awake wondering where Elijah is, who he's with, and what he's doing. By the time I hear the car pull up outside, I'll be furious and sad and too proud to show any of it. I'll finally fall asleep at five a.m. with eyes as red as a baboon's ass. It's not a great option.

I tap my nails against the side of my glass and look over at my husband. Harper's granddaughter has crawled up onto Elijah's lap, her pretty pink dress frothing over his legs. She's playing a game—tugging at his beard with pudgy fingers. Libby is three years old, a gorgeous blond-haired barrel of fun, and her dimpled cheeks crease from laughter as he pretends to cry. She tugs, he boo-hoos. She stops, he grins. On repeat. He's an absolute natural with kids. When Harper's older daughter Shannon comes to retrieve her, it's obvious how reluctant he is to hand her back. He says something to Shannon that makes her laugh, then gives Libby one last hug before her mom carries her away. As he waves goodbye, there's a wistful look in his eyes. I've seen that look before, and as ever, it feels like a fist slamming into my solar plexus.

Elijah should have that. He should be a dad—he'd be so damn good at it. He deserves to have a house full of kids running around, his own toddlers tugging his beard. He should be playing ball in the park and attending his own child's wedding one day. He should have it all—everything that I will never be able to give him. Everything he so desperately wants, no matter how hard he pretends he doesn't.

"Darling," I say to Martha, turning my full attention back to her, "I actually do feel a little off-color. Not even a lie, I swear. I'm going to make my excuses and leave, but we must do lunch very soon, yes? Just the two of us."

She looks disappointed, but she raises her glass and puts on her best smile. "Abso-fucking-lutely." We mwah-mwah without touching, and I slink past her to make my escape.

I was right the first time. I cannot stand even one more minute of this.

FIVE

ELIJAH

I knew exactly where she was until that cutie-pie Libby came over to visit. She's a doll, that one, with her impish smile and those killer dimples. Pretty good grip when she's pulling a beard as well, as I can now testify. I hope to god they don't take her to a Santa's village this Christmas—she'll have him unveiled as a fraud as soon as she sits on his lap.

I was with my assistant, Luisa, and Libby's grandad Harper when she tumbled over, a whirlwind of giggles in a frilly pink dress. We were discussing a potential takeover of a software company in Seoul, which probably wasn't appropriate bearing in mind the occasion. Still, I was enjoying it a lot more than the rest of the day. It felt good to lose myself in the safety of business talk. I can win that game hands down because I know what I'm doing and I'm very, very good at it. Unlike being a husband—I clearly suck at that. Amber's been erratic all day, lurching from laughter to barbed comments in a way that's left my head spinning.

Talking to my colleagues was a fucking relief, truth be

told, because Asian financial markets are a lot less complicated than my wife.

But no matter what else I'm doing, she is at the back of my mind. It's annoying—like having emotional tinnitus—but I've learned to tolerate it. Like any addiction, I can't quite quit Amber, but I also know she's not good for me. That woman is my heroin, and my time with her has been one of incredible highs and ball-busting lows.

So, although I was paying attention to Luisa's impromptu report, I also kept an eye on Amber, hopefully without her noticing. I try to always be aware of where she is in a room, even if only so I can avoid her.

She was talking with a bald dude, who I vaguely remembered is a doctor of some kind, and nodding a lot, widening her big brown eyes in that way she does when she wants to look impressed. I lost track of her after she joined Martha Kemp at a table. I feel sorry for that woman. Her husband is an asshole divorce lawyer who snorts half the product of Colombia on a daily basis. He also treats his wife like crap, but then again, maybe Amber says the same about me. Who knows? Maybe the two of them blow off steam by bitching about their shitty spouses over their boozy lunches.

Then Libby tottered over, and I got distracted by the simple pleasure of being in the company of a toddler. I love kids, love how they live in the moment, how easily pleased they are. My nephew has recently taken his first wobbly steps. Nathan assures me he's a prodigy and will play for the Knicks. I don't know about that, but I love the look of delight on Luke's chubby little face when he manages to stagger all the way to my arms and his squeals of laughter when I scoop him up and spin him around. So yeah, I got distracted.

By the time Libby waves bye-bye and my head is back in the game, Martha is sitting alone, gazing at one of the buff young servers as though she's planning on eating him instead of the smoked salmon canapés on his tray. Amber, however, is nowhere to be seen. I tell Harper and Luisa I'll see them later and walk over.

"Elijah," Martha says, unashamedly raking her eyes over me. This woman really needs some attention tonight. "You look divine in that suit, darling. Join me? Don't worry, I won't bite. I know you're a happily married man."

Do I detect some sarcasm there, or am I being paranoid?

"You look beautiful too, Martha. Love the new hair color."

Her hands fly to her head as light reflects off the subtle gold tones highlighted into her tresses. "How nice of you to notice," she says, sounding genuinely pleased. I'm guessing compliments don't often fall from Freddie's lips, and I'm glad I could put a smile on someone's face.

"Do you know where Amber went?" I ask, gazing around the room.

"Oh, she said she felt a migraine coming on. Didn't she tell you she was leaving?"

I make a show of pulling my phone from my pocket and checking it, then smile as I read a message that doesn't exist. "Ah, there it is. Must not have felt it vibrate. She said she didn't want to spoil my fun. You know Amber, always putting others first."

I'm not totally sure Martha is buying my act, but if she isn't, she's been in this world long enough to know to go along with it. We're all acting to some extent, and Amber and I have built a public persona that has far outlasted our private one. My family knows the truth, but to the rest of the world, we seem like the perfect couple. We play our roles, attending functions together, hosting charity events, networking in the business world. We present a united front, then we go home to a wall of silence and separate bedrooms. It's fucking exhausting.

"I might call it a night myself," I tell Martha, who isn't even listening. She's watching her husband make a fool out of himself, and her, on the dance floor with a blond half his age. "Go home and check in on her."

"Good idea." Her reply comes a second too late, the practiced smile on her lips the tiniest bit strained. The poor woman is dying inside. I can relate. "You two take care of each other so well."

Do we? I think as I stride toward the exit. We certainly used to, but that was so long ago now it's like a dream sequence in a film. An emotional muscle memory of feeling safe and loved. My heart still remembers those days. The days when I still had my mom around, and my marriage was full of hope and potential and tenderness. When everything felt right with the world.

My heart needs to go fuck itself though. Remembering that shit hurts. These days, the only thing right in the world is my work, and it's not enough. It was never enough.

If Amber left, it's because she doesn't want to be near me. I should let her go, give her the chance to exorcise whatever demons are battling inside her right now. Time has a habit of smoothing over our spats. In all likelihood, she'll wake up tomorrow and act as though nothing happened. As though she wasn't stretched tight as piano wire all evening. Some-times I wonder if she's a robot, the way she reboots overnight. She has more control over her feelings than anyone I've ever met. It's like the discipline she learned from doing ballet for so many years became as deeply embedded in her mind as it did her body. She was forced to learn early on not to show weakness and not to expect much from the people who allegedly loved her because Amber was raised by wolves. Very rich, very successful wolves, but wolves all the same.

She never had the unconditional love and comradery that my brothers and I had when we were kids. Her childhood lacked the chaos of siblings and the warm glow of a mom who made her the center of the universe. My dad worked a lot, but we never doubted that he would do anything for us. Our childhood wasn't perfect, but it was rich with love, and every single one of us boys felt cherished. Amber had none of that, and despite her active social life and packed roster of charity events, she can be an incredibly solitary person by nature.

If she's upset about something, she won't thank me for pushing her on it. She's like an animal when she's hurt—she slinks off and licks her wounds in private. Still, when it comes to my wife, knowing what I should do and actually doing it are two different things.

After pausing in the lobby and giving it approximately eight seconds of thought, I decide I'm going after her whether she wants me to or not. I must be jonesing for my next hit.

Anyway, who knows, she might have a migraine for real, and I don't like the idea of her being out on the streets alone at night. This might be an upscale neighborhood, but there are always risks. It's my job to look after her, even if she'd rather walk home alone than be in my company for ten minutes.

If she stopped to collect her coat from the checkroom, I reckon I won't be far behind her. I don't bother getting mine because it will only delay me. I have a lot of coats, but I only have one wife. I'm not totally sure why I feel compelled to track her down. Maybe protecting her is part of it, but she's a big girl, perfectly capable of getting a cab or calling Gretchen. Even if she stays on foot, she's unlikely to get mugged or abducted around here. So why am I really doing this? Why am I chasing her, still, after all these years? She's made it perfectly clear she won't be caught.

Is it so we can fight some more? So we can torture each other? So I can look into those miraculous eyes of hers and wish it was all different? Am I some kind of emotional masochist? Fuck knows—I just know I need to find her.

The reception is being held in a hotel on Fifty-Seventh Street, and heavy rain slaps the side of my face as soon as I step outside. It's late October, and the weather is having mood swings. All day the sky was a crisp, clear blue, but now the heavens have opened. I should probably go back for my coat, but screw it. It won't kill me.

I stop right outside the hotel. Would she have called our car? That would make sense, but for some reason, I don't think so. I suspect she's very much in one of her reclusive moods tonight.

I quickly check in with Gretchen anyway, and she tells me she hasn't heard from Mrs. James. She goes on to ask if I need her to pull the car around, but I tell her not to bother. In fact, I tell her to head home for the night because I've just caught a flash of crimson out of the corner of my eye. I shove my phone back in my pocket and run along the sidewalk as she turns off onto Park Avenue. Or I think it's her. I could be chasing a random lady in red and be about to get a face full of pepper spray for my troubles.

No, I think as I close the distance. It's her. Nobody else walks quite like she does. Her long legs gracefully eat up the sidewalk, her high heels clicking against the concrete in a confident way that screams "don't fuck with me." Her red cashmere coat is belted tightly around her narrow waist, and even the torrential rain has done nothing to dampen her effortless elegance. Everything Amber does, she does with style—including running out on me at a party.

"Amber! Wait!" I shout, wanting to warn her—no woman appreciates a strange man ambushing her from behind.

She clutches her purse and speeds up. How the fuck does she move so fast in those goddamn shoes? And more to the point, *why* is she moving so fast? She must have heard me, but she's still accelerating. She's almost at a run now, her legs blurring in a desperate trot that makes it obvious she's trying to put some space between us. Where the hell is she going? And does she actually think she can outrun me?

A taxi approaches, its tires throwing up spray from the water-logged street, and she raises her hand to hail it. If she gets into that cab, she can definitely outrun me, and I'm not going to let that happen. Because now I am mightily pissed. She dumped me at a wedding we were supposed to be attending as a couple without saying goodbye, and now I'm running through the rain, shouting her name like a fool while she pretends I don't exist. Even by Amber standards, this is big bitch behavior.

When I increase my speed, the soles of my dress shoes slip and slide on the wet sidewalk, and I reach the yellow cab as she pulls the door open. I don't try to reason with her—I'm not feeling reasonable. I smack the partially open door closed and glare at her. "What the fuck, Amber?" I'm soaked to the skin and cold, and I have no clue what the hell is going on here. How did we go from admittedly bad but within-normal-boundaries bickering to this?

The driver of the cab winds down his window and takes in the scene before him. "Are you all right, missus? If you need to get in, get in. You will be safe with me."

Even sitting down, I can tell this guy is a good eight inches shorter and a hundred pounds lighter than I am, but he looks at me in a way that suggests he'd take me on anyhow. He has balls. I should probably recruit him, fuck knows what for, but something.

"She's fine," I reply, trying to rein in my temper. It's not his fault, after all. "She's my wife."

"I don't care if she's your wife or not, sir, if the lady wants to get into my car, then you will not stop her. I can always call the police to help us sort this out." He holds his phone up like it's a grenade and he's about to pull the pin.

Jesus. All I wanted was to talk to my damn wife, and now a vigilante cab driver is threatening to call the cops on me. This is fucking insane.

"That won't be necessary," Amber says, finally breaking her silence. She turns her face away from me and hides behind the length of her hair as she peers into the window. "Thank you, so much ... What's your name?"

"My name is Sanjay, miss."

I can't see Amber's face, but I can see his, and his reaction tells me she's pulling her hypnotism trick. Her eyes are so big, so expressive, that they overcome all resistance. Man, woman, beast—all are powerless against her. Me included. She will now use his name fifteen times in one sentence, and he'll be so flattered by the attention that he'll practically have cartoon Tweety Birds fluttering around his head.

"Well, I'm Amber, Sanjay, and I'd like to thank you for being such a gentleman—who said chivalry is dead?" She infuses some real warmth into her voice, and Sanjay's chest puffs up a little. As it should, because if my wife had been in actual danger, I would have wanted someone like him to make a stand for her. "Thing is, though, Sanjay, this is actually my husband. We just had a little disagreement—you know how that is, don't you?"

"Oh yes, indeed I do." He smiles and flashes her his wedding ring. "Thirty-two years married."

"I thought so. You understand, then, Sanjay, how it can be sometimes. I was just blowing off steam, and my husband here quite rightly didn't want me to disappear off into the night alone. In his own clumsy way, he was being chivalrous too."

Clumsy? Really? She never misses a chance to put me in my place, this woman. Sanjay drags his eyes away from Amber and scrutinizes me. I try to make myself look as nonthreatening as possible, and finally, he nods. "Okay, if you're sure? I can still take you wherever you want to go. No charge."

"Sanjay, you're a darling, you really are—but I think my husband and I might stroll home together, give ourselves the chance to cool down and talk. I won't forget your kindness though, Sanjay—you have a fabulous evening, now, you hear?"

A very slight taste of the South creeps into her voice with those last few words. Amber grew up in and around Washington DC but spent summers with her grandmother in Charleston. Sometimes it shows up without her noticing when she's angry or otherwise distracted. Sometimes, though, it shows up when she needs to come across as humble and approachable. Like a regular human being rather than the ice-queen wife of a billionaire. Tonight is possibly a combination of all three.

I slip Sanjay a twenty. "Thank you," I say simply. "You're a good man."

His eyes narrow slightly, as though he's still trying to make up his mind about me, but he takes the cash anyway. A beep of his horn, a little finger wave from Amber, and away he goes in a cloud of fumes and a spray of rainwater. A white knight in a yellow cab.

I turn to face my wife, but she's already on the move again. Those heels are back to clicking, her stride lengthening. I quickly catch up, grab her arm, and spin her around. She slaps my hand away but finally stays still. We're beneath a streetlamp, the arc of light shining over our heads like a golden umbrella. She clamps her lips together, stares at the sidewalk, and swipes rain from her cheeks. Except ... it's not rain. Amber is actually crying. What the fuck? Amber never cries—at least not in front of me.

Just like that, all my rage disappears. I want nothing more than to take her in my arms, to hold her close and comfort her. Now I understand why she was running—she didn't want me to see her like this. Shedding tears in public?

She's simply too tough, too proud, too practiced at hiding her feelings. In fact, she hides them so well, I sometimes forget she has them at all.

We're both silent, our bodies inches apart, drenched by the downpour that's growing heavier by the second. If I try to touch her, there's a very real risk that I will lose a limb. Her anger and sorrow are clear by her downcast expression and the way she's holding herself. The way she's refusing to meet my eyes. She has shown weakness in front of me, and to Amber, that is the greatest sin she could commit.

"Are you okay?" I ask, recognizing how inadequate those words are, but I'm unable to come up with anything better.

"Do I look okay?" she snaps back.

"No. You look miserable, baby."

"Don't 'baby' me, Elijah. I'm forty years old."

"True. So why are you behaving like a teenager sneaking away from daddy?"

She snorts slightly and finally looks up at me. Amber is five nine, and when we first met, one of my biggest assets was my height and size. She appreciated that she could wear heels and I would still be taller. Back in the days when she loved everything about me.

"Daddy?" she repeats, the ghost of a smile on her face. "If you say so. Do I have a curfew? Are you going to take away my allowance? Am I *grounded*?"

"No, but you are behaving like a brat. Why did you leave like that? Why didn't you tell me you were going? It's not safe for you, walking these streets at night, looking so ..."

"Rich?" she supplies for me. I was going to say beautiful, but her bitter tone tells me she wouldn't appreciate it. That she'd prefer a fight to a compliment.

"Whatever, Amber. Apart from anything else, it was embarrassing."

Now I'm speaking her language, and a flicker of remorse crosses her exquisite features. "Yes. I can see that. I apologize if I embarrassed you."

"Fuck's sake, Amber, I don't actually give a damn about that—I give a damn about you. Why did you leave? And why are you crying?"

She squeezes her eyes shut, her long lashes moist and clumped together, her hands balled into tense fists. "I left because you were flirting with Shannon."

What the hell? I was flirting with *Shannon*? Shannon, Harper's daughter, who is both Libby's mom and five months pregnant? Who, as far as I know, is happily married? Never once have I looked at her in that way. And I barely spoke to the damn woman tonight.

I bite my tongue and take a deep breath, letting my brain catch up before my mouth opens. This is a required skill set when spending time with Amber. My wife is a complicated woman and an absolute mistress of misdirection. She has a knack for making people believe what she wants them to believe, for convincing them her ideas were theirs, for deflecting away from anything that might not suit her. She wants me to react to this. She wants me to focus on her unfair accusation. But why?

She's genuinely upset, more upset than I have seen her in many years, but it's not about Shannon. It can't be about Shannon. Me snapping back at her and escalating this fight would be counterproductive and possibly exactly what she's hoping for. If we end up screaming at each other, I won't probe any deeper. I won't ask again about her tears, and she won't be forced to admit they even exist. But if it isn't about Shannon, what is it about?

The answer comes to me in a flash, and I feel like I've been sucker punched. She's not upset about Shannon; she's upset about Libby. If I had to guess, I'd say she saw me playing with the little girl. She saw me laughing and cuddling her, and in Amber's mind, she saw me regretting every single thing about my life since we got married. That's the way her brain works, whether it's logical or not. She can't have children, and I love children—therefore, I must be miserable with her.

Fuck. Honestly, sometimes I am miserable with her. But it doesn't have a goddamn thing to do with kids. It's because I wake up every single day wondering if I'm going to die of frostbite.

"I wasn't flirting with Shannon," I say quietly, taking all the challenge out of my voice, out of my body language, giving her nothing to fight with. "But I'm sorry if you thought I was. I'm sorry if I upset you. Forgive me. Let's walk home, like you said. Let's cool down. Maybe we can stop somewhere for a drink, just the two of us—coffee at the Moonlight Diner or a late-night cocktail, like we used to?"

"You really think a strawberry daiquiri is going to fix this?" she asks, her eyes still shining with tears. She lets them spill down her cheeks and doesn't try to wipe them away. It's so unlike her that I feel a jolt of fear shoot through me. It's physical, a tingle of dread running up and down my spine like nerve pain.

"Well, a daiquiri never hurts." I reach out and stroke the side of her face. She leans into my palm, her cheek soft against my skin, and for a moment I have hope. "Amber, sweetheart, we're both soaked through. Let's go to a bar, or even better, go home. You must be tired."

She gazes up at me, and her eyes are so big and luminous that I swear I can see the city backdrop reflected in them.

"I am tired, Elijah, yes. I'm exhausted, and I know you must be too. Why do we keep doing this? Why do we keep dancing this dance? Why don't we just … let go?"

My nostrils flare and my hand drops to my side. "What do you mean?"

Her sigh speaks of bone-deep weariness. "I mean I think I'm done, Elijah. I want a divorce."

SIX

ELIJAH

We're back home and in our perfectly decorated living room. This house has several rooms for entertaining where Amber and I have hosted dinners, charity events, and parties over the years. It's also big enough that we have our own space, allowing us to coexist in distant harmony.

Tonight, though, we're sitting together—sitting together as we discuss how to be apart. She's on one couch, I'm on another, and I fucking hate everything about this whole setup. I want to drag her into my arms and kiss her so hard she can't breathe. I want to tell her how much I love her, how much I want this marriage to work. How much I need her.

"So, are you thinking a separation first or straight to divorce?" I say instead in a calm, steady voice, needing to keep a grip on my emotions because I can tell that she's barely holding it together. She's curled up with her legs underneath her, dressed in her silk pajamas with a blanket over her lap, her hair towel-dried and shaggy against her shoulders. She looks nothing like the glamorous creature who emerged from this same house earlier today, but I love this version as much as that one. We were soaked through by the time we got back, and we immediately went to change. Logs are burning in the fireplace, the drapes are closed tight, and the lights are down low. Despite the size of the room, it's cozy and intimate and warm. The very opposite of our conversation.

She bites her lip and swipes at her eyes. Her makeup has been removed, but a random smear of mascara has clung on, straggling over her left cheekbone in a forlorn black smudge. She looks frail, and I know she'll hate that. She stays silent, sipping from the mug of hot cocoa between her hands. She made me one as well, which is a rarity—how ironic that it takes discussing a divorce to bring out such kindness. I added a glug of good Scotch to mine—I have a feeling I'm going to need it.

"You're doing your fake-calm voice, Elijah," she finally says, gazing at me over the haze of steam. "Or maybe it's not fake, I don't know. Maybe this is all a relief to you. You finally get rid of me but you don't have to be the bad guy who dumps his barren wife. The coldhearted bitch who made your life a living hell. I can be the villain of the piece, as usual."

The words are harsh; she's lashing out because she's hurting. This will all be easier for her if it turns into a fight because it will validate her choice.

"I'm not calm," I reply. "I might sound it, but I'm not. I'm all kinds of things right now, but calm isn't one of them. I'm pissed. I'm shocked. And I'm ... Fuck, Amber, I'm sad, okay?

I'm just fucking sad. I never wanted this, so don't act like I did. I'm not the one asking for a divorce, am I?"

"Not in words, no—but in actions, yes. You've been asking for one for years in your own way. The amount of time you spend at the office. Moving into your own bedroom. Your devotion to your family, who hates my guts."

I keep my face impassive as I examine those comments. I want to argue with her, tell her it's all bullshit, but there are enough grains of truth in her words to stop me. It's more complicated than she presents, but I can't deny any of those accusations. Maybe I can at least try to explain them though.

"Amber, I hear you. I do work too much, I know, but in my defense, you seem to prefer it that way. If I'm hanging around you too often, it seems to make things worse. The bedroom ... well. Yeah. I'm only human, and there was only so much I could take. Having you lie there next to me but completely untouchable? Turning your back on me every night as though you couldn't bear to look at me? I had to end that because it hurt, Amber. It fucking hurt. It still does."

Each sentence gets louder than the last, and the final one seems to ring in the air for several long seconds as she stares at me, her eyes wide. There's a little tremor in her hands, and I take a deep breath. Shouting won't help either of us.

"As for my family ... Look, is there any point rehashing this? You don't get along. It's not the first time that's happened in the history of the world, is it? I still don't understand it, but it is what it is. Do you want me to choose between you? Do you want me to cut them out of my life? Would that make you happy?"

Would I do that? She's never outright asked me to, but

would I? There was a time she loved being a part of my family. Somewhere along the way that changed, and I have no idea why. And I never fucking asked her. I just accepted it, letting the gap between them grow wider until it was too big to bridge.

It's an impossible choice. I love Amber, but I love my family too. We share the same blood; we're bonded by the same memories. I run the company my dad built, and I'm the oldest of the clan, the big brother and now the doting uncle. Could I turn my back on all of that? I've always hoped things would change. That something would eventually give. It's been tough, being stuck in the middle, but I was okay with that if it meant keeping both halves of my world happy. Except happy isn't a word I would associate with Amber. Or me, for that matter. We've both been fucking miserable for years, and I'm not sure there's a way to change it. Shit. Maybe she's right. Why am I even fighting this? Is it only because I'm stubborn—because I don't like to fail? Or do I really think there's hope for us?

"I would never ask you to make that choice," she says, her voice small. "I'd never ask, but even if I did, I'm not sure you'd choose me. I'm not a fool, Elijah. I'm aware of how difficult I am and how little I have to offer. I'm aware of how hard all of this has been for you. So maybe it's time to stop trying. We're both exhausted. Drained. And it's not too late to salvage some happiness from life. You're young enough to find someone else, someone who can give you what you want."

"And what would that be, Amber?" I ask, knowing exactly what she's talking about, but I need to hear her say it.

I don't know why. It will hurt us both to discuss this, but perhaps we need to. Perhaps we should have discussed it years ago.

Fresh tears spring to her eyes, and I instantly feel like shit.

"That, Elijah, would be children. You can't pretend you don't want your own. The way you talk about Luke, the way you were with Libby … It's still there in you, that paternal instinct. And there's nothing wrong with that, nothing at all. It's one of the things I loved most about you when we met. You were so strong, so protective—I knew you'd make a great dad. And we planned that, didn't we? We planned our family. I wanted two, you wanted as many as we could manage." She gives me a weak smile, a peace offering.

I will always remember those late-night conversations, back in the days when we talked until the early hours, so fascinated with each other that we never ran out of things to say. She wanted a boy and a girl, wanted to name them Margot and Mikhail after her favorite ballet dancers. I said I wanted a minimum of six, but we compromised and agreed to settle for three or four.

God, we were so naive. So confident that we could make plans like that—that we were in control. In hindsight, I see that's where things started to go wrong between us. After years of expecting it to happen naturally, sex became more regimented. We did it at certain times of the month, even certain times of the day. It was less like making love and more like a medical procedure. Amber tried herbal remedies and drank foul teas and banned me from booze and riding my bike. We ate a god-awful diet with walnuts and salmon in every damn meal, and there was a strict no-jerking-off policy to keep my swimmers in prime condition. Despite it all, despite all the research she did and everything we tried, she would emerge pale-faced and tearful from the bathroom every month when she got her period. One time, she was a week late and so excited to do a test—but again, crushing disappointment was all that followed. I was upset too, but Amber was distraught.

When we finally saw a specialist, we found out that her fallopian tubes were too badly damaged for her to conceive naturally. We were devastated. And exhausted. There were alternatives—surgery and IVF, surrogacy, possibly even adoption—but at that point, I think we were too wrung out to make any decisions. We agreed that we'd give ourselves a break, try to break our obsession with it.

Then my mom got her cancer diagnosis, and all our energy became focused on that. It was an absolute double whammy, and truthfully, I don't think our marriage ever recovered. Clearly, Amber didn't. She refused to discuss it later and retreated further and further every day. Now she's sitting opposite me, so close but a world away, crying into her cocoa as we discuss our divorce.

I want to go to her, to comfort her. Hell, I want her to comfort me as well. I want a time machine, to go back to those early days so I can figure out what went wrong and fix it.

I make to stand up, but she holds up a hand and shakes her head. "No! Please don't. I can't ... I can't cope with you being kind right now, Elijah. I just can't. I'm sorry. I know this isn't only about me and that this is a shock—but it's the right thing. We hurt each other so much, don't we? Every single day. It's like a war of attrition that neither of us can win. I'm so fed up with all of it. I want to stop scoring points. I just want ..." She blinks down at the mug in her hands and murmurs, "I want to be happy," and it's as though being happy is such an alien concept that she wonders if she used the right word.

"And you don't think you can be happy married to me?"

"Based on the last year, I don't think either of us can. I don't blame you, and I'm not saying any of this to make you feel bad. We've both tried, and we've both failed, and I hate what we've become. I want better—for both of us. You deserve to have children. And I deserve to stop feeling like such a failure, like someone who's let you and your family down. And neither of those things can happen if we stay together."

I bury my face in my hands, feeling like crying myself. Is that really how she's felt all this time? Like a failure and a disappointment not only to me, but to my entire family? Fuck. That's too much pressure for anyone to carry. "Baby, I don't see you as a failure. I have never seen you as a failure," I tell her, my voice cracking. "Was it me? Have I made you feel that way?"

"No. Don't do that to yourself, Elijah, it's not all down to you—you're a good man. It's ... God, it's complicated, isn't it? But if I'm being honest, I never quite believed you when you said that I was enough. I never really thought I was, and I know your family resents me. Your parents wanted you to have kids. You were the oldest, and there was this weight of expectation because you were lined up to take over the business. You were supposed to produce an heir. I couldn't give you that, couldn't give them that. I couldn't give myself that.

I've felt that loss every day and also felt … I don't know, guilty?"

She has never spoken like this before. Never shared these feelings, this pain—at least not with me. Why not? And why now? She might say I'm a good man, but I don't feel like one. I let her retreat when I should have been fighting harder for her. I suppose I assumed that she would always be around, that there would always be more time to fix things. To find our way back to each other. Was I wrong?

"Amber," I say softly, overwhelmed with emotion. "I didn't know. I didn't know that's how it made you feel. That you were going through so much. Why didn't you say anything?"

"To start with, because I needed time to process it all. I was so upset, and I knew you were too. But then, not too long afterward, your mom got sick." Hand shaking, she brings the mug to her mouth and takes a small sip. "That was a long, hard battle that we all fought, especially her. Then she died, and … well, the time never seemed right. You were hurting, I was hurting. Your whole family was broken in so many different ways. Do you remember? It was like you were all made of glass and someone threw you from the top of a building. You all shattered, and the last thing you needed was me bleating in the background while you tried to glue everyone back together." She grimaces, those brown eyes full of suffering. "I spoke to my parents about it though."

I recoil, shocked. Amber and the wolves are not close and never have been. The only family member who ever showed her any love was Lucille. Amber seemed way fonder of my mom than she was of her own, and she used to tell me all the time how much she loved being part of our family.

"What did they say?" I ask, dreading the reply.

She raises her eyebrows at me. "Well, as you can imagine, it was a very inspiring talk. My dad basically told me I was lucky you still wanted me, considering I was defective, and that I should be grateful for whatever scraps I could get. My mom very helpfully added that he was right and that no other man would want me now either. Then they both asked about the terms of our prenup."

"You're not *defective*," I say, snarling, my hands balling into fists at my sides. I should fly to DC and put Ronald Warwick's fat head through a window for saying that. How dare he?

"He didn't use that word, honey, don't go all macho on me. I think he actually said 'subpar,' which now that I come to think of it isn't much better."

I love it when she calls me honey. That hint of Southern belle peeks out when it slides from her lips, and it makes me feel warm inside. There are so many things I love about this woman, but apparently there are also many things I don't know. Am I really going to lose her?

"He's an idiot, whatever word he used. And we never had a prenup because I believed in us. I still do. I don't want this, Amber. I don't want a divorce. I want to work things out."

She gives me a sad smile. "That's the shock talking, darling. And maybe your pride. You know you don't like to lose. But ask yourself this—how many times in the last month have you enjoyed a peaceful hour in my company? How many times in the last month have we laughed together? How many times have you genuinely looked forward to coming home and seeing me? Now compare that to how many times we've fought, cursed, glared, or avoided each other ... The math doesn't lie. I know this hurts right now, but the truth is we've been hurting for a long time. I've come between you and your family, and I don't even make you happy. It's like ... death by a thousand paper cuts, every damn day. I can't go on like this, and I don't think you should either, Elijah."

Jesus fuck, my head is all over the place. I'm so shocked I can barely think. She's being way too open, way too reasonable, way too honest. I don't know how to handle this Amber.

"Today was not a good day, admittedly." I scrub my hands through my hair. "But it wasn't any worse than usual, not by our standards."

Her laugh is a delicate sound that seems so out of place in the middle of all this. "Oh, sweetie. Are you listening to yourself? You just proved my point. I don't think either of us should be settling for 'no worse than usual,' do you? Do you really, truly want to spend the next few decades measuring our days by how bad they *weren't* rather than how good they *were*?"

I stare at her, this wife of mine. Wrapped in a blanket, hair a mess, face clear of her normal glamorous mask. I have loved her since the day I met her. Since I saw her sprawled on a picnic blanket on the college lawn, listening to music on her iPod, a daisy chain in her hair. Eyes closed, singing along to that Dido song "White Flag" so badly that I had to laugh. On our very first date, I knew she was the woman I would marry, the woman who would be the mother of my children. The woman I would grow old with. Now it looks like only one of those predictions came true.

The worst part is, I can't even deny what she's saying.

We do torture each other and bring out the worst in one another. We are a fucking disaster zone, and I spend as much time despising her as I do adoring her. She's right— we don't share peaceful evenings in or laugh together, and yeah, sometimes it's a goddamn relief when I get home and she's not here. How many times have I ducked out of her charity events for work or dumped her when one of my brothers needed me? How often have I really tried to talk to her, to reach out and connect? When was the last time I genuinely put her first? *When did I last tell her that I love her?*

"Let's leave," I say. "Right fucking now if you like. Pack a bag and head off somewhere new. Somewhere nobody will find us. I'll give up work and my family. I'll give up anything, Amber. I love you, baby. I don't want this to end."

She can't hide her surprise, and for a moment I think she'll go for it. For a moment, I'm exhilarated and terrified and pumped up all at once. But then she shakes her head, smiles that sad smile, and says, "And what would we do, Elijah? Run a beach bar in Mexico? Hide out in a cabin in the woods? Live the rest of our lives in barefoot bliss?"

"Yes. All of those things. Any of it. Whatever and wherever you want."

"And what happens when you start to miss your brothers? When you see a headline about Jamestech stock plummeting? What happens when your dad's health gets worse? You would hate missing out on Luke's childhood. How long would it be before you resented me for taking you away from your world? No, it's not realistic. I'd never ask that of you. I'd never ask you to change who you are just for a shot at saving a marriage we both know is already over." She takes a deep breath and then says, in a voice so heartbreakingly tender, "But for what it's worth, honey, I love you too."

Her rejection hits me like a hammer to the heart, but again, she's only speaking the truth. I am not that guy. I have responsibilities here—to my family, to my business, to my employees.

But if she's right, then why does this feel so wrong?

CHAPTER
SEVEN
AMBER

It killed me to leave him and make my way on shaky legs back to my own room, but it needed to be done. Emotions were running high on both sides, and I was determined not to let the situation get out of hand. We would have ended up in a brutal fight or tearing each other's clothes off, or both, and it would not have been good. I shocked him—hurt him—and I'm in pain too. There was nothing to be gained from discussing it any further. We both needed to let the idea settle and wake up with clearer heads.

Except I don't wake up with a clear head. I wake up smiling, rolling under the covers, still halfway between sleep and the real world. In my dream, Elijah slipped into my room in the middle of the night and climbed into bed with me. He stroked me and played with me and made me come with his tongue. After that, I pleasured him with my mouth, taking all of him in and sucking him dry as he screamed my name. It was so realistic that I can almost feel his beard on my thighs, taste his cock on my lips. I'm so aroused, my panties are damp.

It takes a minute or so for the memory of what really happened last night to nudge aside the dream. When they do, it all crashes down on me like a ton of bricks, burying me in rubble and choking me with dust.

Did I really do it? Did I really tell Elijah that I want a divorce? The soreness of my eyes and the heaviness of my heart tell me that I did, and the contrast between my fantasy and my reality is awful.

I lie in bed and weep. I weep for the sorrow in his eyes and for myself. For the future together that we will never know. I wanted to grow old with this man, to spend the rest of my days with him, but now that won't happen. I hate the way that makes me feel, but I must stay strong. Because if I don't, we *will* grow old together—and we will despise each other. That would be the worst fate of all.

Some of the things he said last night nearly convinced me that we could pull through, that we could mend and rebuild. I know he loves me, and I love him right back—but it's not enough. There are too many pressure points, too much history, too many ways we have discovered to hurt each other over the years. The issues will never go away. I won't miraculously become fertile, and he won't stop wanting children. Even if he claims he doesn't anymore, I would never believe him. I'll always feel like I've held him back. Like I've deprived him of the opportunity to be a father, that he has had to sacrifice a role he was born for to stay married to me. Maybe I could tolerate that if we actually made each other happy, but we don't. We're like two cage fighters, trapped together in the most luxurious of cages.

I don't know why it all came to a head last night, but it did, and now we have to deal with it. There's a lot to talk over, a lot to decide, and it will be hard and exhausting. I have zero enthusiasm for any of it, so I allow myself a little longer to huddle under the covers. It's okay to feel sad, and it's okay to cry. It's even okay if I do those things in front of Elijah.

I don't want to pretend anymore. I've been faking my way through my own life, and I can't stomach it any longer. I make a promise to myself that from now on, I won't be afraid to show the world my true face. I can't even remember what it feels like to wake up with genuine enthusiasm for the day ahead. Something has to change, and it starts with me setting Elijah free. I should have done it years ago, when his mother first told me to. Verona James was right all along.

When I get out of bed and pull back the drapes, the glorious autumn day makes itself known. The little pocket park across the street is already bustling with dog walkers, birds are singing, and the sky is a cloud-streaked swath of pastel blue. This is the first day of the rest of my life, and I have no idea what comes next.

I shower and dress in yoga pants and a baggy sweatshirt, deliberately avoiding the call of my makeup kit, but I do give in and apply some moisturizer. My whole face feels sore and puffy from all the crying.

A sense of dread curls in the pit of my stomach as I leave my room and tiptoe along the landing like an intruder. I have no idea why—this is still my home, at least for now, and there's no point in trying to avoid Elijah. Ironically, we now need to spend more time with each other than we usually would.

There's no sign of him downstairs. Our cocoa mugs sit in the sink, and I absentmindedly wash them. I don't usually wash the dishes, and I'm aware of how pampered that makes me. I'm aware of how privileged I've been in many ways.

But I often find myself wishing I could swap my life for the one that Dionne, our housekeeper, leads. She's a woman in her fifties, married to a man named Edwin who drives a subway train. They have four children, two of whom are teenagers and still live at home. The others are married with kids of their own. Her whole world revolves around her family, and she's forever smiling as she talks about their achievements, shows me graduation photos and baby pics, and simply basks in the glow of their love. They don't have endless piles of money. No Bentleys or drivers or private Caribbean islands. What they have is priceless—they have happiness. I would give up every bit of my wealth and influence for that. Maybe that's what I need to do.

It's half past seven, and Elijah's normally up by now, either already at Jamestech headquarters or working in his home office if it's the weekend. We both keep busy schedules, and I'm pretty sure I'm supposed to be somewhere for a breakfast meeting soon as well. I'll have to look it up so I can cancel.

In fact, I think I might just cancel everything. I'll probably lose a lot of my appeal as a charity fundraiser once I'm no longer Mrs. Elijah James. It'll be interesting to see who still wants to do lunch with me once the news is out.

Oh god. Managing the rumors is going to be a nightmare. The James family is famous, and I'm no stranger to page six myself. The press will have a field day with it—social media even more of one. I've spent decades perfecting my image as the alpha female of polite New York society, and now I'm going to be pitied. It sucks, but I can't stay married to avoid gossip. I'll have to work on cultivating at least an illusion of apathy.

None of this will be easy for Elijah either, but at least he'll have the support of his dad and siblings. Hell, they'll probably throw some kind of parade to celebrate and toss an Amber-shaped mannequin onto a bonfire. Only Drake will see this as bad news. I wish I could reach out to him and tell him what's going on. We're close, but he's Elijah's brother, and Elijah will need him. I can't put my friend in the position to divide his loyalty. I want him to be firmly Team Elijah on this, and I'll only muddy the waters.

After making myself a cup of coffee, I lean against the counter and sip the scalding liquid, grateful for the pain on my tongue that distracts me from the turmoil in my mind and the empty feeling that grows bigger with every second. How will I get through this? How will I live without him? My whole adult life has been dominated by my marriage, and I have no clue who I am without it. I'd like to be invigorated by all the possibility before me, to feel brave and hopeful about this new adventure, but I'm none of those things. I'm just anxious and flat and starting to cry again.

No. I will not stand here and sob. I won't give in to despair. I don't have to be a superhero, but I also don't have to throw myself a pity party. After pouring the rest of my coffee into the sink, I head back upstairs and keep going until I reach Elijah's floor, his domain at the top of the house. I check his office first, but he's not there, the high-backed leather chair and his MacBook showing no sign of recent use.

Taking a deep breath, I pause outside his bedroom. I haven't entered this room in a long, long time. Again, our lifestyle has allowed me to shirk certain duties, the small things that tie most couples' lives together.

Our wealth has allowed us to disengage with alarming ease, and I'm nervous as I stand in front of the dark oak door. He might not even be in here. It's possible he got up and went to the office so early that I didn't hear him.

I quietly twist the handle and push the door open, and what I see inside breaks my heart. My husband is sprawled across his bed, the sheets tangled around his legs after an obviously sleepless night. His hair is all mussed up, and his arms are splayed across the mattress.

An empty bottle of Macallan sits on his bedside table. That bottle was at least half full when I left him. The glass he was using lies on its side in a pool of amber liquid. His clothes have been dumped on the floor, further evidence of his distress. Elijah is normally a neat and precise man. He must have been crying in his sleep because his lashes are damp, and there are red marks where he's been pawing at his eyes.

My hands fly to my chest, and I suck in a quick breath. *Oh god, what have I done?*

Is this permanent, this pain? Or will he recover? Can we both recover? I think so. I hope so. I hate the thought that I've hurt him, that I've possibly broken him—but then I remind myself that I've spent over a decade hurting him. That only yesterday at the wedding, I deliberately goaded him and rejected him. Me leaving will hurt him—but staying will hurt him even more. And he will hurt me right back because we just can't help ourselves.

He suddenly thrashes, mumbling a jumble of words, his

voice cracking, then finally settles on his back with his naked, muscular body on full display.

Despite the emotion of the moment, I still feel the draw. That unique pull of physical magnetism that neither of us has ever quite been able to banish. My vivid dream rushes back, and heat sears my cheeks as I stare at him. Part of me longs to slide under those sheets with him, to slip into his strong arms. To rest my head on that solid chest and tell him it was all a terrible mistake. We would make love, share tender touches, and our bodies would sing together. I want that, desperately.

But what then? We might share a few magical days feeling reborn and relieved, but the same old problems would eventually surface. He'd say something about his family, I'd react like a bitch, he'd push back. Then he would disappear into his work and make me feel irrelevant again. Or maybe I would have a meltdown the next time I saw him interacting with a kid. The next time he held the door for a pregnant woman.

No. There's too much damage. The bones of our marriage are broken. Ending it is the right thing to do, no matter how much I want to reach out and touch him right now.

Silently, I retreat from the room, and I'm forced to admit to myself that my reluctance to wake him has less to do with compassion—after last night, letting him stay unconscious for as long as possible is a small mercy I can grant him—and more to do with cowardice. I'm afraid I won't be able to resist the urge to pretend last night never happened if I have to look into those deep gray eyes of his.

I need to get away for a while. We both need some space.

Half an hour later, I'm packed and on my way to the

airport in a cab. I'll send him a message once I reach JFK. I don't want to sneak off and leave him guessing. He doesn't deserve that, and it would set a nasty tone for what's to come.

I considered writing him an actual letter, but that would have been too much. Another reminder of days gone by, when we used to leave little love notes on each other's pillows. I still have a tattered little stack of them, dog-eared and faded, tucked away in a treasure box with concert programs, ticket stubs, and other mementos from that time in our life. Nothing has been added to that treasure box for a long time now.

The cab drives over the bridge, the East River flowing beneath us as we leave Manhattan and head into Queens. My flight departs soon, and a couple of hours after that, I'll be in a completely different world. I'll be with my Granny Lucille in South Carolina, the place where I spent the happiest days of my childhood. I need comfort and advice, and she is the only person I trust to provide those things.

EIGHT

ELIJAH

To say that this morning sucks ass would be an understatement.

The first problem declared itself as soon as I tried to open my crusted-up eyes. The finger of sunlight creeping around the edges of the drapes was so bright it felt like a grenade going off in front of my face. My mouth was dry and furry, my head pounding, and I could smell my own sour Scotch breath. Classy.

None of that even compared to the dumpster truck of pain that landed on top of me as soon as I was fully awake. Amber running away from the wedding, then crying on a rain-soaked street.

Amber asking for a divorce.

Shit. Is that still what she wants in the cold light of day? Do I have any chance of talking her out of it? And really, truly ... Should I even try to talk her out of it? I press a pillow over my sore head, feeling sick in every possible way.

I love my wife. I have never stopped loving her. But somewhere along the line, I stopped fighting for her. I've taken solace in my work, in my family, in my life outside my marriage. Over the last year or so, things have definitely gotten worse between us. We seem to have only two modes —battle stations or avoiding each other. We are strangers sharing a house who see each other at social events but have barely any contact when we're alone in our home. That's not normal. At least it's not a normal I'm used to—my mom and dad were crazy for each other right up until her last day on earth.

Seeing Nathan and Melanie so happy together, and now Drake and Amelia, has really emphasized how empty my own life is. How cold Amber's and my relationship has become. I'm thrilled for my brothers, but also a little envious. It's like they've finally come alive now that they have the right women in their lives. It's beautiful. Really beautiful.

I should have that too, but I haven't for a long time. The vulnerable version of Amber I saw last night was a revelation to me. For longer than I can remember, she has been a closed book, hoarding her true feelings like buried treasure. Always keeping me at a distance.

My phone beeps, and I flail around with my hand until I find it. Damn, even the phone screen is too bright. The message from Amber has me struggling to sit up. On a standard day, it would be a reminder about an event I needed to attend or a request for a meeting. Because that is how detached we've become—we schedule meetings when we need to discuss something.

Today, though, it's something else entirely. The message says that she's boarding a plane and will be staying with Lucille in Charleston for "a little while." The tone of the message isn't cold or aggressive, which is actually an improvement, but it is still a knife to the heart.

Deep down, I thought we'd talk more today. Maybe go for brunch, take a walk through Central Park, and she might continue to open up to me. Perhaps we'd even find a way through this. A sentimental corner of my brain hoped it was a new beginning, not an end. That we could come alive again and be like Nathan and Melanie, Drake and Amelia. Elijah and Amber.

But that's exactly what she's trying to avoid. Amber isn't a fool. She realizes how easy it would be to fall back into our old routines and pretend last night didn't happen. If she'd woken up this morning and behaved like normal, I would have gone along with it. I'd have carried on as though it was another ordinary day.

It would hurt a shitload less in the short-term and be much simpler all around. We're both perfectly capable of pretending the whole divorce conversation simply didn't take place.

Instead, she chose to fly over seven hundred miles away. That tells me she means business. Amber is done pretending.

Fuck. She's gone. She's really gone.

As for Lucille, we've always gotten along well, but she's the very definition of "feisty old broad," and she will one hundred percent be on Amber's side. I have no clue what being on Amber's side will look like to her grandmother.

When I go to get out of bed, my head throbs in agony at the movement. I look around, disgusted with myself. Spilled booze, abandoned clothes, frat party hangover. For fuck's sake, I'm a mess, inside and out.

Logically, I know she's done the right thing. We do need

some space and time to get our heads straight. And I need to really think about this, about my future. I've taken so much for granted. I assumed my marriage would last, even if it was an endurance test. As far as I was concerned, we were going to be together forever, sparring partners for life. I assumed Amber would be in my world until the end, for better or worse, just like our wedding vows said.

This new reality is tough to accept. Logic is what I need, but I'm not capable of that when everything is hurting, physically and emotionally. A single tear escapes and trails down my cheek. Pathetic. Nausea rolls in my stomach. I have no fucking clue how to survive this day without Amber, never mind the rest of my life.

Forcing my mind to focus on what is rather than what isn't, I ask myself what my life will look like in a year if we go through with the divorce. Would I be happier without Amber? Without the lingering sense of disappointment and disapproval that seem to radiate from her? I'm so weary of it all—she's right, she's not the only one who's tired.

Last night, she told me things she never has before, allowed me a glimpse of the pain she's been in, but does that really change anything? She seems to think it's too late for us to fix things, and I can't fix our marriage alone.

A sudden loud buzzing noise starts up, and for a moment, I wonder if it's another symptom of this hangover from hell, but I realize that it's the vacuum running downstairs. Vicky is here and getting on with her work. Her very noisy work.

It's a Sunday, which is a stupid day to have the cleaner around, but Amber said yes when Vicky asked if she could switch. One of her kids has special needs and her husband's shift patterns changed, making it harder for her to work during the week. I also know from the household accounts that my wife gave her a hefty pay raise while she was at it. Underneath Amber's hard shell is a soft, delicate, kind interior. She'd hate to hear any of those words applied to her, and it's a side to her that very few people get to see.

Double fuck. What the hell am I going to do? Wallow in bed, stinking of booze and feeling sorry for myself all day? Cry alone while I listen to Percy Sledge singing "When a Man Loves a Woman" on repeat for hours on end? That's what I feel like doing, but that's not me. I need to get out of here, out of my own head.

I type out a message to the only people I know I can rely on, and it takes way longer than it should because my fingers aren't working for shit.

911 meeting, Brassington Lounge, one hour.

Finally, I hit send and force myself to stand and go take a shower.

CHAPTER
NINE

ELIJAH

The Brassington is a five-minute walk from the house and isn't usually open on Sunday mornings. I'm not the kind of guy who normally takes advantage of my wealth and influence, but today is far from normal. A quick conversation with the owner ensured it would be open and ready, the kitchen staffed, and the drinks flowing. The place is set up like an English country club, all dark wood paneling and bookcases and top-shelf liquor. It's exactly what I need today. Anything brighter would feel too cheerful and make me want to puke.

This is the first time I've ever sent a 911 message to my family, but by the time I walk into the private room at the back, they're all there. Just like I knew they'd be.

Maddox, my youngest brother, is dressed in baggy sweatpants and a faded T-shirt covered in Sanskrit writing. Drake is reading the *Times*, a coffee on the table in front of him, his hair still damp from the shower, just like mine.

Nathan immediately looks up from his phone, his dark eyes flashing with concern. "You okay?"

"Nothing more Scotch won't fix," I reply briskly, motioning for the waiter hovering by the door. "Could you bring us a bottle of fifty-year-old Macallan?" I ask him. "And food. Lots of food."

"Yes sir, right away. Would you mind me asking, um, what exactly you mean by food?"

I'm on the verge of snapping back with a sarcastic reply, but I bite my tongue. It's not his fault I'm in a shitty mood. "Bagels. Smoked salmon and cream cheese. Fries, lots of fries. Bacon. Waffles. Eggs, sunny-side up and scrambled. Cookies, chocolate chip. And ice cream."

I give my brothers a crooked smile. "What do you guys want?"

The waiter looks dumbstruck, and I quickly assure him that I'm joking and send him on his way. There's a pot of coffee on the table, and I pour myself a cup while I wait for the Scotch to arrive. As soon as it does, I add a couple fingers. The old Macallan reminds me of Amber. In the bottle, the liquid is exactly the same shade of brown as her eyes. Have I always thought that, or is it just today that everything reminds me of her?

I take a minute to enjoy the warm combination of coffee and Scotch sliding down my throat before facing my brothers. I'm about to speak when my phone rings. It's Mason, calling from London. I prop the phone up next to the coffee pot and nod at him as his face fills the screen. The other three gather round so they can see him properly.

"You all right, bro?" Mason says. There's a delay between his lips moving and the sound arriving, but when it does, it's clear despite the distance.

"Yeah. Sorry for the drama. You didn't have to call. I know you're busy."

He shakes his head, and there is a slight blur with the movement. "Don't be stupid, dude. My big brother sends a 911, I'm there for him, no matter what meetings I have to cancel."

I cringe a little inside. Those meetings were Jamestech business and were important. I open my mouth to apologize, but Maddox lays his hand on my shoulder and gives me that little zen-master smile of his. He may be the youngest, but after years of traveling the world, he gives off the vibe that he just might be the wisest of us all.

"It's fine, Elijah," he says. "Mason doesn't mind. None of us mind. You matter more than anything else we had planned today."

"Yeah. What he said," Mason responds, nodding vigorously. It's the middle of the afternoon in London, and he's dressed in a business suit. Sunday meetings—the glamorous life of the corporate world. "So, what's up?"

I pour some more Macallan, see them exchange looks. It's not quite ten a.m. I take a sip and run my fingers through my hair. "Amber asked me for a divorce."

Nobody reacts straight away, which I expected. Maddox will think it through, Mason's on a slight time lag, and the two lawyers are world class at keeping their cards close to their chests. Nathan's nickname is the Iceman, and he didn't earn that by gushing about his feelings. I pay special attention to his face, though, because I know the subtle signs that tell me what's actually going on inside his head. There's a very slight thinning of his lips, and his eyes narrow fractionally. That means he's angry as hell.

"She did *what?*" he asks, his voice low and steely.

"Asked for a divorce. Then left. She flew to Charleston to stay with her grandmother."

Drake leans over and clasps my arm. He's the only one of them who can tolerate my wife. I'd go so far as to say that they're close. I'm not proud of this, but there have been moments when I've felt jealous of their relationship. Not that I ever suspected for even a second that anything untoward was going on between them, but she seems to actually like him. She likes him so much that she voluntarily spends time in his company, the lucky bastard.

"How are you doing?" he asks, his eyes running over my face as though he's searching for damage. "How is she doing?"

"How is *she* doing?" Nathan interjects, slapping his palms down on the table. "Who gives a fuck how she's doing? She has spent years making our brother's life miserable."

"It's not that damn simple, Nathan," he snaps back. "And if you took your head out of your ass for a minute, you'd see that."

This isn't a courtroom, and this isn't a case they're contesting—this is my goddamn life. "Both of you, shut the fuck up!" I exclaim, surprising them. "*She* isn't doing so great, and neither am I. But she's convinced that she's right, that she's somehow, I don't know, setting me free."

"Well," Nathan says, leaning back in his chair and making an obvious effort to calm himself. "At least that's something she and I finally agree on."

I sigh and shake my head. Everything is always so black and white to him. So straightforward. And although he's coming from a place of love, I still feel like punching him in the face.

"Nate, we all adore Melanie," I say, dumping yet more Scotch into my mug. "But what if we didn't? Would you love her any less?"

"That's not the same thing. Mel makes me happy. Amber makes you miserable. Look at you right now—you're practically inhaling that Macallan."

"That's because she left me. That's because my heart is fucking breaking."

I slam the mug down so hard that liquid sloshes out, and Maddox quickly mops it up with a napkin. "We all need to take a breath," he says quietly. "This decision can only be made by Amber and Elijah. That's who it's happening to, not us. Elijah is our brother, and he's come to us looking for support. How about that's what we give him?"

I see a flash of anger in Nathan's eyes, but I also see grudging respect. He knows that Maddox has a point, and he gives a single nod. "Yeah. Okay. Sorry about that." Shaking his head, he sighs. "I just hate how unhappy she's made you for all these years."

It's been hard for him, for all of them, watching my marriage deteriorate. I guess it's easier for him to hate her— like she suggested last night, to make her the villain of the piece. But we've made each other unhappy. I'm as much to blame for the state of our marriage as Amber is, a fact he seems incapable of recognizing.

We all go silent for a few minutes as the food arrives and is spread out on the buffet table behind us. It gives us a break, time for us all to take a breath, like Maddox said. I sit back down with a full plate but don't have the appetite to eat any of it.

"Damn, that looks good," Mason says from the phone. "This is torture."

"What?" Nathan says, holding up a forkful of waffle. "They don't have food in England?"

"Not food like that. The guys are pretty hot, though. Something about that accent does it for me. Anyway, while you're all busy stuffing your faces, here are my views. Elijah, bro, I feel for you, I really do. Gotta admit, when I first heard that news, my initial reaction was ding-dong, the witch is dead ... Because Nathan's not lying. You've been miserable. Amber's made it pretty fucking clear that she has no time for us either, so I don't give a shit how she's doing—but I do give a shit about you. This sucks for you, and you're obviously in pain. But that will pass. Give it time, man. Let it settle, and it won't feel so much like the end of the world. Plus, look on the bright side—you get to come clubbing with me. I can be your wingman."

"Jesus fuck," I say, half smiling. "Is this supposed to be a pep talk? Because that's a fate worse than death."

"It's better than staying at home on your own and jerking off fifty times a day."

Maddox looks up and lays down his fork. "Fifty times a day? Christ Mason, you must be dehydrated."

"*I* don't jerk off fifty times a day, asswipe—I have an actual sex life. We're not all Buddhist saints."

"I'm not a Buddhist," Maddox says calmly, immune to the jibes about his celibacy. "But unlike you, I do at least know how to spell it."

"I know how to spell it," Mason insists. "It's B-U-T-T-C-R-A-C-K."

It's actually helping, seeing my brothers joke around and insult each other in this lighthearted way. It's grounding me, making me feel like the world isn't quite such an empty place after all. This is what I needed. I even manage to eat a piece of bacon.

"Look, I've actually gotta go soon," Mason says, glancing at his watch. "London traffic is as bad as Manhattan, and I promised Dad I'd meet him for drinks. Do you want me to tell him about this?"

Our dad suffered a minor cardiac event a few months ago. It wasn't serious, certainly nothing like the heart attack he had previously, but it worried us all.

"How's he been?" I ask.

Mason pulls a face. "He's an opinionated, domineering old goat who keeps threatening to come into business meetings to 'show me how it's done.' Because, you know, I'm five years old, and I've never actually been to one before."

"Right. Well, that sounds good. Sounds like normal. Tell him, then, yeah, that's fine. We need ... We need to talk about what this means, and how we'll present it. At some point. If it sticks."

Mason deals with everything related to Jamestech's corporate image, and if Amber and I do split up, people will need to know. There will be a press release, and a surge of public interest, and ... Fuck. That is a problem for another day.

"Don't worry about that crap," Mason says. "You just concentrate on getting shit-faced with the others, okay? That's your one job for today."

"Getting shit-faced is my one job?"

"Damn right, and I can tell you're going to ace it. I love you, brother. See you in a few days, okay? Stay strong."

I put my phone back in my pocket and take another long swig of Scotch.

"If it sticks?" Drake says, looking at me intently. "Do you think there's a chance it won't? Do you think there's a chance you could work things out?"

Nathan's knife clatters to the table, but Maddox shoots him a warning look.

"I don't know. It's all been a hell of a shock. I had no idea she was heading in this direction. She might be my wife, but she's a mystery to me. Things haven't been great, especially recently, but I thought ... Fuck, I don't know. I suppose I thought she was as firmly committed to our misery as I was. Which, now that I say it out loud, is totally fucked up. Jeez." I scrub my hand through my hair and groan. "I just don't know what the fuck to do with myself. Nothing feels right without her."

They're all silent for a few moments. I hold my face in my hands and fight against the tears that want to pour out.

"It'll be okay, Elijah," Maddox says. "Mason was right. Time will help. It always does."

"And it hasn't happened yet," Drake adds. "It's not over 'til it's over. You need to keep talking to her. Don't give up."

"Here." Nathan pours more Scotch into my mug. "Drink this."

I do as I'm told and realize I'm topping up last night's excess. Mason was right about that too—I am indeed going to ace my one job for the day.

"We're here," Nathan says, his hand solid on my shoulder. "We're here for as long as you need us."

"Yeah?" I ask, glancing up at him. "I know you mean that, and I appreciate it. But I also know that part of you is wondering about the prenup and already considering the divorce settlement."

His eyes tell me I've hit the jackpot, and he shrugs. "I'm not going to lie—those things have crossed my mind. Those things matter. Nobody expects divorce to get as bad as they almost always do, and even couples who part on good terms can get dragged into the dirt."

He doesn't have to add that Amber and I are hardly a couple on good terms, and I hate that he's right. I also hate that I understand where he's coming from—he's my brother, my family, and he's looking out for me. He wants to protect me the only way he knows how.

"Well, I'm afraid I've got some bad news," I reply, reaching for my Scotch with a shaking hand. "We didn't have a prenup. Dad advised it, you advised, even Amber said she wouldn't mind ... but I never saw the need. I believed in us. I believed in me and Amber. I believed in our future together. Is this where you say I told you so?"

"No, it's not. No amount of I-told-you-sos could make up for seeing you like this, Elijah. I'm sorry, I really am. The way I feel about Amber isn't likely to change, but I do understand better these days. Back then, I was a baby cynic. I never believed in the fairytale like you did, and I hate seeing you hurt like this."

I nod and suck in more booze. Of all us James boys, he's always been the most cynical when it comes to matters of the heart. It's ironic that he ended up with the fairytale he didn't believe in and I ended up with nothing.

I never considered how that must have made Amber feel. She knew the whole story involving my dad's intervention, that he found Nathan a wife specifically so he could produce an heir, which he has gone on to do. In Amber's mind, that should have been her. She will have felt the sting of it, the rejection, the failure. The fact that because she couldn't have kids, Nathan was being asked to step up and fill that gap. Fuck. Now that I know more about what was going on with her, I see things so much more clearly. How hard has all of this been for my wife? How much pain has she been hiding?

She asked me not to contact her for a few days, so it's not like I can ask. It's also not necessarily going to change where we're headed. If she wants out, she wants out—and I have to face up to the fact that it might be for the best—for both of us. It's sad, but in the real world, sad things happen every damn day.

I feel like boiled shit right now, but there's every possibility that once the shock fades, I will feel differently. Who knows? Maybe I'll be out clubbing with Mason. Maybe I'll meet someone else and go on to have a completely different future. A second act.

Hell. I hate everything about this. I raise my Scotch mug to my brothers in a twisted version of a toast. Today, I will let myself fall apart in the safe company of my siblings. Today, I will concentrate on doing my one job—getting shit-faced.

Tomorrow ... Who the fuck knows?

TEN
AMBER

I 've been staying with Granny Lucille for the last three days, and she finally dragged me outside today. Against the odds, I'm enjoying myself, and feeling the fall sunshine on my skin has done me good. The weather in Charleston is perfect at this time of year, and I almost forgot how beautiful it is. I suppose I almost forgot how beautiful anything is.

Waterfront Park is a pretty place with stunning views of the river and the harbor. We strolled here from her house in the French Quarter, waved off by her friend Vivienne, who stopped by for a late lunch. Now we're sitting by the pineapple fountain, watching the sunset. This park, and the crazy fountain that is literally in the shape of a pineapple, was built when I was a little girl. There was always a real sense of excitement coming here. I used to love splashing around in the water and clambering onto the wooden swings under the pier. I would dance and cartwheel over the grassy spaces like a human tumbleweed, and Granny would treat me to ice cream, benne wafers, or crab cakes, depending on what mood we were in.

They were simpler times. Happy times. My memories of this place, of her quirky home in one of the most historic parts of the city, are pure and filled with joy. Granny has always been eccentric, but always felt warm and safe. She looked after me so well, and I knew I could count on her. Life here was the complete opposite of my life at school or at home with my parents. I loved my visits to Charleston and spent the rest of the year looking forward to summers full of endless hot, humid days. I never got tired of spending time with her, not even when I was a teenager.

Today, she is taking no shit. And when Granny Lucille decides to take no shit, she means it. At eighty-nine years old, she needs a cane to walk but is still fit and active. Her silver hair is in a short pixie cut, which suits her perfectly because she looks a little like a pixie at five foot nothing. There are signs of age, obviously—wrinkles and lines, liver spots on her skin, fingers twisted with arthritis—but she still gives off an amazing energy. She laughs easily and has a delicious Charleston accent that sounds like honey. I can't say that I'm enjoying listening to it right now, though.

"You've got to stop feeling sorry for yourself, Bam-Bam," she says, using the childhood nickname that she gave me. "I've let you hide away in your room long enough. It's time to come out into the light, child."

It is light, I think. The sky is streaked with pinks and reds as the sun slides down, the colors reflecting off the water. I wonder what it's like in New York today. This time of year could mean anything from dazzling sunshine to a hailstorm.

Of course, I then start to think about Elijah and what he might be doing. In the dazzling sunshine or the hailstorm. I have no clue how he is, because he respected my request and hasn't contacted me. Or maybe he hasn't contacted me because he hates my guts and has already moved on. Maybe his brothers are taking him to strip clubs and setting him up on dates with women named Sugar Lips or Busty. Maybe ... *No. Stop right now!*

"Yes, Granny," I say obediently, at least showing her that I'm listening. "I know."

"Do you now, Bam-Bam? What is it that you know?"

"That I need to stop feeling sorry for myself. I get it. It's deeply unattractive."

She snorts with laughter and slaps her skinny thighs. "Unattractive? Who gives a damn about that? You've always cared way too much about what other people think. There's a place for it, as long as they're people whose opinions you value—but that's not always the way with you, is it? You gave up ballet because that asshole Billy Kruger said you looked like a giraffe on pointe."

"I was only fourteen. And anyway, he was right—I was already too tall."

"Too tall for what? To be a prima ballerina, maybe, but to enjoy yourself? To love dancing? No such thing as too tall for that. You also listened to your mother when she said you needed to 'drop a few pounds' before your prom, and to your father when he told you men don't like women to be too smart."

I give her some side-eye. She's absolutely right about all of those things.

"I also listened to you, Granny," I say. "And I followed my

heart. I believed in love. I married a man I adored. That didn't work out so well."

"Pah! Nonsense. Your marriage didn't go wrong because you loved him too much. What a ridiculous thing to say. Although you still haven't properly explained what exactly did go wrong, have you? You've just been crying into your pillow for days on end."

I sigh and stare at the sunset. It really is spectacular, like an abstract painting in the sky. If Verona were here, she would capture it beautifully. The wind is knocked out of me when I imagine her wearing the paint-spattered men's dress shirt she favored—Elijah once told me about the time she absentmindedly grabbed one of Dalton's thousand-dollar dress shirts when the urge to paint struck—one paintbrush caught between her teeth and another in her hand, the pineapple fountain splashing behind her. We had a trip planned. She and Granny Lucille met at the wedding but didn't get to spend much time together. They would have gotten along like biscuits and gravy. But then the diagnosis came and the trip never did. I blow out a breath and force away the bittersweet memories.

"It's complicated, Granny."

She snorts again—it's one of her favorite things. "I'm sure it is, Bam-Bam, I'm sure it is. I couldn't possibly understand, could I, because your generation thinks they invented 'complicated.' Tell me one thing then. Do you still love him?"

"Yes," I say matter-of-factly. "But I also can't stand the way I feel when I'm around him."

"What the fig does that mean? And look at me when I'm talking to you."

I turn to face her, and her fierce expression softens when

she sees my tears. She pats my cheek. "Oh, darling. Bless your heart. You're really hurting, aren't you?"

I nod, the gentleness of her tone making the tears spill. Sometimes, I only hold myself together with sheer will, and all it takes is a touch of sweetness to make me crumble. Come at me with an axe, I'll fight you; come at me with a kind word and I'll fall at your feet.

She holds my hand, and we sit together and watch a group of teenagers fly past on rollerblades. Once they are gone, she says, "What do you mean, you can't stand the way you feel when you're around him? What has he done to you? Because I might look frail and old, and he might be richer than Midas, but that doesn't mean I can't whoop his skinny New York ass."

I giggle at the image. She is frail and old, but I don't doubt she would try. And Elijah's ass is far from skinny. Elijah's ass is ... a perfect manly peach of an ass.

How much do I reveal? She knows my story inside and out, apart from one particular part.

I'll never forget that night, not as long as I live. I loved Verona James with all my heart—she was more of a mother to me than my own ever was. She was quick to find pleasure in life, full of warmth and humor. Elijah brought me home to meet his family when I was nineteen, and I was nervous as hell. She took me into her arms and gave me the kind of bear hug that her sons also specialized in. She made me feel welcome from day one, and when I married Elijah, I felt like I gained a mom as well as the love of my life.

That made it all so much worse. Not only was this precious woman dying, but she used up one of her last coherent conversations to tell me that I wasn't good enough. To tell me I was broken—that's the actual word she used.

"You shouldn't have married my boy," she said, "knowing that you were broken."

I've tried to convince myself it wasn't the real her. That it was the drugs and she didn't mean those horrible words. But I've never quite managed to believe it. Part of me has always wondered if the drugs simply removed her inhibitions and allowed her to say the things that were in her heart.

The truth is, even if she didn't really mean what she said, her words struck a chord. They echoed something I was already feeling. Elijah was supportive when we discovered I couldn't have children, but I worried that was how he really felt deep down. For a man who wanted a whole tribe of kids, finding out his wife couldn't give him any must have been a huge blow. I hated myself. Hated the fact that I couldn't do what millions of women have done with ease throughout the history of humanity. Like Verona said, I was broken.

I never told Elijah. He was grieving, and so was I. The time never felt right to add to his already heavy load. That's when the rot started to set in. I was wounded and started to pull away. Only a tiny bit at first, to give my pain some space. I hoped it would go away. Except it only got bigger and bigger, and he didn't even notice. I forgive him for that. The loss of his mom was like a wrecking ball that swung through his whole family.

It was a messy and difficult time, and nothing was ever the same between us again. By extension, nothing was ever the same between me and his family either. Every time I visited their childhood home, I felt Dalton's gray eyes on me and imagined I saw contempt and disappointment in them, like he felt cheated of the grandchildren he deserved. I got the feeling that when I walked into a room, they all went silent because they were talking about me. Poor barren Amber, the woman who trapped Elijah.

How much of this was real and how much was merely paranoia? I don't know. But I kept withdrawing—from them and from him. It all hurt too much, and that was the only way I knew how to survive. Now I see how much worse it made everything. I should have told him. I should have reached out instead of closing down.

I swipe the tears from my face and gently squeeze Granny's bony hand. The sun is finally sinking into the horizon. I have survived another day of this agony, and I will get stronger with each passing sunset.

"You don't need to kick his ass, Granny. Knowing Elijah, he's kicking his own ass already. He doesn't like to fail."

"This isn't about failing, though, is it? It's about happiness. It's about love. And don't you roll your eyes at me, madam, because I'm talking about the most important thing in the world here. You seemed so well suited. You seemed so ... excited about each other. What went wrong, Bam-Bam? Please tell me it's not because you couldn't have children together. Not everybody needs to be a mother, you know. And some women, like your own mom, really shouldn't be. Your pop won't be winning any parenting awards either."

I've never quite understood how Granny Lucille managed to raise a man like my father. She is made of emotion, and he is made of cast iron. He has never loved anything as much as his work. His dad died when he was only six, and Lucille raised him and his brothers alone. My uncles are nice men who pay attention to their loved ones, but my father barely knows they're there.

"That was part of it." Standing up, I hold out my hand to help her to her feet. She slaps me away and uses her cane instead. "But only part. It's been bad for years, and we've both just ... clung on, I suppose. We were both too weak to end things."

"Until you weren't?" she asks as we walk slowly back out of the park.

"Yes, I suppose so. Until I wasn't. Except I'm absolutely terrified, Granny."

"Of losing him? Or of finding out who you are without him? Because there is a difference between the two."

"I know." I follow her lead toward one of the cute little bars that are scattered around this part of downtown. "Where are we going?"

"To get drunk, obviously—woman cannot survive by herbal tea alone. Now, you go and get us a table, and I'll be with you in two shakes of a lamb's tail."

As ever, Lucille surprises me, but I'm more than happy to go along. I order myself a glass of pinot and a Planter's Punch for her. She claims that pickling herself in rum has kept her healthy, and I can't argue with the evidence.

The place is busy, bustling with artsy types and a few tourists, something bluesy playing over the speakers. I sip my wine and glance at my phone. Drake has called a couple times, but I spoke to nobody during my three-day Granny retreat. Now, a message lands from him, and I instantly feel guilty.

> Are you okay? Let me know you're okay for fuck's sake. Why didn't you tell me? Can I help?

A whoosh of air leaves my lungs, and I type a quick reply.

> I'm okay. Sorry for the silence. Stay by his side and make sure he's also okay—look after him for me.

I know he'll have more to say, and sure enough, his response comes through in under a minute.

> Of course. But I'm here for you too, you know that. I can multitask.

I laugh lightly and send back some kisses. I don't want to get dragged into a big heart-to-heart with him, and I don't want to divide his loyalties. After putting my phone on silent, I stash it in my bag. What I don't see won't hurt me.

It takes Granny ten minutes to join me, and she comes bearing a gift bag from one of the nearby galleries. "That lamb shook its tail real slow," she says, passing the bag to me. Inside is a pen and a pretty notebook covered in yellow jessamine.

"What's this for?"

"Well, honey, that's called a pen, and people use them to make markings on paper called *writing*. You might have heard of it, even in New York."

"Ha ha, very funny. Why are you giving them to me?"

"So you can make some lists. Don't tell me you've been running Manhattan for all these years without making lists?"

I raise my eyebrows at her. She's right, and I do love a

good list—nothing is quite as satisfying as ticking things off when they're done. I usually had three or four on the go at any given time, but since my Great Escape, I've abandoned them all. Other than Drake, the only people who have contacted me since I left are connected with the various social events I was either organizing or a guest at. I've been swimming in shallow waters, and I can't say I miss it. I kept so busy to distract myself, to make myself feel useful. To get out of Elijah's way, even. I have no clue what I will do now.

"Okay," I say slowly, then sip my wine and eye her cautiously. It doesn't pay to underestimate Lucille. "What kind of list did you have in mind?"

"Well, for a start, you should make a list of things you need to do next in this new life of yours. And then I'd suggest possibly a list of things you *want* to do. Even a list of things you've never tried before but should. Like, you know, getting a job?"

I choke on my wine. "Granny! I've had jobs."

She dismisses me with a wave of her hand. "Five weeks at the Harbor Club busing tables one summer does not count, Bam-Bam. I know you've been busy with all your charity affairs, and I'm sure you gained some pretty useful skills doing that. You need to put them to good use."

She's right. I can organize events and plan galas, and I can liaise with multiple teams to make those things happen. That sounds great on paper, but I'm under no illusions—it was all made a lot easier by having unlimited resources at my fingertips.

"Plus, you have a degree. You're college educated," she adds. "Which is more than I ever had."

"Granny, I'm a liberal arts grad—I'm not entirely sure

how useful that is. And anyway, I'm not going to starve. Elijah isn't … He wouldn't …"

"Screw you over in a divorce? Nobody ever thinks that. But let's say you're right. Let's say you get a fair settlement. You can live anywhere you want, do whatever you want. What does that look like to you? You're young. You have decades of living left. What are you going to do with all that life, sweetheart? Or are you going to be content playing the poor little rich girl forever?" She sucks up her rum punch, her blue eyes sparkling in her wizened face.

If she's trying to freak me out, it's working. I have never lived alone, technically. I have never worried about money. I've never applied for credit or been to a big box store or gossiped with colleagues at the water cooler. My life has been far from perfect, but it has been privileged. What do I want to do? More to the point, what am I capable of?

"I'm scared, Granny," I murmur, flicking open the pages of the notebook. "Scared of missing him so much I might die. Scared of building a new life without him. Of trying to figure out who I am and realizing I might be … nobody."

"Bullcrap! You'll always be somebody, Amber. You're so much more than just someone's wife or someone's daughter —even someone's grandchild. But it's up to you to figure out what kind of someone you're going to be. You need to be brave. Bold. You need to make a goddamn list."

A few people glance over to see who is making the impassioned speech, and they're probably surprised to see it's a tiny silver-haired woman nearing ninety. I'm not surprised—Lucille has always been a force of nature. When I don't reply immediately, she narrows her eyes at me. "You're what? Forty years old?"

I grimace before I remember who I'm talking with, then prepare myself for the usual you're-just-a-spring-chicken lecture. Instead, she simply nods. "I'm sure it does feel scary, starting over in the middle of your life. But you have to remember that it's never too late to change. To grow. To find what makes you happy. I didn't do it until I was seventy-three."

I frown at her. What the hell happened to her sixteen years ago?

"That got you thinking, didn't it, child? Well, when I was seventy-three, I met Vivienne at the farmers' market."

"Your friend Vivienne? The one who came to lunch today?" Vivienne is in her mid-sixties, with long white hair and the kind of fashion sense that reminds me of the aunties in *Practical Magic*. I can totally see her whipping up a round of midnight margaritas in the blender.

"Yes, she is my friend, Bam-Bam—but she's also my lover. We've been a couple for all these years."

I put my glass down before I drop it. Vivienne is her *what* now? Did I hear that correctly? Did my Granny Lucille just damn well come out to me?

"Close your mouth, sunshine, you'll catch flies."

I clamp my lips shut but still gawp at her. She has a small smile on her face and looks ever-so-slightly smug. If she was aiming to shock me out of my self-pitying stupor, she's achieved her goal. "What ... Why didn't you tell me?" I splutter.

"It was none of your business. Besides, to start with, I was feeling my way through it all. I was perfectly happy with your granddaddy, but I was a virgin when I married him, and I didn't have much to compare it to. There were a few other men after he passed, of course. I'm not a saint, even if I do live in the Holy City. Truthfully, Bam-Bam, I could never figure out what all the fuss was about. Until Vivienne. *Then* I figured it out. Anyway, I'm not telling you this to scandalize you, though that is fun—I just wanted to prove my own point. It's never too late to find what makes you happy."

"Huh." I raise my hand to get the waiter's attention. I'm going to need more wine. "And in your case, that's other women?"

"I don't know," she says, shrugging. "I've only been with the one, and at my age I'm probably not about to go on a dating spree. But I'm happy, yes. More than ever. As you get older, you start to realize how short life is. You need to squeeze as much juice out of it as you can. Maybe add it to your list. The list of new things you should try."

"Being a lesbian?"

"No, you horse's ass—living life to the fullest. Although hey, why not give it a go?"

A big smile spreads across my face. I think it's the first genuine smile I've managed since the night I told my husband I wanted a divorce. "I don't think so, Granny," I say, shaking my head. "I think I might like cock a little too much."

She snorts so hard rum punch comes out of her nostrils, and I laugh out loud. I've managed to shock her, and it fills me with delight. She laughs along with me and wipes her face clean with a napkin.

"Oh Bam-Bam," she says, her eyes glistening with amused tears. "Is it any wonder we get on so well? You're as bad as I am."

That, I decide, is very much a compliment. I look at the

blank pages of the notebook in front of me. All those empty lines, waiting to be filled. All those lists waiting to be made. All that life, waiting to be lived.

I can do this, I tell myself. I can do this.

ELEVEN

I can't do this. I thought I could, but I was mistaken. Being back in New York is harder than I ever imagined.

I stayed in Charleston for two weeks, and everything felt so much simpler there. Elijah and I started to exchange messages about a week ago, and all our conversations are heartbreakingly polite. We're both committed to staying calm and civil, and that isn't something we've ever been good at.

We agreed that we didn't want things to get nasty and decided that the only lawyer involved would be Drake. It's a hell of a position to put him in, but he said he doesn't mind, and he is at least someone we both trust. Nathan would be a different matter, of course—he'd have me out on the streets with my possessions in a shopping cart quick as a flash.

My pride screamed at me to simply tell him I don't want a dime, but that isn't sensible or even fair. I've contributed to this marriage, to Elijah's life and social standing. Being Mrs. Elijah James is the reason I never built my own career. Pathetic as it might sound now, being Mrs.

Elijah James *was* my career. And now things need to change. I've been using the notebook Granny gifted me to make those lists she suggested, and while I was doing that, I felt positive, like I could move forward. Now that I'm back, I'm not so sure.

Hearing his voice when we speak on the phone is unsettling. The low rasp of gravel when he works to hide his emotions, the sound of everyday New York life behind him. I was reminded what I've lost—of what I'm giving away.

Our last conversation was especially difficult. The anniversary of Verona's death always hits him hard, hits all of them hard, and even in our current circumstances, I reached out. I had to. They usually visit her graveside, then go out for drinks to toast her memory. I called him later in the evening to ask how it went.

"It was ... okay, I suppose," he said, the pain clear in every word. "I think Maddox struggled. Or maybe he's the only one of us who shows it so much. I missed you, Amber."

I never went to the memorial gatherings with him, but I always called a ceasefire and made sure he wasn't alone that night. "I kept finding myself wondering what my mom would say," he continued. "About us."

Of course, I have a pretty damn good idea what she'd say —*leave now, son, while you have the chance.* But I kept that to myself, and we navigated our way through the phone call with awkward politeness. Our new normal.

He has asked several times if I'm sure this is what I really want. His neutrality is undoubtedly deliberate, for both our sakes, but I hate it. He's so emotionless when he asks that it feels like he's going through the motions, ticking a box. It doesn't make sense for me to be bothered—how can I be the one who asked for a divorce and also be upset that he isn't fighting for our marriage? I don't know how, but I am.

Drake has filed the initial paperwork and started drafting up agreements, and the whole process will now take on a life of its own. I arrived in the city this evening, and as agreed, came back to the house in Manhattan. Elijah has moved into a hotel until we decide what happens next.

Now, I'm standing in the vast entryway, suitcase at my feet, looking around at the sweeping staircase and grand chandeliers. It's spotless, smelling of fresh polish and wax, white lilies beautifully arranged in vases. Vicky has been at work, and Dionne will have stocked the kitchen for me. She'll have left me a plate of sandwiches, and there will be fruit in the bowl. The wine cellar will be blessedly full, and anything I could possibly want or need will be only a phone call away.

I absolutely hate it here, and I wish I could run straight back to Charleston.

We were happy in this house to start with, Elijah and I, but that happiness has been completely overshadowed. I don't walk around these rooms and remember better times —I remember fights. My memories are filled with the sounds of slammed doors and cold silences and the occasional thrown glass. I remember the distance that grew between us.

When we moved in, we expected to fill our home with children, to make it our own. Instead, it's become the place where our marriage died. I'd trade it all for a walk-up in Brooklyn if I thought we could get that love back.

I don't even like the way the house looks—it's too smooth, too perfect. I trudge up the stairs, feeling weary. After unpacking, I glance at my phone. Martha sent a message asking if I want to meet up for drinks, and I find myself pleased to hear from her. One of my new lists includes "make real friends." Maybe I could start with the ones I already have.

In a normal family dynamic, I'd be friends with Melanie and Amelia, but that feels like too much of a stretch. Amelia will see me through Drake's eyes, but Mel ... that's a different story. No. I need to find my feet outside the James family circle. Martha and I have never been close, but I do enjoy her company. If nothing else, it will fill my night. The thought of being in this house by myself is depressing.

We arrange to meet for drinks, and I take a shower, eat a sandwich, and start getting ready for the night ahead. It's so strange being here alone. It's not new—I've often been here alone when Elijah stayed with his family or was away on business trips. But on those occasions, it was only temporarily. This is permanent—this could be what my future looks like. Me, bouncing off the overly peach-colored walls of the townhouse.

I don't want that, I decide, grabbing a dusky-pink wrap dress from the closet. I don't want this house. I'll discuss it with Drake, and he'll discuss it with Elijah, and maybe he'll keep it. Maybe he'll sell it. I don't know—I can't imagine it has happy associations for him either. One way or another, though, I'm going to walk out those doors one day soon and not come back. What I need is a fresh start, and I'm not going to find it here.

Having made that decision, I feel better as I sit down at my vanity. I got out of the habit of doing my hair and face when I was in Charleston. The cosmetics, the treatments, trips to the salon, the fancy clothes and designer shoes—it was all an added layer of protection. They were a way of shielding myself from a world that could sometimes be cruel. Getting ready for an event was like preparing for battle, and my makeup was my armor.

Tonight, I keep it light and natural, practically naked by my standards. I brush my hair until it shines but don't add any product. On my feet, I go for a pair of dove-gray heels. I do like my heels—if I really were going into battle, at least I'd be able to stab someone with them.

Dammit, what if I eventually meet someone else, and he's not as tall as Elijah? What if I have to wear flats so he doesn't feel too short around me?

That, I tell myself, is a problem for another lifetime. At the moment, I have no interest in finding another man. Or, Granny Lucille's voice reminds me, a woman.

The place where I'm meeting Martha is in Midtown, and I have a moment of confusion before I leave the house. Do I call Gretchen? Who gets custody of her and the Bentley in the divorce? When was the last time I used the subway like a normal person, anyway? I glance down at my heels and decide against that for tonight. Outside, I hail a cab, trying not to think about the night we met sweet Sanjay. My dashing taxi driver with a heart of gold. At least it's not raining this time.

Through the window of the bar, I see Martha waiting for me in a booth and pause before I go inside. Elijah asked his brother Mason to draft a brief press release to announce our separation to the world, but at this moment in time, the only people who know are our families. Can I risk telling Martha? Can I actually trust her, or will my business be broadcasted all over Manhattan society by midnight?

Maybe I can trust her, but it's not my news alone. As I head inside to join her, I decide it isn't worth the risk. The place is bustling and packed with beautiful people, the bright lights and chatter a stark contrast to the darkness outside. Martha looks up from her phone as I slide into the booth, and her face lights up. She looks genuinely pleased to see me, and I'm sad that I need to lie to her tonight. I make a promise to myself that she will be the first person I contact once the news is out.

"Well, don't you look fucking marvelous?" she says, her eyes sweeping over me. "I'm liking this new look."

I didn't realize it was so noticeable, and my hand goes to my foundation-free face. "Why, thank you, Mrs. Kemp. I'm experimenting with going minimalist."

She pours me a glass of wine. "Well, I suppose it beats experimenting with meth. You look great. How's your grandmother? I bumped into Elijah last week, and he said you'd gone to stay with her."

Hearing Elijah's name jars me a little, but I simply nod and smile. "Yes. She's eighty-nine, you know. I needed to spend some quality time with her, and there comes a point where you have to put family first."

Not a word of what I said is a lie—Granny *is* eighty-nine —but the implication is that she's old and sick and I was looking after her. It was actually the other way around, but I can't let Martha know that. I'm glad he mentioned it though —it gives me the perfect excuse for why I canceled my upcoming social events.

"So true, darling, so true. I hope my feral offspring have the same attitude when I'm that age. They're currently at the stage where I can do no right. Even my breathing annoys them. I think they'd quite like it if I stopped doing that altogether."

Martha has fifteen-year-old twin daughters, and I shudder a little at the thought of all those hormones cooped up in one house. "Moms and daughters are like that," I say. "For a while anyway. They'll get through it, I'm sure, and then they'll see you for the miracle of mothering that you are."

"From your lips to God's ears, Amber. So ... Did you hear about Nancy Pearson? She crashed her Mercedes into the back of a police patrol car outside the Rockefeller Center. That's her second DUI."

And just like that, we are back on familiar territory— gossip, scandal, and examining other people's problems. It's ironic really, because neither Martha nor I have perfect lives. I am on the verge of a divorce, and she damn well should be, bearing in mind her husband's behavior. Yet we don't touch on those subjects at all. In its own way, it's actually quite relaxing, like we have come to a mutual agreement to ignore the personal in favor of the public.

I'm not sure this quite fits in with my list goal of making real friends, but it will do for now. Once I can talk about it freely, I'll confide in Martha and see what happens. Assuming she still wants anything to do with me, that is. There's every chance that without the clout of the James family name, I will become a social pariah.

Glancing around the room, I realize that I don't give a damn. Despite being one of the most densely populated cities on earth, New York often feels very small. Would I be bothered if I never saw any of these familiar faces again? If the endless round of invitations and parties dried up? No. In fact, it would be a relief. I might just go and live in a log cabin by a lake and become a crazy cat lady. Maybe I'll learn how to fish and make campfires, live off the grid and brush my teeth with baking soda. Then again, maybe not. There's probably some middle ground I have yet to find.

Martha reaches the end of her story about a competitive baking competition at her twins' school. "I mean, we all buy the damn cakes and pretend we baked them—I know I do. But poor Lindsay Wilmington made the mistake of bringing her choux buns still in the patisserie box. I felt sorry for her, I really did."

"Sorry enough to confess that you fake it too?"

"Fuck no! Why would I do that?" she says, winking at me. I shake my head, and she orders more wine. I suspect she already had several glasses by the time I arrived.

"Don't you ever get fed up with it, Martha? All the ... faking?"

She narrows her eyes at me. "You're not just talking about the baking fundraiser here, are you?"

"No, I'm not. I'm talking about everything."

She finishes off her glass and bites her lip. For a moment, I wonder if she's about to tell me something real. If we might be on the edge of a breakthrough.

"Sweetheart," she finally says, "if I didn't fake it, I'd have nothing left. This is simply the way it is for women like us. Best not to question it or look at it too deeply."

"Why not?" I ask.

She laughs lightly and wags a finger at me. "Because it might cause a rift in the space-time continuum. Or something like that. Nothing good would come of it, anyway. I'm just popping to the ladies' room. Don't drink all the wine when the new bottle arrives."

She slides out of the booth, her form-fitting dress revealing the jut of her bony hips, the flatness of her ass. She looks like a skeleton in Donna Karan. Just as she disappears into the crowd, the wine turns up. I pour her a glass and one more for myself. Tonight is starting to taste sour. I'll wait until she's back, then make my excuses. I need to go home and add to my list: Find some new places to hang out.

I take a sip and glance around. So many familiar faces, but nobody I'm interested in talking to. There is nowhere as lonely as a crowded room.

I'm about to get out my phone and check for messages when I see him. When I see *them*. They're standing up, the table in front of them scattered with empty dinner plates and used glasses. Chatting and laughing, comfortable with each other, like all of this is perfectly normal. They're on the opposite side of the room from me, and I'm hidden in my booth, staring with disbelief as I watch them walk to the exit. My husband and a woman—girl, really—that I recognize from photos. Melanie's little sister, Ashley. The one who is *bright* and *bubbly* and getting her MBA at Harvard. The one who is gazing up at my husband with an adoring smile, hanging on to his every word.

His hand goes to the small of her back as he guides her through the crowded bar, and it's like someone has stabbed me in the heart. He's smiling too, looking relaxed and happy and, naturally enough, drop-dead gorgeous. Ashley is holding several shopping bags, and he's carrying a couple too. What the actual fuck? Am I seeing what I think I'm seeing here? Is my husband out on the town with a twenty-something child? Is Elijah a goddamn *sugar daddy*?

They reach the exit, and he takes her coat from her hands and holds it out for her to put on, like the gentleman he is. She giggles and thanks him, and I can see her eyes shining from here.

My heart feels like it's going to explode, and I realize I haven't taken a breath in way too long. I'm huddled up in the booth, watching them leave. Watching them stroll together along the busy city street, shopping bags swinging, stupid smiles on their stupid faces. I can't believe he would do this to me.

All that talk about keeping things civil. All those times he asked if I was sure. The way he cried the night I told him I wanted a divorce. I'm starting to think none of that was real. If it was, he's clearly consoling himself in the arms of Ashley Edison. Who is young, gorgeous, and obviously besotted with him.

I am devastated, but I'm also furious. How dare he? How dare he parade his new plaything like this, in a place where he's known? He's flaunting it, and it hurts. I would never do this to him.

The thought of Elijah being with someone new fills me with a sharp, pulsating pain. I feel like I'm being skinned alive. Maybe it's not even new—maybe it's being going on for ages, right under my nose. It could be why he moved into his own bedroom. Is he only pretending to be upset about the breakup? Is he playing nice to make sure I don't hire a killer divorce attorney and skewer him?

Concentrating on my anger is far better than giving in to the pain. I jump to my feet, grab my purse, and scamper out into the night. I keep one eye on the happy couple, and one on my phone screen as I type a hasty message to Martha, telling her I had to leave. I'll make it up to her later, if she even cares. The chilly air assaults me, and it dawns on me that I left my coat behind, but I don't give a damn.

I feel ridiculous as I trail them, like I'm in a bad spy movie. I hide in doorways and dodge behind a group of office workers on a night out, making sure I never get too close. Elijah glances behind him a couple of times, as though he senses someone watching, but he never spots me. After a few minutes, they stop outside the lobby of a grand hotel. A familiar car pulls up beside them—the Bentley. I guess that solves the mystery of who gets Gretchen in the custody battle. My heart contracts as he opens the car door for Ashley, the same way he used to open it for me. He laughs at something she says and gestures for her to get in. Then he leans forward, his head and shoulders disappearing inside the vehicle. Is he kissing her? Is he fastening her seatbelt? Is he telling her he loves her?

He emerges again, closes the door, and pats the roof before the car drives away. Then he stands there for a moment, checking his phone, rubbing his hand over his beard and smiling. They're probably sending each other messages. It'll be all "miss you already" and rows of kisses. Probably some heart-shaped emojis too, because she's twelve.

I'm disgusted to find myself on the edge of tears. Where is my backbone? I might have asked for a divorce, but he's still my husband. He could have shown me some respect and waited five minutes before he found a replacement.

Elijah puts his phone in his pocket and wanders into the

lobby of the hotel. I wait for a few seconds, making sure those tears don't fall, and then I follow him. He heads straight for the elevator, where he presses the button and waits for the car. He's wearing a charcoal-gray suit that fits snugly across his broad shoulders, a few buttons of his white shirt open at the collar. He looks so damn good, and I hate him for it.

I have no idea what I'm going to do or what I'm going to say. All I know is that I'm going to do something. The elevator doors open, and he waits to let a gray-haired couple out first. I run across the marble floor of the lobby, and the doors are already closing when I stick my hand into the gap.

TWELVE

ELIJAH

Ashley is charming, but she's also kind of exhausting. Her endless enthusiasm, the constant questions, the harmless flirting—it's hard to keep up with her. I'm not sure if it's the age gap or just that I'm not firing on all cylinders right now, but I'm glad to get her packed away into the Bentley. She's staying with Mel and Nathan and spent the day doing some early Christmas shopping before we met for dinner. I tuck her bags in beside her and tell her I'll be in touch soon.

I agreed to mentor Melanie's younger sister, and she'll be joining her family company, Edison Holdings, as soon as she finishes her MBA, with a plan to become the new CEO when she's ready. She'll be an asset to her family's company. Ashley is ambitious, bright, focused, and eager to learn. I'm a little concerned that she's interested in more, but I'm probably overthinking it. I've known Ashley for a while now, and she's naturally flirtatious. I'm sure she doesn't mean anything by it. I hope to hell she doesn't, anyway, because she's only twenty-two. I am not remotely interested in screwing someone young enough to be my daughter.

Frankly, I'm not interested in screwing anyone at all. Apart from my wife, that is—the one who wants a divorce. It's been a tough couple of weeks, and I keep waiting for that moment when I decide I'm okay with it. I keep waiting for the day when I wake up and know for sure that this is the right thing to do. Still no dice. Instead, I wake up and miss her. Wonder what she's doing. What she's wearing. If her pussy still tastes as delicious as it used to.

Fuck. I really need to stop thinking like this. We've spoken several times, and she's remained firm. She's been polite and pleasant, so unlike her normal self that it freaks me out. I'd prefer it if she acted like a bitch; it would at least show me some fire was still burning.

Then again, as I watch the Bentley disappear into the night, I realize I haven't exactly been effusive myself. If I miss her so much, why haven't I done anything about it?

The answer isn't one I especially like. I'm still not sure. The hurts we've inflicted on each other for so long are still fresh in my memory. The scar tissue runs deep and is painful. Plus, I still don't know if part of me only wants her because I can't have her—if the competitive streak that all us James men have is leading the way. It wouldn't be fair to convince her to carry on being my wife if my motives aren't pure.

I don't want to rush into either us divorcing or us getting back together—because neither of those options feels completely right. Drake has told us that as the divorce is straightforward, with neither side contesting terms, it could go through in as little as six weeks. I could be officially single by Christmas, though I welcome the delays that will inevitably be caused by the holidays because I have no desire be single just yet.

My phone beeps with a message from Melanie, and I click on the sweet shot of Luke at the dog shelter where she volunteers. He's sitting next to a goofy-looking brindle pit bull that is licking his head like it's a lollipop. Grinning at the cuteness overload, I walk into the hotel.

I plan to have a soak in the tub, drink some Scotch, and catch up on some work. My split from Amber hasn't been good for my professional life. The South Korean deal is looking promising but still needs some final polish. Luisa and I have face-to-face meetings in Seoul the day after tomorrow, and I need to prep. I can't fuck it up by mooning over my probably-soon-to-be-ex-wife all the time.

Mason also needs me to get back to him on the statement he drafted about me and Amber. I haven't even opened the damn thing. It will make it all too real.

The elevator pings, and the doors slide open. I stand back to let an elderly couple out, noticing the way they're holding hands. Almost as cute as Luke and the pit bull, but not something that improves my mood. Old love is even more precious than young love. It's easy to be in love when you're a kid and life is a breeze. Standing the test of time, though? A whole different matter.

I hit the button for the penthouse suite, so distracted I barely notice when someone slides their hand between the slowly closing doors just in time. They open in response, and my eyes about fall out of my head when Amber slips through the gap. I knew my wife was back in town, but we didn't arrange to see each other.

My first thought is: Holy shit, she looks amazing. My

second: Fuck, what have I done wrong? Her extraordinary eyes are fixed on me like I'm prey, and her skin is flushed with emotion. She's not even trying to hide it—she's absolutely furious. She stalks toward me and shoves me in the chest. Actually fucking shoves me with both hands, so hard I take a step back. I have never seen her so incensed, and truthfully, it's really fucking hot.

"How long has it been going on?" she snaps, her voice taut, her face inches from mine.

"How long has what been going on? You're going to need to be more specific, Amber."

"You and Ashley, that's what. I just saw you, dripping with shopping bags, laughing away together. You had your hands on her, Elijah, so don't pretend there's nothing between you."

I take in her flashing eyes, the low-key makeup, the natural hair, the dress. The fucking dress. Perfectly wrapped around her slender figure, the color of a dark pink rose. It's like a petal, begging to be peeled away. It's cold outside, and I can see her nipples standing proud through the silky fabric. I gulp and drag my gaze back to her face.

"The only thing between me and Ashley is friendship and mutual professional interest. I'm mentoring her as a favor to Melanie. If I did put my hands on her, it was completely innocent, and whatever you think you saw, you didn't. But may I remind you that you asked me for a divorce. Why the fuck do you care what I do with my hands?"

"I don't!" she cries, her words and actions completely contradicting each other. "I don't care. I just ... I *hate* you right now!" Her hands clench into fists at her sides, and her nostrils flare as she glares up at me.

Wow. This is a night of firsts. I'm used to her being pissed at me, but I'm not used to her showing it so obviously. So unashamedly. What the hell has gotten into her? Where is all this passion coming from? And if our marriage was truly over, would she care this much?

"You hate me?" I repeat slowly, taking a step forward, desire for her snaking through my veins.

"Yes, I fucking hate you, okay? How many times do I need to say it?"

She raises her hands again and tries to push me away as I bear down on her. I capture both of her delicate wrists in my grasp. "How about you say it one more time."

I drag her toward me, and she fights it. She tries to pull free, but I tighten my grip and slam her body into mine. "I hate you," she whispers, her whiskey-brown eyes filling with tears, her lips trembling with emotion.

Her back is reflected in the mirrored walls of the elevator, and I groan at the sight of her long legs and her luscious ass. Her ridiculously high heels. I pin her up against the glass and hold her hands up on either side of her head, ignoring her struggle. Then I grind myself into her, my hips hitting hers, my dick hard as iron.

She lets out a soft moan, and it makes me even harder. I nuzzle into her neck, nipping at the soft skin of her throat as she groans and purrs. Fuck, she smells amazing. I let go of one of her hands and tug open the front of her dress. Her beautiful tits are right there in front of me, perched on the balcony of a lacy pink bra. I suck in a breath and groan with need. Her fingers flutter up to my arm, a halfhearted protest dying on her lips as our eyes meet. Her pupils are blown, and I know mine are too.

She might hate me, but she also fucking wants me as much as I want her. Jesus fuck, this is all such a shitstorm. I should back off and give her the chance to leave. I definitely shouldn't take advantage of the need I see shining in those astonishing eyes of hers. Ironically, this would all be a lot easier if we weren't married. If we were just two strangers looking for a casual fuck.

Maybe ...

Maybe we could be?

"I see there's a wedding band on your finger," I murmur, running the pad of my thumb over the lace of her bra, much more pleased than I should be about the fact she's still wearing my ring. She leans into my touch, her rigid nipples begging to have my mouth on them. "Are you married?"

The spot between her brows pinches in the cutest hint of a frown, but then her eyes sparkle with realization and mischief. "Yes." She lifts her chin and writhes against me as I kiss her neck. "I'm ... I'm a married woman."

"Right." I trail kisses along her jawline, relishing her little mewling noises. My fingers slide under her dress and along her thigh. I press the palm of my hand against her pussy. Jesus fucking Christ. I can feel how wet she is through her panties, and she shamelessly rubs herself against me. "And does your husband know that you like being felt up by a stranger in an elevator? Does he know how wet it makes you? What a filthy little slut you are?"

What the hell are we doing here? What kind of twisted game are we playing? And really, do I give a shit? I need inside this woman now. Nobody else has stopped the elevator, but we're playing Russian roulette with every floor we pass. Somehow that makes it all the more exciting.

"No, he doesn't ... He doesn't know. But I am a filthy little slut, you're right. I love being fucked by strangers."

Fuck! This is so hot I think my dick is actually going to explode. I slide my finger inside her panties and run it along the wet line of her slit. She shudders against me, and I pull away slightly and hold my glistening finger up. She immediately takes it into her mouth, licking it clean. Then her arms go around my neck, her hands twine into my hair, and she pulls me down for a kiss. This is not a gentle kiss. It's teeth and lips and need, our tongues fighting against each other, neither of us bothering to breathe. If this were to be my last kiss ever, I'd die a happy man.

I force myself to come up for air, look down, and see a new Amber. A wild, reckless, completely uninhibited Amber. There is no way on god's green earth I am going to be able to stop whatever the hell this is. I can only hope that she feels the same.

"I'm married too," I say, holding up my ring finger. "But tonight, I'm staying at this hotel. How about you come back to my room with me? No strings attached, no commitment. Just sex. Fast, hard, filthy. Your husband will never find out, and neither will my wife. It'll be our little secret. What do you say?"

The bell pings as we arrive at the penthouse. She looks up at me from underneath her long lashes, her breasts heaving. She pulls her dress back together.

"I say yes."

THIRTEEN

ELIJAH

Wordlessly, I use the key card to open the door to my suite. This was supposed to be my sanctuary, a way of giving Amber and me some space. Now she's here, invading that space, and I couldn't be more fucking thrilled about it.

I gesture her in, and her huge eyes gaze up at me as she skims past. There's something different about her. It's not only the minimal makeup and the simple hairstyle. It's in her expression, in the way she moves. She seems more ... free? I'm not sure that's the right word, but whatever it is, it's better. Yeah, she was screaming at me only minutes ago, but then she melted beneath my touch. Kissed me with more passion than she has for years. It's like the brittle New York veneer has been washed away by her time in Charleston.

Or maybe it's the excitement of fucking a stranger. Either way, it works for me.

She stands in the center of the room looking around as I take off my jacket. She is so damn beautiful, and all I want to do is take her in my arms and tell her I love her. Then, yeah, screw her senseless. But the stranger from the elevator wouldn't do that. Not the first part, anyway.

I pour us both a Scotch and pass one to her. Our eyes lock as we sip from our glasses, and she grimaces slightly but swallows. Amber prefers wine, but I don't want to ruin the moment—a stranger wouldn't know what she likes to drink.

"What's your name?" she asks, her tone completely deadpan.

"Elijah. You?"

"Amber."

"Amber," I repeat, letting my eyes devour her like she's on display in a store window. I linger on her breasts, those still-stiff nipples. I swear to god, they pop a little more as I stare. "Pretty name. Take off your dress, Amber." She looks momentarily surprised, her eyebrows rising. "I said take it off," I growl. "I want to see you naked. I don't fuck what I haven't inspected."

I have no idea where the hell this is coming from. I have always treated women, my wife especially, with respect—and now I've turned into this asshole? I can't deny that it's working for me, though. My cock throbs inside my boxers and my pulse races. It's working for her too—she hesitates, blushes, then she tugs the belt that ties her dress together, and the two halves fall apart. Face blazing, she slides it off her shoulders, and it slithers to the floor. She stares up at me, obviously embarrassed but also defiant.

Jesus. She is gorgeous. Her long, toned legs tremble slightly in those crazy high heels. Her tits heave in the pink lace of her bra. Her panties are the same shade of pink, and I suck my upper lip as I stare at the damp triangle they barely cover. My wife has always been beautiful, but right now, she is spectacular.

"All of it," I say calmly, sipping my Scotch. "Or have you changed your mind? Do you want to go running back to your husband? Don't you want me to sink my hard cock into that tight, wet pussy of yours?"

Her eyes widen, and she shakes her head. "I haven't changed my mind, no," she replies, her voice low and husky. With unsteady hands, she reaches behind her back and unhooks her bra. Her tits roll free, and blood rushes to my head at the sight of those perky nipples unleashed. My hands itch to touch them, but I force myself to play my part and keep my distance, watching as she hooks her fingers into the waistband of her panties. She looks up at me, licks her lips, then turns around to present me with the rear view. And what a view it is.

She works the panties down her legs, inch by teasing inch and bends down to tug them over her high heels. She stays folded over like that, holding her ankles, and slowly sways her bare ass from side to side. I cannot take my eyes off her, hypnotized by the motion. Her pussy is shiny with moisture, her ass a perfect peach. Everything I want is right there on display. Holy fucking Christ, who is this woman?

She straightens up and glances at me over her shoulder. When she bites her lip, I realize that she's nervous. She's put on a show, and now I need to step up and retake control.

I close the distance between us and wrap my arms around her from behind. She staggers in her heels when I drag her back, and I hiss when her hot flesh makes contact with my body, warming me even through my clothes. My cock is hard against her naked ass, and my hands roam her supple skin. She leans against me, and I softly kiss her neck. "You are sexy as hell, Amber. I'm so glad I met you in the elevator."

"So am I," she murmurs.

My fingers find her nipple, and she cries out, arching into my touch. I squeeze more firmly than I normally would, and her knees buckle. If I weren't holding her up, she would have hit the floor. Biting down on her shoulder, I squeeze harder, capturing the tight bud between my thumb and finger. With my other hand, I part her pussy lips, and my fingers slide along her opening. "Fuck. You're so wet. You really want this, don't you?"

"Yes. I want it. I want you. Please."

She whimpers as I find her clit, swollen and soaked, desperate for attention. I gently roll it between my fingers, and her whole body shudders. She's practically there already. Fuck. I need to taste her. I need to make her come on my tongue. When I take my hand away, she bleats in protest. "Elijah, please ..."

"Don't worry, baby, I'll make you come. But I'll do it when I'm ready." I spin her to face me. "Go stand with your back against the wall. Hands flat and spread your legs." She wavers, uncertain now that I'm not touching her. "Do it now or get out of my room. You're here for one reason only. You're no good to me for anything else."

Would I kick her out if she didn't go along with my every instruction? Fuck. No way I'd normally do that, but I have no clue who I am right now. Maybe this version of me would.

I don't have to find out because this version of Amber complies. She puts her back to the wall and slides her feet apart. Still wearing the pumps. Still dripping wet. Still needing to come.

I stand in front of her and run my hands over her body. Her skin is so warm and soft, and the way she trembles beneath my touch ... Fuck! It's too much. I look into her eyes and see the desire shining in them. She wants me. I want her. So what if we have to play this game, as long as we both get what we need?

Her fingers fumble with my buttons, but I grab her hands and press her palms flat against the wall. "On the wall, Amber, like I said."

Her lower lip wobbles, and it is the sexiest thing I have ever seen. I lean forward to kiss it, then suck it into my mouth. A little nip, and she squeals beneath me, her body squirming. I seal my lips over hers and crush her body with mine. She's trapped, completely enclosed by me. Naked, trembling, and helpless. Her tongue swirls with mine, the heat between us blazing hotter with every second of contact.

I pull away, leaving her gasping and moaning with disappointment. "My mouth has better places to be." My voice is dark with desire. I kiss my way down her neck, along the fine line of her collarbone. I lick the valley between her breasts, then suck her nipples until she starts to slide down the wall. She is boneless with need, and I grab hold of her, keeping her up. "Stay there, Amber. I haven't even started yet."

"Elijah," she groans as I drop to my knees. "Oh god! I need ... please ..."

"I know what you need, my dirty girl, and I'm going to give it to you. Legs nice and wide. Let me see all of you."

I kneel before her, worshipping at the altar of her perfect pussy. The scent of it drives me wild. I inhale the aroma and drag my fingers up her quivering inner thighs. Skin like silk, soft and luscious, glistens in the dull light of the hotel room. I smooth over them with my palms, then lean in and lick them clean of the creamy fluid that's seeping from her. Fuck, she tastes like heaven.

I run one finger along her opening, her neat blond bush slick and curled as I part her. She's wet and pink and needy, her swollen clit shining and her hips swaying slightly. I blow gently, and the warm breath makes her sigh. Her hands curl into fists at her sides.

"This," I say, my lips a millimeter away from paradise, "is the most beautiful cunt I've ever seen. Are you ready to come for me, baby?"

"Yes! Please, yes."

In this moment, I own her. She is made entirely of need. She will do anything I ask as long as I put my mouth on her soaking wet pussy and make her scream.

Lucky for her, that's exactly what I intend to do.

I run my tongue along her seam, keeping it flat and soft and steady to start with. She groans, and her hands go from balled-up fists to splayed fingers slapping against the wall. I pick up the pace and increase the pressure, taking my cues from the rhythm of her gasps. Her hips jut forward, and my nose is buried in her. Exactly where I want it to be. I keep her still with my hands on her hips while I unravel her with my tongue.

I plunge it inside her, curling and uncurling, lapping away at her delicious center. I can feel the vibrations building. A low moan falls from her lips. She's so damn close. After replacing my tongue with my middle finger, I sink in and out of her, loving every filthy wet sound she makes as I drive her crazy.

Her fingers curl in my hair, breaking my rules. But I don't push her hands away. I want them there now. I want to feel her nails on my scalp, to feel her thighs trembling around my face. I want to experience every sensation while she falls apart. Sucking her clit into my mouth, I lash it with my tongue over and over again, matching the pace with my finger thrusts. Her pussy walls clench around me.

"Elijah!" she shouts, even her voice shaking now. She comes in a glorious rush, the muscles of her pussy contracting and pulsating as her arousal floods my senses. I carry on eating her, milking every last second of pleasure, helping her ride it out right to the very end. She continues to quake as I run my tongue along her one last time, and her whole body sags in the aftermath.

Gently, I stroke her trembling thighs and lay one final kiss on her pussy, then I climb to my feet in time to catch her as she starts to slide down the wall. Holding her in one arm, I use my other hand to wipe my mouth and beard. I'm dripping with her, and I fucking love it.

She smiles up at me hesitantly, that endearing flush back on her cheeks, eyes sparkling. "So what now?" she whispers. "Are you going to fuck me?"

"Is that what you want, Amber? You want me inside you? You think you can take me?"

Her tongue darts out and moistens her lips, her weak arms snaking around my shoulders. "Yes. I can take you."

"Good girl." I lift her, and she wraps her legs around my waist. Her soaking wet pussy rubs up against me, and I decide I'll never wash this shirt again. I carry her through to the bedroom and throw her down on the mattress. She lands in a tangle of long limbs and giggles, and my heart gives a dangerous lurch. It has been too damn long since I heard my wife laugh like that.

No, I remind myself as I strip off my clothes. This woman is not my wife. I am not her husband. We only just met. The game allows us both the freedom to take this pleasure from each other without any of the complicated shit that normally comes between us. Tonight, nothing is going to come between us.

I climb onto the bed and crawl between her spread thighs. She lies there before me, bare and brazen, everything a man could want. I lower my mouth to hers and kiss her so deep it feels like I could lose myself. She tugs me closer, wrapping her legs around me. One of her shoes falls to the floor, and she laughs, a sound almost as beautiful as she is.

I pull back, take the other shoe from her foot, and throw it to the ground. Then I simply study her, drinking in the curves and angles that make up her gorgeous body. This is a sight I will never get tired of. It seems to unnerve her, the way I sit there silently, my eyes wandering across every exposed inch. Her gaze shifts to my rock-hard cock. She gulps in a breath and swallows. Her laughter fades, and she seems less sure of herself. "How ... How do you want me?"

Every damn way.

"Lie on your front. Ass in the air." Her lashes flutter, and I know she's nervous. And I like it. I enjoy seeing this woman who is always so stoic, so confident, knocked off-balance. That probably makes me a jackass, but I'm too busy admiring the way she smoothly slithers onto her belly to give a shit. I'm too busy looking at her juicy ass, a perfectly shaped peach.

When she glances at me over her shoulder, something in her eyes touches me deeply. This is the most intimate we've been in over six months. I smile reassuringly—I might be a jerk, but I want her to feel safe. She smiles back, and the warmth that spreads inside me has nothing to do with sex.

"Well?" she says cheekily, emboldened once more. "Are you just going to stare at my ass, or are you going to fuck me?"

I love the challenge in her voice almost as much as I love her jitters. I slap her ass with a sharp crack, and she shrieks.

Then I pounce, grabbing hold of her hips and driving my cock straight inside her. She yells, obviously not expecting the sudden invasion. "Does that answer your question?" I snap back, slamming into her so hard she flies a foot up the bed. Her pussy is still wet, still so tight from her orgasm. It's like fucking velvet and honey, and my cock can't get enough.

I slide my hand around to her clit and gently rub it in little circular motions. "No, Elijah, I can't ..." she protests.

"You can and you will. I promise, baby."

I nail her as hard as I can. I'm not going to last long myself. My cock is ready to explode, and feeling her ripple around me as I play with her isn't helping. I curve my body around hers, kiss her neck, nip her shoulders, driving into her faster and harder. My fingers slide and stroke through her wetness, and she takes in a big desperate breath and cries out my name as she comes again. Her head is turned to one side, pink cheek flat on the pillow, plump lips parted. I watch her closed eyelids flutter in ecstasy, her caramel hair flowing over the sheets as she shakes and shudders. It's all I need. Fuck! With one last driving thrust, I finally let go. My climax is so powerful I feel like I might black out, and she's not the only one shaking now. I keep hold of her hips, empty every last drop inside her, then finally fall at her side on the bed.

We're both slick with sweat, in various stages of come-down from that mind-blowing sex. I wish we could stay like this forever. My hand creeps along the sheets, and I nudge her little finger with mine. She nudges back, then rolls onto her side to look me in the eyes. Fuck, she really is something. Still-dilated pupils in her whiskey-brown eyes, hair stuck in damp strands to her flushed skin. A small smile on her lips. I stroke back the hair and run my palm over her cheekbone. "What happens now?" I say, then curse myself for it. I've broken the spell.

She kisses me once, softly, and gets to her feet. The bed feels empty without her. I feel empty without her. I don't want her to leave, but I don't feel like I can ask her to stay. Maybe that was one last bang for the road. A farewell fuck for old times' sake. Keeping my expression neutral, I watch her retrieve her scattered clothes and put her dress back on. She runs her fingers through her hair in an attempt to tidy it, but it doesn't help much.

She props one hand on her hip. "Do I look like a woman who's just been fucked?"

"Yep," I reply, smirking. "One hundred percent. People will probably point at you on the street."

"Ha! Let them. I don't give a damn." She looks down, then back at me. "Well, this was … interesting. Actually, it was kind of amazing. But it can't happen again—you know that, don't you? We *can't* let this happen again. I'm not in the market for an ... affair? Is that the right word?"

"I suppose it is," I say, stretching my arms over my head. I see her staring, her eyes running over my body and lingering on my abs.

As though trying to clear her thoughts, she shakes her head, then slips on her shoes and forces a benign smile. "Whatever it was, like I said, it can't happen again."

"Worried your husband might find out?"

She gives me a wicked grin. "No. I love my husband, but he wouldn't even notice I was having an affair unless his assistant sent him a memo about it."

I raise an eyebrow and grin right back, but I'm gutted by the truth in her words. "He sounds like an asshole."

Her face softens. "Oh, he has his moments."

"Goodbye, Amber."

She gives me a tiny wave. "Bye, Elijah."

As I watch her beautiful ass swaying like a pendulum as she walks out of the bedroom and listen to the door close behind her seconds later, I am certain of one thing: This will definitely be happening again.

FOURTEEN

AMBER

I sink down onto the sofa, clutching my mug of chamomile tea, still wearing a stupid, post-orgasmic smile on my face despite having showered and changed into my pajamas since I got home an hour ago. But it has been a long time since I had sex of any kind. And I haven't had sex that good in ... Well, now that I come to think of it, forever.

Elijah and I always had a powerful physical connection, and in our early years together, there were no issues at all in that department. We began to lose our way when the fertility problems started. Sex became scheduled rather than spontaneous. Then, when the doctors told me I wouldn't get pregnant no matter how much sex we had, something inside me died. I struggled to readjust. If I couldn't have a baby, why was I having sex? Flawed logic, but I was a mess at the time.

Verona's illness came too soon after, and I couldn't bear the thought of burdening him further with my neediness. I thought I was being kind, doing him a favor by suppressing my own needs in favor of his. Instead, I was contributing to the slow decline of our marriage.

Later still, years after Verona's death, after Elijah and I had grown further apart, sex became something else entirely. Our conflicts were usually ice rather than fire, but every now and then, a fight would end with us fucking. It would be quick, desperate, and hot—and yet another way to hurt each other. It was like competitive fucking, both of us ferocious and full of fury. No matter how satisfying it was in the moment, it left me feeling hollow afterward.

Tonight, though ... Wow. Tonight was something else entirely. Elijah has always been dominant in bed, and frankly, I've always liked it. But tonight was next level. It was so far out of our usual comfort zone, but I loved every damn second of it. I know I should feel like it's wrong, but it sure didn't feel wrong. I don't think I've ever come so hard in my entire life.

And while the sex was spectacular, there were also moments of genuine tenderness. The way he smiled at me when he knew I was feeling uneasy, the way our fingers touched afterward. Despite everything, he's still the only man who has ever made me feel so safe and secure.

I was certain that the divorce made sense for both of us, but now I'm not as sure as I was. Can our marriage really be completely over when such a strong spark remains between us?

On the TV, Gracie is wearing her ridiculous Bavarian milkmaid outfit and beating the crap out of Eric on stage at the beauty pageant in *Miss Congeniality*. Learning how to fight should definitely go on my list of "things I've never done before but want to." Making myself stronger in every way I can is a top priority. It will be a lot easier to work on my body than it will be to work on my mind. These days, my mind is all over the place, and right now, it's still in bed with Elijah.

I told him it can't happen again. Except ...

Even thinking about what we did is making me squirm. There's a dull but insistent ache building between my thighs that has me wriggling around on the couch, wishing I had something to rub against other than the seam of my PJs. My fingers might be a poor substitute for Elijah's tongue and huge cock, but they're a lot less complicated.

My phone beeps to tell me I have a message. It's from Martha, telling me she's home after a fun night out with some strangers she befriended after I left. She included a photo of her wearing my coat and drinking a cocktail, raising the glass to the camera. It makes me smile, and I quickly type out another apology, promising to set a new date very soon. I owe her.

As I finish up, a new message lands. This one is from Elijah, and I suck in a deep breath before I open it. What if it's a dick pic?

It won't be. Elijah isn't that kind of guy, but part of me wishes he was. Maybe I should take a photo of myself with my hand inside my panties to get the ball rolling ...

No! *Stop right there, Amber.* This is madness. I need to get control of my brain, my libido, and my life in general. My hands shake slightly as I touch the screen.

> I've left something for you on the step. And just to be clear, there is nothing going on between me and Ashley. There is only one woman I have any interest in.

That's me, right? With a flutter of nervous excitement in my belly, I put my phone down and head to the front door. It's been a long time since Elijah gave me a gift, and given the turbulent state of our relationship right now, it could be anything. Diamond ring. Giant vibrator. Eviction notice. Rattlesnake. All of the above.

I do believe him about Ashley though. I was caught unaware by seeing him. And seeing him with another woman snapped something in me I didn't even know was there. But his shock when I confronted him was genuine. Besides, Elijah is many things—a liar isn't one of them.

I pause at the front door before I open it. I probably shouldn't be prancing around outside in my PJs this late. Maybe I should go to the control room and watch the video feed to find out what's out there waiting for me. We don't have live-in staff, but we do have a lot of cameras and alarms. We're rich, and rich people apparently need these things.

I smile at the memory of when a personal safety specialist came to the house a few years ago. He was here to review our security arrangements and was concerned at my lack of bodyguard and how I roamed around New York without protection. He told Elijah I was a kidnapping risk. Elijah looked at me and, completely deadpan, said, "I can guarantee you that anyone foolish enough to kidnap my wife would end up offering *us* a ransom to take her back."

Even then, I thought it was funny. And true. Now, though, as I hesitantly open the door, it crosses my mind that I feel more vulnerable than I used to. This house is too big, and I really don't want to stay here alone. The street is predictably quiet, in the heart of the city but secluded from the usual urban chaos. There's a small cardboard package on the top step, and I crouch down to collect it.

After locking up, I take it back to the living room and find a phone inside. Why has he given me a phone? And not even a particularly nice model. It's a simple thing, the kind you pick up in a convenience store. It's unpackaged and, I see when I switch it on, charged up. There's already a message from a number I don't recognize. I click on it.

> This is Elijah. We met earlier. If you want to see me again, use this number. It can be our secret. Nobody need ever know.

Fuck. My own husband sent me a burner phone. My own husband is offering to keep our hookups a secret.

My own husband is inviting me to have an affair with him.

A thrill of excitement shoots through me.

My answer should be no. It should be an emphatic *hell* no. I should throw the damn phone in the trash and forget tonight ever happened. It's a crazy idea, and it won't end well. So why is there a smile on my face and a kaleidoscope of butterflies in my belly?

I feel like I'm being torn in half. My head is telling me one thing; my heart—and a few other body parts—are telling me another. Could we actually do this? Are we capable of having an affair? Can we put our emotions and the complications of our life together in a neat little box and keep them separate? There's no denying the appeal of his offer, and the idea of it being clandestine makes it all the more alluring. I've never had an affair—and isn't this supposed to be a time in my life where I rack up some firsts? Something to add to, and subsequently tick off, my bucket list.

I stand here in the middle of the room, biting my lip. I'm so nervous, but in a good way. Like when Elijah and I first met. When I was really into him but wasn't sure how he felt about me. I was a teenager then, though, and now I'm forty. I shouldn't be standing here hopping from one foot to another, wondering what to do.

But I knew my answer as soon as I read his message. Hell, I knew as soon as I walked out of his hotel room earlier. It's probably all kinds of insane, but god, I want it. And don't I deserve to get a little of what I want? Don't we both?

Nobody will know? Not even my husband?

I stare at the screen after I've hit send, imagining him waiting for a response from me. Is he as excited as I am? Is he as worried and nervous and turned on?

Especially not him.

Then I'd like to see you again. But promise me you won't tell anybody.

I promise. This is just for the two of us. The rest of the world can go to hell.

I clasp the phone to my chest and press my lips together, suppressing my excitement. Until I realize I'm completely alone and can kick my feet and squeal like a teenage girl all I want. So that's exactly what I do.

FIFTEEN

AMBER

F ive days later, back in the "real" world, we finally agree on a statement about our separation. We've already filed, so there's no point in hoping that nobody will notice—eventually, they will. The statement was drafted up by Mason with our input, and it's short and simple.

"After more than two decades together, Jamestech CEO Elijah James and his wife Amber have agreed to part ways," it reads. "The decision has been made jointly and amicably and is grounded in mutual love and respect. Amber and Elijah remain close friends and will continue to support each other as they enter the next stage of their lives."

Then there's some extra flimflam about respecting our privacy, which we all know in the age of instant social media and online news is unlikely to happen. Mason is going to post it on the company website tomorrow morning, and it won't take long to spread after that.

It feels odd, knowing those words will be out there. That it will all become real. Journalists will contact me for comment, and acquaintances will be surprised. Our marriage will become part of the rumor mill. People will gossip about us over lunch, wondering what went wrong for the apparently perfect Mr. and Mrs. James. What we don't provide in fact, they will supply in fiction. And by the end of the week, Elijah will probably be having an affair with his secretary, I will have discovered God and joined a convent, and both of us will have "possibly" been spotted at sex clubs with a dominatrix.

Tongues will wag so hard they might fall off. I know all of this because I've been guilty of doing it myself. Never maliciously, I hope, and never in a way intended to spread harm, but I've gossiped over cocktails. I've reduced other people's lives to entertainment. I'm sure most people have.

Interest in our separation will fade, though, because that's the way these things work. As long as we remain quiet and dignified, people will soon get bored of us and the fuss will die down.

I am surprised at how much pain I feel. After the other night, part of me wondered if things would change course. If either of us would have second thoughts. Obviously, we didn't, and while I might know that's for the best, this feels awful. I don't give a damn about the gossip, but this is a step closer to the end of my marriage, to the end of something I once thought was sacred.

I hit reply all to the email chain I'm part of—me, Elijah, Mason, and Drake—and confirm that I'm happy to go ahead. Happy, of course, is not really the right word. I'm terrified. Uncertain and anxious. Although I instigated this turn of events, it still hurts. I keep the tone of my response polite and businesslike, but inside I am unbearably sad.

Our strange and magical interlude in Elijah's hotel room definitely showed that there is still something between us, and we've exchanged a few sexy messages since. That's certainly been fun and exciting, but clearly neither of us feels it's enough to sustain a whole marriage.

Drake contacted me separately to ask if I want to delay the statement, assuring me that there's no rush at all. Bless his heart, he's trying to give us the opportunity to rethink. But he would have asked Elijah first, and my husband obviously didn't draw the proceedings to a halt.

Yes, there is still something between us, but that's only natural after so long together. Maybe it's simply a leftover, a reminder of what once was. Whatever it is, it's not enough to reverse all the damage we've done to each other.

I don't quite understand how one version of us is calmly discussing logistics with Drake, and another version of us is using burner phones to carry on our illicit "affair." Then again, there's a hell of a lot that I don't understand about the world.

After I've approved the release, I message Martha and ask if she wants to meet up for drinks soon. I don't really want to, but the news will be out tomorrow, and she's the closest thing I have to a friend in Elijah's and my shared world. She'll have questions, and I owe her after abandoning her to go fuck my husband. Interestingly, now that I think about it, we both studiously avoided talking about our men during our night out.

That's not unusual—we're not exactly soul sisters—but Freddie's name did not pass her lips even once, and I didn't discuss anything about my own marriage. I know why I stayed quiet, but she was equally close-mouthed.

Freddie is one of the toughest divorce lawyers in the country. He has a reputation for ruthlessly championing his clients and skewering his victims on their behalf, but he is, ironically, also a lousy husband. His constant cheating is well-known to our entire social circle, and I don't know how Martha tolerates it. I guess we all make compromises in life. At least Elijah didn't do that to me. He cheated with his work, with his family, but never another woman.

One day, though, he will meet someone else. That is what I want for him—at least it's what I told him, and myself, that I wanted. But I'm realizing how devastated I will be when it happens.

Shit, my life is a mess. I go with the flow of that thought and get another crappy task done—I call my parents to warn them that the news is breaking tomorrow. When I told them about the split, predictably enough, their only concern was how much I'd be taking away with me financially. The whole conversation was full of dire warnings, stories about women who were left homeless and missing a kidney after brutal divorces. There was pretty much zero concern for my wellbeing, and in my mom's case, a cynical tone of voice implied she expected this. She even uttered the immortal words, "Well, at least there aren't any children to make it more difficult."

I long ago came to terms with the fact that my parents are emotionally incompetent, but sometimes I still find myself hoping for their support, and it's a painful shock when I realize yet again that not only is it not available, but it never was. Granny Lucille makes up for both of them though.

It's midafternoon now, and I'm at home alone. I've paused all of my social engagements for the foreseeable future and have way too much time on my hands. Elijah has been in Seoul for work, and I've been trying to keep busy and tick off some of the things on my list. I thought "learn a new skill" would be a fairly easy item to start with. However, I've already taken up crochet, jewelry design, painting, and needlepoint. Quickly, I realized I neither enjoy nor have the talent for any of them.

So instead, I organized the contents of my entire closet and donated an embarrassingly large pile of barely worn designer clothes to charity. I've also organized every other closet in the house—except for Elijah's. It didn't feel right to go through his things.

I need a job, a purpose of some kind, or I'll go mad. I need to find something that ignites my passion or at least does some good in the world. Melanie, Nathan's wife, still works as a veterinary nurse, and Amelia is still Drake's secretary. That makes me feel even worse. They both have billionaire partners and managed to keep their own identities. It is a bit different for them, though—they were already in their thirties when they met their James boys. I was only nineteen. I grew up with mine, molded my life around him. It's daunting, this whole unraveling, but as Granny Lucille said, it's never too late to change.

I sit down with my laptop and look up examples of résumés on employment websites. I am ashamed to say that I have never needed to write one. Elijah proposed to me when I was still in college. I didn't possess any driving ambition to build a corporate career, but I did have some grand ideas about changing the world. Maybe working for nonprofits or setting up my own charity. But then, marrying Elijah presented me with a new role—being the perfect corporate wife and mom. The next Verona James. And it was a role that I wanted. One I truly relished for a short time. I made it my own, and while I didn't do any of the changing the world stuff I envisaged, I did make a difference.

There are plenty of people who look down on society wives and their charity work, but I took it seriously. I chose to make a difference the best way I knew while maintaining my most important role as Mrs. Elijah James. Perhaps it was an old-fashioned idea, too old-fashioned for a woman like me. But I adored Elijah and wanted nothing more than to build our world together. I was happy to simply be a wife and a mother, to play my part that way. As it turned out, I wasn't great at the former, and I was never given the opportunity to try out the latter.

I browse the advice on the website I'm currently on and pull a face. Even the made-up people populating the résumé templates seem a lot more impressive than me. I'm sure I could get some dreadful figurehead job just because of who I am—who I was?—but I don't want that. I want something real. My life from now on, I have promised myself, will be real.

My own résumé is pretty thin, so I decide to explore the "getting back into the workplace" suggestion by doing some voluntary work. Except in my case, it's getting in, not getting back in. It makes sense. Volunteering will give me the chance to gain experience and find out what I might want to do in the next stage of my life, as Mason put it. I start to scout out some opportunities but quickly find that filling out a résumé is harder than it seems. How do I succinctly say what it is I have to offer?

I do have a little hands-on work experience from the

soup kitchen I volunteer for every Thanksgiving and all the dinners, auctions, and galas I organized. Plus, I've literally raised millions of dollars for charity and boosted the funds of hundreds of different causes, from hospitals to theaters to retired circus folk. But nearly all of that has been done at a distance. Sure, I cajoled and convinced and used my position of influence to make all of those events a success, but I rarely got involved in the grassroots work. I rarely contributed in any way other than financial and as a representative of the James family. The vulnerability required to offer myself up like that on a regular basis was outside my wheelhouse and probably still is, but I'm done keeping walls up between me and the rest of the world.

I'm not an idiot—I'm aware that most charities would prefer a nice big check to someone like me turning up on their doorstep. I mean, what use am I, really? I have no tangible or practical skills. I can't build a wall or tend a garden, fix a broken toilet or drive a bus. I'm a society wife who has good contacts and enjoys organizing. Or at least, that's what I have been up until now. It's time to find out what I will be next.

Granny Lucille knew what she was doing when she bought me that notebook and told me to make my lists. It's helped, even if only by showing me what I don't want to do. I carry it with me everywhere, and right now I turn to my "learn a new skill" list and grimace at all the things I've crossed off—and not because I learned them. Perhaps I should change it to simply "try new things." I jot down "do something hands-on and make a difference" under the crossed-out needlepoint. Then I add in parentheses, "and stop feeling sorry for yourself." I feel more determined as soon as I've done that. Like I now have to make it happen or I'll be letting Lucille down.

When I turn back to my computer, I decide to register with a website that matches volunteers to roles in New York and soon realize that my initial self-assessment was completely incorrect. I have a whole plethora of skills that plenty of recruiters are looking for. I just need to figure out how to sell myself in a whole new way. It might take me a little time, but time is one thing I have plenty of.

If nothing else, it's a distraction from the gnawing sadness that's eating away at me. This is a time of transition, and it's natural to feel upset, but I can't sit around like this forever. There needs to be more to my life than missing Elijah.

I'm still looking online when our cleaner arrives. Vicky stands before me with her feather duster, obviously surprised to find me at home. She really is a great lady. A brunette in her mid-thirties, she always has a smile on her face and a song on her lips despite the challenges that life has thrown at her. "Oh! Mrs. J," she says. "What are you doing here?"

"I live here, Vicky," I reply, grinning so she knows I'm joking.

"Oh yeah. I forgot," she jokes back. "How was your trip?"

"It was really good, thanks for asking. How are things with you and the family?"

She chats away for a few minutes, updating me on the state of affairs in Vicky-land, and I realize that I will miss her. I'm the one who manages coordinating and communicating with the team of people who work for us, and I hope I have been a fair and supportive employer. I very much enjoy the friendly relationships I've fostered with everyone. Who knows? As people keep warning me, divorces can turn nasty. I might end up knocking on Vicky or Dionne's door one night asking for a spot on their couch.

In all seriousness, I really don't want to stay in this house, and that will eventually mean change for my staff. That gets added to my mental list of things to do—make sure they are treated well. Elijah is a good man who would never knowingly screw a hardworking person over, but it also might not occur to him to think about the housekeeper, the cleaner, or Stuey, the guy who handles general maintenance. I'll talk to him about it. That and a million other little details need to be ironed out. Huh. Ironing. Another thing I suck at. My life skills are seriously subpar.

"You all right there, Mrs. J?" Vicky asks. "You seem a little ... out of whack."

I have no clue how much she knows. Probably more than I'd imagine. Our staff has access to the intimate details of our lives. The separate bedrooms. The separate meals.

"I've been better, truthfully, Vicky, but that's a story for another day. But I have been thinking about doing some volunteer work. Please sit, will you?"

She nods and takes the chair opposite me. When we do chat, it's usually while she works. She's an energetic soul who sees sitting still as a waste of her valuable time. "Don't you already do enough, Mrs. J? I mean, all those committees you're on, all those events you organize."

"I'm thinking of something a bit more ... practical. I'd like to meet different people. Get out of my comfort zone. Feel like I'm helping. I want to actually *do* something, you know?"

She frowns as she turns it over. I probably sound like a

lunatic to her. My life must look so perfect, so carefree, with all its wealth and privilege. Even with the separate rooms, she must think I have it made while she zooms around, caring for her kids and working.

"Yeah, must be boring, mixing with those snooty women with the sticks up their butts. You never really seemed like that."

I have to smile. It's not the world's greatest compliment, but I'll take it.

"What did you have in mind?" she continues. "What are you into?"

"I'm not totally sure, but I'm open to ideas. I used to like ballet and trained in it for years. I enjoy wildlife, as long as it's not too wild—I love watching the squirrels in the park. I, uh, I suppose I'm pretty interested in people? You know, in their stories?"

"You mean you're nosy?" she says, giving me a cheeky wink. "In a good way. You listen to me ramble on, Mrs. J, and not all my clients even see me as a human being, so I really appreciate that. What about kids, you like them?"

"Is this the part where I say something like 'yes, but I couldn't eat a whole one'?"

She laughs, and I bite my lip as I think it over. I have raised money for children's charities, but I have avoided spending much time with little ones. To start with, it was simply too hard to be around something I wanted so desperately and couldn't have. Then, as my contemporaries and college friends started to have their own families, I struggled even more. It's not something I'm proud of, but seeing them with their big pregnant tummies and then their beautiful babies was too much. I was jealous and resentful. It's a big part of why I don't have any genuine friendships these days—there was a natural divide. Their lives became about playdates and preschools and houses in the suburbs. Mine would never be that, and their journey into motherhood took them farther and farther away from me. Our shared experiences shrunk, and I started to find them unbearably smug. They weren't, I see that now, but it was how I felt.

I nod at Vicky, who is waiting patiently for my response. "Yes. I do like kids." It's the truth. I adore them in all their noise and mess and joyous chaos. And maybe I'm ready now. More mature. Able to cope with being around them.

"Well, look, Mrs. J—"

"Please, call me Amber."

"Okay, so, Amber … There's a community center near where we live in Queens that's always looking for people. Not gonna lie, it's not your usual type of place."

"I'm not looking for my usual. Go on," I say.

"LOJ isn't the kind of organization that gets a lot of attention, you know? Nobody's going to be planning fancy dinners to raise money for it any time soon, but it does a lot of good. The neighborhood ain't the best, but that just means there are more people in need, if you know what I mean."

I nod, interested. "Did you say LOJ? What does it stand for? And what kind of things do they do?"

"Yeah, it's the Leslie Odom Jr. Community Center, and they offer a bit of everything. They hold coffee mornings, bingo, art classes, self-defense, coaching for various sports, and they run a community garden. You name it, they do it. A lot of the older folks rely on it for company, and it keeps the kids out of trouble. Some of them, anyway. They do their best. How do you feel about motorcycles?"

It's an abrupt swerve, but I ride it out. "Never been on one. No plans to. Is that a deal-breaker?"

"Nah, just wanted to mention it because some of the guys who hang out there are bikers. Rough around the edges but good hearts."

She stops mid-flow and shakes her head. "It ... Look, Mrs. J—Amber ... Now that I say it all out loud, I'm thinking it's not the place for you. I don't think Mr. J would like you being there either."

I say nothing in response to that one. What Elijah would and wouldn't like is irrelevant, but those are muddy waters I don't want to dive into.

Vicky obviously thinks her world would be too tough for me. She probably thinks I'm soft and weak, and that her community would eat me alive. Like most people, though, she doesn't really understand how tough I actually am. There are many different types of strength, and I'm not even remotely put off.

"But do you think I could be any use?" I ask her. "Not just ... donate? I mean, it sounds great, and I will do that as well. Really, though, I'd like to find something more active."

She raises her eyebrows and looks surprised. "Yeah, they could use you. The kids love dancing, and their teacher just left. Maybe you could you do that."

"I don't know. I'm not a teacher. I haven't danced for years."

"Well, there's no harm in giving it a shot. There's other stuff too. Hey, you could always do the cleaning." She raises her feather duster in the air, and we both laugh at the idea.

Except, I wouldn't mind. I might not have Vicky's skills, but I'm guessing I could swing a mop if I needed to. "Speaking of which," she says, "I really better be getting on. You want me to call the center, tell 'em you might be in touch?"

"Yes, please. And Vicky? Thank you. I really appreciate it."

"No worries, Amber. Us girls have to stick together, right?"

I feel oddly uplifted by our conversation. She didn't dismiss me or write me off as deluded, and her suggestion energized me. I should try this asking-for-help thing more often.

I have no idea if this LOJ Community Center idea will work. I'm not sure I've ever even been in Queens. I've certainly driven through it, but shamefully, my world has been mostly limited to Manhattan. Perhaps this is all part of my life rehab—expanding my horizons.

I listen to Vicky singing away in the background—"Bad Romance" by Lady Gaga—and glance at my phone. It is still only midafternoon. I'd go for a walk, but the weather is dreadful. November is behaving badly, with lower-than-normal temperatures and lots of violent wind and rain. I wonder how the squirrels are coping and spend a few moments of worrying for them. Should I take them some food, try to set up some kind of shelter? I remind myself that the squirrels have survived for many years without my interference, and they'll undoubtedly be fine.

I wonder what Elijah's doing right now. Is he as sad as I am about the breakup statement? Probably not. He doesn't have the time to sit around being self-indulgent. He might have meetings, even though it's the weekend. He could be with his family, playing with little Luke while Dalton hosts them all for a day-long brunch. I suspect he hasn't even given it a second thought.

I hear a beeping noise, and at first I don't recognize it.

When I remember where I've heard that sound before, I dig the burner phone from the pocket where I keep it hidden in my purse. Only one person has the number, and it's as though I was thinking about him so hard I manifested him.

My heart rate speeds up, and I look at the screen.

I'm free tonight. Are you?

SIXTEEN

AMBER

We arrange to meet in Greenwich Village. The village is perfectly pleasant, but not a place we usually socialize. That's the whole point—if we were really having a top-secret affair, there's no way we'd risk being seen together in our usual haunts. He messages me the address, and it all feels so exciting and mysterious.

Normally, if we were meeting up at night, he'd send Gretchen to collect me. He's always been very protective like that, from the very first day we met. He walked me home after every date and made sure I was safe on campus. A complete gentleman in so many ways, just as his mama raised him. Even in more recent times, when we've been at our coldest toward each other, he maintained that level of concern for my physical safety. Tonight, he doesn't send Gretchen, but when I leave the house and go to find a cab, I discover one already idling outside with its engine running. The driver's window winds down, and a familiar face gazes up at me.

"Mrs. Smith? Hey, is that you, Amber? You're Mrs. Smith?" he asks, grinning. It's Sanjay, the chivalrous cabbie who so bravely defended me on the night of Elodie's wedding. One of the few positive memories from that brutal evening. This is obviously Elijah's work, and the Mrs. Smith thing is a nice touch. I suppose we are having an affair, after all.

"Sanjay!" I exclaim. "How lovely to see you. Is this a lucky coincidence?" I clamber inside the car, grateful to be out of the wind. My hair has already been whipped into a frenzy after thirty seconds outside. It's usually styled and sprayed, but tonight it's a whirling dervish. I'm wearing a pair of black skinny jeans paired with spike-heeled ankle boots and a plain black button-down shirt. I've added a long necklace with a silver fabric tassel on the end to glam it up a little. It's a nice outfit, but it's not by any means sophisticated.

"I don't think so, Mrs. Smith. I was booked specifically for this address at this time. You are looking very lovely tonight, if you don't mind me saying."

"I don't mind at all, Sanjay, thank you. How have things been with you?"

As he drives, he tells me about his daughter who recently gave birth to triplets. "Three babies," he says, the glee obvious in his voice. "All healthy. Such a blessing."

"And how is your daughter doing, coping with her blessings?"

"Oh, well, of course, she does not always see it as such a blessing. Her whole life is diapers. But we are helping, and she is very happy, really. Our son, also Sanjay, has three children too, but he did it the old-fashioned way, one at a time."

He continues to talk, so proud and delighted with his

family, and it warms my heart to hear his tales. I wonder how long it took Elijah to find him. Did he call every cab company in New York trying to find the right Sanjay? Or did he get one of his many minions to do that? Probably the latter, but knowing Elijah, he would have double-checked the information himself to make sure he had the right man. He has enough money to simply buy a new car and hire a new driver, but I can see that this would appeal to him more. Sanjay has already proven he can be trusted to look after me.

We make our way along the windswept city streets, surrounded by people battling with umbrellas and scurrying between cars and buildings, and into Greenwich. The place we pull up in front of is a pretty townhouse, glowing with light behind shuttered windows. I'm not quite sure what it is —bar, restaurant, hotel? It's so discreet it doesn't even have a sign, and so quaint it could simply be somebody's home.

Sanjay turns around to face me and passes me a piece of folded up paper. "That's my number, Mrs. Smith. You call me any time you need a ride. An account has been set up with the cab company, and I'm available to you twenty-four seven."

"But what about the diapers?" I ask, widening my eyes in mock horror.

He winks. "Well, truthfully, it is nice to escape them sometimes. You call me, though, any time at all. I am at your service."

I thank him and tuck the number away in my purse. Elijah probably paid for his exclusive services for the foreseeable future, and Sanjay must be wondering what the hell is going on but hasn't embarrassed me by asking. I'm not sure I could quite explain it even if I tried. *So, it's like this—the man I was arguing with the night we met is my husband, and we're getting a divorce. But we're also having an affair, and my name isn't Mrs. Smith. Confused? Me too.*

Sanjay assures me he'll have his phone with him all night if I need a ride home, and I climb out of the car. Immediately, a smartly dressed man appears from the townhouse and holds a huge golf umbrella over my head to protect me from the elements.

"Mrs. Smith, please follow me." He gestures toward the steps into the building. "Mr. Smith is already here."

Inside, I'm shown through to a small room furnished with tables and chairs. We pass a sleek mirrored bar, the shelves lined with expensive brands. It's super stylish, small but perfectly decorated—and also completely empty. The place is probably usually bustling, but tonight there's nobody but Elijah. He's waiting for me at the back of the room, away from the door. Exactly where somebody having an affair would sit.

He stands, looking completely edible in jeans and a fitted short-sleeve white shirt that makes his muscles pop, and I try not to swoon. It's a laid-back look for him—seems I'm not the only one recreating themselves. He's also wearing a new cologne, something spicy and masculine as hell. It flies directly from my nostrils to my lady parts. They are subtle changes, but enough to keep up the illusion that this is a sexy stranger.

"Amber." His gray eyes rake over my face and body. They linger on the foxy spike-heeled boots, just as I thought they might. "You look stunning."

I find myself blushing at the compliment and smile as he holds a chair out for me. Two bottles of wine are on the candlelit table, one white and one red, along with his glass of Scotch. I've already eaten, which is lucky because there's no sign of food. I had no clue what our "date" was going to look like—dinner, drinks, straight to fucking? Damn. I blush even harder, imagining the fucking.

"Thank you. Mr. and Mrs. Smith?" I say, arching an eyebrow. "Really?"

"I thought it was fitting, no? This is certainly the right kind of place for it."

I look around, putting two and two together. No sign outside. Heavily shuttered windows. A secluded spot away from the busier thoroughfares.

"Mr. Smith, have you brought me to a high-class by-the-hour hotel?"

"I don't think that would be on their marketing brochure, but yes, that's exactly what it is. An exclusive venue designed specifically for couples who need their, uh, privacy." As he speaks, he holds up the white wine. He's obviously messing with me—he knows I prefer red. I point at the other bottle—my favorite pinot noir—and he grins as he pours.

"Well, we've definitely got our privacy tonight. Why is it so empty?"

"Because I booked the whole place out," he answers, giving me the lopsided smile that always makes my heart leap.

I raise my glass in acknowledgment and offer a slight nod. "That's quite ambitious, Mr. Smith."

"What can I say? You bring out the best in me, Mrs. Smith."

If only that were true, I think, sipping my wine. The same thought seems to cross his mind as well, because his eyes, stormy with emotion, meet mine over the flickering candlelight. I don't look away, and we simply stare at each other for a few moments. I love this man. I really, truly love him. So why couldn't I be happy with him?

"Why is it," I ask, knowing that I risk breaking the spell, "that we had to pretend to be strangers to have the best sex of our lives?"

"I don't know." He picks up his Scotch and takes a small sip. "I've been asking myself the same thing. This may make me an asshole, but could we carry on pretending? Even if only for tonight? I hated today, Amber. And I know I'm going to hate tomorrow even more."

The pain in his voice is real, and it does at least answer one of my earlier questions—yes, he's also sad. Just like me.

But also like me, he's not making a case for giving our marriage another shot. It seems we both know that ship has sailed, and right now, we're clinging to the life raft of what's left between us. He runs his hands through his hair, and his eyes look haunted.

I pick up the wine bottle and stand. "Yes, we can carry on pretending. Come on. Let's go and see one of those rooms, Mr. Smith." His smile transforms his face, and he takes my offered hand.

The guy from earlier—concierge, maître d', pimp, whatever his job title is—sees us on the move and gestures us through a red velvet curtain into a hallway lined with wood paneling. He hands Elijah an old-fashioned metal key on an oval fob and nods politely before disappearing. We climb the stairs together, and Elijah lets us into a grand room that's dominated by a spectacular four-poster bed. Everything is deep red and black, from the sheets to the canopy to the carpet, and the room is scented with something musky and spicy. I briefly wonder if there's a specific aroma made for places like this—Classy Hot Sex No° 9 or something.

Elijah takes the bottle of wine from me and sets it down on a mahogany end table. His eyes shine with dark delight, and he closes the distance between us in a split second. Delicious nerves dance along my spine as he slides his arms around my waist and tugs me toward him. A little gasp escapes my lips at the feel of him pressed against me. The firm length of his cock leaves me in no doubt that he's ready for us to take this to the next level. His big hands run over my backside, squeezing possessively as he crushes me closer.

He buries his face in my hair, inhaling. "I want you so much," he whispers, his breath warm on the skin of my neck. "I've been hard since the moment you walked in. I can't wait to be inside you." His words and his tone and his touch all combine to flood me with need.

"I can't wait either," I murmur, circling my hips against his. My clit is already throbbing from the contact.

I pull his shirt from his waistband and slide my hands up his back. God, I forgot how good he feels. His skin is soft over the steely strength of his body, like velvet over iron. Muscles ripple with every movement, and as ever, he makes me feel small and protected, but also vulnerable. Vulnerable in a way that has me achy and wet.

I draw back, unbutton his shirt, and pull it off. At the sight of his ripped torso, I sigh. Firm pecs, defined abs, bulging biceps, the delicious plume of dark hair that disappears into his pants ... He's a work of art, this man, and I could stare at him all day long.

He pulls me against him and seals his lips over mine. His tongue is in my mouth, and his fingers twine in my hair. We lose ourselves in the kiss, both of us alive with fire and passion. He tastes of fine Scotch and need, and he groans loudly when I finally come up for air. My eyes run over his bulky shoulders, his heaving chest, down to the bulge in his pants. I lick my lips in anticipation. "I want to taste you." My voice is unrecognizable, low and husky. Alien. I don't even recognize it myself.

His nostrils flare, and the bulge gets even bigger. He slowly unbuttons my shirt, gazing hungrily at my breasts. "You want me to fuck your mouth, Amber?"

He wouldn't normally speak to me like that, but it's so exciting when he does. And yes, I do want him to fuck my mouth. I haven't tasted him in at least a year, and I yearn to have that salty tang on my tongue. To lick and suck and stroke in the way I know he likes. To feel the intoxicating power of making him come undone.

Elijah wasn't the first man I had sex with, but he is the only man I've enjoyed it with. He made me feel like a virgin because it was all so new, so very different from what I experienced before. Those experiences were disastrous in various ways, ranging from disappointing to damaging, and it was only when I met Elijah that I realized what all the fuss was about.

It was Elijah who showed me how much pleasure the human form is capable of giving and receiving. He was the first man to make me come, the one who unlocked all my body's secrets. He was also the one who taught me how to deep throat, and I loved it. I loved how powerful it made me feel, how much it affected him. I'll never forget the first time I managed to take all of him, the way he looked down at me with a combination of pride and passion. I want that again right now.

"Yes, that's what I want."

He nods but still takes his time removing my shirt. "Then that's what you'll get. Eventually."

He unhooks my bra and throws it to the side. His eyes eat me up, and his tongue flicks out across his lips as he gazes at my tits. I think they're too small, but he's always told me how perfect they are. When he says it again now, the way he looks at me—I can tell he means it.

He holds my breasts in his palms as he leans down and gently kisses each nipple, making me groan at the contact. His tongue skims them, and I'm desperate for more. This is too soft, too teasing. I want him to suck them, to squeeze them, to sink his teeth into them. He moves his mouth away but continues with his hands, gently massaging my sensitive breasts until I'm a quivering mess before him. My response elicits a smile from him. The man knows exactly what he's doing to me.

I moan, arching toward him, and he picks up the silver necklace I'm wearing. The chain is long, hanging down between my breasts. He lifts the tasseled end of it and brushes the silky strands over my nipples, staring at them in fascination as they pucker even more. Quickly, his touch follows, and the sight of his big hands all over me is so hot I already feel well on my way to orgasm. He rolls my nipples between his thumbs and fingertips, and I squirm beneath his skilled hands, putting mine over his to encourage him.

"Harder?"

I bite my lip and manage a desperate nod. Looking straight into my eyes, he does as I ask, increasing the pressure. Exquisite pain shoots straight from my nipples to my pussy, and I murmur his name, lightheaded from the divine shock of it all. After one last squeeze, he removes his hands from my skin, leaving me bereft and dizzy as I look up at him in confusion.

"I want you down on your knees now, Amber," he commands. "But first, take off your jeans."

I do as I'm told, kicking off my boots first and then sliding the denim down my ass and legs.

He spots the slinky black thong I'm wearing and his breath hitches. "Leave your panties on."

I'm so turned on, so completely at his mercy, that he could tell me to eat the damn things and I would.

My knees sink into the plush carpet as I kneel before him. He circles around and crouches behind me. A shudder runs through me when he lifts my hair from my neck and brushes his lips across my shoulders. I lean into the touch of his lips as he whispers, "I love this necklace you're wearing. I'm going to use it to tie your hands together. Okay?"

I suck in a surprised breath. We've played around like this before, but only a little, and it's been well over a decade. I loved it then, and it seems I still love it now.

"Is that okay, Amber?" he repeats, his tone stern. "I need to hear you say it."

I nod shakily. "Yes. That's okay."

Satisfied, he gently pulls my arms behind me so my

wrists lie at the small of my back, then he uses the long silver chain to tie them together. It's not too tight, and I could probably break free, but absolutely no part of me wants to. I remain on my knees, waiting and trembling, nipples erect. With my hands restrained behind me, my pussy pounds a needy rhythm that drums through my core.

He moves back in front of me. Turbulent gray eyes roam my body, and his devilish smile makes me shiver. "You are so damn perfect," he says as he removes his boots. "Eres tan hermosa."

I haven't heard the Spanish words in so long, but I recognize them. *You are so beautiful.* He unbuckles his belt and slides his jeans off. The unbuckling makes my pussy quiver even more, because I know what's coming next. I swallow audibly as he pulls out his cock, feeling a rush of nerves as he holds it in his hand. Long, thick, as hard as I've ever seen it. Can I still do this? I want to, I really do, but I'm uncertain.

Elijah strokes his impressive length, and a pearly drop of pre-cum glistens on its head. I lick my lips, practically tasting it. Yes, I can do this.

"You want this, Amber?" he growls. "Do you want my cock in your mouth? Will you suck me like a good girl?"

As he speaks his filthy words, he circles me, and I try to follow him with my gaze. "No," he says firmly. "Eyes forward. I just want to admire this rear view for a while before I give you what you've asked for. Fuck, you look amazing ... Your hands tied up like that? Sexier than any woman I have ever known, Mrs. Smith. And your ass is sensational in those panties."

Kneeling behind me, he scoops my breasts up in his hands and caresses them. The way his hands and lips skim my flesh has me aching for more. For everything. His chest feels firm and warm, and my heart thrums as his hands float down my body. He slips his fingers inside the black silk of my thong and slides one along my seam. It's electrifying. "Oh, Elijah …"

"Jesus fuck. You're so damn wet, baby. I wanted to make you wait, but I don't think I can resist you. You want to come?"

"Yes!"

"Yes, what?" He probes my opening.

"Yes, please. Please, Elijah."

He wraps one arm around my torso, holding me close and steady while his fingers slowly demolish me. He's always understood my body, always been able to play me like a maestro plays his chosen instrument, but this is incredible. My hands are trapped between us, his hard cock pressing into my back. My head falls back against his shoulder, my breath coming in desperate pants as he works his magic. "Look down. Watch what I'm doing to you. See how wet you are."

I do as I'm told. My knees have spread without me noticing, and he has the thin fabric of my panties pushed to one side. Two thick fingers slide in and out of me. They're covered in my creamy arousal, and the scent fills the room. He speeds up as I watch, his thumb rolling over my clit with every movement, making me shudder. "God, I love that smell … that sound … the sound of your needy little pussy sucking me in."

He's right. I am needy. I'm so wet. So close. Every cell in my body is screaming, and I can barely breathe. The beat pulsating from my core spreads all through my body, darkening my vision and pounding in my ears like the sound of the ocean. He nips at my shoulder and focuses on my clit. Rubbing at that tiny bundle of flesh, murmuring my name over and over as he takes me higher and higher. He teases and plays, taking me to the edge and pulling me back again, so many times I'm sobbing with desperation.

"Please, Elijah ... I need to ..."

He growls and strokes my swollen bud, holding me tight against him as he brings me to the brink and finally lets me topple over. The world explodes in a flash of light and sound and sensation, bliss flowing over me in wave after wave of pure pleasure. "That's it, baby, that's it," he murmurs, keeping his fingers deep inside me as I clench and contract around them.

I'm floating halfway between consciousness and blacked out, nothing existing in my universe apart from Elijah and the way he made me feel. Nobody has ever pulled an orgasm like that from my body. Not even him. He lets me settle, kissing me and whispering to me, his fingers circling inside my tight pussy, touching my still-quivering walls. When he finally pulls them out, his whole hand is covered in my cum, and my face blazes from embarrassment. He runs his fingers along my lips until I open them, then pushes them inside my mouth. "Lick me clean, Amber. Taste yourself. You really are a filthy little slut, aren't you? Tied up and helpless, and you fucking loved it."

I suck his fingers, and he gently twists my head around to the side with them and meets me there at that awkward angle and kisses me. His fingers and tongue fill my mouth, swirling and exploring and dominating. His other hand goes around my neck and up to my throat, holding me there while he explores me. I'm in pieces, but I still want more. I want his cock inside my mouth. I want it all.

"Fuck!" he says with force, pulling away from me. He climbs to his feet and moves to stand in front of me. "I almost came in my fucking boxers just from the taste of your cunt inside your mouth."

I gaze up at him, his muscular legs planted wide before me, his big cock throbbing in his hand. "That would have been a waste," I say, finally regaining the power of speech, "when you could come down my throat."

I shuffle toward him, my movements hampered by the fact that my hands are still tied. He groans and grabs up a fistful of my hair, tugging my head backward. "You've got a dirty mouth on you, Mrs. Smith. And now I'm going to fill it."

I manage to nod slightly, and despite my earlier nerves, I open my mouth to take him. He starts gently, letting me get used to his size. Flicking my tongue over his slit, I lick up the salty pre-cum and make him moan. When I suck him farther in, I wish my hands were free. I want to cup his balls, grab his ass, pull him deeper. I struggle slightly, hoping I can disentangle my wrists from the chain.

"No," he says, burying both his hands in my hair now. "Leave them be. The sight of you bound is fucking sexy as hell."

As he speaks, he forces himself deeper inside my mouth. Tears sting my eyes, and I breathe through my nose. I can do this. I just need to relax and let him fuck me. I want to do this. His pace builds, and I glance up to see him completely lost in the moment. His eyes are fixed on mine, his mouth open as he rams himself into me. His grip on my hair never lets up, and his hips slam backward and forward. Saliva runs from the corners of my mouth, and tears flow down my cheeks. "You're so damn good at this, baby, such a good girl. Your mouth feels amazing. Oh, fuck!"

He slams into me deeper than ever and holds my head rigid as he cries out and shoots his creamy load inside me. His cum fills my throat, and I breathe through my nose as he shudders his way through his climax. When he's finally done, he pulls out of me and leans down. He kisses my face clean of everything—my tears and spit, drops of his cum.

"That was fucking spectacular." He staggers behind me and unloops the chain that binds my wrists, then helps me up to my feet. I fall against him, shaky after kneeling for so long. We're both unsteady, and he laughs as we stumble toward the big four-poster bed. He falls back onto it, pulling me down on top of him.

I giggle as he grabs hold of my ass, our legs tangled and our breaths mingling as we roll around the bed together. When he pulls me into his arms, my head comes to rest against his chest. With gentle strokes, he untangles my hair, and my fingers curl around his waist. He snags one of the sheets and drapes it loosely over us.

We both simply lie still for a few minutes, settling our breathing and letting our hearts steady. It's intimate, tender, and I'm not sure how I feel about that. Elijah and I have spent so many years hurting each other—it still doesn't feel safe to be so open to him. Is he feeling as exposed as I am?

"If we were really having an affair," he says quietly, his fingers still in my hair, "do you think we'd be ... what would you call this? Snuggling?"

I laugh lightly and feel him smile against my head. "Snuggling? Yes, I suppose that is a good word for it. As for whether people having an affair would snuggle, I can't answer that. This is my very first. I'm actually doing a lot of things for the first time this year. I have a list."

"Really?" he asks, repositioning us so he can see my face. "Tell me more."

"Well, Granny Lucille gave me a notebook and told me to make a list of things I want to change and things I want to do. For starters, I've had it with my suit of armor."

He doesn't reply immediately, but then says, "You mean the way you look? I noticed the change in style. I really like it."

"Thank you. I do too."

"What else is on this list of yours?" He sounds genuinely interested.

"Um, well, some of it is a work in progress. But I'm going to take self-defense classes and learn to cook. I want to make new friends. I've also realized that I have a limited range of skills, so I'm planning to do some volunteer work, then get a job."

He nods as I run through them—right until the last one.

"You know you don't have to do that, don't you?" He frowns, gazing directly into my eyes. "Get a job? Look, if you want to, go for it—I have faith in you. I'm sure you'd make a success of whatever you put your mind to. But financially, I'm ... we ... Fuck. I hate saying this. Saying it makes it real."

I place my palm on his cheek, understanding exactly how he feels. "I know, Elijah. But it is real. No matter how much we pretend when it comes to Mr. and Mrs. Smith, it is real."

He nods and kisses my palm. "You're right. So, what I'm trying to say is that financially, you won't ever need to work. I'll always look after you."

I don't know whether that's sweet and reassuring or patronizing and insulting. I suppose it depends on how I choose to interpret it. "Thank you. I do appreciate that. But there's more to life than money. I need a purpose, to be more than your wife or a member of the James family. I need to find out who I am without you. I'm sorry if that hurts, and I hope you understand."

"Not completely, but I want to," he says, genuine honesty showing on his face. "Help me understand, baby."

In recent years, I resented him calling me baby, but now ... It feels so natural when we're lying here like this. "Are you sure you mean that? Isn't this supposed to be all about fun? Isn't that the whole point of being Mr. and Mrs. Smith?"

"Yes, I mean it, Amber. And we both know who we truly are, no matter how much we enjoy pretending we're not. Talk to me," he says firmly. "I want to understand what's going on with you."

I hesitate for a moment. Can I trust him with this piece of me? I have no idea—it's been so long since I let another human being *really* see me. But Elijah is one of the few to have had the privilege. Besides, I remind myself, I vowed to make my life more real. This is a good first step toward that goal.

"Okay, I'll try," I reply, my hand drifting to his shoulder. "But I'm not sure I totally have a grip on it myself yet. There are still things I'm piecing together, forcing myself to face up to for the first time. I suppose I've been trying to figure out where things went wrong, you know?"

"I know. I've been doing the same. Go on." He nuzzles my hair and holds me closer.

"Okay. Well. It's hard to describe, but I feel like ... like I've been sleepwalking through life for years now. I stay busy, and I play to my strengths, but I'm faking it. Inside, I've been so hollow. When I found out I couldn't have children, I think I lost my sense of purpose. I couldn't see the point of me anymore. I was sad and angry and eventually bitter, and that's not a good combination. It was a huge loss, and I never really grieved for it because of the timing."

"My mom?" he asks, his voice catching.

"Yes. She found out she was sick, and that took priority, as it had to—and believe me, I don't hold that against you. But I didn't have the chance to grieve the fact that I couldn't be a mother myself—that we lost the life we always imagined. I bottled it all up, and you probably did too, and we ended up lashing out at each other. Now we're finally escaping that cycle, and you still have everything else that makes you *you*—your family, your work, your friends and colleagues, Jamestech. You're passionate about those things. I don't have any of that, and I have no clue what I'm passionate about. And I'm not saying this to make you feel sorry for me. I'm saying it to explain—I need to find my own way. I need a world outside yours. Does that make any sense?"

He throws his leg over me, and I run my fingers along his thick thigh. "It does make sense. And you're right—I don't think either of us really processed that loss." He gently kisses my bare shoulder. "I was overwhelmed, and you were too. We should have … Well, I don't suppose that matters now. As for you finding your own world outside mine, if that's what you want, I'm here for you. On the sidelines, cheerleading." His voice is heavy with emotion, and I know he'll take what I told him to heart. He will think it over and look at it from every angle. That's the kind of man he is.

"I really can't see you in the uniform," I say, trying to lighten the mood. This, I suppose, is the trouble with snuggling—it opens up too many doors.

"You'd be surprised. Maybe that could be one of *my* firsts."

He's trying to lighten the mood too, and I gratefully grab hold of it. "I'm not sure I'd be into that—you and pom-poms. If we're going to be dressing up, I'm sure we can find something better for you. Sexy doctor. Gladiator. Pirate. Fireman. *Magic Mike* stripper ..."

"Whoa, easy tiger. You've been thinking about this way too much."

"What?" I protest, faking outrage. "And you haven't? What kind of an affair is this?"

He laughs and then gazes up at the ceiling, nodding slowly. "I could go for any of those, to be honest. Sexy doctor is a good one. I like the idea of your gorgeous legs in stirrups while I give you a thorough examination."

We're only joking, but the image is vivid ... and I like it. A lot.

"We already seem to be trying a few firsts in the bedroom, don't we?" he says. "I'm not sure Granny Lucille would approve."

"Ha! Granny Lucille is a lot more open-minded than you might suspect, sir. But yes, we do. You seem to have developed a very dirty mouth for one."

"And you fucking love it."

I do indeed fucking love it. Along with the role-playing,

the hand tying, and what the *hell* is going on with my nipples? It's like they're, I don't know, supercharged.

"What on earth are we doing here?" I look up at him, genuinely puzzled, and he laughs.

"Baby, I have no idea. But whatever it is, it's working for both of us. This is the best sex we've ever had."

"It is, isn't it? Probably not a good idea to analyze it too closely."

"No. Let's not do that. Let's treat it like Tinkerbell and just keep believing."

I lightly smack him on the chest. "Don't compare our perverted sex life to a Disney character. Disney should never be sexy."

"What? That's blatant bullshit—have you seen *Maleficent*? Anyway, that's a role-play for a different day. Tell me more about your list. Where will you be volunteering?"

"I'm not sure yet. Possibly at a community center in Queens."

I feel him stiffen, and not in a good way. He falls silent, and I can practically feel the cogs turning. Just like that, the lighthearted mood from moments ago has shriveled away. I should have guessed that he'd react like this. He probably expected me to stay in my safe little Manhattan-society bubble, and now I've knocked him off-balance.

"Queens?" he repeats.

"Yes, Elijah. It's a borough of New York, situated on Long Island."

"I know where it fucking is. But it's also … Are you sure it's safe? What about security? It's one thing to ignore it when you're hosting charity dinners on the Upper East Side, but Queens?"

I take a deep breath and try to stay calm. I don't want to fight, but I can't let myself be controlled. Elijah is saying this because he's still protective of me. Because he still sees that as his responsibility. But we both have to accept that we're getting divorced, and keeping me safe is not his job anymore. It's mine.

"It's not set in stone yet, Elijah. I might not even get the role, so don't freak out. But yes, I'm sure it's safe. Millions of pcople do live there, you know."

"Yes, but they're not ... you."

"You mean they're not connected to the James family? They're not kidnapping risks? Targets because of their billionaire ex-husbands?"

"All of that is true, but it's not what I meant."

We're both getting annoyed now, and I can hear the effort he's making to stay calm, just like I am. This affair can't work if Mr. and Mrs. James are constantly lurking beneath the surface, waiting for the opportunity to get embroiled in our old ways.

"What did you mean, then?" I ask, telling myself to listen. To not snap and not judge—to not smother him with snark like I usually do.

"I meant that none of those millions of people are you, so I don't give a shit about them. You're the only person I care about, Amber, and signing some papers won't change that. Nothing will ever change that. You can leave me, divorce me, never speak to me again, but I will always look out for you, whether you want me to or not. It's the way I'm made. I protect the people I love."

I bury my face in his chest again because I cannot bear to look at him. I cannot bear to see his expression or for him to see the sheen of fresh tears in my eyes. This is all so intense, and my feelings are so conflicted that I'm worried I can't contain them all. Worried I will explode like a grenade filled with emotions instead of shards and splinters. He squeezes me tight, completely wrapping me up in his body. He knows exactly what I'm doing—that I'm hiding.

His breath dusts over my hair. "I'm sorry, baby. We're a fucking mess, aren't we?"

"We really are, and I'm not sure all this honesty is helping. Maybe this isn't such a good idea. Maybe we should stay away from each other."

"You're probably right," he says, his hand running over my hip and coming to rest on my waist. "Except ... Well, I don't fucking want to."

His tone is petulant, and despite my tears, I have to laugh. "You know you sound like a kid about to have a tantrum, don't you?"

"So what? Maybe that's how I feel. Look, I know this is screwed up. I know we're going ahead with the divorce. But I have felt more alive in the last hour than I have since the night in my hotel suite. I don't know if that's because of the affair, the pretending, or the mind-blowing sex we seem to keep accidentally having. But I don't want it to stop. What about you?"

My fingers trace the silky hair on his chest. This is a crazy rollercoaster ride, and even in the past few minutes, we've been up and down, veering between mischievous and way too serious. But I can't deny that I also feel alive. "No. If I'm being truthful, I don't want it to stop either. But as of tomorrow, we're officially separated in the eyes of the world, and we genuinely will need to keep this a secret.

We'd have to keep sneaking around, find other places like this."

He shrugs. "I'm fine with that. And anyway, I like *this* place. I might buy it. Or book it out for a year."

He's perfectly serious—I can tell from his expression. I grew up without money worries, but Elijah's level of wealth is next level and still manages to surprise me at times. "Really? You'd buy this place just so you could have sex with your ex-wife here?"

"Yeah, why not? I like this bed. I'd like to tie you up to those posts and play with you. I'd like to spank you 'til your ass shines. To screw you in the shower and take you in the tub."

I grin at his words, and the playfulness helps ease the tension that was building between us. "That's very eloquent, Elijah."

"What can I say?" he shrugs. "I have the heart of a poet."

And the body of a Greek god, the mouth of a sailor, the hands of a magician ... It's a pretty tempting mix. "I mean it, Amber. I'd like to explore some of those firsts with you. I'd like to do all kinds of things with you. This place is safe and private, and it would make the perfect playroom."

I won't pretend I'm not intrigued. My pussy is already throbbing a little, and the jut of his cock tells me the images are working for him too. We might have been together for more than two decades, but this feels brand new and thrilling. It's the best of both worlds—we know each other's bodies inside out, but we're also taking steps into the unknown. "That's very ... Christian Grey of you."

"Yeah, it is, isn't it? And you fucking loved those books."

I actually blush. I wasn't aware he knew about that.

Those books were fun and escapist and hot. But when I made myself come after an especially erotic scene, it wasn't Christian Grey I pictured in my fantasies—it was the drop-dead gorgeous billionaire lying next to me. The one now sliding his big hand between my thighs.

He props himself up on one muscular arm and smiles as he slips a finger inside me, making me moan.

"Mrs. Smith," he says, his voice husky. "I think we've done enough talking. I do believe you're ready to be fucked."

Hell yes I'm ready, Mr. Smith.

CHAPTER
SEVENTEEN
ELIJAH

Luisa is talking to me about the Kim deal, but I am once again finding it hard to concentrate due to a severe case of Amber Syndrome. My assistant glares at me and waves her hands in front of my face, snapping her fingers. "Earth to Elijah, come in," she says in her usual assertive tone.

"I heard you." I glare back at her.

Luisa has an incredibly bright business mind. She is smart, driven, and ambitious—but she really doesn't know how to read a room. Or rather, she does; she just chooses to ignore what she reads. "What did I say, then?" she asks.

She stands in front of me with her hands on her hips, her dark hair swept up into a brutally tight bun as usual. She's been with Jamestech for six years, working her way through the ranks, and has been my right-hand woman for the last eighteen months. She is a pain in my ass, and she gets away with talking to me in a way nobody else would. She gets away with it because her constant challenge makes me better. It's like having one of my brothers around, only without the banter. She's unafraid to speak her mind and keeps me on my toes. If she sees bullshit, she calls it. Which she's doing right now.

"You said ... something about Mr. Kim's granddaughter being a Taylor Swift fan?"

She nods abruptly. "Almost. I said we should look into getting her tickets to her show, and possibly a meet and greet if it can be arranged. She's twelve."

"Taylor Swift is only twelve?"

"Dios mio. No, Ji-min is twelve. What the hell is wrong with you today?"

Wincing, I shake my head. She's right, and one of the things I appreciate most about Luisa is her lack of butt-kissing.

"Everything is wrong with me today. I'm sorry, my head's not in the game. Talk to Mason about the Taylor Swift thing. He probably plays volleyball with her on the weekends or something. It's a good idea. Those little touches help swing a deal in the right direction."

"I know. That's why I suggested it. I saw on your schedule that Amber is coming in—is that the problem? It's been a tough few days, and I know I don't always pick up on that stuff. I'm, uh, sorry?" She looks almost confused as she says the word, like it's completely alien to her lips.

I laugh at her discomfort but appreciate the sentiment. "Nothing to be sorry for, Luisa. And yeah, she's due in any minute. I'm distracted, and I shouldn't be. It's good that you keep me on track, so don't apologize for it."

She nods, her big brown eyes on mine. "Okay. I'll leave you to it. I have work to get on with anyway."

Of course she does. The woman does nothing but work.

Apart from Drake before he met Amelia and got a life, she's the only person I know who puts in as many office hours as me. I at least have the benefit of being the CEO of Jamestech and my surname being in the title of the company—she does it because work is her whole world.

I was raised to work hard, but I've taken it to the extreme the last few years. The split has allowed me to see things with more clarity, and I recognize the mistakes that were made. As Amber and I pulled away from each other, seemingly separated by a rift too deep for either of us to cross, I sought solace in my work. As she's implied, Jamestech was my mistress, and I could rarely resist her siren call.

Ironically, since we agreed to part, I've thought about Amber more times per minute than ever before. That might be because I'm missing her. It might also be because I'm banging her senseless on the side. Work might be seductive, but it can't compete with my wife's delicious pussy or the brain-shattering orgasms we give each other.

I look down and see a massive tent in my suit pants. Fuck. Even thinking about her gives me an erection, and now I'm stuck here. The phone on my desk rings, and I pick it up. "Amber's in reception," Mason says. "Shall we meet in the boardroom?"

"Uh ... yeah, okay. Give me five minutes."

"All right, but don't leave me there alone with her for long. I might start being honest."

He hangs up, and I try desperately to ignore the party going on in my pants. I adopt a tried-and-tested method and picture Dr. Braithwaite, the dentist we went to as kids. She looked about a hundred years old, had ironic and extreme halitosis, and when she leaned over you, all you could see was nostril hair. Not only did she keep our teeth in great shape, I've been using her as the mental equivalent of a cold shower ever since my dick grew up and got a mind of its own.

She works her magic yet again, and I make my way to the boardroom. Jamestech headquarters is in Midtown, a few blocks from Nathan and Drake's law firm. Mason and I have a suite of offices on the top floor, along with Harper O'Brien and a couple other key personnel. I take the elevator down to the next level and inhale a deep breath before I go into the room.

Amber has been on my mind pretty much constantly since I took her to that private hotel last week, and I've seen her another three times since. I can't stay the fuck away from her, but it's our first night together that continues playing on my mind. She shared more with me that one night than she has in over a decade. I want her to be satisfied with her life, to be happy. I just don't want it to involve a community center in Queens. She's led a sheltered life, and while I'm not exactly from the 'hood either, I do at least know how to look after myself. Our mom insisted we all learn how to dance when we were kids, and my pop insisted we learn how to box —both have come in handy over the years.

All those worries need to go into a box while we meet with Mason. They won't help. Neither will the whole hard-on thing that seems to happen every time I see her or think about her. I can't shake the image of her on her knees, hands tied behind her back. The way she took my cock so well. I slam my hand against the wall of the corridor. Shit, I need to get control of my thoughts.

We're here to discuss media strategy, I remind myself.

The reaction to Mason's press release about our split was predictably rabid. My phone has been blowing up for days with calls from people I actually know expressing genuine concern and journalists looking for comment. Both Amber and I have cultivated a lot of press relationships over our years together. For me, it's part of my job leading one of the biggest tech companies in the world. For her, it's on behalf of the various causes she fundraises for, but it was also part of her role as my wife—as Mrs. James, specifically. A role she, from a business standpoint, truly excelled at, regardless of our personal issues.

Neither of us is a stranger to the limelight, but this is different. This is deeply personal in a way that a business story or a photo of Amber cutting the ribbon at a new hospital wing is not.

We expected the announcement to attract attention, but not quite as much as it has. As head of corporate communications, Mason has been fielding calls too, and he thought it would be a good idea for us all to sit down together and discuss it. This is straightforward and necessary, and I need to deal with it. Standing outside thinking about my wife's incredible pussy is not going to help matters.

As I drag myself together and prepare to go in, the frosty pitch to Amber's voice from inside the boardroom reaches me and pulls me up short—like a swift kick to the balls. I haven't heard that particular ice-cold tone since the day of Elodie's wedding. That day, she used it to great effect, but since then? Not even once. Since then, she has cried and been angry and screamed my name as she's come—but not once has she frozen me out. I don't miss it at all. It's like the ghost of everything that was wrong with our marriage has come back to haunt me.

I school my face into neutral and walk into the room. Mason's secretary has already set us up with coffee and pastries, none of which appear to have been touched. Amber is dressed in a fitted black dress and a pair of knee-high boots with pointed heels that could kill a man. She's also wearing that tasseled necklace she had on a couple of nights ago, and I narrow my eyes at her when I see it. She gives me a mischievous wink as Mason stands up to greet me. She knows exactly what she's doing, the minx.

Mason's face is red and his knuckles are white, and I can tell he'd really like to punch the shit out of something. "She's refusing to cooperate, which is no fucking surprise at all."

"I'm not refusing to cooperate," Amber says, that patented ice of hers dripping from every word. "I'm simply refusing to do what you've asked of me, Mason. Mainly because it's a stupid idea. Perhaps you could consult with a PR person who actually knows what they're doing."

His nostrils flare, and he whirls around to face her. Nathan has no patience at all for Amber either, but he's the Ice Man. Mason is not. Mason is quick to laugh, quick to lose his temper, quick to forgive. Amber knows all of this, and she's pushing his buttons—what I don't know is why. Just for fun? I suppose that's possible.

I place a calming hand on my younger brother's shoulder. "Before we escalate to DEFCON 1, how about you tell me what it was you suggested?"

Nodding, he takes a seat and throws a quick glare at my wife, then pointedly ignores her. Her lips curve as she pours herself a coffee. Yeah. Definitely pressing his buttons.

"I think part of the reason this whole thing is getting way more attention than we expected is because people want to know more," he says. "You're both public figures in your own right. Elijah, because you're the successful CEO of a multi-billion-dollar corporation, and Amber, because you look good in a cocktail dress and pretend you give a shit about good causes."

I bite back a laugh. Mason is also very sharp and damn funny. Amber's response is priceless—her head lifts and tilts very slightly to one side. She fixes him with those irresistible eyes, the very picture of classy Jackie O elegance, then abruptly gives him the finger. Even his mouth twitches at the corners.

"Will you two quit acting like kids?" I say, remembering that I haven't eaten all day and grabbing a Danish.

"I will if she will." Mason sticks his tongue out, and she responds in kind, but then she holds her hands up in a gesture of peace. "Look, I'm here, aren't I? I'm not enjoying all this fuss either. My phone hasn't stopped ringing, and I've had several journalists come knocking on the door. I was even caught by a paparazzi during my walk around the park this morning."

"Christ, I hope you didn't give them the finger too." Mason follows my lead and picks up a croissant.

He's joking, but I don't think it's funny at all. I'm fucking furious. "That's not happening again. We need to get security in place. I'll make some calls, get someone there by tonight. The cameras aren't enough to deal with this." I'm thinking she needs someone living there twenty-four seven. "You shouldn't be in that house alone, with fuck knows who hanging around outside."

We have a security company on retainer, but I'm not sure they're good enough. Ideally, I'd have a Navy SEAL team outside the house. Or Nathan could talk to his clients the Ryans—they're basically Irish Mafia, and they'd definitely keep her protected. Legal doesn't mean shit to me when it comes to my wife. I hate being away from her anyway, but the thought of her alone and under siege makes my blood boil.

"Hold it right there, Sir Plans-a-lot," she says, interrupting my train of thought. "None of that is necessary. For a start, it was nothing I haven't dealt with before. They were polite enough, and nobody showed any signs of bundling me into the back of a van. Even the photographer was apologetic once he got his shot. Plus, and most importantly, I'm not staying there. I've decided to move out."

When the hell did she decide that? She hasn't mentioned it any of the times I've seen her, but Mason knows nothing about our affair, so I keep my voice steady as I say, "What do you mean, you're moving out? When did you decide that?"

"I've been considering it since I got back from Charleston, to be honest. The house ..." She shakes her head. "It's too big for me on my own. I need somewhere new."

Our eyes meet across the table, and I wish like hell that Mason wasn't here. I wish like hell I could simply say, "Fuck it, I'll move back in. Let me look after you." But that's not what she wants, and it's not sensible. Seeing each other as pretend strangers in clandestine hotel rooms is one thing—resuming our life together is quite another.

"Why the fuck didn't you say that to start with?" Mason snaps at Amber, then glances at me and explains. "I wanted you two to do an interview together at the house. Show a united front, stress the continuity, answer a few scripted questions. Basically overfeed the press and public enough niceness that they lose interest in you. Nothing is more boring than a conscious uncoupling."

"I didn't say it because you didn't give me the chance," she drawls. The slower she speaks, the more annoyed she is. "Plus, it was something I preferred to tell the organ grinder, not his media monkey."

I shake my head and blow out a breath. These two. They've barely seen each other in years, and I almost forgot how much they make me want to bang their heads together. I slam my hands down on the table to stop their incessant bickering. "Amber, where are you thinking of moving to?" I ask, far more concerned about her next moves than what a gossip columnist has to say about us. "You're free to choose any of the properties Jamestech owns—we have the apartments we use for visiting guests and staff. Or I could contact our realtor and see what's available that would be suitable for you."

"Suitable?" she repeats, a distinct and dangerous glint in her eyes. It's another signature Amber move that I haven't seen from her since we decided to divorce, and it makes me feel exactly the same as it always has—frustrated, misunderstood, and like a complete fucking idiot. "What do you mean by suitable, Elijah?"

"Suitable as in safe. As in somewhere you feel comfortable," I say, keeping my voice even, knowing I'm on thin ice.

But no, screw that. The Amber from my hotel suite, the Amber from Greenwich, is gone and has been replaced by the coldhearted automaton who can destroy me with one word, one look. Replaced by the Amber who seems to enjoy inflicting pain on me. I understand why that Amber exists a lot better than I ever did, and I appreciate that she isn't actually coldhearted at all—but I don't want to go back to that life. I lived it for too damn long. "Jesus Christ, you know what? Live wherever the fuck you like."

Mason's head snaps up, his eyes wide. Amber herself simply nods and sets her coffee cup on the coaster in front of her with a click. She stands, smoothing down her dress with efficient, deliberate motions, and grabs her coat. "Right. Well. Thanks so much gentlemen. This was productive." She spins and walks out of the room, her heels clicking on the floor, and it feels like they're sinking into my heart with every step she takes away from me.

Mason meets my eyes. "Do not go after her," he says firmly. "She's not worth it."

I glower at him. He was at least partially responsible for the way she behaved. She's under no illusions about the way Mason feels about her, and she has always felt second best to my brothers. Upset, she retreated back into her frigid-bitch act. It's an act, but it's an act that still has the power to hurt me.

"Mason, I love you dearly—but fuck off." I get to my feet so quickly I knock the chair over. The elevator doors close as I approach them, so I take the stairs, galloping down them two at a time. I emerge into the lobby as she leaves the building. A few members of the staff look confused when I dart past, racing to catch her before she can jump into a cab.

"Amber," I shout. "Wait!" She freezes on the spot, and I'm relieved I don't have to chase her this time. Her hands go to her face, and I swear under my breath. She's fucking crying. Whether they're angry tears or sad tears or a bit of both, I have no idea.

She whirls around, her whiskey-brown eyes flashing at me, that damn tasseled necklace swinging between her breasts. "What, Elijah? What do you want?"

"I want to talk to you. I want us to speak like human beings again. I want us to be Mr. and Mrs. Smith for a few damn minutes."

"Really? And what exactly do you have in mind? Want to sneak down a dark alleyway and screw like animals? Maybe you could shove me up against a wall and fuck me from behind."

"No, that's not what I had in mind. But hey, if that's what turns you on, baby, I'll be happy to oblige."

She is visibly furious. I'm not sure if she's angry with me, with Mason, or with herself for showing weakness and crying. This damn woman and all her defenses. The real Amber hides behind so many walls, it's almost impossible to reach her.

I sigh and close the distance between us. It's after five, and office buildings are emptying around us. We're committing a New York crime by blocking the sidewalk, but I couldn't give less of a fuck. I stroke her tears away, swiping her cheeks clear of mascara. My touch seems to calm her.

"Panda eyes?" she asks quietly.

"Not anymore." I want to take her in my arms and hold her. To kiss her and tell her I love her. Shit. I'd quite like to take her up on the alleyway idea too. None of it is feasible, though, not in public. She pulls herself together and steps away from me.

"I'm sorry I turned into a prize bitch back there," she

says, biting her plump lower lip. "It's being around Mason. Being in your office. It's ... I don't know. My head got all messed up. I didn't mean to tell you like that, about moving out."

"That's okay. I get it. We're both under pressure. But are you sure, Amber? About the house? It's yours—you know that, don't you? For as long as you want it. Forever."

"That's the thing, Elijah—I don't want it. Not anymore. When's the last happy memory you have of that place? It's not exactly filled with them."

I shake my head because she's right. I'd have to go back a long time to find one. "No, it's not. And I can see what you mean. Just promise me that you won't, you know ..."

"Move to Queens?" Her lips twitch.

"Yeah. That. Or if you do move to Queens, at least tell me. I'm not trying to control you ... but I also can't just flip a switch and stop caring about you. You're part of me, and you always will be."

She nods and wipes her eyes as more tears appear. "I know. Thank you for that." Her lips curve in a wobbly smile and she takes a small step back. "Look, I'm going to head out. I arranged to see Drake and Amelia for drinks after ..." She motions at the Jamestech building. "I had an idea I might need to decompress."

Her plans are a reminder of how separate our lives have been for so long. I haven't been invited to drinks with her and Drake in as long as I can remember. And as much as I'd like to go with her now, she needs her space. Plus, truthfully, I need mine. She might have apologized, but I'm still shaken by how easily we both slipped back into our old personas. I love the hell out of her, but I won't go back to living like that.

"Okay. Well, be careful. Call Sanjay if you need a ride. And call me if anyone bothers you around the house. I mean it."

Her smile does nothing to hide the sadness in her eyes. "I will, I promise." She steps up and kisses me briefly on the cheek. "Now you'd better get back to Mason. He needs you." Her lip wobbles, and for a second I think she's going to say something else, something profound. But she shakes her head and plasters on a smile I know from years of experience is fake. "No doubt he's up there putting a price on my head."

"Nah, Nathan tried that years ago," I say, forcing a grin. "Nobody would take the job. Even John Wick was scared of you."

She rolls her eyes and waves goodbye as it starts to rain. I stand in the drizzle, surrounded by office workers heading home for the night, and watch her go.

I glance behind me at the Jamestech building, the place where I spent the majority of the last ten years of my marriage. Mason needs me, she said. Does he need me more than she does? Deep-seated regret gnaws at the pit of my stomach. There must have been a time when she needed me more. And was I there for her when she did? I honestly don't know.

A few minutes ago, when she swallowed whatever it was she was going to say ... Habit kept me from pressuring her to tell me, but I should have pushed. Would we be here now if I had pushed more? If I had forced her to confide in me all the times sorrow flashed in those incredible eyes of hers but her icy expression told me not to pry?

She turns the corner a block away, and it takes every ounce of self-control I have not to chase after her and ask.

CHAPTER
EIGHTEEN
AMBER

'm cautious as I approach the James and James offices, my head on a swivel. It's the end of the workday, and a lot of the staff are leaving. Nathan is unlikely to join the mass exodus, but you never know. My encounter with Mason was bad enough, and Nathan makes him look like a pussycat.

In the before times, when I felt like I was part of the James family, I got along with all the brothers, but Nathan was the most reserved. The most naturally cynical of them all. Elijah and I had a big, flashy wedding, and I remember Nathan looking around at all the ribbons and chintz and chiffon with something akin to amusement. I think even then he had his doubts, and I do rather hate to have proven him right.

I successfully make my way to Drake's part of the building without any upsetting encounters. I'm early, and Amelia's workstation outside his office is empty. I knock on the door, announcing myself.

"Come on in," Drake shouts after a second. "Quick meeting?" he asks when I walk in.

"Yes. We went from civilized to barroom brawl in about sixty seconds."

He nods sympathetically, and Amelia brings me a coffee from his machine. I stand and look through the window as I sip it. I always forget how magnificent the view is from here. "How are you two doing?"

Amelia blushes slightly, and I notice that Drake's normally immaculate hair is a little mussed up. Ah. I see. They're doing very well, thank you.

"While you're here, I need you to sign some papers." Drake grabs a file from his desk drawer. "If you're still sure, that is?"

His lovely brown eyes meet mine, and I see a glimmer of hope there. He loves his brother and is fond of me, and he would like for us to give it another shot. He's the only other person who knows about that night in Verona's room. The things she said to me, and the damage it caused. He doesn't understand, though, quite how bad things have been the past few years.

I thought they'd gotten better since Elijah moved out, but it seems old habits die hard. Today, for example, and how quickly I became my old self again, including the way I dressed, the makeup, the styled hair. Yes, I'm going out for drinks, and yes, I can look however I damn well please—but going into Jamestech, knowing I'd see Mason, felt like marching into enemy territory. I needed that suit of armor again. It didn't take long for us all to descend into back-biting and sniping, either. I felt so isolated, so attacked. The same way I have felt for years.

But I gave as good as I got and didn't let any of them, including Elijah, see how much it hurt. In all our years together, I never asked him for backup or showed any weakness—because I am Amber James, Ice Queen Super Bitch. Hard as nails.

Except I'm not, deep down. And just once, I would have loved to hear Elijah tell them to go screw themselves. But I've spent way too much emotional energy on this subject, and I don't want my life to look like that anymore. I don't want every day to be full of petty squabbles and point scoring. Sad as it is, my marriage is over.

"I'm still sure, darling," I answer Drake. "Just tell me where to sign."

We handle the paperwork while Amelia uses the bathroom in Drake's office to freshen up. "Can we go somewhere different for drinks?" I ask. "The usual Manhattan fishbowl won't be ideal for me at the moment."

"Trouble?" Drake cocks an eyebrow.

"Nothing serious. Just a lot of interest after the statement was released. Some overzealous paparazzi. And goodness, a million divorce lawyers offering their services—I was not prepared for that."

He laughs. "Yeah, I should have warned you. Sharks sensing blood in the water. And while we're on that subject, I need to say something. The way we're going about this is unorthodox. I'm one hundred percent committed to making the process as fair and painless as it can be for both of you, but this isn't the way a divorce normally works. I'd go so far as to advise you to sign up with someone else, or at least find someone willing to oversee the final settlement on your behalf. Just to make sure that my conflict of interest isn't detrimental to you in any way."

"But we've already agreed on everything and signed what we need to sign, haven't we?"

"Yes, but nothing is irrevocable yet—you could still get external counsel. You probably should."

I have, of course, been told this by several people. My parents were horrified when I told them Drake was representing us both, and even Granny Lucille lodged a protest. I'm aware that the traditional approach to the legal ending of a marriage is like a battlefield. Wife on one side with her troops, husband on the other with his. They either go full berserker and fight to the death, or they meet in the middle and hack away at each other until they sign a peace treaty. I don't want any of that. I've had enough conflict with Elijah and his family to last me a lifetime, and I just want this over with as amicably as possible.

"Drake, it's fine," I say. "I appreciate you bringing it up, and I know it's not conventional. But what can I say? I trust you, and I trust Elijah. Whatever has happened between us, I believe in his basic human decency. He won't be looking to screw me over, and there's no way on earth that I'll be looking to do that to him either. I can't imagine Nathan is thrilled with the arrangement though."

"You got that right," Drake says, shaking his head. It must be causing problems between them too, and I regret that. But there's also nothing I can do about it. "He's worried about Jamestech."

I frown and turn that idea over in my mind. It didn't occur to me that I might have a claim to any part of the James family business. Perhaps that is naive of me. Given that we have no prenup, it would be fair game—but I don't want it. The James family has enough independent wealth for this to all be settled without having to take a penny from the company. "I see. And Dalton—is your father concerned about that too?"

I never felt the same emotional connection to Dalton as I did to Verona. But his health hasn't been great, and I'm eager to avoid adding anything stressful to his life. He's no longer a young man, and he has a heart condition. We don't need to have a soul connection for me to not want to be the cause of any further health complications.

Drake nods. "He is. You know what he's like. Jamestech is part of him."

"The great James family legacy. Look, this potentially risks blowing my hard-earned reputation, but could you please do your best to put his mind at rest? I'm happy for you to let Nathan suffer, obviously, but not your father. Please reassure him that I want nothing whatsoever to do with Jamestech. I haven't asked for that, and I'm not going to. Frankly, I can't think of anything worse than being tied to that company for the rest of my life. I know they all think I'm evil personified, and that will probably never change, but I don't want your dad's blood pressure going up because he's worried about me stealing his precious business. If you'd like, if you think it would help, I'll sign something to that effect right here and now."

Amelia has come out of the bathroom, and she looks between us but stays silent. This must be strange for her. She's settled into the James clan so naturally, and all she must see is their kindness, their generosity and warmth. I hope that's all she ever sees. But there is another side to them. People don't get to be billionaires without a ruthless streak.

"No, there's no need for that. Not today," Drake says firmly. "But I will tell him, and I think he'll believe it. He doesn't see you as quite the ogre you think he does, Amber."

"Damn. I must try harder. Anyway, enough." I shimmy my shoulders and shake out my arms. "I need wine, and I need it now."

"Shall I call Constantine?" Amelia offers. "I was thinking we could take Amber to my old neighborhood."

"Good idea." Drake flashes his wife a charming smile. "I'm pretty sure nobody there will recognize her or care who she is."

"Are you sure?" I ask when we're in the elevator. "I could always go in disguise. I have a fake nose and an Elvis wig in my purse."

"I'm positive, but you could wear them anyway, just for fun?" Amelia says.

We clamber into the limo, and I say hi to Constantine before he drives us over the bridge and into Brooklyn.

We head to a small Italian place, and I smile as I watch Amelia chat excitedly to the owner. "Does she know everybody in this neighborhood?"

"Pretty much, yeah," Drake answers, looking at her fondly. "At least her little corner of it. She grew up here, still has an apartment here. We've moved into the Tribeca loft as you know, but her lease isn't up for a few months. She also has her mom's house, which she's almost cleared now and plans to eventually fix up so she can rent it out. That will be the start of her property empire. She'll be running the world soon."

He sounds so proud, and I can practically see the connection between them. It's like an invisible string, binding them together. Her hazel eyes are bright and lively as she walks back to us, waving to a few other people.

"Donny's going to bring us a couple pizzas to go with the beer. Or would you prefer wine, Amber?"

"Usually, I'd say yes, but tonight I think beer will be perfect. What was it like, living here?"

"Oh, it was great," she says enthusiastically. "I loved it. There's a real sense of community, and people really look out for each other, you know?"

I nod, but I actually don't know. I study the groups of friends, families, and older couples who occupy the tables around us. Everyone looks as happy as Amelia. Nobody seems to be inspecting each other's outfits or wearing a Rolex, and they're all relaxed as they eat messy food and laugh and chat. It's a far cry from what I'm used to.

"I'm moving out of the Manhattan house," I announce right as the waitress arrives with our beers. I take a tentative sip and nod in appreciation. It's better than I thought it would be.

"Why?" Drake asks, frowning. "You've lived there since you got married, and Elijah was planning to let you keep it."

"I don't want it *because* we've lived there since we got married. We expected to fill it with children, and that didn't happen."

I can tell from the way Amelia looks away, her pinched expression, that she knows I can't have kids.

"It's okay, Amelia." I pat her hand on the table. "It's fine for you to know, and it's fine for us to talk about it. I should have talked about it more in the first place. If I had, maybe people wouldn't have kept asking. It was like torture—the constant questions. 'When will we be hearing the patter of tiny feet?' I felt ashamed, for absolutely no reason, and that made it worse. By the time I was in my thirties, I was getting asked about it so much I considered taking an ad out in the *Times*. Some kind of announcement of infertility, right in there with the births, marriages, and deaths."

Drake's expression darkens. I never told him how much it bothered me either. "And how do you feel about it all now?" Amelia asks, her tone cautious but interested.

"I will always feel sad about it, truthfully—but I also don't want what I can't do to define me."

"That makes sense," she says. "And moving out of Manhattan, that's part of your plan?"

I didn't actually say that I was moving out of Manhattan, but really, why not? What is left for me there? Fake friends, meaningless social events, shopping? Once the divorce goes through, there's no real reason for me to stay in New York. I could go to Charleston or anywhere I like. Not a day has passed when I haven't thought of heading back to Lucille's to lick my wounds. But there's a difference between running and relocating, and I will not run. For the time being, I will stay in the city. Besides, I'm having quite the satisfying affair, and I'm not sure how far Mr. Smith would be willing to travel.

"Moving out of the house is, for sure. I need to look for a place. The problem is, I've never had to do any of this stuff. I haven't signed a lease or had to figure out how to get the power connected."

"Life stuff, you mean?" she asks.

"Exactly. I went from my family to college to Elijah. Pathetic but true. I'm sure I can figure it all out."

"Of course you can," Drake says. "You can do anything, Amber. Don't underestimate yourself."

The pizza arrives, and it's pretty much the best damn pizza I've ever tasted. We lose ourselves in a saucy cheese coma for the next twenty minutes. Afterward, I slump in my chair with my beer. I might even break the rule of a lifetime and belch in public.

As the plates are cleared away, Amelia wipes her face with a napkin and laughs at my expression. "You think that was good, wait 'til you try Mario's exploding donut balls."

"I'm not sure. They sound dangerous."

"They are." Drake rolls his eyes. "Dangerously good. This place is sinful food heaven."

"Huh. Maybe I should move here, then."

Amelia taps her fingers on the table and narrows her eyes at me. "Maybe you should. How about my place?"

"Which one? I believe you're a budding property mogul."

"Hardly. But my mom's place ... it's a nice house on a nice street. It's not big, and it's not fancy, but it might be okay for you."

Drake lets out a surprised laugh, and I turn my gaze to him. Smirking, he holds his hands up in surrender. "Sorry. I just ... The thought of you living in Brooklyn? No way."

"What happened to not underestimating me? Do you think I'm some kind of pampered princess who might faint if she's too far away from her nail salon?"

"Uh, well, yeah—a little bit. I'm sorry if that hurts your feelings. Look, I get that you're looking for a fresh start. And it is a nice street, but it's really not what you're used to."

"Darling, I'm used to feeling miserable every single day. Anything will be an improvement on that. Can we go and look at it? Or are you worried that your big brother might disapprove?" I'm messing with him, and he knows it. Drake is the middle sibling and has always worked crazy hard for his place in the hierarchy.

"Oh, I'm pretty sure my big brother will disapprove. You know full well that Elijah will want to have a SWAT team on standby twenty-four seven if you leave Manhattan." He leans back in his chair and stares at me. I know I have him.

"You're doing your not-blinking thing, Amber. Are you hypnotizing me?"

"I don't know—am I?"

"Well, I am feeling sleepy, but that might be the beer. Come on, then. Let's walk this off. I warn you, though, the entire house is roughly the size of your closet."

"That's okay. I'm downsizing on that front as well."

After Drake pays the bill, we stroll the few blocks to the street where Amelia grew up. She gives me a running commentary as we go, showing me Wanda's bakery, the deli, and the dive bar that has live music on weekends. It's very endearing, and Drake doesn't let go of her hand once.

The earlier rain has stopped now, but there's still a chill in the air, and I'm glad when Amelia finally tells us we're here. It's a quiet street, lined with neat houses. Small front yards are well-kept, a few feature swing sets, and the cars are all at least ten years old. There's a yellow cab and a plumber's van, signs of people who have real jobs in the real world. A front door opens and the red tip of a cigarette glows in the dark.

"Hi, Mrs. Katzberg," Amelia shouts, giving her a wave.

"Hi, Amelia. I watered the plants for you, honey. You doing okay?"

A face comes into view behind the cigarette, and it belongs to an elderly woman with a tight gray perm. She looks wiry and strong and reminds me of Sophia from the Golden Girls. I give her a big smile in case she ends up being my neighbor. She looks unimpressed, but I like a challenge.

Amelia chats with her for a few moments, then leads us into the house. She must have the heating system on a timer, because it's warm and cozy. It is, as Drake said, very small by my standards. It would take Vicky a half hour to clean from top to bottom, and Dionne would be horrified by the kitchen. Or maybe not—it's small but spotless and perfectly ordinary.

A framed picture of Amelia and her mom hangs on the living room wall. It was obviously taken at a party, as they're both holding wine glasses and wearing paper hats. It immediately makes me smile. "You look so similar," I say. "And you look like you're having a lot of fun."

"We always did." Amelia comes to stand beside me. "She was a terrific lady, and I miss her every day. Are you close to your mom?"

"Ah, no. Not at all, sadly. But I am to my Granny. She lives in Charleston."

Amelia kisses her fingertips and presses them against the picture of her mother. "So, this is it." She gestures around herself, slightly flustered. "It's not much, I don't suppose, compared to what someone like you is used to."

Now that we're here, it seems she's regretting her suggestion. "It's gorgeous," I quickly reassure her. "It's cute and cozy, and it has a great energy. It feels like a home, not only a house. If the offer is still open, I would love to live here."

Her face lights up. "That's amazing. I'm so happy." She claps her hands together. "Most of Mom's stuff has been cleared out—my friends Kimmy and Emily helped me. You know Emily, don't you? Emily Gregor?"

I nod, surprised. Emily is old money—Manhattan nobility—and it's hard to picture her in this little house with trash bags and a broom. Looks like I'm as guilty of judging a book by its cover as anyone.

"I made a start on the painting," she continues, gesturing toward a wall full of brush strokes in different shades of yellow. "But I couldn't quite make up my mind. I love painting. Do you enjoy it? Maybe you could carry on for me."

I reach out and touch the wall, needing to feel it under my fingers for some reason. "I don't know," I reply, gazing at it in wonder. "I've never actually painted a wall."

"Well, this will be a whole new experience for you." Her bubbly laugh fills the homey space.

I try to imagine myself living here. She's right, it's not what I'm used to—I think it might be better. I can picture myself curled up on the couch, eating takeout pizza—or exploding donut balls. I could watch TV alone like I do now, but I wouldn't feel anywhere near as lonely in a place like this. Maybe I'll take up smoking and join Mrs. Katzberg on her stoop at night. And I could paint walls, damn it.

It would get me out of my current prison, set me free from the empty shell of my Manhattan world. This would be the total fresh start I need.

Drake shakes his head. "What's wrong?" I ask.

"Nothing's wrong. I just ..." He smiles. "I don't remember

the last time I saw you look so hopeful. But I can only imagine how Elijah is going to react when he finds out."

Ah. Elijah. I try to picture him here, curled up on the couch with me. Painting those walls. Strolling through the lively streets of this pleasant working-class neighborhood. I can picture it, but I quickly chase the images away. Whether he is Mr. Smith or Mr. James, I can't let him influence my decisions anymore.

For the first time in my life, I need to make choices with only my own thoughts and feelings in mind.

NINETEEN

AMBER

When I arrive at the Greenwich Village hotel a few nights later, I follow Mr. Smith's instructions and head straight upstairs. We're in a different room than usual, and nerves skitter up my spine as I walk along the corridor, looking at the numbers on the doors.

I haven't seen him since the meeting with Mason, but we've spoken on the phone. I told him about my plans to move to Brooklyn straight away. Drake is stuck in the middle enough as it is, and I didn't want him to feel like he had to have that conversation with his brother.

"Brooklyn?" he repeated.

"Yes, Elijah, it's a—"

"Yeah, let's not start with that again—I know where Brooklyn is. Why do you want to move there?"

"Because I like it and Amelia offered to rent me her old house. I meant it when I said I was leaving our place. Please don't make a big deal of it. Please … just try to be happy for me."

He went silent for a few moments, and I pictured him googling Brooklyn crime statistics with steam coming out of his ears. "Okay," he finally said. "I will try to be happy for you. Are you free tomorrow night?"

"Me or Mrs. Smith?"

He laughed. "Oh baby, most definitely Mrs. Smith. Tell her not to bother with underwear."

Now, I'm here, wearing a slinky, low-cut black dress and no underwear. I feel slutty as hell, especially because I'm already damp between my legs. I have no idea what he has planned for me, but I'm certain I'll enjoy it.

Once I find the right room, I pause outside for a moment, running my fingers through my hair and taking deep breaths. It's game time. He tells me to come in after I knock, and I step inside with more confidence than I feel and close the door behind me. I'm barely in the room when he grabs hold of me. I squeal as he spins me around and pushes me face-first against the door. He presses his chest to my back and pins my hands, palms flat above my head.

He nuzzles my neck and kisses my earlobe. "Mrs. Smith. You're late."

"I'm not," I protest, struggling against him. Well, no more than a few minutes.

"If I say you're late, then you're late. That's your first warning. Do you understand?" He presses his hips closer, and his hard cock pushes into me.

"I understand, Mr. Smith. I'm sorry."

"Good. Now, stay where you are. I need to check that you've obeyed the rules." He slowly runs his big hands down my body, slipping and sliding on the satiny fabric of my dress, exploring every curve. Being searched like this feels incredibly sexy, and I almost wish I hadn't obeyed the rules. I wonder what he would have done to me.

He pushes the skirt of my dress up and over my thighs, exposing my bare ass. Strong hands skim my flesh and roughly palm my breasts. I cry out when he nips my bare shoulder.

"Very good. No underwear, as instructed."

I hear a rustling sound, and then the world goes dark. I gasp and protest, but he ignores me, tying the blindfold behind my head, the fabric cool and soft. He turns me around so I'm facing him but still trapped against the door. I reach out and lay my hand on his shoulder. "Elijah, I'm not sure about this."

I'm even more nervous now, caught between excitement and discomfort. Being unable to see makes me feel vulnerable. He gently strokes my cheekbone, then runs his fingers along my jaw. Without any visual cues, I'm surprised when he kisses me. His tongue slides into my welcoming mouth, and his hands roam my body. He tugs down one of the straps on my dress and moves his mouth there, tracing kisses along my collarbone. I lean back against the door and moan as he works me over.

I jut my hips out slightly and rub myself against him, and I'm momentarily confused when he pulls away. "Did I tell you that you could do that?" he asks.

"No, but—"

"No, I didn't. Second warning."

"How many warnings do I get?" I bleat, sounding bratty even to my own ears. I'm off-balance here, and although my body is very much enjoying this, my mind is still unsure.

"As many as I choose to give you. Now, kick off those heels and remove your dress."

I tremble at his commanding tone. He sounds like a complete stranger, and maybe that helps. With quivering hands, I pull the dress over my head and stand naked and blindfolded before him. I have no idea where he is or what he's doing, and it's unnerving. I shriek when I feel his hands on my ass and his breath on my neck.

"You're shaking. Are you scared?"

"A little bit, yes. What are you going to do to me?"

"I'm not entirely sure yet." He slides his hand between my thighs and probes me with one long finger. My legs automatically spread wider to let him in, and I lean back against him, gasping as he circles my clit with deft strokes. "You're absolutely fucking soaked, Amber. You're a dirty girl, aren't you?"

"I am, yes. Please don't stop."

He wraps his other hand around my throat, and not seeing it coming makes it more thrilling. Then he gently squeezes, a mild restriction that drives me crazy. Everything feels heightened because of the blindfold, like all my other senses have gone into overdrive. Keeping his fingers around my throat, he kisses my neck, all the while keeping up the perfect level of pressure on my swollen clit. "Don't come, Amber," he whispers darkly.

"What?" I murmur, confused and hazy and too close to the edge to pull back.

"I *said* don't come."

He carries on stroking the sensitive bud between my legs, continues fucking me with his finger, doesn't stop biting my neck and gently gripping my throat. It's too much, and he must know that. "If you come, I'll have to punish you."

The raw growl, the promise wrapped up in a threat, is what pushes me over. He's too skillful to resist, and this whole scenario is too hot for me to survive. My orgasm rips through me, tearing from my pussy to every single cell in my body. I throw my head back, my hands grasping, my pussy walls clenching around his fingers. He holds me steady and helps me wring every last drop of pleasure from that orgasm. But as soon as I'm done, I feel his breath on my ear. "I told you not to come, Amber. You disobeyed me again. No more warnings."

I try to pull away as he leads me by the hand. "What's happening? W-what are you going to do?"

"I'm going to punish you. You've been a naughty girl, and we all know that little brats need discipline, don't we?"

"Oh god ... B-but what if I don't want to be punished?"

He tugs on my hand, and I slam into the solid wall of his chest. My hands fly up to his shoulders to steady myself. "If you don't want me to, tell me to stop. Or you use a safe word. In your case, let's use 'princess,' shall we?"

"No, I don't like that safe word."

I sound petulant, like a spoiled teenager, and I am amazed at how easily I slip into the game. "Well, you've just proven my point, Amber—princess it is."

I stagger along, completely unable to see where I'm going, my bare feet sinking into the plush carpet. He keeps hold of my hand until he drops lower, and I assume he's sitting on the edge of the bed. He pulls me toward him, and I feel his thighs on either side of me. My flailing hands find his head. He tugs me closer and wraps his arms around me. "I'm going to spank you now, Amber. Would you prefer to be on your knees or over my lap?" He squeezes my ass hard as he speaks, making me jump.

"I'd prefer neither," I snap. "I'm not a child."

"No." One finger slides along my pussy. He flicks it over my sensitive clit, then pushes it inside me. "You're really not. You're all woman, but tonight, we are playing a game, and we're playing by my rules. Now, on your knees or over my lap?"

I bite my lip. Fuck, I really don't know. I've never done this before. "On my knees."

"'On my knees,' what? Show a little respect." He pulls his finger out of me with a wet sound.

"On my knees, sir. Please."

"That's better … But I could tell you didn't mean it. I supposed that means we'll do this my way."

Before I know it, I'm lying across his lap, spread over his powerful thighs. My head falls to the bed, and I wriggle around, trying to escape. He keeps one big hand between my shoulders, holding me in place. "Just say the word. Princess."

"Fuck you."

"No, that's not it, but don't worry, I will most definitely be fucking you. Your ass, by the way, is incredible. You could base a whole religion on this ass. People would come from miles around to worship it."

He runs his hands down my backside, gentle and reverent. He takes his time, and it's sexy as hell. Without any warning, he slaps me so hard I squeal. The sound of his hand hitting my flesh makes a cracking noise, and he follows it up with another. It hurts, but I enjoy it far more than I thought I would. There's something so liberating about him holding me here, his palm coming down on my skin, me yelping and writhing while he focuses on what he's doing. I'm still blind-folded, but I can picture his face: the look of solemn concentration as he spanks me, pupils dilated, fire in his deep gray eyes.

He stops as suddenly as he started and smooths his hands across my sore flesh, tenderly rubbing away the sting. "Oh baby, you should see your ass now ... bright red. I'm tempted to take a fucking picture."

I think he's finished and try to push myself up.

"Oh no, not yet. I think this fine specimen can take a little more, don't you?"

Shit. It really is sore now. But I want to please him, and I want him to touch me more. And I need to see where this leads. "Yes," I whisper.

"Yes, what? I didn't hear you."

"Yes please, sir," I murmur, raising my backside slightly, my hands clutching the sheets beneath me.

"Good girl. You're better behaved already."

When the next slap comes, it's on the back of my thighs, and I shout my surprise. He works his way back up to my backside and continues to deliver his stinging blows. By the time he finally finishes, tears are trickling from my eyes and I'm trembling.

Again, he rubs his hands softly over my skin, stroking and reassuring. "You look perfect like this. I know you're sore, baby, but you're so wet. I can feel you through my pants."

My cheeks blaze, and I try to squirm away. I am clearly a pervert on top of everything else. "Don't be ashamed," he says, holding me still. "I'm sure you can tell how much I'm enjoying this too."

I can. His cock is rock hard, pressing into my belly. He pulls me up into his arms, where he cradles me and kisses my forehead. I hiss as my ass makes contact with his legs, but it's not intolerable. In fact, I kind of like it. He kisses my neck, making me purr, then lays me down flat on the bed. "Just stay there."

I'm still wearing the blindfold, and although I could take it off myself at any moment, I don't want to. The sense of anticipation is glorious, and I lie here, listening to him move around the room. I hear his belt unbuckle and slide out of its loops. The image is all too clear in my head: him standing next to the bed, his belt in his hands. It scares me, but the warm liquid seeping between my legs says I also like it.

He crawls along next to me, and I tremble as he runs the belt up my body. The buckle bumps over my nipples, and he continues upward to my face and holds it under my nose. It smells of leather and him, and I feel my pulse racing.

"You like this, baby, I can tell. You want to feel my belt on you, don't you? You're even dirtier than I thought. I'm not going to give that to you tonight. Your ass has taken enough, and when I use my belt on you, I want you to really fucking feel it. For now, we'll use it for something else."

He takes both my arms and raises them above my head. With one wrist crossed over the other, he ties them together with his belt. "How does that feel? Because it looks fucking sensational. You on those black sheets, your hair all wild. The blindfold, the belt ... You're like a wet dream come to life."

Without my vision, all I can do is feel. His hands on my

body, on my breasts. His mouth on my nipples. "Oh god, Elijah, it feels ..."

"What, sweetheart?" He pulls away, leaving me desperate. "How does it feel?"

"It feels amazing. What ... What are you going to do to me?"

"You keep asking that. You'll have to wait and see."

From the sounds I hear, I can only guess that he's taking off the rest of his clothes. Then comes the familiar sound of ice and liquid clinking in a glass, and I try to picture what he's doing. "Are you ... Are you drinking a Scotch?"

"I am. An especially fine glass of Macallan. The perfect accompaniment to this fine view. Spread your legs for me."

I don't react immediately, and when he speaks again, his voice is dark and commanding. "Spread your legs. Now." I do as I am told this time, and he growls as I reveal myself.

"Fuck. You're so wet. So fucking needy. I could look at this all damn day. Stay exactly like that for me."

The glass is set on a wooden surface. A drawer opens. Blindfolded, my arms tied above my head, I lie here with my most private parts on display like an exhibit in a gallery. My pussy weeps for him to touch me again.

When he does, it's not what I expect. He takes my legs and spreads them wider. Then, with quick hands, he uses a length of silky fabric to tie my ankles to the wooden frame at the corners of the four-poster bed.

"Wh-what are you doing?" I splutter, raising my head with some difficulty.

"What do you think I'm doing? I'm tying you up to keep your legs nice and wide. Then I'm going to play with you and make you come. And then I'm going to fuck your brains out. Objections?"

Oh my god. This is really happening. He moves to my other leg, and I let my head fall back to the bed. My heart pounds. "Amber. Speak to me. If you want me to stop, you know what to say."

I shake my head. "I don't want you to stop."

He slides his hands up my inner thighs, and I feel so ridiculously exposed. I'm completely at his mercy, and I love it. "That's what I thought, my horny little slut. Look how wet you are. If I touched this pussy now, I think you'd come immediately. I think you're almost there from being spanked and restrained. You're desperate for me."

"Yes, please—touch me."

He laughs, and I'm flooded with disappointment when he removes his hands from my skin. I hear the sound of his glass again and feel the weight of him sinking into the mattress next to me. He runs his hand over my bound wrists, down my arms, around my throat. I almost jump out of my skin when he presses something freezing cold against one nipple, then the other.

"What is that?" I shriek. My nipples pucker.

"Ice from my Scotch. Nothing that will hurt you, so settle down." He moves the ice cube around, making circular motions around my taut nipple. It's painful and perfect, and he follows it up with his mouth, sucking the bud between his lips. The contrast between the cold of the ice and the warmth of his tongue is mind-blowing, and he clearly enjoys torturing me.

My breath comes in heavy pants as he works his way down my body, running the ice cube along my skin, leaving a chilled, watery trail behind him. He reaches my pussy, and I cry out as he slides the melting cube along my center.

"Oh! That's so cold. It ... Oh, god." I shiver, cold water dripping inside my center and mixing with my own juices to flow down to the sheets under me.

"This is missing something," he murmurs, climbing off the bed again. I feel liquid pouring over my pussy, warmer than the ice. A familiar scent reaches my nose. "Is that Scotch?" I ask. "Did you just pour fifty-year-old Macallan on my pussy?"

"Yeah. The perfect cocktail—Scotch, ice, and your cunt. And now I'm fucking thirsty."

His mouth settles over my sensitive flesh, and his tongue starts to lap at me. He licks up all the liquid, then buries his face there, his nose running up and down my opening, his tongue going inside me to curl and play against my inner walls. He holds my hips steady, and I realize I'm bucking and writhing beneath him. My whole body is on fire. Being tied up, the ice, the heat ... It's all too much. He sucks my clit into his mouth and holds it there, lashing it with his tongue, driving me wild. He sucks harder, and I explode. The orgasm rockets through me, and I scream his name, my belt-tied hands thrashing against the bed, my eyes rolling in my head behind my blindfold. He works me some more, licking every drop of Scotch and cum from me, letting me shudder against his face. It feels like it lasts forever, and I am a wreck by the time he finally pulls away.

"Jesus fuck," he says, and I picture him wiping his beard. "Best drink I ever tasted. And now I get to fuck you, baby."

He slides his huge cock inside me and groans. "Christ. So fucking tight." His hands land on either side of my head, and

I turn to kiss his arm. I can't move much, and I can't see anything, but I can do that. "Does your husband fuck you like this?" He slams into me, fast and hard, his breathing speeding up as he chases his own release. He sure does now, I think, but I'm unable to form the words.

When he finally comes, he cries, "Fuck! Amber!" Then he falls down on top of me, laughs, and eventually rolls off to one side.

It's not bright in here, only one lamp is lit, but I've been in darkness for so long that it takes a few moments to adjust after he takes the blindfold off. I'm lying in the biggest wet patch ever—water, Scotch, and cum from both of us—and my ass is still sore from my spanking, but I don't think I've ever felt better.

He unbuckles the belt and kisses my wrists and then scoots down to do the same for my legs. Once I'm free, he rolls me into his arms, and I curl up into his chest. "That was ... uh, different," I say quietly.

"Yeah. And fucking fantastic. I can't wait to use my belt on you." I blush and bury my face against him. "What? Why are you embarrassed? If you want it and I want it, what's the problem?"

"I don't know—I feel a bit ... surprised, I suppose. I know we've played a few of these games before, but not for a long time, and not this intensely. It's a lot. I think I'm a little overwhelmed. Plus you got my pussy drunk and made me come so hard my brain has turned to mush."

His laugh, deep and rich, makes me smile. And makes me feel like all will be well in the world. "Okay. Well, while your brain is mush, can we talk a little about Brooklyn? And Amber—do not start describing where Brooklyn is to me."

"I think I need to, Elijah. Your knowledge of geography is abysmal." I laugh when he pinches my side. "Okay, okay. What do you want to talk about? I don't need your permission to move there—you do know that, right? I might follow orders in the bedroom, but you can't control where I live."

"I do know that, yeah. But I also have some concerns, and if you carry on being a brat about it, I might have to keep you tied up to a bed forever, so quit it with the smart mouth. You're still my wifc. I'm allowed to ask."

I take a deep breath and remind myself to stay calm. He's right. He is simply asking for a conversation.

"It's a very nice place, Elijah. A real nice neighborhood, one where people look out for each other. I'll be careful, and I'll make sure I take precautions. I'm not streetwise, but I can learn. Plus, I'll use Sanjay when I need to—hey, did you know he actually lives three streets away from Amelia's?"

"I did not know that, and I've got to say it does make me feel better. Okay. Like you said, you don't need my permission. I just ... I need you to be safe."

I wrap my arms around his waist, and he buries his hands in my hair. I have no clue what the hell we're doing. The way we move between the most adventurous sex we've ever had and these intimate chats is so confusing.

"I know, Elijah," I say, kissing his chest. "And I am, I promise you."

At least I'm safe physically, I think as I close my eyes. The biggest danger to me right now is the way I feel about my own husband.

TWENTY

AMBER

"Thank you, Sanjay." I pass him a twenty-dollar tip and climb out of the car.

He pokes his head out of the window, glancing at the building behind me. "You be safe now, Mrs. James, won't you? Call me when you need picking up."

"I can get a ride home with one of the other volunteers, Sanjay. You go home and enjoy your Thanksgiving."

He eyes me with suspicion. "You call me if you need me. Okay?"

I nod and wave him off before spinning on my heel and heading toward the entrance to the building, passing a few stragglers on my way. "Afternoon, Miss," one of them says, his salt-and-pepper hair unkempt and his face drawn.

"Good afternoon, sir. Are you coming inside?" I jerk my head toward the double doors. "You have to get in early for a good seat. I hear all the best pie is gone by four."

His smile makes his eyes crinkle at the corners, and the kindness in his expression makes me wonder about his story. So many people here have heartbreaking stories, and they make me truly thankful for the privileged life I lead. "I've never been here before. A bit nervous, I guess."

I open the door. "You'll love it here. Everyone is super friendly." I gesture for him to go inside, but he holds the door for me and insists on ladies first.

"Amber!" Andréa says as soon as she spots me. "Ricky is in the kitchen. He could use some help with the mashed potatoes."

I give her a quick salute and show our new visitor to a table before heading to the kitchen. I'm not a great cook by any stretch, but I can mash potatoes.

I've known Ricky and Andréa Hernandez for ten years now. We met during a fundraiser I organized. They're both veterans who are heavily involved in their local community. I became a patron of their charity, and during my first year, they suggested I volunteer on Thanksgiving so I could experience firsthand the kind of good they were doing. At the time, it seemed a hell of a lot better than being with Elijah's family or spending the day on my own like I usually did. I've spent every Thanksgiving since volunteering here.

So when Elijah asked me if I had plans today, I told him I had my usual plans with friends. He didn't push—he never does—and I suspect he was relieved that he didn't have to pretend to want to make plans with me.

"Hey there." Ricky greets me with a smile and an apron in his hand. "Potatoes are waiting for you." He jerks his head toward the pot on the stove.

"Wouldn't be Thanksgiving unless I mashed the potatoes." Grinning, I slip on my apron and pull my cap over my hair.

"It would not, Miss Amber." He heads back to the counter and continues rolling out the pastry dough.

We chat for a while about everything and nothing, and it's nice to have a slice of normalcy, a conversation that doesn't involve divorce or Elijah and his family or anything to do with my other life. I get to be an entirely different person here, and that's a big part of why I love it so much. Soon, Andréa joins us along with a couple other volunteers, and between us we prepare a Thanksgiving feast that will feed at least two hundred people today.

When it's time to serve, I plaster on a huge smile and dish out food to the various people who came out today, from individuals to families who have no place else to go and don't have the resources to feed themselves or their children. It's heartbreaking and truly humbling, and every year I make a bigger donation to the charity.

Despite their circumstances, most of the people here are still filled with hope and the promise of a better tomorrow. And as well as tears, there's always laughter too. I listen to as many stories as I can and provide a willing ear, a soothing word, or an appropriate dose of humor. It makes a difference when people know that someone's listening. That someone cares.

Today, as I serve food and wipe tables and mop the floors, it hits me that I have the privilege to make choices that will make me happy, and I am more determined than ever to do something with my life that will make a positive difference in the lives of others.

TWENTY-ONE

ELIJAH

Sitting in the den, full of turkey, surrounded by most of my family—my dad and my brothers, Mel, Amelia, and Luke, and Tyler and Ashley, Mel's cousin and sister who've become as much a part of our family as she has —I should feel nothing but joy. So why is that not the case?

I've spent every Thanksgiving of my life with my family, and Amber hasn't been to a Thanksgiving here in well over a decade. So why the fuck does it bother me that she's once again spending the holiday with her friends instead of me? I don't understand why I miss her so much. Why I can't stop thinking about her.

When we went around the table and shared what we were thankful for at dinner, I gave my usual answer—my family. In my mind, that's always included her, but tonight, she was the first person who popped into my head. I am most thankful for this second chance we're getting, no matter how long it lasts. But I couldn't say that aloud.

Nathan hands me a Scotch. "At least we don't have to

worry that Amber might show up tonight, huh?" He laughs and Mason joins in.

"What's that supposed to mean?" I try to keep my tone even, but inside I'm already burning up with anger.

"Mase and I used to make a pact every year—if she showed up and ruined our Thanksgiving, we said we'd pretend to have the stomach flu and go drink Scotch in the wine cellar. This is the first year we haven't had to make it." He says it so casually, like he's not talking about my damn wife.

I scowl at him and Mason, my jaw clenched tight. "Are you fucking serious?"

Mason at least has the good grace to look contrite. "It's not as bad as it sounds. It was a joke. Of course we'd never actually fake having the stomach flu."

I jump up from my chair, ignoring Nathan's outstretched hand and the offer of a good Scotch. "Jokes are supposed to be funny, assholes. That's my fucking wife you're talking about." I look to my dad and my other brothers. "Did you all feel like this?"

Drake instantly declares that he didn't, Maddox reminds me this is his only his second Thanksgiving in years, and Dad simply shrugs noncommittally.

"Jesus Christ. It's no wonder she never wanted to be around any of you."

"Hey," Nathan says, frowning. "This started long after Amber froze us out."

Stepping away from him, I take a calming breath before I say something I regret. Is this how she feels when she's around them? Belittled? Like she's someone to avoid at all costs?

"It really was just a joke, Elijah," Mason says, sounding apologetic.

I shake my head, swallowing down the anger burning in my throat. "She is still my fucking wife, and I expect you to treat her with some goddamn respect." I snatch my jacket from the back of my chair.

"Where are you going, son?" Dad asks with an exasperated sigh.

"Home." I ignore their protests and Mason's and Nathan's half-assed apologies. "I need some fucking space," I shout as I march out the door, thankful that no one tries to stop me.

I climb into my Bacalar, a gift from Nathan for my fortieth birthday. If I didn't love it so much, I'd go back inside and shove the keys up his ass. Instead, I pull out my cell and send Amber a text on her regular number rather than the burner phone. Tonight, I want to spend time as Mr. and Mrs. James.

> Hi, baby. I know you're busy, but is there any way I could see you tonight?

I stare at the screen, wondering if she'll reply or if she's too busy having fun with people who actually want to be around her. My heart beats a little faster when I see the dots that signal she's typing.

> Is everything okay?

No. Everything's gone to shit, and you're the only person who can make any of it feel better. I don't type that though.

> I just really want to see you. I can wait until you're done with your friends. Maybe pick you up and give you a ride home?

There are no dots to say she's replying, and I quickly add.

> No expectations. I just want to see you.

> I'll be done in an hour. You can give me a ride home if you'd like.

A smile spreads across my face, and the tension slips away from my shoulders.

> I'll be there in an hour. Where are you?

> I'll drop you a pin. I really have to go. x

The kiss makes my smile wider, but when the pin drops, I'm sure she must have sent me the wrong location because it's a soup kitchen in the Bronx. I check her phone location, and it matches what she sent. She might be on the board of directors ... I've never been able to keep up with all the organizations she's involved with. But that wouldn't explain her being there on Thanksgiving. A dozen scenarios run through my mind involving my wife working in a soup kitchen in the Bronx. With no security. No protection. And no clue how to defend herself if something should happen.

Fuck. As much as I love this new Amber, she's going to end up giving me a heart attack before I'm forty-five.

. . .

I PARK across the street and send her a text to let her know I'm outside. Feeling like a privileged prick parked outside a soup kitchen in a two-million-dollar car, I half expect her to call me and say I've got it all wrong, that she's actually at some fancy Manhattan restaurant. But less than a minute later, she walks out of the building, pulling her coat tighter around her.

When she sees me, her face breaks into a smile that makes me feel better than I've felt all damn day. A baseball cap is pulled low on her head, her ponytail popping out of the back, and she doesn't seem to be wearing a scrap of makeup, but she's fucking glowing. And are those sneakers on her feet? Amber James is out in public wearing sneakers.

I jump out of the car and open the door for her.

"The Bacalar? Really? You couldn't have tried to be a little less conspicuous?" Her smile has transformed into a wicked grin that has my brain misfiring, and I'm bombarded with images of the time we had hate sex on the hood of this car. From the twinkle in her eyes and the way she's biting down on her lip, I assume her memory is replaying the same thing.

It was on my birthday, and she was livid that Nathan had bought me such an expensive gift and, in her mind, tried to upstage her. We were in our private parking garage, and I told her she was acting crazy. She called me a giant dick, and then the next thing I knew, I had her pinned to the hood and was shoving my dick inside her.

Glancing at the silver sports car, I'm about to explain that I would have called an Uber if I knew I was going to be driving to a soup kitchen tonight. But I'm enjoying this playful side of her too much, so I play along. Perhaps being

Mr. and Mrs. Smith is easier than trying to be Mr. and Mrs. James. "I wanted to drive you home in style, Mrs. Smith."

I gesture for her to climb inside, and she gives me a sweet kiss on the cheek before she does. The twitch in my cock becomes a full-blown ache.

We're headed back toward the city, and she's taken off the hat and settled back against the leather seat with a contented smile on her face. I have several questions, some of which are likely to piss her off, so I ease in gently. "So you started volunteering at a soup kitchen?"

She hums. "Not started, no. I only work there on Thanksgiving. It's their busiest day of the year, and it's saved me from spending it alone."

There are so many things I want to unpack about that statement, but I don't know where to begin. Again, I choose to play it safe. "You've done this before?"

She nods. "Every year for the past ten years."

"What?" I almost crash the damn car. "How did I not know? What were you ..." I clamp my mouth closed before I say something that will start an argument.

Her lips curve with a smile. "You remember that time I organized a benefit for the soup kitchen, don't you?" she asks, and I hope she's not waiting for my reply because in truth, I don't. She's organized hundreds of fundraisers and benefits. It would have been impossible to keep track of them all. Thankfully, she continues. "Well, I got along well with the people who ran it, Ricky Hernandez and his wife, Andréa. They invited me to volunteer, and I enjoyed it so much that I've done it every year since."

"But how did nobody know? The press? How did *I* not know, Amber?"

She shrugs. "Hiding in plain sight, I guess. Either that, or a baseball cap is a better disguise than anyone gives it credit for. But truthfully, I don't think anyone would expect it of me, so nobody ever looked for me there. And Ricky and Andréa would never out me—they're too cool to do that."

She's got a point. I can't imagine anyone searching for Amber James in a soup kitchen, at least not the Amber James I used to know. "And you didn't tell me because ...?"

"Why would I have?" She sounds genuinely confused. "You would've worried about me being there, and it's not like we had plans to spend Thanksgiving together. I told you I was with friends, and it was the truth."

Guilt and regret, compounded by my brothers' asshole behavior earlier, eat up my insides. "But if I'd known you were spending Thanksgiving alone ..."

I steal a glance at her and find her scowling. "I wasn't alone."

"Okay, you obviously weren't alone, but I didn't realize you didn't have plans. If I knew, I would have—"

"Abandoned your family?" I don't miss the ice that's crept into her tone. "And I did have plans. I'm quite happy with the way I've chosen to spend my Thanksgiving."

"You should have told me, Amber," I say quietly.

"Why? It's not like you would have changed your plans and stayed with me instead of spending time with your dad and brothers."

Now she's being unfair. She can't assume that when she didn't give me the chance to prove otherwise. My knuckles turn white on the steering wheel. "Of course I would have!"

She snorts. "That's a lie, and we both know it."

"Don't make me out to be some kind of monster. I never would have knowingly left you alone on Thanksgiving."

She turns in her seat, and when I steal another glance at her, she's glaring at me, her whiskey-colored eyes full of fire. "You really believe that, don't you?"

I pull the car over to the side of the road so I can give her my full attention. "And you don't? It's no wonder we're getting a divorce when you believe me to be that cruel."

"Not cruel, darling, simply ..." She sighs and shakes her head.

"Simply what?"

"Simply what you are. A devoted big brother who needs to be needed by your family. Remember the time I invited you to come to Charleston with me and you said you couldn't leave them?"

I can't believe she's rewriting our history so egregiously. "One time, Amber. That was one time, and it was thirteen years ago."

"That was one of a whole series of incidents. I stopped asking you to do anything or go anywhere with me because it hurt too much when you chose them over me. Every single time."

Is that really how she's felt our entire marriage? Like she's second best?

"It really doesn't matter now anyway. It's ancient history. I actually had a lovely evening tonight, and I wouldn't have chosen to spend it any other way. Will you please just take me home?"

I screw my eyes closed and take a deep breath. "I want to understand, Amber. Please talk to me."

She shakes her head. "You'll get upset and defensive, and

then the evening will be ruined. So, no." The words are brutal, but her tone is bland.

I put my hand on her arm and wait for her to look into my eyes and see how sincere I am. "I promise I'll listen with an open mind."

She licks her lips and then flashes me a well-you-asked-for-it-jackass look. "Your brothers always seem to need you, and I wonder sometimes if they really do or if they're so used to you being there for them that they think they do."

"It's called being a good brother." Immediately, I regret my words and my harsh tone. I just proved her point about getting upset and defensive. I lower my voice and keep it neutral. "Shouldn't I be there for them if they need me? Even if they might not really? I don't get how that's a bad thing."

"Of course you should be there for your brothers, Elijah, but not at the expense of ..." Her throat works as she swallows, and tears fill her eyes. "There are four of them and only one of me."

What the hell is that supposed to mean? "You truly think I prioritized them over you?"

She looks incredulous. "You *don't?*"

A wave of guilt crashes over me at the naked, unvarnished pain in her eyes. "Okay, I did do that. Sometimes. But only when they really needed me. What was I supposed to do? I'm their big brother."

"And you're my husband. And it wasn't sometimes, Elijah, it was every single time."

"Like when?"

She rolls her eyes. "I could write you a list longer than the phone book, but off the top of my head, the benefit for Zoo Animals in the Arts a couple years ago—you blew me off at the last minute to go to dinner at Nathan's. The dinner party I organized for the hospital board, which you didn't attend because Mason needed you to go over some notes with him for a meeting. A meeting he was more than prepared for. Three months ago when Maddox asked you to take him to an NA meeting out of state when I had that follow-up with my doctor after an abnormal pap. Would you like me to continue?"

An argument is perched on the tip of my tongue, but I swallow it down. She assured me the abnormal pap smear was nothing, that she didn't need me fussing around her. But of course it wasn't. She must have been scared. Anxious as hell. I was terrified. Despite her assurances, I stared at my phone the entire time Maddox was in his meeting, waiting for her to tell me everything was okay.

But she wouldn't have known that because I was too afraid of her cutting rejection to tell her how badly I wanted to be there for her. I genuinely believed she didn't need or want me around for any of that stuff. But that's no excuse. It was my job to know that she needed me. My job to make her my top priority. "Amber, I … I am so sorry. I didn't realize … didn't know … I should have known you needed me."

She brushes a tear from her eye. "The truth is, I learned to stop needing you a long time ago—I realized I couldn't rely on you. But I never stopped hoping that you would choose me anyway."

Her words are sharper than a knife to my heart, and I can't deny the truth of them. Any one of my brothers would have been happy to take Maddox to his NA meeting, but I had to step in and be big brother of the year. Meanwhile, I was in contention for shitty husband of the decade.

Reminded of how I felt at my dad's earlier and how she must have felt around them all the damn time, I take her hand in mine again and squeeze her slender fingers. "I'm sorry for every single time I didn't prioritize you and every single time I made you feel second best."

Her smile is wobbly but so beautiful. "I appreciate that."

"Fuck, I was a crappy husband."

She nods. "And I was a crappy wife. But not all the time. We worked in our own messed-up kind of way. And like I said, it's ancient history." Her expression changes completely, a light coming to life behind her eyes. "I had such an energizing and eye-opening day today, Elijah, and it truly made me thankful for so much. So let's not dredge up our past hurts any more. How about we enjoy each other while we can?"

The sparkle in her eyes emboldens me. "And where would you like to do that, Mrs. Smith? I am entirely at your disposal."

Her eyelashes flutter against her pink cheeks. "Is the room in Greenwich Village available?"

I press her knuckles to my lips. "For you, mi amor, always."

She sighs, and I pull her in for a lingering kiss, unable to recall the last time I called her my love. I regret that as much as anything else she's accused me of tonight. As much as all the ways I failed her the past twenty years. I've always prided myself on being a good man, and at least in other people's eyes, I probably am seen as such. But none of that matters when I failed to show up for the one person in this world who should have been able to rely on me.

It's a bitter pill to swallow, but I'll beat myself up over it tomorrow. For tonight, there's a smile on her face, and I will give her every ounce of my attention. It's no less than she deserves.

I CALLED AHEAD to the hotel and let the manager know we were on our way so he could prepare our room. There are other patrons here tonight, and I wanted us to be able to head straight to our room unnoticed. He was waiting for us when we arrived, and he slipped our usual room key into my hand.

There's no residual hostility from our fraught conversation in the car, and as I clasp my wife's hand in mine and pull her into the room, I'm overcome with desire. Judging by the way her pupils blow wide when I push her against the door, so is she.

I slide off her coat and let it drop to the floor, and she sinks her perfect white teeth into her pillowy bottom lip before looking down at herself. "I don't think I'm properly dressed for a romantic liaison."

My gaze hungrily devours her body. It's true that she's dressed down compared to her usual attire, in sneakers, faded jeans, and a plain baby-blue cashmere sweater, but she looks incredible to me. "I don't intend for you to remain dressed for much longer, baby."

She twists the end of her ponytail between her fingers and grimaces. "I smell like kitchen grease."

Running my nose over her throat, I inhale, but all I can smell is her. Intoxicating. Addictive. "Then how about a shower first?"

She purrs and slowly works her hips against my hard

cock. "I think that's a good idea. You'll wait until I'm done, won't you?"

Tease.

I pick her up and wrap her legs around my waist. "The fuck I will."

She giggles, wrapping her arms around my neck as I carry her to the bathroom. It takes me no time at all to relieve us both of our clothes and get us under the hot water. She stands with her back to me, and for a moment, I watch the droplets meander down her spine and over her perfectly round backside. With a hard smack on her ass, I silence her insistence that she can wash herself, and before long, she has her eyes closed and her lips parted while I wash and condition her caramel-colored locks.

When I'm done with her hair, I squeeze a generous amount of soap into my palm and slide my hands to her front, palming her breasts and massaging them slowly. She moans, pushing back against me until my throbbing cock is nestled between her ass cheeks. I nip at her flesh, enjoying the sounds she makes as I soap every part of her body. When the soap has almost washed away, I slip a hand between her thighs and palm her sweet pussy. "Time to make you really wet, mi amor."

She rests her head on my shoulder as I sink one finger inside her. "Elijah," she whimpers, her thighs trembling. "Please?"

"You want to come, baby?"

She sinks her nails into the muscle of my forearm. "Yes."

I add a second finger and drive deeper and harder, relishing her tight heat squeezing me, her velvety wetness coating my fingers as I bring her closer to the edge. This right here is when she gives me complete control—when she's trembling with need. I would live in these moments forever if I could, the moments when there's nothing in the world but the two of us. I rest my lips against the shell of her ear. "I've got you. Let me take care of you, Amber."

Using my free hand, I work her sensitive nipples, and a keening moan pours from her throat as she comes for me. Creamy wet heat runs down my palm, and my cock jumps, desperate to take over. While she's still trembling, I spin her around and lift her. With her back pressed flat against the cool tiles and her legs around my hips, I have my cock inside her before she can take a breath, completely filling her tight pussy.

"Nobody will ever fuck you as well as I do, will they?"

She wraps her arms around my shoulders and buries her face in my neck.

Unable to bear the thought of losing her, I growl. The idea of her ever moving on from me is like a million blades slicing open my heart. I pull out slowly and drive back inside her with one smooth thrust. "Will they?"

"No, Elijah," she whimpers, clinging to me as I nail her to the wall.

"That's my good girl." I fuck her harder, channeling all the frustration that has built up inside me. Nathan and Mason acting like jerks. Our argument in the car. The guilt I feel knowing everything she said was true.

She takes it all. Every punishing thrust. Until all the anger and hurt fades away and once again, it's only the two of us against the world. Here, where nobody can touch us.

Heat builds in my core and spreads down my thighs as

my own release draws near, and I slide a hand between us and circle her clit with my thumb.

She cries out my name, and I can't hold back another second. I fill her tight channel with my release, and we pant for breath, foreheads pressed together as we ride out our orgasms. When I can finally speak again, I brush her hair back from her forehead and ask, "Will you stay here with me tonight?"

Her whiskey-colored eyes sparkle, and she bites down on her lip. If she says no, I might tie her to the bed anyway, but she smiles and whispers, "Yes."

I gently lower her trembling legs to the shower floor and smile against her skin. I'll order food and wine and we'll eat and drink and make love again before she falls asleep in my arms. It's the most perfect way I can imagine spending an evening. As much as I love spending time with the rest of my family, I don't recall being this happy or this thankful in a very long time.

TWENTY-TWO

ELIJAH

I glance at my watch and realize I need to get going. My nephew has very different ideas, though, and is repeatedly hitting me on the head with a Jenga block. Every single time he makes contact, Luke laughs hysterically. He sits up on his mat like a sturdy Buddha statue, shrieking with delight, his arms waving in the air. It's one of the best sounds in the entire world.

Few things could tempt me away from this spot, but Amber is one of them. I let Luke take one final slug, and he lands a whopper right on my nose, then laughs so hard he actually falls over. On his back now, he rolls around, kicking and gurgling, and tries to get his foot into his mouth. I tickle his tummy, and by the time I sit him up again, he has tears of laughter streaming down his round, ruddy cheeks.

"Little dude, you are the coolest person I know," I say, climbing to my feet.

Nathan and Melanie are in the kitchen, and they've been missing for a suspiciously long time. I make sure I knock first and find them looking way too disheveled for "getting the baby a snack." I raise an eyebrow, and Nathan gives me a smirk. Smug bastard.

"You'll stay for dinner, won't you?" Mel asks me, smoothing down her hair. "Please?" My whole family has been inviting me to dinner, brunch, and breakfast pretty much every day since I told them about the divorce.

They seem to think I would starve without them, but it's their way of showing their support and making sure I don't have too much time alone to feel sorry for myself. It's sweet and a hell of a lot better than none of them giving a damn or having no family around me. Which, it suddenly occurs to me, is exactly the position Amber is in. Fuck, why am I just now realizing this?

"You okay, brother?" Nathan asks, his hand on my shoulder. I nod and force a smile. "I'm good, thanks. I can't stay for dinner though, sorry."

All three of us walk back into the living room to keep an eye on Luke. He can get into all kinds of mischief now that he's more mobile.

"Why not?" He scoops up his son and blows a raspberry on his neck, and Luke lets out a full belly laugh. "Is it because your nephew is better at Jenga than you?"

"He cheats. Must get it from his dad. No, I'm, uh, busy. I've got a thing."

Nathan and Mel exchange looks, and my brother raises his eyebrows. Melanie gives me a sweet smile and says, "Oh. A thing? Is that what they're calling it these days?"

"I don't know what you mean," I reply, keeping my voice neutral.

"She means we know you've got a date, jerkwad," Nathan answers. "And we've noticed an extra spring in your step recently. The kind that gets put there by a woman. There's no need to be so defensive about it. You're a single man now. You're allowed to go on dates."

I shrug and grab my jacket.

"So, is it serious?" He pries Luke's fingers out of his hair and continues. "Or is it just a, you know, rebound from Amber?"

I fight to keep a neutral expression. "I don't know if it's serious or not at this stage. It's definitely not trivial."

"What's she like?" Melanie asks. "Is she nice?"

"Yeah. She really is." Despite how much she tries to convince people she's not. But I don't say that. "She's also funny and kind and intelligent."

"Is she also smoking hot?" Nathan says, winking.

"Fuck yeah." I can't keep the smile off my face. "The hottest woman I've ever known."

Mel shoots us both a look. "Can I remind you two that Luke's brain is currently soaking up language like a sponge. I do not want his first word to begin with f and end with k. Understood?"

"Yes, Mom," says Nathan. "Though I don't see what's wrong with our kid's first word being flapjack."

Melanie rolls her eyes, and the two of them walk me to the door. Nathan shakes my hand and holds it for an extra second, looking me in the eyes. "I am really pleased you've met someone, brother. I know the Amber situation is tough, but believe me, you're better off without her. We all are."

His words come from a place of genuine love, but they piss me off. "Don't talk about her like that, okay? You can think what you like about her, but at least show me the respect of keeping your mouth shut on the subject."

He looks surprised, then annoyed. Mel lays a calming hand on his arm before he can say anything else. It has an immediate effect, and he takes a breath. "Message received and understood. But she's your ex—you don't have to defend her anymore."

I don't reply because nothing that comes out of my mouth right now will do any good. Instead, I pass baby Luke the Jenga block I found in my pocket. Delighted, he lets out a demonic giggle and whacks it solidly into his dad's eye socket.

As I close the door behind me, I smile at my brother's exclamation of "Fuck!"

I've given Gretchen the night off, as I always do when I'm meeting Amber. I trust our driver completely, but it's not fair to put her in such a difficult position of having to keep Amber's and my secret. I hail a cab and check my phone on the drive into New Jersey. Tonight, we're making this a federal crime and crossing state lines. It was Amber's idea—since she moved into the Brooklyn house a week ago, she's fallen in love with the idea of trying new places. Being a gentleman, I certainly don't want to discourage her spirit of adventure. Especially as it seems to translate into every aspect of her life, including the bedroom.

I was initially resistant to the idea of her living in Brooklyn. And by resistant, I mean absolutely fucking horrified. Drake bore the brunt of it, and he was typically Drake throughout. He listened, his face completely unreadable as I ranted and raved, and he let me get it out of my system. Then put me in my place. "You're being a dick," he said. "There's nothing wrong with Brooklyn, and there's nothing wrong with the house my girlfriend grew up in. Get your head out of your ass and admit that you just don't want her out of your sight and out of your influence."

There wasn't much I could say to that without proving him right, but I took a halfhearted stab at justifying my concern on security grounds. He was having none of it. "She'll be fine. Mrs. Katzberg lives across the way, and that woman would scare the shit out of Chuck Norris. Plus, Amber's going to learn Krav Maga and buy a semiautomatic."

I gaped at him, and he finally cracked a smile. "Joking." He cleared his throat, obviously fighting the urge to laugh when he added, "She's more of a pearl-handled pistol kind of gal, wouldn't you say?"

Ultimately, I had to face the fact that I couldn't control Amber or her decisions—and the fact that she is so much happier now that she is making decisions with only her own wants and needs in mind. She's lighter now, like a snake who shed her skin along with all the expectations and glitzy trappings of her previous lifestyle.

When she made the move to Brooklyn, I moved back into the townhouse and I immediately understood where her desire to get out of there came from. The place is far too big for one person. Hell, it was too big for two, and all that extra space really does seem to taunt me with the life we planned for when we bought the house.

Maddox has stayed over a few nights, which has been great. I've enjoyed spending quality time with my baby brother and getting to know this version of him better. He spent years traveling and dealing with his own demons, and he's different from the rest of us because of it. Healthier than the rest of us, no doubt. I'm hoping he stays put for a while now for all our sakes, but especially Dad's.

It's nice having him around, but nothing compares to this—to the thrill of a secret night with Amber. My wife and my mistress, all wrapped up in one intoxicating package.

We're traveling out of the city to meet in public for dinner, like any other cheating couple I imagine, and I can't wait. She suggested a little town on the river that's known for its quaint community feel and historic buildings. It's highly unlikely we'll see anybody we know in New Jersey, and the media interest predictably died down after we released a short video that we filmed on neutral territory in Drake's office. As Mason predicted, we bored them to death by being so damn civilized. Ha, if they only knew.

I chose the specific place we're meeting, and I have an extra surprise waiting nearby. I find myself grinning in the back of the cab, excited to see her reaction. We draw up outside the restaurant, and I'm amazed at how different this little town is from Manhattan. Only a forty-minute drive, but a whole world away. Amber arrives at the same time, and I see her chatting to Sanjay through the window of his cab. She waves him off with a laugh, and when she turns and sees me, a huge, surprised smile transforms her whole face, making her radiant.

I warned her to dress casually. It's part of my surprise for her, and she's taken me at my word. Her endless legs are encased in pale gray skin-tight leggings, and she's wearing a baggy pale-blue sweater that comes down to her thighs. It's casual, but it's also Amber—she's matched it with heels and yet another long-chained necklace that takes my mind to dark and dangerous places.

"You look like you're going to a yoga class at Buckingham Palace," I say, sweeping her into my arms. She lands against me with a little squeal and wraps her arms around my waist.

"Excellent. That's exactly what I was aiming for. How are you, Mr. Smith?"

My heart rate spikes as I seal my lips over hers. Our tongues slide hungrily against each other, and she groans and melts into me like hot wax. "I'm better now, Mrs. Smith," I say once I come up for air.

She rubs herself against me and smiles. "Yes. I can tell. You'd better start thinking about Dr. Braithwaite or we might get arrested for public indecency."

"Well, that would count as one of your firsts, wouldn't it?" I take her hand and lead her inside. "Getting arrested?"

"As far as you know," she quips, grinning up at me. Fuck, she's so beautiful. It seems like every guy in the room turns to look at her, and I feel like the luckiest man alive. Because I get to touch as well as look.

We're shown to a table by the window with a view across the river. It's December now and dark already. Yellow light from the town and headlights from the cars on the bridge reflect on the glassy surface of the water.

"I think this is another first," I say after we place our order. "You actually showing up for something on time."

"Oh, I know. I was almost early—that would have been a disaster." She pauses, then says, "It was never on purpose, you know." Her eyes fill with tears, and she blinks them away, offering me a sly smile. "Well, maybe sometimes."

She's obviously trying to keep the conversation light, so I play along. "I suspected as much. You really were a frightfully spoiled brat."

"Hey, less of the 'were' if you don't mind. I still have my moments." Her huge eyes shine as bright as the lights on the river, caramel-blond hair lying in loose waves on her shoulders. She's wearing a little makeup, but it's less of a suit of armor and more of a playful mask. This new life she's building for herself suits her. I feel the sting of that, because her new life is one she's building without me, but I also admire her. It takes guts to do what she's doing. It took guts to end the toxic crazy train we were stuck on together.

"You look amazing," I say quietly, pouring her wine. "You are amazing. I don't think I've ever seen you look so stunning." My voice comes out especially deep, and color infuses her cheeks.

"Thank you," she says on a light laugh. "But I'm not sure you're right. This whole low-maintenance look isn't always good for the ego. I see a lot more lines than I used to. I guess I'm at the age where most women we know have work done."

"No, you're not," I say firmly. "You'll never be at that age. You'll always be perfect the way you are."

"Really? Even when I'm old and gray and crinkled up like a raisin?"

"Even then. You'll still be beautiful. You'll just have a little more ... patina."

Her smile is breathtaking, and I am completely helpless before it. "Patina," she says, turning the concept over. "Like the Statue of Liberty. Works for me. Speaking of precious things that show their age ... Did I tell you that Granny Lucille is a lesbian?"

I spit out my wine, and she laughs as I dab at my beard

with my napkin. "Did you deliberately tell me that after I took a sip?"

"Of course. It wouldn't have been funny otherwise. But it is true. She has a girlfriend named Vivienne."

"Wow. I'm not sure I want to run with that image." I'm fond of Granny Lucille, but as a general rule, I try to avoid thinking about the sex life of octogenarians. "What does she think, about ... everything?"

The waiter arrives with our food, and she gives him the big eyes and the hint-of-the-South honey as she thanks him. Unsurprisingly, he trips over his own feet when he turns to leave.

"Well, she doesn't know about Mr. and Mrs. Smith. I didn't think she needed to know how hot you look in a fireman's outfit." Her pupils dilate at the memory of our last little session in our Greenwich hotel.

"I'm surprised *you* know how hot I look in a fireman's outfit. I only had it on for thirty seconds."

"What can I say? Sometimes a girl needs a hero. A naked one. It was fun, wasn't it?"

The time we've spent together since she got back from Charleston has been so far beyond fun—it has been some of the best, happiest moments of my life. Which makes me seriously question why we spent so many years living in hell.

I almost jump out of my skin when her toes skim my inner thigh and gently land on my groin. Her smiles turns wicked as she lightly rubs my dick. "Do you walk around like this all the time, or am I special?"

I reach under the table and firmly remove her foot. I can't return the favor from this angle, but I will get my revenge at some point. And she'll enjoy every second of it.

"You are most definitely special. My cock is always ready for you, baby. We're sitting here in this pretty little place, pretending to be civilized, but all I can think about is being balls-deep in your tight, wet cunt."

I'm keeping my voice low, but the dirty talk has the desired effect. She flushes bright red and bites her pillowy lip. I know she's wet right now, and I wish I could crawl under this table and taste her. Bury my tongue in her pussy and lick her until she comes all over my face.

We stare at each other, and then we both laugh at the same time. "This whole being out in public thing is a challenge," she says. "Maybe we're more of a behind-closed-doors couple."

"Maybe we are." I wonder if she noticed that she called us a couple. Her hand trembles slightly as she forks up a bite of salad, so I assume she did. I take pity on her. "How's Brooklyn? And when do you have your interview at the community center?"

She grabs hold of the offered way out and fills me in on life in Amelia's old neighborhood. She talks with real enthusiasm about the food, the bars, the sense of being somewhere real. As she chats, her hands fly and her eyes sparkle. Brooklyn has ignited something inside her, and I am gripped by unreasonable jealousy. She knows my world, every inch of it, but she's moved into a whole new one that doesn't involve me. I don't know if she picks up on my irrational jealousy, but she pauses. "You could, I don't know, come and visit? I mean, if you want to."

We're on uneven ground here. This whole situation is already completely cracked—having an affair with the partner you're currently divorcing is strange enough. But at least we both know what it is. It's fantasy. It's our way of finding closure on a relationship that has held us both in its thrall for over two decades. But visiting her in Brooklyn? Seeing her new world? I'm not sure if that's a good idea.

"Maybe I will," I say simply, making no commitment but also not rejecting her. She nods, and the moment passes. She probably regretted the invitation the second it passed her lips anyway.

"The community center interview is the day after tomorrow." She quickly moves on. "It's taken forever because they had to run all kinds of checks, make sure I'm not a hardened criminal or anything. In the meantime, I've been watching dance class videos on YouTube, and I think I might be able to do it. It doesn't need to be ballet or anything that structured. It's more about having fun and inspiring them. It'll be different from anything I've ever done before, but ... that's a good thing. That's what I want." Her voice gets quieter, and her intoxicating gaze locks on my face. "Am I crazy?"

"Definitely. But of course you can do it. I don't doubt it for a second."

After doing my own research and talking with Vicky about it, I still have my concerns, but it's clearly a well-respected organization, run by a former nun. If she ends up volunteering there, I'll definitely be paying it a visit myself.

Changing the subject, she asks me about work, and I fill her in on the South Korean deal. She asks all the right questions and even makes a few suggestions. Amber has a shrewd mind for business, and she played the role of corporate wife exceptionally well. Whenever we had to entertain guests or take visiting dignitaries out on the town, she knocked it out of the park. Together, we put on a fantastic show. It was only when we were alone the barbs started to fly and the claws came out.

We move on to Luke, and I show her the pictures I took this evening. He's holding on to the couch and standing on wobbly legs, a slobbery grin on his face. "Oh my, look at those thighs," she enthuses, scrolling through. "I love those rolls of fat. He's scrumptious, isn't he?" Her tone is pure joy, no hint of sarcasm, sadness, or underlying snark.

Once we're finished with our drinks and our food, we emerge into the chilly night air. She brought a big faux-fur coat with her, and it looks sensational, even with her casual outfit. Her hand slips into mine as we stroll along the riverside, and I grasp her cold fingers. We walk, talking about everything and nothing, and it is simple and joyous. I can't remember a time we were so at peace with each other.

"You ready for your surprise?" I ask her. She gazes up at me contentedly, and it's clear that she feels the same.

"Always," she replies, leaning up to kiss me. "As long as it's a pony."

Damn. Why didn't I think of that?

TWENTY-THREE

I glance at the map on my phone, suddenly nervous. "Yeah. I bought you a pony, and we're going to keep him in a stable in New Jersey and visit on weekends."

"Yay! Just what I always wanted."

Does she mean that? Like most girls with her background, she had riding lessons when she was a kid, and she loves animals. I've never known her to express a real interest in horses though. But fuck it—if she wants a pony, I'll get her a goddamn pony. There's just no way I can arrange that in the next five minutes.

By the time we reach our destination, I'm half worried she will be disappointed. I pause near the building we're headed for and hold both her hands in mine. "Look, it's not a pony."

She tips her head back and laughs. "I didn't think it was."

I nod, trying to keep the relief from my expression. "Right. Well, I'm going to blindfold you now."

"It's going to be that kind of night, is it?" Her lips curve seductively. "I'm game if you are."

Fuck. My dick is hard again. I'm going to develop some kind of medical condition if this keeps happening. "Maybe later." I pull a blindfold from my coat pocket. "For now, it's so the surprise isn't ruined."

She lets me tie the fabric around her eyes, and I inhale her shampoo as I lift her hair from her shoulders. Even that smells different, subtle with a hint of coconut. I lead her inside the building, telling her when there are steps and guiding her along the corridor. The room is shadowed when I open the door, and I remove the blindfold.

She keeps a tight hold of my hand and blinks a little as I flick a switch. The overhead lights buzz into action, and her eyes go wide when she sees where we are. Her hand goes over her mouth, and she spins around, taking it all in. I'm not interested in the room—I only have eyes for her. I want her to be happy, to see delight on her face. I want her to have everything she needs in life and more. This might not be a pony, but she looks pretty fucking thrilled with it anyway.

"Oh my god, Elijah! This is gorgeous." She immediately slips off her high heels and coat and runs around the room, seeming to float across the blond wood floor. Stopping suddenly, she points at me. "You didn't buy this, did you? Because I really don't need my own dance studio."

"No," I assure her. "I just booked it for tonight. Thought you could get some practice in."

She races back to me and throws her arms around my shoulders. "Thank you. I love it."

I lift her up and give her a twirl, overjoyed at how excited she is.

As soon as I put her down, she gallops away. She spins and swirls and jumps, laughing like a little girl on Christmas morning. My heart cracks wide open, and I wish I could hit pause on this one perfect moment. There is nothing more miraculous than watching my beautiful wife act like the carefree young woman she was when I first met her. Before life dragged us both down like wounded animals.

She skips over to the barre, runs her hands along the polished wood, and immediately takes up a ballet position. Her toes point outward, and she drops down low, one arm gracefully stretching out beside her. She continues through a range of moves, and I'm content to look on as she flows and flexes from one position to the next. I pull up a classical music playlist on my phone, and she nods at me in thanks before putting her hands up high and performing a pirouette. She pauses and pulls the soft blue sweater over her head, revealing a strappy white tank underneath.

"I haven't been in a place like this for years." She does a little run and then leaps into the air, legs splayed and toes pointed. "It's amazing how my body remembers all this stuff. I've done dance exercise classes and kept up with Pilates, but nothing beats this. Even if I look like a baby elephant, it feels wonderful."

She looks absolutely fucking incredible—long, lean, and luscious as she dances around the room, reflected versions of her following every move like backup dancers. Her hair flies around her face in a golden tornado as she builds up speed in a spin, and she laughs as she rotates faster and faster. She does a spirited circuit of the whole room, takes another leap, then slides down onto the floor, landing in a split. Jesus. That should be illegal.

When I applaud, she looks up, face flushed, blond strands sticking to the sheen of sweat on her forehead. She climbs to her feet and gives me a little bow. The long silver necklace dips and touches the floor. Ballet is an art form, but looking at her like that, bent pretty much in half, her ass reflected in the mirror ... Well, let's just say that my mind doesn't turn to culture.

"Come on, your turn." She comes over and grabs my hands, then pulls me to my feet and drags me toward the barre.

"Uh, no way," I say firmly, shaking my head. "Ballet's not for me."

"Oh. Too much of a chicken, are you?" She flaps her arms at her sides and makes squawking noises. "I suppose ballet is only for the strongest of men."

"Stop goading me. I grew up with four brothers. I'm ungoadable."

"Okay, but are you unconvincible? Because I'd really love it if you gave it a go. I'm doing all these new things for the first time. You should try one too. Or don't you think you can lift me?"

I know exactly what she's doing. She's getting her own way, something she's very good at. Her big eyes maintain their innocence, and her chest heaves a little as she recovers from her exertions. The white cotton top clings to her breasts, her erect nipples clearly visible through the flimsy fabric. She isn't wearing a bra, for fuck's sake. That should also be illegal. She sees me staring and gives me a flirtatious smile. "What can I say? Ballet makes me horny."

"Okay. I'll give it a go." There's a rasp to my voice that has nothing to do with wanting to dance.

"Fabulous. Warm up a little first, though. I don't want

you to pull a muscle. Try to copy what I do, but don't worry if you can't. Do your best, and if anything hurts, stop."

She runs through a few basic dips and stretches, nothing I wouldn't do at the gym or during a sparring session, then leads me the barre. I try to mirror her movements with limited success. There's no way I can get my leg as high or as straight as her, and she knows it. I swear, she is on the verge of laughter all the way through.

"You know," I say as she effortlessly swoops her hands down to the floor and I only make it part of the way there, "this isn't fair. I should get you in the boxing ring and see how you cope with that."

She slowly rolls upright again, her arms reaching high, and I do the same. My back tweaks and spasms, but I ignore it. "I'd love that," she says enthusiastically. "Name the date and I'll be there. Okay, are you ready for a lift?"

"Are you? I could drop you on your head. I don't know what the fuck I'm doing."

"Yeah you do. I've danced with you before. You've got moves. Besides, you're a big, strong guy, and I trust you. You won't drop me."

She's still limbering up, and her top keeps riding high, flashing her smooth abdomen and the bottom of her rib cage. I want to lay my hands on her right now. I want to run my fingers along every inch of exposed skin and kiss those perky nipples and grab her perfect round ass in both my palms. But first, it seems, I must dance. She picks up my phone and changes the music.

"Really?" I groan, protesting her song selection as I unbutton my shirt and roll my shoulders in preparation. Her eyes graze appreciatively over my bare torso, which makes me feel a damn sight better about the whole thing.

"*Really*," she replies.

"Okay, fine. But which one of us is Patrick Swayze?"

She places both hands on my shoulders, and as she leans in and kisses my chest, she slides my shirt all the way off. I can see us in the mirror, and fuck, it's so hot watching her touch me. Her hands run up my arms and trace the outline of my pecs. "You," she says huskily. "You are most definitely Patrick."

"So." She pulls away, eyes blazing. "We won't do the run. Maybe next time. You hold the sides of my hips, like this." She guides me as she speaks, checks the positioning, and then places her hands on my shoulders. Her touch is soft and warm, her expression full of trust. "Now, the key to this lift is for you to get down low—let your legs give you extra power. Then as I jump into you, on the count of three, you simply ... make me fly. Once I'm up, lock your elbows, and I'll do the rest. Come on. We can do this."

Fuck. I really don't want to, but I guess this is what happens when you rent a dance studio for your soon-to-be ex-wife. A soon-to-be ex-wife who is currently going through a "doing it for the first time" stage of her life. The blatant joy she's exhibited since we got here is a painful reminder of all the dreams she had back when we were in college. The dreams she gave up to become the perfect corporate wife I needed. She was going to change the world, that beautiful wide-eyed Amber who was so full of hope and promise. I failed her in so many ways. She lost herself, and I failed to notice.

The music builds up to its familiar crescendo, and I give her a nod. "Yeah. Of course we can."

She grins and counts. As she hits three, she seems to levitate from the ground, upward and forward, saying, "Now now now!"

I power up through my bent knees and lift her. She zooms up into the air, and her arms and legs straighten out. Her core strength is astonishing, and she actually giggles while holding herself rock steady, defying gravity. An angel in flight. I manage to move around on the spot for a full turn, and she maintains her balance, laughing the whole time. I smile up at her although I'm feeling the strain. My wife is slender, but she is also tall, and she does not weigh nothing. My arms start to protest, but a stubborn part of me refuses to show any weakness.

Eventually, it's her who wobbles. "I'm coming down," she says, sliding down my body. She props her hands on my shoulders, and I wrap my arms around her ass and hold her pressed against me. Her breasts are right there in front of my face, her breath making them rise and fall temptingly. Fuck it, I'm only flesh and blood. I suck one nipple into my mouth and can feel every rigid line of it through her top. She groans and buries her hands in my hair, pulling me closer. I suckle hard, moving from one nipple to another, loving the sounds she's making. After a few moments of torture, I slowly lower her onto unsteady feet, and she holds onto me, her eyes full of need as I peel her tank off and let it fall to the floor.

When I glance down, I can't help my smug smile. Her pale gray leggings highlight a dark spot between her legs, her pussy already so wet it's seeping through. She blushes slightly. "Don't be embarrassed. Just let me take care of you."

I grab her big fur coat and lay it on the wood floor before I lift her into my arms and gently place her down on top of it. Her hands don't leave my body. They explore my muscles, stroke my chest hair, toy with my nipples. I nestle above her, push her damp hair away from her face, then pause to simply look at her, to glory in her disheveled beauty, her perfect tits, the light sheen of sweat on her body. I really am having the time of my life.

I drop soft kisses on her eyelids, her cheekbones, her exquisite neck. I kiss my way down her breasts, her belly, and she writhes beneath me. "Elijah," she murmurs, her husky voice going right to my balls.

"I'm here, baby. Exactly where I should be."

I hook my fingers in the waistband of her pants, and she lifts her ass to make it easier for me. Her panties come off at the same time, and she lies before me naked apart from that tantalizing necklace of hers, dangled onto her faux-fur coat. Jesus fuck. I've never seen anything so sexy in my entire life. I run my hands along her legs, sliding in the moisture at the top of her thighs. Pushing them apart, I stare down at her pussy. Pink, perfect, pearled with creamy fluid. Growling, I slip one finger inside her. Her pussy walls contract, and I can tell it won't take much to push her over the edge.

"Fuck, Amber. Ballet really does make you horny. I've got to taste you."

She squirms and sighs as I lean my face down between her legs. The smell of her is mind-blowing, all that desire, all that need. All for me. I lap at her slit, slow and smooth, eating her up as I trail my tongue along her seam, opening her up and exploring. Then I flick the swollen bud of her clit and suck it into my mouth, gently pulsing it until her moans deepen. Her hips grind into my face, and I hold her down while I lick her into a frenzy. "Come for me, Amber."

She screams my name, and her back bows as ecstasy shoots through her. I keep my face exactly where it is, arousal rushing from her and onto my lips, my beard, my nose. Her body quakes while I sweep my tongue all over her pussy, cleaning her up and savoring every last drop. With trembling thighs bracketing my head, I nuzzle her damp curls and smile. "Fuck. Can I stay here forever?"

She props herself up on her elbows and laughs, a big, dopey smile on her face. "Well, you could, honey, but I'm not sure it'd help swing that South Korean deal in your favor."

I wipe my face clean and crawl up to join her. She waits until I'm lying flat on my back and then straddles me. My cock is fucking delighted when she rubs herself against me, and she sighs and squirms some more. "Oh, honey, we really need to do something about this swelling."

"Yeah, we do, don't we? How about you go and stand by that barre for me?"

Her eyebrows shoot up. "You want to fuck me while we watch in the mirror?"

"I've wanted to do that since the moment we walked in here. That is what the mirrors are for, right?"

"They are tonight," she replies, getting to her feet. Her legs are still a little wobbly from her orgasm, but she soon steadies, and I look on as she saunters, completely naked, to the wooden barre. She holds onto it with her palms and bends over, presenting her ass to me. She glances over her shoulder. "What are you waiting for, sir?"

Fuck. For a second, I was so mesmerized by the sight of her that I lost the ability to move. I jump to my feet, get rid of my shoes and pants, and stand behind her. I'm desperate to get inside that tight pussy, especially when I see it's still glistening, but I take my time. I run my hands over her juicy, round ass. "Some other night, Amber, I'd love to fuck this ass as well. It could be one of our firsts."

She gulps but sways her backside more firmly into my hands. She had a bad experience with anal before she met me, and that stopped her from being open to trying again. Now, though, she's a very different woman.

"I'd like that, Elijah. I really would."

There's a slight catch in her voice. She's still nervous about it—nervous, but willing to try. Fuck, she is incredible. I make a vow that I will make it as pleasurable as it possibly can be for her when I take her ass. I will show her a whole new way to fuck.

I lean down and plant two smacking kisses on her backside—one for each cheek—and she giggles. For now, I'm more than happy to fuck her pretty pink pussy. I hold her hips and dip my rock-hard cock inside her. With all the buildup, she expects me to take her hard and fast, so I take it slow instead, enjoying the look of confusion on her face. It's torture for me as well, but I ease myself in inch by leisurely inch. She grips the barre, her knuckles going white as I fill her, and I watch her face in the mirror. Her eyes close, her tongue flicking out to lick her lips. Yeah, she's enjoying this. She's going to come again, and I'm going to enjoy every second of it.

I run my hand over her hips and slide it around to her clit. My dick is all the way inside her now, completely buried in the soft velvet of her pussy, and I keep it there while I stroke her swollen bud. She doesn't protest about being too sore anymore. She knows that won't stop me, and she's learned that she's capable of tolerating the sensitivity until she climaxes again. "I think we should do an experiment." I watch her face change in the mirror as she gets closer. "We should see how many times in a row I can make you come. How many times I can build you up and break you apart."

"Mmmm ... okay ..."

I smile at her mumbled reply. I wouldn't be doing my job properly if she were capable of coherent speech. "Open your eyes, Amber. Look at me while you come."

She does as she's told, and it melts me. She looks so beautiful, so trusting. So completely at my mercy. "Good girl." I speed up my fingers. It's killing me to not slam my dick in and out of her, but it's worth it. The feeling is fucking spectacular. She keeps her eyes on mine in the mirror, and I see and feel the moment her climax starts. Her full lips part, she calls out my name. The contractions of her inner muscles around me are so strong it's like she's jerking me off. Unfuckingbelievable. I wait until her orgasm runs its course, and then I put my arms around her, pulling her upright. She leans into me, the back of her head resting against my shoulder as our eyes meet in the glass. We're still and silent for a moment.

"Fuck me, Elijah," she demands.

I don't need to be told twice. Keeping one arm wrapped around the front of her body, I put the other on the wooden barre and rail into her like there's no tomorrow, listening to her cries and moans and watching her tits bounce in the reflection. Her thighs glisten with cum, her nipples stand at attention. The necklace jiggles between her breasts. She's trapped between my thrusting body and the barre, leaning into me. Strands of her hair stick to my chest and back, and her huge eyes never leave mine. I slam into her two, three more times, then fall apart. My climax rockets through me, and the pleasure is so fucking powerful that I see stars. I groan her name, my mouth falling to her shoulder as I come. She reaches back and places her hand on my neck.

"I fucking love you, Amber," I murmur.

"I know. And I love you too, Elijah."

I look up again, and her reflection gives me a small smile. One moment of pure, perfect connection. In its own way, that shared look is more intense than the orgasms.

Then she slips out of my grasp and starts to get dressed. The moment is gone, our connection shattered. She moves around the room, hiding behind her hair, her shoulders shaking.

I want to go to her, to drag her face out from behind that curtain of hair. I want to force her to look at me and tell her again that I love her. These emotions are so strong, so powerful, they threaten to overwhelm us. This isn't just sex, and we both know it. I should scoop her up, carry her home with me. Tell her I won't ever let her out of my sight again.

Instead, I do exactly what she's doing. Burying my emotions deep, I gather up my clothes and get dressed. I hear her on the phone asking Sanjay to come get her, and when she finally turns around, she's managed to compose herself. She tidies her hair, refusing to look at herself in the wall of mirrors. "He was visiting his sister in Hoboken while he waited," she explains. "He'll be here in five. Do you ... Uh, do you want a ride?"

The situation is so awkward, but she is polite and calm, not at all aggressive, and that only makes it hurt all the more.

Her shutters are down. Playful, passionate Amber has left the building. The woman I unraveled with my tongue and fingers is gone to hide behind her impenetrable walls.

"No, that's okay," I answer. "I'll get myself home. Before you leave, though, I have a gift for you."

I'm not sure it's the right move now, but what the fuck—I arranged for it to be left here, so I might as well give it to her. "Oh?" She attempts a grin. "Is it a pony?" The effort she puts into her attempt to restore the lightheartedness from earlier seems to drain her completely. Shoulders slumped, she looks like a breeze could knock her off her feet.

I go to the corner of the room, find the box, and pass it over. New life comes into her when she sees what's inside, and she lifts the white satin ballet shoes to her face. With eyes squeezed tightly shut, she rasps, "Thank you," then clears her throat. "They're beautiful. I need to build up my strength before I'm back en pointe though."

"Well, if there's one thing you're good at, it's building up your strength. And you're welcome."

She kisses me on the cheek, thanks me again, and turns to leave. After switching off the lights, I follow her out and wait in the doorway until she's safely in Sanjay's cab before calling an Uber.

The journey back to Manhattan passes in a blur, the Uber driver playing loud music and singing along the whole time. It all feels surreal, like it's happening to a different person.

On autopilot, I enter our home—the townhouse we moved into together when we were full of youthful optimism. Over the years, it became less of a home and more of a battlefield. Our optimism was replaced by cynicism, our hope wiped out by mutual frustration. I fucking hate it here now. She had the right idea when she got out. I imagine her in Brooklyn, safe and warm in Amelia's little house. Maybe she's trying on those ballet shoes. Or maybe she's curled up in a ball, crying, which is exactly what I feel like doing.

I pour myself a large Scotch and head up to the rooftop garden. It's a cold, beautiful night, and I sink into one of the chairs and gaze out at the incredible view. Central Park is spread out below, and the curves and spikes of the iconic Manhattan skyline are as familiar and as stunning as they've ever been.

I don't care about any of it. I don't care what I can see or how stunning it is. All I care about is what I can't see. Her. Amber. My wife. What the fuck are we doing? Our marriage isn't over. A divorce? I don't want a divorce. I want to start again. I want her at my side, in my bed, in my home. She's already in my heart, and I realize now that she always will be.

Tonight might have ended abruptly, but it showed the depths of emotion still running between us. It showed me that our love story is still being written. We can't give up on it now. I love her too much, and I know she feels the same.

The way we chatted over dinner, the way we held hands as we walked along the river. It was perfect. Everything I am is alive and radiant when I'm around her—mind, body, and soul. Everything about her calls to me. She is the person who completes me. Who completes my life.

Our relationship won't be easy to rebuild, but we are worth the effort. Few people are lucky enough to meet someone who makes them feel like this, and it would be criminal to throw it away.

I sip my Scotch and gaze at the city lights. I love my wife.

I love her, and I want her back. I don't care what compromises I have to agree to or how many changes I have to make. Amber is mine, and I'm determined to keep her.

Tension flees my body once I've made that decision, and I smile to myself. I have a goal, and I am not the kind of man who fails to achieve his goals.

I pull the burner phone from my pocket and type out a message to the only contact in there.

Can I see you tomorrow night?

After an interminable, torturous wait, one word arrives.

Yes.

TWENTY-FOUR

AMBER

I'm meeting Martha for a late lunch—in her case probably liquid. We've been in touch sporadically since the news broke about Elijah and me, and I made sure to contact her the minute Mason posted the statement. We might not be soul sisters, but she is one of the few women from my socialite life that I truly enjoy being around.

First, though, I am doing a little work in Amelia's yard. Nothing major, because it is December, just some tidying and leaf-clearing. It keeps me busy. Last night was a lot, in every possible way. The dancing, the sex.

The gift.

When he told me that he loved me, I felt so raw and exposed. It was like we were no longer Mr. and Mrs. Smith—it felt like we were Amber and Elijah from twenty years ago, the world at our feet.

He was upset when I left so quickly, but I didn't have a choice. I couldn't think straight with him so close. It was too intimate, and there was a real risk of me losing my resolve and telling him I don't want us to be over.

I miss him, and I'm still sad that my marriage is ending, but I am finding glimmers of hope in my new life. I like living in Brooklyn and getting to know this quirky neighborhood. I enjoy chatting with Mrs. K across the street and buying my own groceries. I've even been learning how to cook with the help of some YouTube videos. I'm putting in the work on myself, and I need to figure out if the way I felt last night is compatible with that.

Sanjay dropped me back here, and I made myself a mug of hot cocoa and settled down on the couch. My body was still singing from the orgasms and the dancing, and I took the ballet shoes out of their box and sat with them on my lap. I love the smell of new ballet shoes, the hint of leather and glue. They start to stink real fast, I remember.

They are beautiful shoes, and the more I look at them, the more I understand that what they represent is especially beautiful. I might be overthinking it, but I believe they represent acceptance. Elijah was worried about me living here and volunteering at the community center, but gifting me the shoes tells me he has accepted both. I told him what I want to try next in my life, and he's supporting me.

I took a final happy sniff before I put them down and flicked on the TV. Exhausted mentally but too wired to go to bed, I was half watching an old episode of *True Blood* when I realized how much I want to be with him. Not back in that house, the way we were. But somewhere new for both of us. Was I crazy to think like that? Would opening my heart to him again mean sacrificing all the progress I've made? The shoes, I decided, said otherwise. The shoes said he could also adapt and accept that I had changed, that we were changing.

I was still turning it over in my mind when my burner

phone pinged. My logical brain told me not to reply until morning. I was off-balance, confused by awesome sex and the simple pleasure of being wooed by my own husband. The logical part of my brain was a wuss though. It couldn't hold out against the part of me that was overjoyed at the thought of seeing him again so soon. So I told him yes and went to bed feeling giddy.

The giddiness was still there when I woke up this morning, but so was the doubt. The affair is getting out of hand, at least for me. I am starting to feel far more than I should. I wonder if he's feeling the same kind of uncertainty and that's why he wants to see me tonight.

Overwhelmed by the myriad of questions without answers in my mind, I slam the lid down on the trash can so hard it makes a big metallic clang. "Hey Amber," Mrs. K calls from across the street. "What did that trash can ever do to you?"

"It looked at me funny, Mrs. Katzberg."

She waves her cigarette at me and cackles. "Well in that case, have at it, girl."

I head back inside with a smile on my face, shoving aside thoughts of Elijah and focusing on getting ready. I take a quick shower and blow-dry my hair. I'm more comfortable in casual attire these days, but I make the effort to choose a nice outfit from my vastly reduced wardrobe. I'll probably go straight from meeting Martha to seeing Elijah anyway, so the effort won't be wasted. Not that he seems to care what I'm wearing or like I wear anything for long in his presence.

Still, I think he'll notice this, I think as I study the red dress I chose. It's slinky and a little lower cut than I normally wear, but I'm feeling it. I add the spike-heeled boots and another dangly necklace. Both will drive him wild. Martha will probably think I took the trouble to dress up because I'm newly single and looking to mingle. Nobody would ever guess the truth—that I have a date with the man I'm divorcing.

Last night, Sanjay let me know he wouldn't be available today as he is on triplet duty with his wife, but I pick up a cab without any trouble. As we drive into the city, the burner phone goes off.

> I can't wait to see you later. I miss you so much. I really think we need to talk.

He's right—we do need to talk. I want my independence and to learn to live in the real world and find my passion, but I also want him. There's no denying it—I have fallen in love with my husband all over again. And as ever when falling in love, the feeling is complicated. It fills me with both joy and terror.

> I can't wait either. I agree we need to talk xxx

I add the kisses since I won't be able to kiss him in person until tonight. Nothing has technically changed, yet I feel completely different. Like I'm floating on air. When I see him tonight, when I kiss him for real, I will be honest and tell him how confused I am. I'll tell him about the changes I want to make in our lives, but I will make sure he understands that if he wants it, there is still the potential for this to be *our* life. That we could give this another shot.

Another beep sounds from my purse, and the crazy-lady grin stays on my face as I pull out my other phone, the one that the rest of the world uses. It's Martha, asking me to meet her outside Freddie's offices because she's running a little late after stopping by to talk to him about something.

I tell her no problem and let the driver know the new address. It's in Midtown, near the cluster of high-class law firms and businesses that includes Jamestech and James and James.

I'm not sure how I'll play it with Martha. We've previously managed to have incredibly boozy fun times out together without talking about anything personal at all. I'm hoping we can do the same today, except maybe with less booze. What I really don't want is to spend the whole time talking about the split.

I'm dropped off right outside the building that houses Kemp, Michaelson, and Chambers, and right after I step into the lobby, another message lands from Martha.

> Come up to Freddie's office, this is dragging on. There will be coffee waiting for you.
> Sorry, you know how it is.

I do know how it is to be married to someone you have to schedule time with. If Elijah and I decide to give things another shot, we'll both need to make each other far more of a priority than we ever did before.

I've never been in Freddie's office, but I follow the signs and ride the elevator up to the correct floor, and I'm greeted with a smile from a sleek-looking assistant. "Mrs. James?" he says when he spots me. "I'm Tom. Let me show you through."

I follow the man toward a corner office, and he holds the

door open for me. I walk through, looking for Martha, and he closes it behind me. Freddie Kemp jumps to his feet from behind his desk. Still no sign of Martha. Maybe she's in the bathroom.

Although I'm decidedly off-balance, my normal instincts kick in. My face instantly schools itself into a friendly smile. "Hi Freddie, how are you?"

"All the better for seeing you, Amber. You look gorgeous, as usual."

As he walks toward me, I immediately regret the low-cut red dress. His eyes are like laser beams running over my figure, and a sleazy smile forms on his slug-like lips. I have never liked Freddie Kemp, and not only because of the way he treats Martha. There's something off about him, a predatory vibe. He is a touch shorter than me, especially in these boots, and apart from a flabby little gut that hangs over his belt, he's skinny. It's unbelievable really, the lengths that Martha goes to in order to keep the interest of a man like this.

"Is Martha here?" I ask, backing up slightly. He's come too close too quickly, and I notice that all the blinds in the office are closed. The only natural light comes from his balcony.

"No, she's not. I'm afraid that was a little ploy we cooked up to get you here."

"Really?" I'm starting to freak out, but I manage to keep my voice haughty and in control. "And why is that?"

"Please, will you sit?" He gestures toward a big couch at the back of the room.

"No, I don't think I will. I came here to meet your wife, and if she's not here, I really must be going."

"Oh, don't be like that, Amber. We're old friends, aren't we?"

We are not old friends, no. We are old acquaintances, and that is very different. He puts his hand on my elbow and attempts to steer me toward the seating area. I resist, but he's stronger than he looks, the little turd. Years of social conditioning kick in, and I start to yield. Making a scene is one of the worst sins a girl can commit—I had that drummed into me from birth. Even as a toddler, I knew to cry in private.

"Um, actually, I'm in a bit of a hurry. What was it that you wanted?"

"I want to make you rich, Amber. I want to make you one of the richest women in the country."

I stare at him for a moment, completely dumbfounded, and I finally manage to pull away. "Freddie, I don't want to be rude, but I don't have a clue what you're going on about."

He sighs and shakes his head as though I'm a silly little thing who doesn't understand the real world. A horrible grin splits his face, full of overly white veneered teeth that make him look like a crocodile. "I want to represent you in the divorce. I'm the obvious choice. Elijah has all the money, all the power—he's bound to screw you over. With me on your side, you can be sure that won't happen."

I've received multiple offers of representation from many different divorce attorneys, but Freddie was not one of them. Apparently, this particular shark simply had a different approach and used his wife to lure me here. A flare of hurt bursts inside me at Martha's betrayal, but I clamp it down.

"Thank you, Freddie, but that won't be necessary. I

already have representation, and the proceedings are well underway."

He's still pushing, still getting closer. Every time I take a step back, he takes a bigger one forward. I really do not like the manic gleam in his eyes, not one little bit. Something is off about his pupils, and I realize the rumors about his cocaine addiction are undoubtedly true. This is the first time I've ever been alone with Freddie Kemp—and it will certainly be the last.

"Who?" he asks, dispensing with all attempts at charm. Spittle flies from his mouth as he rages. "Who have you signed with? You know I'm the best! The rest are all garbage compared to me."

"My divorce is none of your business, Freddie. Now, get out of my way."

He has backed me all the way to the corner of the room, and my ass hits the wall. There is nowhere else for me to go, and a rush of fear almost chokes me. What the hell is happening here? Freddie can be aggressive, and he's used to getting what he wants in both his personal and professional life, but this is insane. The man is out of control. His eyes are fixed on my cleavage, and he licks his lips with his fat tongue. His hands go down to his groin, and I'm horrified at the sight of the erection that is clearly visible through his suit pants.

I raise my hand to shove him away, but he catches hold of my wrist and pins it against the wall. He squeezes it viciously, painfully grinding the little bones together. I want to scream, I should scream—there is an office full of people just through that door. Someone will hear. Someone will help me.

As his leering face comes closer, though, I'm paralyzed. I

269

can't scream. Can't run. I am frozen. Immobile. All I can do is shrink away from his fetid breath. "You're a stuck-up cunt, did you know that, Amber? You've always looked down on me, just because I'm from a small town in Michigan and don't have the same fancy manners as you."

"Freddie, I don't know what you mean. I didn't even know you were from Michigan. Let me go!"

"No, I don't think I will," he says, and I shudder at the sensation of his hard penis grinding against me. "Beautiful Amber James, always thinking she's the queen bee, looking down her nose at the rest of us. I don't suppose I'm good enough to represent you, am I? What about this, though, is this good enough for you?" He grabs my hand and forces it down to touch his hardness. His face dissolves into an expression of ecstasy as he rubs my fingers over his groin, and he closes his eyes and smacks his lips together. This man is utterly revolting. Why the fuck am I standing here taking this? His smug expression finally unfreezes me.

I snatch my hand away and slap him firmly across the face. He is so shocked at me fighting back that it's his turn to freeze. I push him as hard as I can, and he topples backward, trips over a glass coffee table, and eventually lands on his ass on the floor. He stares up at me for a long moment before scrambling to his feet and stalking forward. "You fucking cunt!"

I dodge, too quick for him to catch, and race out of his office as fast as my feet will carry me. I need fresh air and to be as far away from Freddie and his grasping fingers and crazy eyes as I can get.

Tom the assistant jumps up to talk to me, but I keep

walking, desperately seeking the ladies' room. I'm just about holding it together, fighting back my tears and my nausea, when a horribly familiar voice calls my name.

"Amber, Stop!" I close my eyes. Every muscle in my body tenses. I keep walking, hoping to get to the elevator before he reaches me. No such luck—I press the button, but the car is on the ground level. Rolling my shoulders back, I stand up tall and remind myself who I am. Amber James, stuck-up cunt. He might be the Ice Man, but I am the Ice Queen.

I whirl around, and Nathan James bears down on me. I fight the panic gripping my throat. He's always angry when he sees me. He cloaks it with sarcasm and biting comments, but beneath that is pure fury—I hurt his beloved brother. I am the enemy.

I force myself to stay exactly where I am. I have given up enough ground today, and I will not let another man bully me. "Nathan," I say coldly. "What are you doing here?"

"I had a meeting with Cynthia Chambers about a case we're working on together. What are *you* doing here?"

"None of your goddamn business," I snap. He looks taken aback. I am usually calm and frosty, but I can't fake it that well today.

The elevator arrives, and I wait while a young woman gets out. "Take the stairs, Nathan," I say after stepping inside.

"Fuck you, Amber." He holds the door open and keeps his voice low—we are in public, after all—smiling as he speaks. "How does it feel to be replaced?"

"What do you mean?"

"I mean that Elijah has met someone else. He's been

271

seeing her for a while now, and she's good for him. Much better than you were. In fact, he's the happiest he's ever been. You have a real nice day now." He says the last few words in a mocking Southern accent and looks unbearably pleased with himself as the elevator doors slide closed on him.

I stagger back against the wall, finally letting my proud expression fade. The adrenaline rush has left me weak and shaky, and as soon as I get to the lobby, I head straight for the ladies' room. I splash my face and scrub my hands with scalding hot water for several minutes, trying to scour away every trace of Freddie Kemp's filthy touch.

I knew he was a cheat, but I had no idea he was a predator, and I'm not sure what to do about it. Should I call the cops? Talk to Elijah? Go back upstairs and kick the shit out of him? I am not naive—if he behaved like that with me, he has undoubtedly done it before. Which is why I'm shocked I've never heard a whisper about sexual misconduct. How has he kept it a secret?

My reflection stares back at me, pale and drawn. Elijah will make me feel safe, if nothing else.

I take a few deep breaths and find my burner phone.

Any chance you can meet a little earlier?

I hit send and lean against the marble vanity while I wait for his response. He doesn't keep me waiting long.

For you, anything. See you at five?

I reply with kisses, feeling relieved at the prospect of

seeing him again, especially now. I need his hands to replace the lingering crawling sensation Freddie left behind. I need Elijah to hold me until the horror of it fades.

I need my husband.

TWENTY-FIVE

ELIJAH

I sit back in my seat and punch the air. She wants to see me early, and her most recent message had more kisses than the last. So what if I'm acting like a goddamn teenager—I'm fucking thrilled at her response. I'm so happy that I push my chair back from my desk, lift up my feet, and whirl around in a circle. The only reason I resist the urge to shout "Yippee!" is because the walls to my office aren't soundproofed. The CEO of Jamestech is expected to conduct himself with a modicum of dignity.

I can hear my secretary talking to someone on the other side of my door, so I'm glad I reined it in. Beverley's playful tone tells me it's someone she's familiar with, but I grab my desk to stop my spinning and pick up a pen, hoping I look like a serious man doing serious work. I damn sure don't feel like one.

When I reached out to Amber last night, I genuinely wasn't sure which she would leap. It was entirely possible that she would retreat further away from me. When she agreed to meet, I knew there was a chance—and a chance is all I need. Our follow-up messages so far today have done nothing to discourage me. Kisses—text message kisses. I don't think Amber has sent me kisses in a message for over a decade, and now it's twice in one day. Fuck. I can't believe how good I feel right now. And I can't believe I have to hide it from the world, at least until Amber and I have had the chance to talk properly.

We have a lot to discuss, but I feel confident we can make it work. For the first time in forever, I can see a future for us. One where we chat over dinner and go for walks and have amazing sex and support each other with love and kindness. A future where we are allies in life. It's the path we were on when we got married, and we took it for granted. Never again.

I send a quick email to Luisa canceling the strategy meeting we had planned for later and vaguely wonder who Beverley is talking to. She laughs and says, "Oh my. He's absolutely gorgeous."

Seconds later, there's a quick knock on my door and Nathan strides in.

"Were you showing her pics of Luke or Jason Momoa?" I ask, grinning at him.

"Well, I deleted all my shots of Jason when Mel started getting jealous," he jokes as he walks toward me. Despite the banter, it's clear he has something on his mind.

He sinks down into the guest chair opposite me and runs his hands through his dark hair—a sure sign of distress. I subtly glance at my watch and hope that whatever this is, it leaves me enough time to reach Amber by five. Turning up late because I was dealing with Nathan's drama would not go over well. Those are the exact kinds of choices that helped us into this mess in the first place. It's never easy though, being tugged in two opposite directions.

He grinds his teeth and clenches his fists. He's not just upset, he's raging inside.

"Bro, what's wrong?" I ask, and he slams one of those fists down on the desk so hard it shakes. "Nathan, what the hell is going on? Is everything all right with Mel?"

"What?" Confusion flickers in his eyes. "Yeah, of course." He shakes his head. "Look, Elijah, there's no easy way to say this. She's screwing you over."

"What? Who is?"

"Who the fuck do you think I mean? Amber! I knew she was a bitch, but I never thought she'd sink this low."

"Nathan, I have told you before—stop bad-mouthing her." I stand up, my own temper flaring now. I'm sick of this constant tug-of-war. I'm sick of my own family refusing to see any good in the woman I love.

He jumps up too and leans over the desk toward me. "It's not bad-mouthing if it's the truth, and you really need to stop defending her. She's not what you think she is, Elijah— she's got you fooled. You should have made her sign a prenup."

Making a visible effort to calm himself down, he sucks in a breath, plops back into his chair, and rubs the bridge of his nose between his fingers. "Sit down, will you? We need to talk."

Something is very wrong here. I haven't seen him this upset in years. He does a good job of presenting a cool, calm front to the world, but inside, Nathan is a deeply passionate man. He loves his family, and he would do anything to protect us. The conflicted expression on his face tells me that he is about to say something he knows will hurt me.

I sit, forcing myself to match his calm. "Go on, then. Spit it out. But make it quick, because I have somewhere I need to be at five."

With my wife. With the woman he hates. I have no idea how I will ever resolve the two halves of my life, but I have to find a way. And that means putting Amber first—every single fucking time.

"You both agreed to use Drake for the divorce, correct?" he asks.

"Yeah."

"So, you're both using the same lawyer. There is no prenup. Nobody is looking out for just you. Do you have any idea how dangerous that is? Not only for you, but for Jamestech?"

Where the hell is he going with this? "So you think I'm a dumbass. You've made that abundantly clear already. Is there a fucking point to any of this, or did you just want to come by and make me feel like shit? All of this is hard enough without you weighing in and pointing out my flaws."

He bites his tongue, his nostrils flaring. He is working damn hard at controlling himself. "I did not come by to make you feel like shit—I came by to tell you she's not playing by the same rule book as you. She doesn't have a scrap of the honesty and integrity that you have, and I don't want to see you get fucked in the ass."

"Charming image—but where is this coming from?"

His eyes meet mine, and his voice is a low growl. "She's not being repped by Drake alone. She's gone to Freddie Kemp."

The words are like a slap across my face, and I sag back into my chair. There's got to be some mistake. Freddie Kemp is ... Well, he's an asshole, but he's also damn good at his job. Probably the most vicious and ruthless divorce attorney in the States. He has represented movie stars, crime lords, billionaire bankers—and their spouses. In every single case, the end result was the same. Freddie's client came out on top. Not just on top, but completely dominant. Their other halves were either wiped out or severely financially depleted. No, Nathan can't be right. She wouldn't do that to me.

"What makes you say that?" I ask, needing to hear facts.

"Man, I just saw her. I was in their building for a meeting, and she was tucked away with Freddie in his office. And when she saw me, when I confronted her, she knew she was caught—she was all pale and shaky, not like herself at all. Because she knew I'd tell you, obviously. She's been playing you all along, Elijah."

Can he be right? Can this be the truth? I run things over in my mind. Drake advised her to find her own attorney to check over the settlement, and she gave the impression that she wasn't going to do that. But were we both wrong? Has she played us? Why else would she be in Freddie Kemp's office? She doesn't like the man. Always said he creeped her out.

"Maybe she was meeting Martha there?" I say as much to myself as to him. "They're friendly."

He shakes his head sadly. "Martha wasn't there. I saw Amber arrive alone, and Freddie's assistant met her and showed her into his office. I wasn't totally sure at that point. I know I haven't not been her biggest fan, but if I'm honest, I never thought she'd stoop that low. So I hung around and waited. She dealt with Freddie and nobody else. It wasn't a social call. You need to wake up and take action. Without a prenup, and with that scumbag in her corner, she could take you for everything. All this time you've been playing nice, she's probably been gathering information. Information Freddie Kemp will use against you."

Last night at dinner, she did show a lot of interest in the Seoul deal. Was that more sinister than it seemed?

"When was this?" I ask, trying to get the timing straight.

"It was maybe twenty minutes ago. I came straight here."

Her message arrived right after Nathan talked to her. Fuck, does this mean he's right? She was trying to get in front of it, altering our arrangement so she could get to me before he did. Maybe come up with some bullshit story to cover her ass. Her perfect heart-shaped ass.

There really is no other reason for her to be alone with Freddie Kemp in his office. Or to be talking to his assistant. If this was a Martha thing, they'd be sipping cocktails in that place they like off Fifth Avenue, not holding business meetings.

Still, I ask, "You're positive?"

He nods, staring at me intensely. "Yeah. I can't think of any other explanation. I wish I could, for your sake. I know you wanted this to end differently and that you still have feelings for her."

"Feelings?" I echo. The word is wholly inadequate. "*Feelings?* I have loved that woman for over twenty years, Nathan. You do know what love is, don't you?"

Hurt and angry, I can't help lashing out, and I don't give a damn.

"Yeah, dickhead, I know what love is," he snaps back.

"Maybe you do now, Nathan, but you didn't back then. When I brought Amber home, you made zero effort with her. And then after Mom died, you really drank Dad's Kool-Aid— that whole 'never fall in love' bullshit he fed us. You saw love as a sign of weakness. Do you ever wonder if that's part of why it took you so long to find someone?"

"So what if it is? It doesn't make me wrong about this. No, I don't like Amber, but that doesn't mean I'm wrong. Like I said, I wish I were wrong. I really do. I'm sorry, Elijah. I am so goddamn sorry. But she's planning to destroy you."

It's the genuine sympathy that undoes me. It's in his eyes and his voice, clear as day. This has been hard for him, and he didn't do it out of spite or because he doesn't understand what love is. He did it because he loves me.

"Okay," I say quietly. "I hear you. I ... Damn it, I believe you. I just don't want to." I sound as broken as I feel.

He comes around to my side of the desk. "Get up, you asshole. How am I going to hug you if you're all the way down there?"

I do as he says. He wraps me up in a bear hug, and we slap each other on the backs once it's done. I don't feel awkward—I am one of life's huggers—but I am eager for him to leave. I need to be alone with this for a while.

"Get home to Mel and Luke," I say firmly. "And thank you."

"What are you gonna do?" he asks. If he had his way, there'd probably be flaming torches and pitchforks involved.

"I don't know yet."

He opens his mouth to speak, but I hold up my hand to silence him. "Nope. Don't. Leave it with me for now."

Something in my voice or my expression must convince

him I mean it, because he gives me a nod and a final pat on the shoulder and leaves.

I sit back down, my legs weak and my heart heavy. First of all, I pick up the phone and call the firm of Kemp, Michaelson, and Chambers. I do not doubt that my brother saw what he says he saw. He might despise Amber, but he wouldn't lie about something like this. He has too much integrity, and he knows the damage it would cause. But before I do anything else, I need to be absolutely sure.

Once I explain who is calling, I'm put through to Freddie straight away. "Elijah James." There's an edge to his voice, but he doesn't seem at all shocked to hear from me. It's almost like he was expecting my call. "I thought I might hear from you. I can explain."

"Explain what?" I keep my tone even and polite. There is nothing to be gained at this point by antagonizing him. He doesn't really need to explain why he's taken on my wife's case, although I guess it might be awkward socially as we run in some of the same circles. I'm surprised that bothers him, but Freddie always was on the unpredictable side.

It takes him a while to reply, and there is a hesitant note in his voice when he does. "Anything you like. What can I do for you, big man?"

"Well, for a start, you can tell me if you're representing my wife in our divorce proceedings."

There's a pause, and then he lets out a delighted cackle. "Well, Elijah, you know I couldn't possibly tell you if I was— I'd be bound by client confidentiality, would I not? But between you and me, because we're friends, your lovely wife did pay me a visit earlier today. We talked over a few things in my office. That's really all I can say on the matter. I'll leave the rest to your imagination."

He sounds unbearably smug, and I'd dearly love to punch his lights out. Instead, I take a deep breath. "Thank you Freddie. I appreciate that."

After hanging up, I scrub my face with my hands. They come away damp. I am a forty-two-year-old man sitting in his goddamn office, crying because his wife lied to him.

No, she didn't just lie to me—she has, like Nathan said, played me for a fool. I should have known. I've always said the woman could win an Oscar. She pretended to want a nice, civilized divorce. She even pretended there was hope for us, presumably to keep me distracted and softened up. Fuck, and it worked all too well. All I've thought about for the last day is how I can win her back. Apparently, all she's thought about is how much Freddie Kemp can take from me.

My hands tremble as I pour myself a Scotch. Could it all have been a lie? The sex, our connection? The love? I bite my lip and taste blood.

It must have been a lie. Freddie Kemp confirmed it. It was a sweet, sultry lie—one I fell for hook, line, and sinker. She told me what I wanted to hear. She baited me and reeled me in. I am a fucking idiot. A fucking idiot with a broken heart.

I take the burner phone from my pocket and put it on the floor. Channeling all my anger and heartbreak, I power it through my body and slam my foot down, smashing the sole of my shoe onto the screen and grinding it to pieces with my heel.

Mr. and Mrs. Smith are over.

TWENTY-SIX

AMBER

I check my phone again. It's ten minutes after five, and there's still no sign of him. I'm sitting at our usual table in our place in Greenwich. Also as usual, it is completely empty apart from me.

Aaron, the manager, brought me a bottle of pinot, but I'm only a few sips in. I haven't eaten, and I still feel jumpy from my encounter with Freddie.

Encounter ... That's not the right word for it.

I need to call it what it is. Sexual assault. It may not have gone as far as it could have, but it was still an assault. I shiver when I remember it, the way he forced my hand onto his groin. The look of ecstasy on his face. It was disgusting, and there is no way I could have eaten after that. I have been sick several times, and it was with a huge sense of relief that I arrived here. Knowing that I would be with Elijah soon gave me the strength to get through the last couple hours at home.

I still can't believe I let it get so far. Why did I let him back me into that corner? Why didn't I trust my instincts?

Why didn't I scream? I have never considered myself to be a passive person, but this is not the first time I have been abused without striking back.

Many years ago, when I was only eighteen, my so-called boyfriend tried to persuade me to have anal sex with him. I said no, and he seemed to accept it—but later that night, after plying me with alcohol and weed and making me feel oh-so-sophisticated, he did it anyway. I woke up from a drunken stupor, only half-conscious, face down on his bed. I can still recall the taste of the pillow against my lips, his hand on my neck. The stinging pain, and the animalistic grunting noises he made. Afterward, he told me it was all my idea. That I woke him up and told him I wanted him to do it.

I knew he was lying, but I wasn't sure what to do about it. He was a "nice" boy from a good family, and I was certain nobody would believe me. I didn't know if I would have believed a girl in my situation either. A huge scandal would have erupted had I reported it, and my parents wouldn't have tolerated that.

I tried talking to my mom about it, pretending a friend had ended up in a difficult situation, and she just snorted over her gin glass. "Tell your friend to forget about it, would be my advice," she said. "That kind of thing happens to women all the time. She needs to be more careful who she associates with."

I've never known if she saw through my asking-for-a-friend ruse, and after her response, I wasn't tempted to find out. She reinforced my belief that it was somehow my fault, and I lived with it. Pushed it to the back of my mind and tried to behave as though it didn't happen. And now here I am, yet again, feeling sick with shame and self-loathing. Did I send out some kind of signal that made Freddie Kemp think I was interested? Did I ever flirt with him at a party or give him a reason to believe I found him attractive? I'm sure I didn't—and anyway, the way he spoke to me was abusive. The names he called me were not seductive; they were aggressive. It was not my fault.

No matter how many times I repeat it, though, I still don't quite believe it. I need Elijah here with me. The thought of being in his arms again is the only thing keeping me sane. Seeing Nathan straight after Freddie didn't help, but I did take some comfort from what he said—that Elijah's new woman was making him so happy. Unintentionally, Nathan offered me consolation, and that gave me something to cling onto until now.

I take another sip of wine and look at my phone again. Only a few minutes have passed since the last time I checked. Has something awful happened? If he were stuck in traffic or caught in a meeting, he'd have called me. Perhaps he simply got the time wrong. There's got to be a simple explanation for it. He's the one who initiated this date, and he seemed as excited as I was to meet again. So, where is he? It's not like him to be late—he's not me. We joked last night about the way I used to torture him with my tardiness—perhaps he's returning the favor, thinking it will be amusing? He has no clue what happened to me today, that the joke will fall flat.

No. That doesn't feel right either. I check both my burner phone and my normal phone. No messages, no missed calls. I was wondering if Martha would be in touch, but she hasn't. That's probably for the best, at least for today.

Ten minutes later, I give in and message him, a just-checking-in kind of thing. I stare at the screen, my heart sinking further with each passing second it remains blank. After that, I try actually calling him on both his numbers. The burner phone rings out, and his regular phone goes to voicemail. Hanging up, I die a little more inside.

He's now almost an hour late, and he is incommunicado. Something could be seriously wrong—a car crash, his dad, anything—but if that were the case, Drake would have told me. The others, no, but Drake would have called.

This day is not turning out like I hoped it would at all. I hoped Elijah and I would have a proper conversation about the future. Then, after what happened with Freddie, I needed him to comfort me and counsel me and keep me safe. Now, I'm sitting alone in an empty room with a bottle of wine, wondering where my husband is and hoping that he's safe, while having a sinking feeling that he simply stood me up.

I decide to give it one last shot and type out a message on the burner phone.

> Are you on your way? Something terrible happened to me today and I need you, Elijah. I love you. Please don't let me down.

More minutes pass. More silence, more pain twisting in my gut. I wave to Aaron, and he is immediately at my side. He looks pained when I ask if Mr. Smith has called or left a message. "I'm afraid not, Mrs. Smith, other than by email, and it certainly didn't mention any changes to tonight's reservation. Maybe he was delayed?"

"It would certainly appear so. Do you mind me asking— did my husband, um, buy this place?"

He smiles and shakes his head. "No. But he did book it for your exclusive use until ... Well, he paid for three months in advance, but that email I mentioned? He said we were free to open to the public again as of tomorrow because he no longer needed us. I assumed the two of you had found a new meeting place." As soon as the words leave his mouth, he looks really uncomfortable and is obviously wondering if he's made a terrible faux pas.

His words knock the wind out of me, but I am too experienced to show it. I let out a small laugh and give him a coy look. "Well, that would be telling, wouldn't it?"

He laughs along with me, then asks if I need anything else. I tell him no and keep up the pretense until he leaves.

As soon as he retreats back to the bar, I let myself crumble, but only on the inside. I have to face reality. Elijah isn't coming. He canceled his booking here and is ignoring my calls. He's made it as clear as he can that this thing between us, whatever it was, is now over. I hate feeling like this again, so sour and disappointed. My trust for him was starting to rebuild, and I was beginning to believe we could find a way to make things work. Now, all I want is to run away, to hide from all this pain and angst.

I don't usually misjudge situations so badly, and this is yet another hammer blow to my confidence and self-respect. I genuinely thought he wanted to talk about us trying again —as Mr. and Mrs. James, not Mr. and Mrs. Smith. Clearly, I was mistaken. Clearly, I am the world's biggest idiot. I rub my wrist, which is still sore from where Freddie grabbed me. A physical reminder of what happened.

Elijah isn't coming. He doesn't love me. He couldn't even be bothered to turn up and end things himself, face-to-face. I reached out, told him how I feel, and he ignored me. I don't know why I expected anything more—I have never been first on Elijah's list of priorities, and that was never going to change.

I wrap my own arms around myself and squeeze. It would be so easy to fall into this bottle of pinot and numb myself to all the pain. But I will not become my mother. I will not use booze as an anesthetic. I stand up and make my way toward the exit on shaky legs.

I will not fall, I tell myself. I will put one foot in front of another. It's time to go back to Brooklyn and learn how to make myself feel safe.

TWENTY-SEVEN

ELIJAH

The thought of her sitting there alone, disappointed when she realizes I'm not coming running like a pussy-drunk idiot, makes me feel marginally better. I ignore her call with a smile. She probably tried the burner first, but that is well and truly dead. By now, she must be getting increasingly desperate. Maybe she's figured it out —she's far from stupid. She'll probably guess that Nathan put two and two together and came to tell me. She'll probably have been trying to calculate the odds, though— wondering if Nathan actually saw her in Freddie's office or if there could be some other explanation. Wondering if she could come up with a decent excuse and continue with her sly game.

By now, she knows the answer to that is a solid no. She won't be able to manipulate me ever again. She may have signed with Freddie Kemp, but he doesn't scare me. Tomorrow, I will sit down with Drake, and we will come up with a strategy. This will hurt him too. The bitch doesn't know what she's let herself in for. We'll destroy her in exactly the same way she planned to destroy me. I will fucking ruin her the way she's ruined me. Well, not exactly the same way, given that she's torn my fucking heart to shreds. Her lack of heart makes it impossible to do the same, but I can and will ruin the only thing she cares about—her reputation. Freddie Kemp might be a shark, but he's never come up against Nathan and Drake before, and they will eat him for fucking breakfast.

This is exactly what we hoped to avoid—all-out warfare. At least it's what I hoped to avoid—she was pretending to my face while plotting with Freddie in private this whole time. Keeping me pussy blind so I wouldn't see it coming.

I'm back at the townhouse now, filled with anger and welcoming it. Anger is better than what came before. Give me good old-fashioned rage over heartbreak every damn day.

I strip down to workout shorts and a T-shirt and head to the gym in the basement, needing to punch some shit. Once my hands are wrapped, I start with the speed bag. I build up power until it's a blur in front of me, then move onto the heavyweight punching bag that hangs from the ceiling. I put my gloves on and lay into it. Every blow I land comes with a satisfying thud, and I work up a healthy sweat. Eventually, though, even that isn't enough.

Fuck it. I tug my gloves off and throw them to the floor. I need to feel some real pain.

Twenty minutes later, I'm done. I sink to the concrete and pour half a bottle of water straight over my head. I'm sweating hard, my face feels like someone took a blowtorch to it, and my lungs are bursting.

I swallow down the rest of the water and look at my

hands. My knuckles are scraped and bloody, my fingers swollen and red. That was fucking stupid, but I needed it. I needed the distraction of the physical, because the emotional is threatening to knock me out. I clamber to my feet and notice my back is still sore from that stupid ballet bullshit last night. Jesus fuck. Was it really only last night? It seems impossible that so much changed so quickly. How long was she going to keep up this charade, anyway? The legal process would have shown her true colors before much longer. Maybe she and that fucker Freddie Kemp were planning a big reveal. Who knows—it's pointless trying to figure it out.

I take the world's hottest shower, torturing myself with the spray on its most punishing setting and then change it to freezing cold. It's the only way I know to keep my mind off her. Even now, my bastard memory is messing with me, flooding me with images of her in the shower at the Greenwich Village place. I fucked her in there the last time we met, with her long legs wrapped around my back, her ass in my hands. She came so hard around my cock, screaming my name, her eyes fluttering and rolling. The water flowing off her slender shoulders and cascading over her rigid nipples ... Fuck!

My hand is on my dick, and despite the icy water, I'm still hard for her. I still want her. I'm nothing but a goddamn animal.

She used that against me, and I hate that I was such an easy mark. I hate that despite it all, my stupid, soft heart is still in pieces. I dry myself off, throw on sweats, and pour another Scotch. I don't know what to do with myself. I can't stop thinking about her, about what she's done. My thoughts are ricocheting around my head like a pinball on acid. I have too many fucking feelings, and I don't know where to put them all. I also have too many fucking questions and no way to answer them.

Unless … It's only ten o'clock. Too early for me to try to sleep, and I don't want to be around my family. Nathan agreed to keep this whole situation quiet for now. The last thing I need is pity or more questions. Worse, the subtle sense of I-told-you-so that I will imagine is there even if it's not.

I genuinely believed Amber and I were finding our way back to each other, and I wanted it so much. Each time I saw her during our "affair," my feelings for her deepened. I witnessed her opening up and softening, and I watched myself open up right alongside her. Tonight, I planned to lay it all on the line for her—ask her to come back, promise her the world, give her my whole heart.

I still don't understand why she felt the need to pretend and deceive. Except I suppose I do. She made her feelings about my family very clear. Apart from Drake, she cannot stand them, and vice versa. Over the years, that attitude has hardened inside her, made her bitter. It's like scar tissue, hidden beneath the surface. She saw a chance to strike back, to screw them over the way she thinks they screwed her over, and she seized it. Fuck, maybe I've got it all wrong. It could have been good old-fashioned greed. I clearly don't know my wife as well as I thought I did, so why would I think I could figure out her motivations on my own? There is only one person who can provide the answers I seek.

I'm self-aware enough to know I'm looking for an excuse to see her one last time before things get nasty, but I need this. I need to look her in the eyes and call her out. Only then will I be able to fully turn my back on her.

I BANG on Amber's door with my fist, ignoring the doorbell with its dreamcatcher hanging over the buzzer, twirling in the wind. There's no answer, and I bang again. I realize as I stand here that I haven't really thought this through—she might not be home. For all I know, she's found herself a new man already. My breath freezes in my lungs, and I slam both fists on the wooden door.

Finally, lights come on inside the house, and I hear footsteps on the stairs. If she has found another man and he's here with her, I won't be fucking responsible for my actions.

"Hey, asshole!" someone shouts from behind me. It's the voice of a two-pack-a-day smoker, full of gravel. "Shut the fuck up. Some of us are trying to sleep."

I turn around to see a vicious-looking old crone glaring out at me. Fuck, this must be the famous Mrs. Katzberg, the woman Drake thinks is former Special Forces. At only five feet tall, she still manages to be terrifying. Before I can respond, Amber opens the door, and I turn back, coming face-to-face with my wife. She doesn't look like a monster, but clichés are clichés for a reason—looks really can be deceiving.

"Amber, hon, you okay?" Mrs. Katzberg shouts. "You want me to call the cops or shoot him in the ass?" I have no doubt she's the kind who keeps a handgun next to her dentures, and I prepare to hit the ground.

"That's all right, Mrs. K," Amber calls back. "I appreciate it though. You go on and get back to sleep. I'll come by tomorrow so you can give me that recipe we talked about."

"All right, dear. You know how to reach me." This last part seems pointed, a threat, and as I turn to watch her close the door, the look that old woman sends my way has my balls crawling up inside my body. Jesus. If I still gave a fuck about Amber's safety, I would be sufficiently reassured by the presence of the vigilant battleax across the street.

Shivering in only a T-shirt that ends at mid-thigh, Amber glares up at me. That's my fucking Ramones T-shirt from a million years ago. "I thought you said you threw that in the trash."

"Yeah. Well. I lied. You'd better come in or Mrs. K will have a fit. She wasn't joking. She has a Mossberg shotgun in there."

She walks away without another word, and I follow her into the small house. Someone has been painting, and the smell of cocoa is in the air. The space is chintzy and cute, definitely the domain of women. I try to imagine a heartless, scheming bitch living here and struggle to make the two halves fit.

She leans against the kitchen counter, and I work hard at not noticing the legs. Or the hard nipples. Or the deliciously mussed-up hair.

"What do you want, Elijah?" There's no aggression in her tone. None of her signature frost either. She simply sounds sad and tired.

I look at her face, really look at it, and see how pale she is. Her eyes are red rimmed, and there are dark circles forming underneath. I don't think I've ever seen her look so broken, and I fight the urge to comfort her. "I want to know when you were going to tell me."

"Tell you what?"

"Fuck it, Amber, you know what."

She rubs at her eyes again and sighs. "Elijah, it's late, and I'm too tired for this. I can't play these games with you anymore. It's sick and it's cruel. So just ask what you want to ask and leave me in peace."

Huh. This is not the reaction I expected at all. I thought she'd be spitting like a cornered tiger, ready to scratch my eyes out.

"I agree. No more games. So how long has Freddie Kemp been representing you?"

She looks up at me sharply, her eyes huge. "What?" She's trembling, and her legs look like they're about to give out. Her skin goes even whiter, and as she tries to straighten up, her knees buckle and she starts to fall. I catch her under her armpits and heft her toward me. She sags against my body, then immediately starts flapping her hands like she's trying to fight me off. What the fuck is this? Some kind of act? She's pretending to be sick now?

"Let me go, I'm fine." She pushes away from me with weak shoves, but as soon as I loosen my hold, she staggers again. Shit. This isn't an act. She's a mess. I scoop her into my arms and carry her like a child into the living room, where I lay her on the couch and cover her with the pink crocheted blanket draped over the back of it. Brushing her hair back from her face, I note her unfocused eyes and wobbling lips.

"When's the last time you had something to eat?" I ask briskly. I'm still angry, and I still have questions, but she won't be answering them if she's unconscious.

"I don't know, breakfast maybe ... It doesn't matter. Just leave, Elijah, leave me alone like you did earlier. I don't need you." The words come out in an uneven flurry, and as she speaks, tears spill from her eyes. She bats me away, but I don't budge.

"I'm going to get you something to eat and some tea. I'll be right back."

As soon as I stand up, she curls into a ball under the blanket and buries her head in her arms, sobbing uncontrollably. I have no clue what's happening here, so I concentrate on the basics.

It doesn't take long to find what I need, and I whip up some buttered toast and a cup of the chamomile tea she likes, then add a couple chocolate chip cookies on the side. The cocoa I smelled earlier is still sitting in its mug, completely cold now. She must have made it and left it there when she went to bed.

I take in the signs of her life here: the colorful jars of tea and cocoa, a bowl of kiwi, a pile of paperwork. It's an invasion of her privacy, but I rifle through the pages. The top page reads "Leslie Odom Jr. Community Center Volunteer Application and Questionnaire," and her elegant handwriting fills every page. I study her answer to the question of why she wants to volunteer there, and her apparent naked honesty, her desire to have a lasting impact on the world around her, fills me with doubt. Why bother taking the time to complete a twelve-page questionnaire if this whole moving to Brooklyn and finding herself thing was a ruse?

Determined to get answers, I carry the food and tea back to the living room where she is still curled in a ball but has stopped sobbing.

"Amber, come on. You need to eat." I gently pry her hands from her head and encourage her to sit upright. She lets me maneuver her but pulls her knees up and refuses to meet my eyes. I tuck the blanket around her and pass her the plate. Her hands are shaking so damn much she struggles to get the food to her lips, and I don't think having me here is helping. "I'm going to use the bathroom, but eat and drink your tea. You need to get your strength up."

She doesn't respond, but she does nibble at the corner of a piece of toast, so I leave her and go find the bathroom, giving her a bit of space. After closing the door behind me, I let out a harshly whispered "Fuck!"

I came here full of self-righteous fury, and now she's gone and blown that all away. Nathan would say she's faking it, but I know my wife, and she is in real distress. Whether that's because she's been caught or for some other reason, I don't know yet.

This small, unmistakably feminine room oddly seems to fit her in a way none of the rooms in our house ever did. I absentmindedly pick up a bottle of shampoo from the side of the tub and sniff the coconut fragrance she uses these days. The budget-store brand toiletries are another glaring disparity, more evidence that there are way more pieces missing from the puzzle I came here looking to solve tonight.

Dead set on learning the truth once and for all, I splash my face with cold water and head back downstairs.

Giving her a moment paid off. She's eaten most of a slice of toast and nibbled at a cookie, and she is now sitting with the tea in her hands, steam forming a cloud in front of her face.

"You feeling better?" I ask, sitting down next to her.

She scoots her feet away as though she's scared of touching me. "Better, yes. Thank you. Now will you leave?"

"No. I won't. Not yet. I know you're not at your best, but I'm not leaving until I have answers. How long have you been cooking up this thing with Freddie?"

Again, the mention of his name makes the blood drain from her face, and she swallows hard before speaking. "I haven't been cooking up anything with Freddie, and I don't know what you're talking about. If that's all you're going to keep asking me, it's going to be a long night for both of us."

I suck in a breath and try to calm myself. Yelling at her when she's in this state won't help.

"Nathan saw you there, Amber. You must have known that he'd tell me."

She frowns up at me, looking confused. "What did he tell you?"

"That he saw you. That you had an appointment with Freddie Kemp, in his office, alone—that he's your attorney."

She looks at me like I've grown an extra head and sips more tea. Probably buying herself time. "I should have known he'd interpret it like that and that he'd come running straight to tell you what your big, bad bitch of a wife was getting up to." She shakes her head and huffs a humorless laugh. "I would have thought of it if I'd been thinking straight. It didn't even occur to me ... I'm so stupid." Her big brown eyes are glassy, but no tears fall. "Did you just ... just believe him?"

She sounds so fucking disappointed in me. I would rather her throw the damn tea in my face than hear that defeated tone in her voice.

"Of course I believed him. Nathan is many things, but

he's not a liar. If he says he saw you, he saw you. But I did also call Freddie."

"I see." She nods. "And? How did that go?"

"Well, he basically backed up what Nathan said. Said you'd been to see him, and he couldn't confirm you were his client because of confidentiality but that I could figure it out myself."

She laughs bitterly and puts the tea down. Her arms disappear under the blanket when she tugs it up over her shoulders. "Okay. I get it now. You think I've been pretending to go along with the civilized divorce plan, and all the while, I was secretly sneaking around behind your back. Plotting what exactly? To steal all your money? Your precious Jamestech?"

Her tone is calm and even, and I don't know what to think, so I simply shrug. "Something like that, yeah."

"And you think I've been sleeping with you for, what, spite? To pump you for information? To make you underestimate me?"

Those are all things I considered. She still isn't angry, and it's confusing the hell out of me. Maybe she simply lacks the energy, and as soon as the sugar hits, she'll be across this couch with her claws bared.

"Oh, Elijah. What have we become?" She drops her head back and closes her eyes. "How far have we fallen for you to believe that about me?" When she looks at me, the grief in her eyes guts me, but it doesn't match her resigned tone. "The irony is that I thought ... I thought we might actually make it, you know? I thought we might get back together. But here we are. Again. Me on one side, and you and your family on the other. You never even asked me. You didn't give me the benefit of the doubt. Instead, you automatically believed your brother, who hates me, and then you believed Freddie Kemp, who ..." Her voice falters, and she pulls the blanket up to cover her mouth. Tears fill her eyes again, and she stares down at where they fall in beads on the brightly colored yarn.

"Who what, Amber?" I say gently. I want to reach out and touch her, but her closed-off body language stops me. She needs her space right now. Eventually, she looks back up, and the pain in her expression sucks all the air from the room. She bites her lip and then nods—almost to herself, as though she's found some inner strength and is acknowledging it.

"Freddie Kemp, who assaulted me today."

TWENTY-EIGHT

ELIJAH

My brain freezes and time stands still. All I can do is stare at her. Finally, after what feels like hours, I find my voice. "He did *what*?"

"He assaulted me, Elijah. The man you're so convinced I'm in cahoots with tricked me into coming up to his office. I was supposed to be meeting Martha for drinks, and he got her to ask me to meet her there instead. I didn't think anything of it. I thought I was meeting a friend. Like I said, I'm stupid."

She sounds pissed now, but with herself. Not even half as angry as I am with myself though. "You're not stupid, Amber. Now tell me what happened. Please."

"Are you sure you want to know?" she asks, a flash of emotion in her eyes and a tremor in her voice. "Are you sure you'll believe me?"

This is a fucking shitshow. My wife is in pieces before me, and something horrible has clearly taken place. And now she doesn't want to tell me about it because she's worried I won't believe her. I came here so convinced I was in the right. I'm such a fucking dick.

"I'm sure, Amber. And yes, I will believe you, I promise."

She looks away from me again, squeezes her eyes shut tight, and starts to talk. "He said he wanted to represent me in the divorce. That's why he got Martha to lure me up there. That's how it started—he wanted to sign me, told me you were going to screw me over and only he could protect me. When I told him no, that I already had an attorney, he ... he changed. He was so jacked up, so on edge. He took my refusal as some kind of personal attack and started saying all kinds of crazy things. Calling me horrible names. And then, he backed me into a corner, and ... he ... Fuck! Why am I *crying* again?" She swipes at her eyes, and I can almost hear the pep talk she's giving herself.

Rage is eating away at my insides, but I force myself to stay calm. "It's okay, baby. Take your time. I'm not going anywhere."

She runs her hands through her hair and takes a deep, steadying breath. "Okay. I can do this," she mutters to herself before continuing. "He backed me into a corner. I tried to shove him away, but he pinned my wrists against the wall. He hurt me. Then he ... He rubbed himself against me, and ... ugh! He was hard. He made me touch it. He held my fingers there while he rubbed it into me. It was ... God, it was disgusting! That brought me to my senses, and I managed to get away, but up until then, I was paralyzed. Useless. I can't believe I let that happen to me."

She shudders and closes her eyes. I know she's reliving it right now. Today was probably one of the worst moments of her life, and I didn't give her the chance to tell me about it.

Instead of being there for her, I stood her up. Abandoned her when she needed me most. My stomach churns, and I can barely breathe through the fury I feel for myself. I'm going to fucking kill Freddie Kemp. But her needs come first.

I gently place my hand on her blanketed knee. She's shaking, but she doesn't pull away. "You didn't let it happen, Amber. It was not your fault. You know that, don't you? It was nobody's fault but his."

"I know that logically, Elijah. But I also feel like I should have stopped him. Like I somehow, I don't know, asked for it."

"No, baby, you didn't. I'm so sorry, if I had known ..." I don't finish that sentence, because there are no words to convey how fucking wrong I was and how goddamn awful I feel that I let her down. Again.

She stares at my hand on her knee, and I wonder if she'll let it stay there. She does. When she looks back up, though, there's such pain in her expression that it feels like she's torn my heart out of my chest.

"I wanted you to know, Elijah. The first thing I did when I got away was message you—after seeing Nathan, of course. That was lucky, wasn't it?" She lets out a hollow little laugh, and I remember my brother saying she was pale and shaky and not herself. We both assumed it was because she'd gotten caught.

"It had just happened when I asked if you could meet me earlier," she continues. "I was in the ladies' room, about to throw up. It wasn't something I wanted to talk about on the phone, and I was in shock. I was desperate to see you. Desperate to be with you and feel your arms around me and to feel ... safe again. Like I keep saying, I'm stupid."

No, it's me who's stupid. "And like I keep saying, you're not. I'm the asshole here, not you. Fuck, when I called Freddie, he was so weird with me …"

"He probably thought I'd told on him and expected you to tear him a new one."

I nod, narrowing my eyes as I replay the conversation. Yeah, that tracks. Technically, everything he said was true. He made implications that confirmed what I already feared, and like an idiot, I was ready and waiting to accept his lies. Primed by Nathan and my own underlying worries, I swallowed them whole.

Freddie must have known I'd eventually find out it was bullshit, but there was glee in his voice when he told me she'd been there. I gave him the opportunity to cause trouble, and he took it. He probably hoped it would scare her, show her how he could mess with her life. That he could distract us by setting up this conflict. The little shit is probably terrified of a visit from the cops. And that might still happen, depending on how things work out. Right now, though, I'm thinking the cops are too good for him. Justice might come a little more up close and personal. But that will all come later.

She's rubbing at bruises on her wrist. Bruises put there by Freddie Kemp. I bite down my fury at the thought of him touching her and take her hand in mine. I raise it up to my mouth and gently kiss the discolored skin.

Not only did I not show up for her today, but I deliberately left her there on her own. I knew what I was doing. I was torturing her, getting petty revenge for something she didn't do. I wanted her to suffer. And I got what I wanted.

"I messaged you … on the burner phone. I told you something terrible had happened. I told you I loved you. That I needed you. You never replied. That was ... This will sound silly, but that hurt more than what happened with Freddie."

My heart cracks in two. I let her down in the worst possible way, and I wouldn't blame her if she never forgives me for it. I will never forgive myself. "It doesn't sound silly. But I didn't get the message. I ... I was so angry, so upset. I destroyed the phone."

"Oh. Well. I hope that made you feel better." The hint of snark in her tone actually does make me feel a little better. I fucking deserve it.

"It didn't. Look, I'm so sorry, Amber. I'm so fucking sorry. About everything. I had no right to treat you like that. I listened to Nathan, and I listened to fucking Freddie, and I listened to my own insecurities, when I should have been listening to you. I know it's not an excuse, but I was so damn broken, baby. I was planning to ask you to come back to me. I wanted us to get back together. I was terrified you would say no, but I was willing to risk it. I hated being apart from you."

She nods and lets her hand stay in mine. "That's what I wanted too, Elijah."

"Wanted?" Past tense. My heart, already broken, shatters. "Is there no way past this? I know I was wrong. I was the world's biggest jerk. Something awful happened to you, and I wasn't there when you needed me—but I love you, Amber. With all my fucking heart, I love you."

"Maybe you do, Elijah, but ..." She squeezes my fingers and pulls her hand away, back under the pink blanket. "Nothing is ever going to change. You'll always have Nathan and the others pouring poison in your ear. You chose him over me, again. Do you know how that makes me feel? It makes me feel small and pointless and pathetic. I'll always be second best, and I don't deserve that. I don't deserve it, and I won't take it. Not anymore."

Her words are strong, but her voice is not. She still sounds shaken, and her lips are trembling again. She's clinging to her self-control, forcing herself to be brave. She's also right. About everything.

"No, you don't deserve that, Amber, you really don't. And believe me, I wish I could go back in time and change the way I handled everything. I can't. All I can do is apologize and tell you I love you and promise you I will never *ever* react like that again."

"Oh, honey." She manages a small smile. "I know you mean that now, I do. But I'm not sure I can trust you to remember that promise. I think maybe too much damage has been done. On both sides. When Freddie ..." Her voice cracks. She clears her throat and continues. "When he touched me like that, my instinct was to reach out to you. To rely on you. You let me down, Elijah, and you know what the truly sad thing is? I wasn't all that surprised."

Fuck. She couldn't have hurt me more if she'd stabbed me in the heart. And I can't dispute a word of what she said.

I kneel on the floor beside the couch and take her face in my hands. Her skin is soft against my palms, and her eyes meet mine. There's still no anger there, and it kills me. She should be furious. She should be raging and ranting and calling me every name under the sun. Instead, she seems resigned. As if this is the only reality she's ever known. All the fight has gone out of her.

I kiss her very gently, a simple touch of my lips on hers, slow and cautious in case the trauma of the day makes even this delicate contact too much for her. We lean our foreheads against each other and stay like that for a long moment.

"I did let you down, Amber. And I have no idea if there's any way I can ever make it up to you, or if you'll let me try. Believe me, I am willing. I will do anything I need to do to prove myself to you. Whatever you want. Whatever you need. I know you might not be able to see a future for us right at this moment. I understand that. I fucked up. There isn't a quick fix for any of this, but tonight, I'd like to stay here with you."

"Why?" she asks.

"Because I can't stand the thought of you being alone, and truthfully, I don't want to be alone either. I'll stay on the couch if that helps, and if you say you don't want me here, then hell, I'll sleep on the front stoop. But I need to be near you. I'm not asking you to make a commitment or a promise, and you'd be within your rights if you wake up in the morning and decide you never want to see me again. But for tonight, please, just let me take care of you."

I feel her tremble against me and wait with my heart pounding as she considers it. Finally, she gives a small, shaky nod.

TWENTY-NINE

AMBER

I wake up in his arms, and for a split second, it's glorious. His solid chest rises and falls beneath my cheek, our legs tangled up together between the sheets, our bodies melted into one. I sigh and slowly awaken.

As soon as I do, the horrors of the day before crash down on me. Freddie. Nathan. Sitting alone in Greenwich Village after Elijah discarded me like a used tissue. The journey back here and my gradual descent into emotional chaos. Being unable to eat or drink and getting sick with nothing but bile to purge from my stomach. I cried until my eyes were gritty and swollen, and as soon as I drifted off into a restless doze, Elijah was hammering on my door.

I don't regret letting him stay—I slept surprisingly well wrapped up in my husband. My mind allowed itself to be hoodwinked, let me feel safe for one night. But now, as the bright winter sunlight creeps in around the drapes, a new day begins. I take deep breaths and try to steady myself before panic can grab hold of me. I'm not at all sure I want this new day.

"Morning, baby," Elijah says, stroking my upper arms, holding me close. I look up and almost melt at the sight of his deep gray eyes brimming with love. His hair is all messy, and he gives me his lopsided smile before dropping a gentle and reassuring kiss on my head. "How are you feeling?"

"I don't really know," I answer honestly. "I'm glad you stayed. Thank you for that. But ..."

"But it doesn't change anything? I know that, baby. I didn't expect it to. I've been thinking about what you said, and you were right. I didn't want to believe Nathan, but I did anyway. I thought I was being impartial by fact-checking with Freddie—that I was doing my due diligence by calling the dickhead who assaulted you. I didn't put you first, and I didn't trust you enough to stand by you. That was a mistake, and I can't promise I won't make other mistakes. All I can say is that I want to try. I want to give us another shot. Give it our best shot. I love you, Amber, and I'm not ready to let you go."

It's a pretty speech, and I have to smile at the thought of him rehearsing it. "You've been awake for a while, huh?"

"Fuck yes," he says, laughing. "I was waiting for you to open your eyes so I could say all of that. But I mean it, every single word. Give me another chance. Give us another chance. At least say you'll think about it."

I lie against him, enjoying the feel of his silky chest hair against my face. I still feel comforted by his presence, but I don't trust him to be present when I need him. "I'm not making any promises, Elijah. Right now, my answer would be no—so if you want it to be yes, you'll need to give me some time and space. And I don't think I'm the only person who needs to think about it. You need to really think about what it would mean if we got back together. For you, for your family—it would cause as much conflict as us splitting up did. That's a lot for you to cope with, being pulled in two different directions."

It would also be a lot for me to cope with, but I don't say that. I don't think I need to. While pretending that we were merely having an affair, we managed to rebuild a great deal of our foundation and to forge a new bridge of trust. In one fell swoop, that has all been swept away. The wound that was healing has been ripped open once more, and I don't know if either of us truly has the energy to start all over again.

"I hear you, but I assure you that I have thought about it, Amber. I will give you time and space if that's what you need, but I don't. You are the one I choose. And I know it will take practice, that it won't be as simple as choosing you every single time, but I will do the work. If it helps, we could, I don't know, maybe look at getting some counseling?" His voice, so confident throughout most of his speech, falters with that last sentence, and I laugh, surprised.

"I'm almost tempted to say yes just to see you on a thera-pist's couch. I see from the state of your knuckles that you've been indulging in your normal therapy and punching things?"

He shrugs and nods. "What can I say? I like punching things."

"I know you do. Ha, you and counseling … You know it would only work if the whole family came along, right? Your dad, Mason, Maddox, Drake, Nathan … Maybe even Luke. All the James boys together."

He grins and rubs his hand over his beard. "Yeah. We're

gonna need a bigger couch." The joke is weak, but it breaks some of the tension. "I love you in this Ramones shirt, by the way. Why did you tell me you'd thrown it away?"

There's no point in lying about it now. "I thought keeping it made me look weak. I didn't want you to think I'd gone soft, so I hid it and only wore it when you were away. It made me feel safe ... even when you didn't."

He swallows, and I know that must have hurt. But it wasn't said out of spite, and I'm so tired of hiding. "Right. And you wore it last night, after I let you down. I promise you, I'll do everything in my power to never let you down again."

"You can't promise me that, Elijah. Just like I can't promise you I'll never be a cold bitch again or that I'll never shut you out again. We've both played our part in where we are now. Breaking our marriage was a team sport."

He murmurs something that might be agreement, and I realize I've started to run my fingers through his chest hair. My leg has slipped over his thighs as we talked, and his breath is coming a little heavier. I can feel his heart booming inside his rib cage. My hand slides down his chest and glides across his taut abs. He sucks in air as I reach lower.

"Jesus, baby, I'm sorry," he mutters. "That's fucking embarrassing."

His cock is solid under his boxers, straining and twitching beneath my feather-light touch. "Why embarrassing?" I ask, a slow flutter thrumming in my core.

"Because of the way I behaved yesterday—because of what you went through with Freddie. I stayed to look after you, but now I have a raging hard-on. I'm pretty damn sure that's the last thing you need."

It should be, I know. I should be running from the room or kicking him out of bed. But, well, I'm not. In fact, my hand has drifted inside his boxers. I stroke his shaft, exploring its rock-hard length. My fingers caress his heavy balls, and he moans. "Amber, sweetheart, please stop."

"Why?" I rock gently against his side, my pussy rubbing against him in a way that makes my whole body pulse.

"Because if you don't stop, I'm going to end up fucking you, and I don't think that would be right."

"Really?" I whisper, rubbing the head of his cock and finding a drop of pre-cum to massage away. "This doesn't feel right to you?"

"Of course it fucking does." He sounds anguished as he places his hand over mine as though to move it away from him. "But—"

"But now I'm too damaged to fuck, is that it, Elijah?" I sit up and look him in the eyes. "Let me tell you something—Freddie Kemp is not going to win. Freddie Kemp is a disgusting pervert, and he is not going to stop me from enjoying sex. I don't want the last cock I touch to be his. I want ... I want *you*, Elijah."

Under the covers, I tug off my panties and pull down his boxers, then climb on top of him. I'm already wet, my pussy slipping along his shaft as I writhe, desperate to be filled. "This might not make sense, Elijah, but I need this. No matter what happens between us long-term, I need this from you now. I need you to help me chase his memory away. Can you do that for me?"

I work my hips slowly, coating him in my arousal. He pulls the shirt off me and throws it to the floor, staring at my pussy all the time. "Yeah, I can do that for you. Fuck, look at you … so wet already. Ride me, Amber. Slide yourself onto me. I'm all yours."

I'm more than ready for him, and I sigh as I hit the right angle and impale myself on his impressive length. I hold my breath, lowering myself onto him completely, feeling deliciously stretched and full. He keeps his big hands on my waist, and his eyes are intense as I move. He normally likes to be more in charge than this, and I can see him battling his own instincts, but he gives me control.

The pressure builds quickly, my clit throbbing with every thrust of my hips. He doesn't even need to touch me there; the friction between us is already setting me on fire. He glides his hands up my body, palms my breasts, and pinches my nipples in exactly the way I like. "God, you're the most beautiful thing I've ever seen in my life. I can feel you squeezing me, baby. Fuck, that's so good."

I love the way he looks under me, his huge, muscular physique splayed on my bed, his eyes hazy with lust. I put my hands on his shoulders and increase my pace. He leans up and sucks a nipple into his mouth, and it's enough to push me over the edge.

"Elijah!" I cry out, my nails digging into his flesh as I come. Ripples of pure bliss wash over me, my hips jerking.

He growls and, in one slick move, roughly positions me underneath him, keeping his cock inside me the whole time. I gasp in surprise, and he pauses. "Is this okay?" he asks softly as I wrap my trembling legs around his ass.

"Yes, it's okay. Fuck me, Elijah. Fuck me hard."

He puts his hands on either side of my head and looks me in the eye. "Ready?" he asks, grinning wickedly.

He doesn't give me a chance to answer—he takes my

breath away as he begins to rail into me. I grab his shoulders, holding on for dear life as he nails me to the mattress. Speed, power, and a massive cock—the lethal combination soon has me screaming his name and coming yet again.

Our sweat-slickened bodies slide together. "I. Fucking. Love. You," he grunts as he thrusts. Then he stills, finding his release, looking magnificent and wild. After he collapses beside me, he immediately scoops me into his arms. He knows I'm a flight risk and doesn't seem to want to let me go.

I settle on his chest, letting myself enjoy the moment. "You seem tired," I tease. "I think you need to work on your cardio." He slaps me firmly on the ass, which is what I was hoping for. I like the pleasant sting it spreads over my skin.

He notices my reaction, of course, and raises an eyebrow. "You in the mood for another spanking? I'm happy to oblige."

He holds up one of his huge hands, and my pussy clenches a little. I laugh. "Tempting offer, but no thank you. I do actually have stuff I need to do today. And I might need to sit down while I do it."

Also, I cannot allow myself to be tempted back into the world of Mr. and Mrs. Smith. We just had sex, and it was fantastic sex—but I need a clear head. This needs to be the last time, at least for a while. I meant what I said when I told him I needed time and space.

"You have your interview at the center, right?"

"More of an informal chat from what I've been told. See if we're a good fit."

"It will go great. They'll be lucky to have you." He squeezes me tighter and plants a kiss on the top of my head. "I heard what you said earlier, and I will give you the time and space you need, but will you let me hold onto you a bit longer?"

I nod and snuggle into him, allowing us both a few more minutes. When I kiss his chest and sit up, he smooths my hair back from my face and gives me a comforting smile. "I know this is bit of a mood killer, but before I go, I need to ask ... What do you want to do about Freddie?" The name causes me to tense up, but Elijah expected it and is already soothing me with long strokes down my spine.

I close my eyes and take a deep breath. "I don't know. I was asking myself that yesterday. I'd be lying if I said part of me doesn't want to forget all about it. That would be easier, but it would also make me a coward."

"No, it would make you human. You had a traumatic experience. Of course you want to forget about it. And if that's what you choose, then I will support you. But ..."

"But I won't have been the first." I sigh. "He was so cocky. So confident. This wasn't the first time he assaulted a woman."

"I think you're right. The way he spoke to me too ... He was laughing. He obviously thought he'd gotten away with it again, and I suspect he's been doing this for years." He grits his teeth, his expression like thunder. "If you're up for it, I'd like to make sure that, although you weren't the first, you will be the last."

"Do you think we should call the police?"

"We could do that," he offers. "Or you could leave it to me."

"What do you mean?" I ask, frowning. "Elijah, I know what you're like, how protective you are—I can't stand the man, but please don't kill him, okay?"

He sucks his upper lip, and I can tell he's considered it. My husband, the psychopath. "I won't kill him. But I will make sure he never hurts another woman. Do you trust me?" I raise my eyebrows, and he adds, "Do you trust me with this one particular thing? I promise I won't end up on death row."

"And also promise me you won't do anything that hurts Martha."

He scowls. "Why do you give a fuck about her? She was part of this."

"Yes, but ... We aren't besties or anything, but I know Martha. She's ... Okay, sometimes she's vapid and self-obsessed and shallow, but most of that seems like an act. She reminds me of a wounded bird, Elijah. Her husband ..." I shake my head. "He hurts women for sport. I can just imagine how much abuse she's taken over the years. And their girls, they're only fifteen. They're innocent in all of this. When I was waiting for you, before— Well, I considered involving the police, but I kept coming back to the same thing: What would it do to those poor girls if their dad was all over the media for being a sexual predator?"

Sighing, he nods. "Yeah. Okay." Then he shakes his head and gazes at me with wonder. "You're amazing, you know that?" Before I can think of how to respond, he continues. "Let me handle it, all right? I promise I will make sure Martha and the girls are protected. But that little shit will rue the day he ever touched you." The quiet, deadly fury in his voice sends a shiver down my spine. He is always civilized on the surface, but when the people he loves are hurt, well.

Freddie Kemp is about to discover exactly what lies under the polished James veneer. If only I could be a fly on the wall.

I wriggle up in his arms and kiss him lightly. "All right, I'll let you handle it. And please, don't tell Drake or Nathan or anyone else. I'm not ashamed—I have nothing to be ashamed of—but I don't want to rehash any of this with them."

"Of course, baby. Anything you want."

"Right now, I want to go so I can get ready for my meeting," I say, jumping out of bed before he can stop me.

He climbs out of bed and stretches. Hell's bells, he really is a work of art. I pick up the Ramones T-shirt and throw it at him. "You can take this with you if you'd like."

"Nah." Giving me a knowing look, he slowly rubs it over his chest. "I think I'll leave this here with you. So you won't forget about me."

I walk away as though I'm not at all bothered.

Fat chance, I think as I escape into the hallway, my cheeks blazing, the image of his gorgeous body seared on my eyeballs. I couldn't forget him if I tried.

THIRTY

ELIJAH

I get dressed and call Gretchen, planning to head straight to see Nathan. Amber promised she's doing better, and I made sure she ate before I left. Sanjay is going to take her to Queens and wait there until she's done, which makes me feel more relaxed about leaving her. I'm hardly in a position to preach about Queens being dangerous, anyway, not after Freddie's assault. Having a Manhattan zip code doesn't mean you're safe—and he's about to find that out himself. The hard way.

My brother's secretary looks taken aback as I stride toward her, which is understandable. I think this is the first time I've left the house in sweatpants since college. "Good morning, Helen. Is he in?" I ask, pausing politely at her desk. The etiquette is more for her sake than his. I'm going into his office no matter what she says.

"He is, Mr. James. He has a call coming from Hong Kong in about half an hour, though."

I nod and smile. "No problem. I'll make sure I'm done by then."

I knock and go straight in. Nathan is staring at his computer screen, a pile of paperwork on his desk. He specializes in criminal law, and that has given him connections that I'm hoping to make use of. He looks up, his dark eyes taking in my outfit. He'll see it as a sign of an impending mental breakdown for sure.

"Jesus," he says, gesturing at my sweatpants with the pencil he's holding. "Did you get mugged or wake up in the drunk tank? You look like you got those from the lost and found."

I bark out a laugh—funny fucker—and sit down opposite him, the painting our mom did of the beach we used to vacation at in Spain on the wall behind him. I wanted to take Amber there once, but by the time I asked, too much damage had been done. She gave me some line about not wanting to be away from her friends, which I now see was bullshit. She doesn't have close friends. She just didn't want to be with me in a place that was so much a part of the James family legend.

"You okay?" he asks, his eyes skimming my scabbed knuckles. He misses nothing and is usually the best judge of character I know. Amber is his blind spot. Or maybe wives are, because he once jumped to a conclusion about his own wife that almost cost him his marriage.

Part of me is pissed at him for the role he played in all of this. The way he jumped to the wrong conclusion about Amber and convinced me he was right. But I clamp down on that, because the only person who deserves my ire is me. I'm her husband, the man who claims to love her. The man who wants her back. It was down to me to do the right thing, not him.

"No, I'm not okay. It was all bullshit, Nathan. She isn't being represented by Freddie Kemp. We were wrong."

His nostrils flare, and the pencil in his hand snaps in half. "I wasn't wrong, Elijah. She was there. You think I'd make that shit up?"

"No, of course I fucking don't, so calm the fuck down. Yes, she was there. But she isn't his client. Drake is her only attorney, and she has no intention of going after Jamestech. It was a setup."

His eyes narrow. He doesn't believe what I'm saying. I slam my hand down on his desk, but he doesn't react at all. Goddamn Ice Man. "Nate, I am telling you the truth. There are things going on that you don't know about, and no, I'm not going to tell you what they are. Not everything needs to be out in the open here. I know you think I'm weak when it comes to Amber, but in this case, I'm right. You need to drop it. You don't have to trust her, but I assume you trust me?"

He waits a beat, then gives a terse nod. "Yeah. I do."

"Okay, well, you're just gonna have to go with that then —I understand why you thought what you did, but you were wrong. And now, I need you to put me in touch with Shane Ryan. Or actually, his wife—or is she Conor's?"

His eyebrows knit together. "Yes, she's their wife. It's complicated. More importantly, why do you need to speak to the Ryans? They're not from your world."

Nathan and Drake both have clients whose relationship with law and order is a tad loose to say the least. The Ryans here, the Morettis in Chicago—neither are what you'd call model citizens. I know this, but I also know my brothers—no matter what kind of reputation men like the Ryans have,

Nathan would not defend them if he thought they were bad people.

"I'm going to keep this simple—I need to speak to them about a little thing called *none of your fucking business*. And I'm not saying that to be an asshole. I'm saying it because as their lawyer—fuck, as my lawyer—you really don't want to know."

"Plausible deniability?" he asks, smirking.

"Exactly. Now, are you going to help me or not?"

"Of course I'm going to fucking help you—you're my big brother. Just tread carefully, all right? These men are not to be messed with—Jessie even less so. She could have you on a terrorist watchlist and shipped to Guantanamo in ten seconds flat."

"Duly noted."

"And speak to Shane first. I'm giving you his number, not hers."

"Why? Isn't she allowed to speak for herself?"

He laughs. "You wouldn't ask that if you'd met her. Yeah, she's allowed to speak for herself, but the Ryans are protective of her."

If anyone can understand that instinct, it's me right now.

He scribbles a number down on a piece of paper, using the stubby end of the pencil he broke, and passes it to me.

"Elijah?" he calls as I'm about to leave.

I turn back around. "Yeah?"

"I'm sorry, okay? If you're right and Amber was completely innocent, I'm sorry I put you through all of that."

I nod my understanding. He didn't do it to cause me pain, but that doesn't make the hurt that's been caused any less real. Who the hell knows if I will ever be able to win her trust back. For now, I will concentrate on what I can control—I am going to fuck up Freddie Kemp's life.

THIRTY-ONE

AMBER

"So, what shall we dance to?" the red-haired woman standing opposite me asks. "A bit of Backstreet Boys? Some old school disco? Oh, I know, I know."

She leaps to her feet, fingers flying over her phone, then grins at me, her blue eyes sparkling. "I love *Madagascar*, don't you?"

I'm pretty damn confused by this point, but I recognize the song as soon as it kicks on—"I Like to Move It" by Reel to Real. It's a terrific song to dance to, but it's really not what I expected at an interview. I was told it would be informal, but this is more of an impromptu party. "Shawn!" she hollers, her voice piercing even over the beat of the music. "Can you make this louder?"

A blond-haired boy of ten or eleven looks up at her from his corner of the room. It's a big space, like a school gym, with various activities going on around us. He nods and takes the phone over to a sound system, and within seconds, the track is blasting from speakers positioned around the room. "Come on, let's get jiggy," yells Sissie, gesturing for everyone to join in. I can't help smiling as children of all ages, shapes, and sizes run to the center of the floor and begin getting extremely jiggy.

She's in the middle of it all, her long red hair flowing, her Crocs stamping the floor as she moves. Nobody seems to have any inhibitions at all, and I decide that I won't have any either. Before long, I'm lost to the joy of dancing. Children swirl and jump all around me, and some offer their hands up for me to hold. I laugh and twirl them around, and for the chorus, I put together a small routine that involves a little shaking of the tail feathers. They all copy me, and when the next song turns out to be the "Cha-Cha Slide," I lead them in an energetic line dance. So what if some of them don't know their left from their right—including Sissie. It's a lot of fun, and we're all laughing as the music fades. Shawn, the gangly youth with the technical skills, comes over to offer me a high five before going back to his corner. He's got a large stack of schoolbooks and pencils scattered on the floor.

"He's talented," I say, nodding in his direction. "He can really dance."

"Shawn? Yeah. He's a great kid. Nice mom, too. She just doesn't have enough of herself to go round, working three jobs to support the family. The dad is long gone, and from the sound of it, good riddance. Shawn really enjoyed the dance classes Esther ran. She always said he had raw talent."

Esther, I have gathered, was something of a legend around these parts. In her eighties, she was still doing the splits at her going-away party. She retired to Florida, where she's apparently teaching her new community a thing or two about the can-can. I have no idea how I could possibly fill such boots.

"Well, Amber, if you're interested, you're welcome to join us here. Assuming you know what you're getting into."

"What?" I follow her out into a quieter part of the building. "But we haven't really talked ..."

She makes a "pah!" kind of noise and waves her hand. "I'm a big believer in instinct, and my instincts say you'll do great here. The kids clearly like you. You know what you're doing on the dance floor, and even though I could tell you were uncomfortable, you joined in anyway. That tells me you've got balls. So, balls plus ability plus gumption ..." Sissie gives a decisive nod. "You'll do just fine."

"Gumption?" I repeat, smiling. "Isn't that the kind of thing Calamity Jane had?"

"Yep, and you need it around here, believe me."

"Okay. I have it. Gumption is my middle name. Sign me up."

She laughs at my enthusiasm, and I grin back at her. I had high hopes, but I like it here even more than I expected. And Sissie is nothing at all like I expected. In my head, former nun translated to her being old and demure. But she's maybe in her late forties and is an absolute firecracker. Short, buxom, and extremely pretty in a wholesome, no-makeup way, Sissie—formerly Sister Bridget—is obviously a woman who wades in wherever she's needed and gets things done. She's the perfect role model for me in this new chapter of my life.

"You do know that I don't have any qualifications, right?" I want to do this so badly, and I don't want any more disappointments. "Well, apart from a useless college degree."

"No such thing as useless. I'm sure you picked up something valuable from it."

Yeah, I think as she leads us to a seating area by the windows. My husband, and not much else. We sit surrounded by battered metal lockers and walls covered in beautiful graffiti art.

"I know you're not an experienced teacher, Amber, but most of the people here don't have formal qualifications. We care more about commitment. If you do want training, we have a small budget and could maybe find you some courses to take."

"If there are any courses that would help me add value, I would love to take them, but I'll handle the costs. Has Vicky told you much about me?"

She tilts her head to one side. "A little. Nothing too personal, don't worry. She's held true to the Cleaners' Code."

"There's a Cleaners' Code?"

Sissie laughs. "No idea, but Vicky isn't a gossip. I do know that your background is a world away from this place. She swears you are good people, and I believe her, but I suppose I do need to ask—are you sure about this? Like I said, I'd love to get you involved, but I don't want this to be something you're doing as some kind of experiment with slumming it, you know? I don't want the kids to get used to you just in time for you to disappear back to your Manhattan mansion. No offense."

I nod and look through the windows. The community garden is out there, and it's obvious how gorgeous it will be come spring. They're growing fruits and vegetables for the neighborhood, and they even have a small apiary.

"That's a fair question, Sissie, and no offense taken. I do actually have a Manhattan mansion, but I swapped it for a two-bedroom in Brooklyn. My husband and I are getting a divorce, and I … I couldn't stand that life anymore. Money buys security, and security is necessary, and I know I'm coming from a place of privilege when I say this—but wealth truly doesn't bring happiness. I'm deeply grateful for the fact that I've never worried about paying for groceries. But I have experienced very little joy in my life. I need joy, Sissie, and I'm making changes that allow me to find it."

"Good for you, Amber." She nods, looking interested and, dare I say, impressed. "Is there any concern about your husband causing trouble? Divorces can get ugly, and it won't disqualify you, but we need to know what we're dealing with so we can handle it."

"God, no. He's … He's great, in so many ways. You definitely don't have to worry about him causing trouble. Truthfully, I still love the man. But it isn't working, and I don't think it ever will. I've reached the stage where I need to accept that and start to build a life that doesn't have him at the center of it."

I feel terrible as I say those words, like I'm somehow betraying him. But their truth is evident in the way I've blossomed since I began centering myself. Who knows how things will play out between us in the future or if we will ever get our shit together.

Whatever happens, I need to have my own life. I need to be the leading lady of my own story, not just play a supporting role in his. Dancing in a community center with a load of kids and a slightly eccentric former nun was liberating—because it had nothing at all to do with my former life.

"You're recreating yourself," she says. "Phoenix, ashes, all that shit. I get it. I did it myself. Well, okay, if you want in, you're in. But before you decide for sure, did Vicky mention the uh, guys who help us?"

"She said something about bikers?"

She chews the inside of her cheek. "So, there are a lot of great people in this neighborhood. The vast majority are decent and hardworking. Normal folks. But there are also problems, bad elements. They harass the neighborhood kids, try to encourage them to get involved in stuff they shouldn't. You know what I mean? We try to offer them an alternative. Shawn's a good example. He's a smart boy, and his mom has been working her ass off to keep him on the right path—but he's also cute and fast and would be an asset."

"Why?" I ask. "I'm sorry to sound naive, but what use could he be to them?"

"Kids like Shawn are useful to some of the less law-abiding folk around these parts. Looking innocent goes a long way. They're also expendable."

I blanch at the idea of any child being expendable to anyone, but I'm not so naive as to believe Sissie is exaggerating. "That's where the bikers come in. Informal security. They help us keep this place nice and friendly. Other than the boxing and wrestling classes. And the baking contests." She laughs. "Those can get pretty hairy."

I'd be lying if I said I don't have a moment of doubt. Not fear exactly, because this seems like a safe place, but more of a concern that I truly don't belong in this world. Never have I considered myself a snob, but I've been accused of it enough times that I can't pretend like the shoe doesn't fit at all.

What if I'm as vapid as Elijah's brothers think I am and I let these kids down by not being able to ignore the siren call of high society, designer shoes, and exclusive dinner reservations? No. That's not possible. I've felt more joy since I moved out of Manhattan and walked away from that life than I have felt in the previous ten years combined.

"Tell me about the bikers," I say.

"Well, they're called Misfits MC—motorcycle club in case you hadn't figured it out—and the clue is kind of in the name. Most MCs are made up of pretty stereotypical macho dudes with big bikes and small dicks."

I laugh at her choice of words, and she winks at me. "These guys are different."

"They have small bikes and big dicks?"

"The bikes are plenty big, and I cannot comment on the dicks. But they're from all over, you know? Different types of people from different backgrounds. It shouldn't work, but it does. Rafael is in charge. He's Salvadoran. He ended up here after doing a stretch in Rikers for smashing someone's head in for kicking their dog."

"I like him already."

"He's easy to like. Not all of them are. They're all tough men who've had hard lives. They're like a family—a really fucked-up family. They're around a lot, and your paths will cross, which is why I'm telling you all of this. They're our protectors. They have enough muscle and enough crazy that even the gangs are wary of them. They help us keep this place safe."

I try to imagine their world—the one these kids live in, where they need bikers to keep them safe from gangs—but I can't. All I can do is try to add something positive to it. "Here's Rafael now," she says, nodding at the window. The throaty roar of an engine is followed by a massive motorcycle pulling up outside the building. "I told him you were coming, and he wanted to meet you. Don't try to get him to dance, okay?"

I laugh, but my mind immediately goes back to that night in the studio with Elijah. The way he tried to match my warm-up, even after he pulled a muscle in his back. The way he held me in that lift, so strong and reliable and so damn hot. The amazing sex afterward ...

Shut up, shut up, shut up!

But I can't help wondering what he's up to right now. I'm worried he might do something reckless about Freddie and get himself into trouble. Deciding I'll call him as soon as I'm done here, I put him out of my mind.

The giant of a man switches off the bike's engine and meets my eyes through the glass. He nods once in acknowledgment, and I nod back, admiring the graceful way he dismounts and strides toward the building with his helmet under his arm, all muscle and tattoos. He wears a black tank underneath his leathers, and every inch of visible skin is inked, right up to his throat. His intimidating appearance is offset only slightly by a classically handsome face—square jaw, high cheekbones, deep brown eyes. His mouth is wide and his lips full, and they quirk at the corners when he steps into the room and greets Sissie. I'm guessing that's this man's version of a full-on grin.

"Mrs. James," he says, his voice deep and surprisingly quiet, a hint of an accent I can't place coming through. "It's nice to meet you. My name is Rafael Reyes." He tugs off a leather glove and offers me a meaty hand to shake. It completely engulfs mine, and his fingers are covered in tattoos.

"Did that hurt?" I ask, staring at the elaborate designs swirling between his knuckles.

"Like a motherfucker," he replies, half smiling. He lets go of my hand and quirks one eyebrow at Sissie.

"As you can see, Amber, Rafael here is not a big talker. That eyebrow just asked me what I've decided about you, whether you'll be joining our merry little team here. And yes, Rafael, she will be—assuming that is what she wants?"

They both turn to look at me, and I feel the weight of their gazes. They both seem like tremendous people in their own way, albeit completely outside my entire sphere of experience. But they give off nothing but positive energy, and I know that this is what I want. I wasn't lying when I said I need joy, and I can find that here. I can make a difference here in a way that has nothing to do with money or the family I married into.

"I'd love to join you," I say. "And I promise I'll do my very best."

Rafael nods once. "That's all we can ask, ma'am."

THIRTY-TWO

ELIJAH

Less than an hour after I first spoke to Shane Ryan, he calls me back. "The information you requested has been delivered to your office," he says. He's no-nonsense, and I like that.

"That was … quick."

"Our girl is the best in the business. Plus, she says this asshole was so arrogant he didn't bother covering his tracks. It was all there on his laptop, waiting for someone like her to come along and find it. Not that there is anyone else like her."

"Well, I appreciate it. How do I compensate Jessie for her time?"

"No need. She'd be insulted if you tried. She considers it her honor to take down scum like this. What are you going to do with this information? I hope I don't have to point out that it can't be used in court, and it can't come back to her."

"No, I understand. And I'm going to use it to fuck him up. It's possible I may also beat the crap out of him."

He laughs, and it's not an especially pleasant sound.

"Sounds like a plan. You need any help with that second part, you know where we are."

As I hang up, Beverley knocks on my door and brings me a thumb drive in the shape of an actual thumb. Huh. I take my time familiarizing myself with its contents, and by the end of it, I have a clear picture of what Freddie has been up to. Amber was far from the first woman he abused, as we suspected. He's done the same thing to several clients and female employees. There are emails about it going back years, and I'm guessing this is only the tip of the iceberg. Most of the women will have done what Amber's first instinct was, try to forget about it, and who can blame them? The man is powerful and rich, a master manipulator.

The ones Jessie found details about are the ones who tried to take him on. Several threatened legal action, and one went so far as to file a police report. That went away because there was no evidence. It was her word against his, and she was an office cleaner who had only recently moved here from Puerto Rico. I wouldn't be surprised if cash exchanged hands with law enforcement also. The other women he basically threatened right back—but bigger, better, and with more bite. He told them he'd take their homes, their jobs, their whole lives. If they told, nobody would believe them anyway, he said—he was too well connected, too well respected.

Fuck, it turns my stomach. I have no idea if he really could have done all the things he threatened, but eventually, they all believed he could and went away. And Freddie just carried on hurting more and more women. I despised him when I thought he was merely an adulterer and a creep— now I'd like to wipe him from the face of the earth. I force myself to sit and think this through, because anything I do now will not be done with a sound mind.

I print out the information, along with photos of some of the women. Once that's done, I sit a while longer. After twenty minutes, I still don't seem to be getting any calmer. My quest for a sound mind is doomed. When I went home to shower and change, I put on one of my favorite shirts, but fuck it. I can get a new shirt.

Freddie's office isn't far and I have a lot of excess energy to burn off, so I choose to walk. Without engaging with the receptionist, his assistant, or anyone else—I'm too mad to behave like a civilized human being—I storm right into his office and slam the door in the face of the spluttering young man chasing me.

"You want me to call security, Mr. Kemp?" the kid yells through the door as I stalk toward Freddie's desk. I loom over him for a few seconds, then sit down in the guest chair, enjoying his confusion. I can pretty much hear the wheels of his brain turning, working to figure out all the angles.

"No thanks, Tom," he calls back. "Mr. James here is an old friend."

"Are ... Are you sure?"

"Yes, I'm fucking sure. Go away, Tom."

Freddie finally gives me his full attention, and I glare back at him, beyond furious but keeping it under control. "What can I do for you, Elijah?" he says, smiling smugly.

I want to put my fist through the little runt's face. Instead, I lay the photos on his desk so they're facing him. "Samantha Salazar. Michelle Lowe. Andrea Sherman. Cindy Hernandez. Charlotte Carter. These names mean anything to you, Freddie?"

He gazes down at them, and I have to admit, he's good. Like Drake and Nathan, he has a superb lawyer face. I wouldn't want to play poker against any of them. Other than the slightest twitch of an eyebrow, there's no reaction whatsoever. He turns them back around to me. "Nope, not a thing. Why are you here, Elijah?" He leans back and folds his hands over his flabby gut. "Drake not cutting it as a divorce attorney?"

Is he fucking serious? Does he actually think I'm here to ask him for representation? Unreal.

"You know why I'm here, Freddie, so let's cut to the chase. You assaulted my wife, and you implied you were her lawyer."

"Be careful with your baseless accusations, Elijah. I could sue you for defamation. As for the other ... Well, I told you the facts. Your inferences are your own. Now, if that's all, I'm a busy man." He gestures toward the door and turns his attention to his computer.

I slam my palm down on the desk, and his chair squeaks when he jumps back. His lawyer face fails him, and as I lean closer, he goes pale. There must be something in my eyes that tells him I'm not fucking around here.

"You. Assaulted. My. Wife."

He stands up, and I know he's going to make a run for it. All the blinds are closed, cutting off any visual contact with the rest of the building. He probably keeps it like this to allow him to play his sick games. To hide what he was doing to Amber, to the others like her. He takes a few steps toward the door, and I block him. I have maybe seven inches and a hundred pounds on this guy—there is no way past me.

He looks scared when he realizes he's trapped, and I

enjoy it. That's exactly how Amber must have felt. I move forward, bumping into him and forcing him to take a step back. Each time he steps back, I step forward. He frantically searches for an escape, his hands held up defensively in front of him.

"There's no way out, Freddie. I have you cornered. Just like you did with Amber. How does it feel? You want me to touch your dick, Freddie? You want me to bend you over the desk and shove a stapler up your ass and tell you you're enjoying it?"

He shakes, and I smell urine. A wet patch spreads across the front of his pants, and he whimpers, "Elijah, please—I can explain."

"Really? Go on then."

Despite his terror, he blusters and splutters, managing a few incoherent sentences about "a misunderstanding" and "mixed messages" and "reading the signals wrong." It's an impressive amount of bullshit for a man who just pissed himself in fear.

I keep him trapped but pretend to be listening. When he's done, he looks up at me, hope shining in his eyes, and I can only laugh. "Nah. Sorry, Freddie, but I don't believe you. Let's get some fresh air, shall we?"

I slide open the door to his balcony and shove him outside. The view is quite impressive from the top floor. I hold him by the bunched-up fabric of his shirt and push him right to the balcony railing, leaning into him so he's bent backward. He clings to my jacket for dear life. It's windy up here, and his hair flutters, lifting away from his bald patch. "Elijah, please," he whines. "You're a civilized man, don't do this."

"Oh Freddie, that shows how little you know me. I'm not civilized. Not when it comes to my wife. My wife, who you laid your filthy hands on. My beautiful, perfect wife, who you dared to touch without her permission, you fucking pervert."

My fury builds as the words pour out, and without thinking it through, I grab his ankles and dangle him over the edge of the balcony. He flails his arms and screams, but the wind carries most of the sound away. "Nobody can hear you, Freddie. And you can't talk your way out of this one, you little shit! How does it feel to be powerless, huh? To have someone touch *you* without permission?"

I shake him a little, realizing as I do that he's a bit heavier than he looks. I'd dearly love to let go, but I promised Amber I wouldn't kill him. Deep down, despite my rage, I know she's right.

He tries to curl his body, but he can't manage it. "Let me up. Elijah, let me up. What do you want from me? I'm sorry. I'm so sorry."

"What do I want? I want to drop you, Freddie. I want to kill you for what you did. But what can I say? I promised my incredible wife I wouldn't commit murder today. So, what you're going to do is this: You're going to reach out to all the women you've abused. Not just the ones I mentioned today, but all of them. You're going to apologize and tell them it wasn't their fault. You're going to give them all, let's see, a million bucks is a nice round number. It doesn't make up for what happened, but it might pay for their fucking therapy, you bastard."

We're so high up here that the cars whizzing through the city streets look like Luke's toys.

"A million?" he cries. "That's too much!"

Is he actually fucking trying to negotiate right now? While he's hanging upside down about to go splat on a busy Manhattan sidewalk? I shake my head. "The price just went up. A million each, and a new car. Bentleys are good."

I let go of one ankle and hold the other with both hands. He screams and jerks, his free leg windmilling through the air. "Okay! Okay! Whatever you say. A million and a Bentley."

"We have a deal then, Freddie? I sure hope so, for your sake. I keep in shape, but I spent a long time in the gym last night, and my arms are tired ..." I shake him a little, just for fun, but my arms really are starting to feel the strain.

"We have a deal. Pull me up, you fucking psycho!"

I haul him back over the balcony, "accidentally" knocking him around a bit on the way, and by the time he's sprawled on his ass, he also has a bleeding nose and scrapes all over his face. "Here," I say, crouching down in front of him, "let me check that nose. Looks like it could be broken."

My jab is hard and accurate, and he squeals. "Yeah. It is now," I say. "Come on, Freddie, in we go."

I drag him back into his office and slide the balcony door closed behind us. It seems weirdly quiet now that we're away from the traffic and the wind. I throw him into his chair, and he slumps there, covered in piss, hair in disarray, bleeding and crying as he holds his hands over his nose. I gather up the printouts and stand over him. "Look at me, Freddie," I command. He does as he's told, a mix of pain and hatred in his beady eyes.

"You might be thinking about calling the cops after I leave or that you'll find a way to screw me over financially—but forget all that. You called me a psycho out there, and you're right. It's a little family secret. All the James men have an inner psycho that we channel when we need it. So let me make something very clear. Are you listening to me?" I slap him across the face with an open palm, smearing blood across his cheek.

He nods and mutters, "I'm listening."

"Good. This is what's going to happen—I'm going to leave now. You're going to set the wheels in motion for the compensation package we discussed. You will email me a copy of your apology first, so I can make damn sure you grovel hard enough. My suggested wording would include something along the lines of 'I'm a fucking scum-sucking asshole who preys on the innocent, and I beg your forgiveness'—you're a lawyer, I'm sure you'll come up with something. You are not going to report any of this to the police or tell a single soul about it—you will explain your injuries the traditional way. You were clumsy and fell down the fucking stairs. Are you with me so far?"

More blood drips from his nose when he nods. "Good man. If you do tell a soul, then I will come back and I will kill you. I might do it myself, or I might hire someone else to do it. I have the money and the resources. You'll never see it coming, Freddie. Also, remember that I now know everything. I will be watching you; others will be watching you. If you touch another woman or so much as look at one inappropriately, I will know. Maybe I'll pay a spy to come work for you. Maybe I'll have secret cameras installed. I could have you tailed. But I'll know, Freddie, and I will end you. And while we're at it, why don't you stop fucking cheating on your wife."

"I won't do it again, Elijah," he croaks out. "I promise I won't. I'm sick, I'll get help."

"Fuck off, Freddie. You are sick, but it's not an illness. You're just a nasty little shit. Right. Well. That was a good chat—very productive. I'll leave you now. You have a lot to do. And don't forget—*I'll be watching*."

I wipe my bloody hands on his shirt and leave him crying in his office.

Yeah. I feel better now.

THIRTY-THREE

ELIJAH

I stare at my cell phone, ignoring the noise surrounding me. It's the usual carnage of the entire James family being in one place together. The entire James family except one, anyway.

The most important one. A lump forms in my throat as I stare at my last message to her. I sent it an hour after I left her house two mornings ago. It simply reads:

> I'll give you your space. And I'll wait as long as it takes. I love you.

She read it but sent no reply. Not that I blame her. Once again, I let her down. Hurt her when she was already hurting too much. I'll never forgive myself for that, so I can't expect her to. Although I suspect she already has. Holding grudges isn't exactly the new Amber's style. She proved that when she allowed me to stay with her the other night and when she sought my comfort the following morning.

Fuck, I miss her.

But now, I'm here and she's there, and I'm doing my best

to give her space. As promised. Even though it's the last thing I want to do.

"Hey, have you spoken with Amber today?" Drake asks quietly as he takes a seat on the sofa beside me.

My head snaps up, and I shove my phone into my pocket, trying my best not to look guilty. "No. Why?"

He glances around the noisy room. "I called to get her bank information for the settlement, and she … Well, she sounded awful. She tried to brush it off. Blamed some reheated takeout she had for dinner last night. But it sounded like she'd been crying. Amelia and I are gonna stop by on our way home and make sure she's okay."

Amber never gets sick. The woman has the constitution of an ox, which is a good thing because she has an extreme phobia of vomiting. A remnant from her time at boarding school when one of her classmates almost choked to death in the middle of the night.

She asked for space and I promised to give it, but I can't leave her alone feeling terrified and vulnerable. "No, I'll go check on her." I jump up, scanning the room for the rest of our brothers.

"You're going to leave in the middle of Mason's birthday brunch?" The incredulity in Drake's tone is further evidence that I've spent far too long not putting her first.

"Yes. Now." When I glance over my shoulder at him, his lips are curved in a smile, and he gives me a knowing wink.

I quickly find Mason and tell him I need to leave because something important has come up. Given his difficult history with my wife, I don't tell him exactly what that important thing is, and once I assure him everything is okay, he doesn't press me on it.

While he's disappointed I'm missing his birthday brunch, he understands. Of course he does, because I'm a good fucking brother, and I get to have a life outside of this family. We all do.

It's that fucking easy ... and that fucking hard.

LESS THAN AN HOUR LATER, I'm standing on Amber's doorstep, clutching a white paper bag containing a box of electrolyte packets. The woman at the pharmacy assured me they were the best thing for replacing essential fluids after a bout of food poisoning.

I stand, my hand suspended in midair, poised to knock. I promised her that I would honor her request for space, and yet here I am. Invading her life. However, any doubts I have because she might be pissed at me are far outweighed by my concern for her wellbeing.

After I knock, it takes a few moments for the door to be answered, and I spend that time shuffling from one foot to the other and hoping I haven't woken her. When the door opens a crack, I'm met with only a sliver of her face, but it's enough for me to clearly see how pale and drawn she is.

"Elijah, what are you doing here?" Her voice is raspy, her tone weary.

"I know I agreed to give you some space, but Drake told me you were sick. And I ..." I scrub my free hand through my hair. "I remember how freaked out you used to get about vomiting, and I didn't want you to be alone."

The door opens a little more, and tears fill her eyes. Her lower lip wobbles.

Shit!

"But what about Mason's birthday brunch?"

I take a step closer, my hand resting gently on the door so she doesn't feel like I'm trying to force my way inside, and I stare into her beautiful eyes. "Baby, nothing is more important to me than you. I know it's taken me far too long to realize that, but believe me when I tell you that you are my first priority. I'm not here expecting anything from you. I know this changes nothing that we spoke about the other day. And as soon as you want me to go, I'm gone. No questions asked. But whether we're together or apart, I will be here whenever you need me."

"Elijah." My name leaves her mouth on a sob that makes my chest ache. I'm not sure whether she's going to let me in or tell me to go to hell until she opens the door a little wider, allowing me inside.

I waste no time taking her into my arms, and she sags against my chest. "I feel awful," she mumbles.

I run my hands over her back, noticing now that she's wearing my Ramones T-shirt—the one that makes her feel close to me, that makes her feel safe even when I don't. It fills me with hope that her instinct is still to want to be close to me.

Resting my lips on the top of her head, I ignore the faint smell of vomit. "Was it something you ate?"

"Uh-huh. I reheated my leftovers from the chicken place on the corner," she says with a loud groan. "I guess I didn't heat it enough, or—" Her hand flies to her mouth, and she pushes me roughly away before bolting upstairs. A few seconds later, I wince at the sound of her vomiting.

After leaving the paper bag on the table, I follow the sound until I find her and drop to my knees at her side so I can rub gentle circles on her back. Eventually, she sits back on her haunches and wipes her mouth. I brush away the damp hair sticking to her forehead.

"I must look so attractive right now, huh?" she manages a laugh.

I stare at her. Cheeks pale. Lips dry and cracked. Hair in a disheveled ponytail. "You always look beautiful to me," I tell her honestly.

Groaning, she closes the lid of the toilet and rests her forehead on the cool porcelain. "Smooth talker."

I find a washcloth and run it under cold water before wiping it over the back of her neck. She lifts her head, allowing me to wipe her forehead too. Her eyes flutter closed. "That feels nice."

"Let's get you off these hard tiles, baby."

I scoop her up off the floor, and she doesn't even murmur any kind of protest. Instead, she curls her body into mine, and I carry her downstairs and sit down on the sofa with her on my lap, wrapping my arms around her. "Do you need anything? Water? Saltines?"

"Nothing right now," she mumbles.

"When you are able to drink a little, I brought some of those rehydration packets."

She makes a fake vomiting noise now. "Those things are vile."

"I know, baby, but they're the best way to replace lost fluids. So you'll be taking some. Okay?"

"You're so bossy." I bite my tongue so I don't remind her that I haven't scratched the surface of bossy. Because if I were to stray close to that territory, I would insist on her having a chef to cook her meals so she doesn't poison herself with dodgy takeout again.

When I place a kiss on the top of her hair, I can't help but smile. Being with her is the only place I want to be, so if being grateful that she got sick and is letting me take care of her makes me a selfish asshole, then that's just what I am.

"This changes nothing, Elijah," she says quietly, burrowing her head against my chest.

I press a kiss to her forehead now. "I know."

"It means a lot to me that you're here though. I really do hate being alone when I'm sick."

"I know."

She rests her hand on my chest, directly over my heart. "Thank you for choosing me."

I did choose her today, and that's a good start, but it's not enough. I should have chosen her every single time, and if she decides to give me another shot, I will never miss another opportunity to put her first.

THIRTY-FOUR

AMBER

T had no clue how much I needed a girls' night until I was in the middle of one. It was all Amelia's idea. She told me it was time I had a housewarming and that she and a few friends would be over on Saturday. I couldn't exactly object—she owns the place. Besides, I told myself, this is my time of firsts, and this is the first time I've lived alone. Hosting friends sounded lovely.

I spoke to Granny Lucille earlier in the day, and she talked me through making Planter's Punch for everyone. I laid out chips and dips, and Amelia assured me that they would bring everything else.

It's a far cry from the society events I'm used to organizing, but as I watch Amelia tie tinsel around her head and down her third glass of punch, I decide that it's a lot more fun.

She arrived first, bearing an armful of cannoli from Wanda's, and soon after, her pal Kimmy showed up with a stack of pizzas. Emily supplied enough booze to get the whole of Brooklyn drunk, and Melanie turned up with the most unexpected item—a Christmas tree.

I was nervous when Amelia told me Nathan's wife was coming. He and I range somewhere between indifferent and archnemesis, depending on the mood we're in. The tree definitely broke the ice. It's massive, and her driver had to help her inside with it. Teddy gave me a respectful nod on his way out, after looking around the small house with interest.

"I wonder," I said to Melanie as she stared up at the monster fir, "if the James family drivers have a Christmas party. Can you imagine the secrets they know? The things they've heard and seen?"

She winced slightly. Hah. I'm guessing Nathan's limo has seen its share of drama too. "My god. I never thought of that. I hope not—they must think we're a bunch of complete lunatics."

"They'd be right. Can I get you a punch?"

She happily accepted, and I felt my tension flee. That was almost three hours ago, and the tree is now decorated—on one side. Amelia brought out every single item she and her mom owned, but it still wasn't enough. Nobody seems to care though, and Kimmy has started hanging silverware from it. Everyone is slightly tipsy, Christmas music is playing, and Emily is asking me about my new role at LOJ. It's odd seeing her in this relaxed setting, but it's nice to see a whole different side to her.

"Well, I've only been there a week, but so far so good," I answer. "The kids are fantastic, and so is Sissie, the woman who runs the place. I've been doing the dance classes and helping out in the kitchens and generally being ... useful. It's nice. I haven't felt useful for a very long time. Possibly ever, to be honest. My Granny Lucille once accused me of being a poor little rich girl, and I suspect she was right—but now, instead of feeling sorry for myself, I'm doing something about it."

"That's fantastic," Melanie says, raising her glass to me. "I'd go crazy without my work. How does Elijah feel about it?"

I quirk an eyebrow at her, and she laughs. "I know, I know—you're splitting up, and it has nothing to do with him. But if, heaven forbid, Nathan and I ever got a divorce—and I think Elijah might be the same—there's no way he'd just stop being, um, how do I put this ..."

"A controlling asshole?" Kimmy suggests helpfully.

"No," both Mel and I say at the same time.

"Well, sometimes," she admits. "But mainly just protective."

"They all are," Amelia adds. "I can't speak to Maddox and Mason, but Drake, Nathan, Elijah are all a little possessive. Gotta be honest—sorry, Kimmy, don't shoot me—I find it kind of hot. When Drake gets that dark and intense look in his eyes ... Yeah." Her lips curve with a dreamy smile. "Like I said, kind of hot." She blushes, and we all laugh with her. "Tell us about the bikers, Amber," she adds, obviously trying to deflect attention.

"Oooh, bikers," announces Kimmy, rubbing her hands together. "Now we're talking. Are they the sexy kind?"

I sip my punch and grin. "Oh yes, they are. If you're into tattoos and muscles and leather."

"Fuck yes," Kimmy cheers. "Can I get an invite to *their* Christmas party?"

"Not sure they have one, but I'll check for you. They've

been really nice, actually. I'm even getting self-defense lessons from them."

Kimmy makes a raucous remark about that, and the hilarity continues, and I make the most of it to escape briefly to the kitchen. This evening has been incredible, but I'm slightly overwhelmed. I'm unaccustomed to this level of intimacy, of being so vulnerable with people. I feel a little like a turtle out of its shell, wondering when a giant bird of prey is going to swoop down and peck me to death.

I check my phone and smile when I see a message from Elijah, but I also feel the urge to hide back in my shell. While it's true that I love him, I also recognize that he's dangerous. I still haven't forgotten how I felt sitting alone in Greenwich Village, and the pain of that is forever lurking beneath the surface. Other than him taking care of me when I was sick, I haven't seen him in a week.

The morning following my digestive system failure, he didn't leave until after he made sure I was okay and told me what happened with Freddie. I'm pleased with the direction Elijah chose to go. Freddie deserves jail time, no doubt, but in the real world, it wouldn't be that simple.

Martha has been in touch, and we're due to meet soon as well. I have no idea how I feel about her now, and this evening has shown me what healthy female friendships can actually look like. Still, I will at least hear her out.

I type out a quick reply and attach a photo of the giant Christmas tree. I've relented a little on the space issue, allowing us to reconnect from a distance. He's become my best friend again, just like the old days, and we talk on the phone and text more now than we have since college.

The poor thing is half naked.

Me too. I just had a massage.

I gulp. A massage? Where is he, and who's he getting a massage from? And how naked is he? God, I bet he looks good, lying spread out and all oiled up, his muscles gleaming ... I decide not to reply. I've had too much to drink, and no good will come of it. I'm interrupted anyway when Mel walks into the kitchen, and I guiltily shove my phone in my pocket. I can tell she noticed, but she simply gives me a small smile and gets herself a glass of water.

"Are you okay?" she asks, leaning against the counter and taking a sip. It's the first time we've been alone together, and I hope it's not going to be awkward.

"Sure. I'm actually a little tired. Truthfully, I'm usually in bed by ten."

"It's only just past that now," she says, glancing at her watch. "But I probably need to be heading home soon. Nathan is great with Luke, but I don't like being away from them for too long."

I nod. I don't want to talk about her husband—things could go south quickly. "Well, thanks for coming, Mel, it was nice to see you."

"It was nice, wasn't it? I wasn't sure at first, when Amelia asked me to come along. Things are ... complicated."

I let out a little laugh. "That's a polite way of putting it."

"Look, just to clear the air, Amber—I am not my husband. I love and trust my husband, and he is usually one of the best judges of character I know. Very few people can read a person as well as Nathan. But I don't make the mistake of thinking that he's God, and I do have my own mind."

"That must annoy him."

"Yes, but he loves it really—gives us something to fight about. And that gives us a reason to have fantastic make-up sex. Anyway. I had a great time, and I hope we see each other again."

On impulse, I lean forward and give her a quick hug. She looks surprised but pleased.

"You should bring Luke to the center," I say, again without really thinking it through. "If you want to, that is."

"He might be a little young for dancing," she says, laughing.

"We actually have quite a few babies and toddlers who come with their older siblings. They seem to really enjoy the music and the motion."

She thinks about it, then nods, smiling. "Maybe I will. Right, I'm going to make a move. I'll see what the mood is like out there."

The mood, it turns out, is mixed. Amelia announces that she's heading back to Tribeca and shares a ride with Melanie. Emily and Kimmy, much to everyone's amusement, decide that they're going barhopping, both wearing tinsel garland as necklaces. They tried to persuade me to join them, but I genuinely am tired. I wave everyone off and then do a quick clean-up, filling a trash bag and putting the glasses in the dishwasher. I snap a picture of the empty punch bowl and send it to Granny Lucille to show her what a success it was.

She replies quick as a flash.

Next time, invite me.

I grin and tell her I will. After making sure pizza doesn't breed bacteria like leftover chicken, I wrap up what's left and put it in the fridge. I'm still not the world's greatest cook, and that will take care of tomorrow. It's a small thing, but one that shows how much my life has changed. I no longer have a housekeeper or a huge kitchen stocked with food that arrived there as if by magic. No more daily lunch meetings either. I no longer have a lot of things I took for granted, and I miss none of them—apart from him.

I sit down on the couch and pour myself another glass of wine. I still miss Elijah, and no matter how much I'm trying to rebuild without him, that tug in his direction doesn't seem to fade. I'm not sure it ever will. Maybe it's something I'll simply have to learn to live with.

To offset the feeling of melancholy that's starting to creep over me, I do what I usually do—turn on the TV. I get lucky with an episode of *Bones*, which has always been a guilty pleasure of mine. Except no, I remind myself, not a guilty pleasure at all—if a single woman in her forties can't enjoy watching a hunky FBI agent team up with a beautiful-but-nerdy forensics specialist, then what is the world coming to?

The will-they-won't-they vibe of their romance while they solve a gruesome murder helps to distract me from thinking about Elijah. If I think about him, I will eventually call him, and that is a terrible idea tonight.

A knock on the door makes me jump so hard I spill my wine. In my defense, it comes at a particularly tense moment when two lead characters are buried alive by a deranged serial killer. Getting up, I remember my self-defense lessons —number one of which is avoid getting into a situation where you need to use them at all. I peek through the drapes and do a double take. Either I drank a lot more alcohol than I remember, or Santa Claus is on my doorstep. I close the drapes, pause for a moment, then look again. He's still there. I stare some more, and as he turns his face toward me, I realize that Mr. Claus is in fact Elijah. Amused, I rush to open the door.

"Ho ho ho," he says, completely deadpan.

"Who are you calling a ho?" I reply, hands on hips. I look him up and down and burst out laughing. He looks ridiculous in his red suit and floppy hat, the fake bushy beard hanging from his face like a comatose sheep.

"Can I come in?" he asks. "This thing is not as warm as it looks. But I shouldn't complain—I got it from a late-night store in Times Square for only twenty bucks. Hopefully the real Father Christmas has better insulation."

I gesture for him to come in, and he stands in the entry, blowing on his hands for a few seconds. "Um, not that this isn't very festive, but why are you here? And why are you wearing a cheap Santa suit?"

"Well, because I didn't have time to buy an expensive one, obviously. You told me your Christmas tree needed help, so I come bearing baubles. Can I interest you in the contents of my sack, young lady?" He waggles his eyebrows at me suggestively, and I roll my eyes. He shouldn't be here. But it's late, and I've had wine, and I was missing him. Plus, he looks hotter than he has any right to dressed up as Santa.

"Have at it," I say, showing him the tree. "And what's that smell?"

"That depends. Do you like it?"

"I do, but I can't quite identify it."

He tugs off the fake beard, which is much better. His own beard is cuter. "Well, I had an appointment with Melanie's cousin, Tyler. He's a physical therapist."

"I see. And he made you smell like that, how?"

"He massaged my back. Gave me some oil to take too. Almond, I think."

I nod knowingly. "Right. The sore back you got from the dance warm-up?"

"I thought I hid that from you pretty well. Now my macho facade is ruined."

Laughing, I poke him in the stomach. "I think this plastic belt ruins any illusion of machismo, pal. Did he help? Tyler?"

"He did. He's very good at his job. Never thought I'd feel comfortable getting my body rubbed down by a man with hands the size of my face, but he talked about football while he worked to make me feel better. He was like a straight-man whisperer, keeping me calm. How was your girls' night?"

"It was great," I say, helping him drape the extra baubles on the tree. None of them are the same color as the ones on the other side, but what the hell. I like the chaos. "Mel brought the tree."

He raises an eyebrow. "How did that go?"

"Really well." I pass him an ornament and gesture at the top branches. "She's nice. If I sound surprised, it's because I am. It's almost enough to make me think Nathan might not be totally evil."

"Whoa, don't get carried away with the Christmas spirit there."

We joke and laugh as we work, and I provide him with

beer—I don't have any Scotch in the house, but he seems happy enough. By the time we stand back and survey our handiwork, a few of the stubby bottles have disappeared, as has the rest of my wine.

"It looks like shit, but I like it," he says, head tilted to one side. He's unbuttoned his Santa suit, revealing a tight white T-shirt underneath. Our eyes meet, and I feel that tug yet again. The need to touch him, the need to feel his body against mine. This is a perfect example of why he's dangerous. Of why I should stay away from him.

The moment builds, and he knows exactly what he's doing to me when he reaches out and gently tucks a strand of hair behind my ear. On the surface, it's a harmless gesture, but any contact at all is enough to unravel me.

"Elijah, don't," I murmur, trying to back away, but I come up against the bristling boughs of the Christmas tree. He freezes, but he's still only inches away.

"You want me to leave?" he asks, his voice deep and husky as his gaze runs over me. "Just say the word, Amber, and I'll leave."

I want to tell him to go. I know I should.

I stay silent. His hand goes to my waist, and he pulls me toward him. "Or do you want me to stay and make you scream my name?"

Our hips touch, and my pussy contracts when I feel how hard he is. Hot. As. Hell. "That's ... You're ... Oh god, I ... Don't leave."

He grins down at me and puts one big hand on my ass, pressing me even closer. I grind against him, already throbbing with need. He tips my chin up, and his grin widens. "Look at you. Your pupils are blown. I know your panties are wet. You're rubbing up on me like a horny she-devil. You are most definitely on the naughty list."

"You're right. This is naughty. We shouldn't be doing this."

"Naughty is perfect for this time of year. Now be a good girl and take off all your clothes for Santa."

THIRTY-FIVE

AMBER

He clears a space for us as I undress, spreading a blanket over the rug to create a nest under the tree. Then he slowly takes off his Santa suit, making me laugh as he does a mock-Burlesque bump and grind with his shirt and hat, eventually kicking his red pants away with a flourish. They end up snagging on one of the tree's low branches.

"You're a very bad Santa," I say, gliding my hands up his chest. I explore his toned and muscular physique, loving the feel of his skin. The power in his arms is luscious, and even looking at his chiseled abs makes me lick my lips.

I drop to my knees and take his cock into my mouth, teasing and toying, flicking it with my tongue. My hands are on his firm ass, and he groans as I play with him. "Fuck, baby, you are so good at that. Nobody has ever sucked my cock like you do."

He thrusts very slowly in and out of my mouth, and I can tell he's holding back. I cup his balls, gently caressing them. I can't get enough of the taste of him. He pulls away suddenly, and when I look up, he is smiling and shaking his head. "I don't want to come yet. It's not polite. Ladies first."

"Always the gentleman," I murmur as he joins me on the blanket.

His gray eyes flash with something primal, and I gulp at the intensity in them. "Not always," he growls. "Sit on my face. Let me eat that delicious pussy of yours." He lies on his back. "Don't be shy. I want your pussy on my mouth. I want to smell it and taste it and see it. Right now."

My face heats at his dirty talk, but I bite back my embarrassment. It makes no sense to be embarrassed. This man already knows every inch of me. I crawl slowly over him, my legs on either side of his body, and trail my pussy over his cock, leaving it coated in my juices. He groans as I work my way up. His beard brushes the inside of my thighs, and he roughly grabs my hips. I hover above his mouth, so close I can feel his hot breath against me.

"There. Exactly there. Fuck. That is a beautiful sight, baby. Look how wet you are, practically dripping for me already. So pink and perfect." He flicks his tongue along my seam, and the sensation from this position is amazing. He works up and down, holding me in place as he explores. He curls his tongue and pushes it inside my opening. I gasp, and he pulls me slightly lower, his nose sliding against my clit as he laps me up inside. The pressure starts to build, a constant throb, a second heartbeat.

His big hands keep me still, controlling the slight changes in angle as he licks and kisses my wet folds, the heat increasing with every shift of his mouth. He sucks on my clit and swirls his tongue around it.

"Elijah," I moan, and his hands move to my ass, tugging

me closer. Every nerve ending tingles, the orgasm coursing through me like an electric shock. My arousal drips from me, and I can't stop shaking. He keeps me there, holding me still, licking and sucking and gently probing. "Fuck, that was spectacular," he says as he rolls me onto my back. He wipes his face with the back of his hand and looks down at me with hunger in his eyes.

I'm still trembling, still recovering from what he just did to me. From what he always seems to do to me. I pull him in for a kiss and taste myself on his tongue. I want more. He growls as he claims my mouth, his hands roaming my body, palming my breasts and sliding under my ass. He kneads my flesh and sucks my nipples, and I am already feeling that seductive rhythm build again. When he pulls back, our eyes meet. His beard glistens with the evidence of how hard I came, and his face is dark with passion. He is terrifying and magnificent, and I want every damn inch of him. I don't care how complicated this is, and I don't care if it's wrong. I need him.

"Tonight, Elijah," I whisper. "I want to do it tonight."

"What, baby? What do you want to do?" His gaze is intense, so hot I can feel it on my skin. His cock is upright and throbbing and huge, and I swallow down a moment of doubt.

"I want to do the thing we've never done."

His Adam's apple bobs as he swallows. "You're sure?" he asks. "It's not something you have to do."

"I don't feel like I *have* to do it, Elijah. I want to. Please?"

"Baby," he says, getting quickly to his feet. "You really don't have to ask me twice. I was just making sure it was what you really wanted. And now that I know it is ..." He rummages around in his red felt Santa sack and emerges holding a small bottle. "Almond oil," he says triumphantly. "I knew that muscle strain would come in handy."

He joins me back on the floor. "Turn over. Let's start with a massage. We don't have to rush, and the more relaxed you are, the better."

I do as I'm told and stretch out on my front. He rubs the oil in his hands to warm it up, then smooths his big hands over my shoulders. I am a little more tense than I realized. Even though I want to do this, I'm also nervous. He's surprisingly skilled, naturally knowing where to apply firmer pressure and where to be gentle. It's relaxing and arousing. Every time his hands glide down my sides, he touches the edge of my breasts. Every time, I want him to touch them more. It is a slow and sexy form of foreplay, and by the time he actually reaches the lower half of my body, I am made of liquid.

He murmurs appreciatively as he kneads my backside. "I've said this before, but baby, your ass ... It's phenomenal. The most perfect ass in the history of asses." He pauses, and his tone deepens. "I cannot wait to be balls-deep in it. You still want that, Amber? You want me to fuck you there?"

His words are filthy, and they make me want him all the more. I wriggle my butt, lifting it slightly as though I'm offering it to him. Which I suppose I am. "Yes, that's still what I want."

"Up on your knees then. Ass in the air. Keep your head down, get nice and comfortable ... Yeah, that's it." He skims his fingers along my slit and easily slides two fingers inside me.

"Fuck. You really do want this. You're soaking my whole hand, you dirty girl." He lazily rubs my clit, building me up to a state of almost-orgasm, but leaves me hanging right as I'm about to come. I groan in disappointment, and he laughs. "Not yet, sweetheart, not yet. It'll be even better if you wait a while. First, I need to get inside this juicy ass of yours."

He pours oil on me, and the sensation is strange but also exciting as the thick liquid runs into my most intimate places. He gently spreads my cheeks apart and sighs. "Fuck. You're even perfect here. I'm going to shoot my load into this gorgeous ass of yours, baby. I'm going to fill you up."

I moan at the image. "Yes, please."

He slides a finger to my back entrance, and with the help of the oil, inserts it. It feels odd, but not painful. It's like nothing I can remember experiencing before. The last time I tried this was against my will, and this is a million miles away from that—this is something I desperately want. Something my husband will do with passion and respect. Already, my pussy is clenching and fluttering.

I push back against the invading finger, and he moves it in and out, building up speed as he goes. "Jesus. That feels so good. You okay? I'm not hurting you too much?"

"No. I'm ready for more, Elijah. I want more."

"Fuck," he says, pulling his finger out and replacing it with the crown of his cock. He holds my cheeks apart, and I feel the big head of his dick pushing against me. "Just relax, baby. Deep breaths and relax."

Slowly, he forces his cock past the tight ring of muscle. There's resistance, and it hurts. I suck in air and remind myself to breathe slowly as he goes deeper. "That's it," he murmurs, stroking my skin soothingly. "You're doing so well. Fuck, you look amazing."

He gives a final firm push, and I squeal as I feel him go all in the way in, then he goes still, letting me get used to the sensation. His fingers dip back inside my pussy, and I cry out with pure pleasure at the way my skin stretches around him.

Very slowly, he starts to thrust from behind, matching the rhythm with his fingers. His thumb pad slides over my clit as he moves, and I'm almost weeping from the heightened sensations that course through me. "I can feel my own cock inside you. I fucking love it, and I can tell you do too. Come for me, Amber. Squeeze my fingers with your tight, wet cunt. Come for me while I fuck your perfect ass."

The pressure builds inside me, pounding away in two different places. I'm full of him, and he's stroking my swollen bud and gliding his fingers in and out of my soaking pussy. His cock is stretching my ass, thrusting and pushing me closer and closer to the edge. He circles my clit with his thumb and curls his fingers inside me, stroking the sweet spot that pushes me over the cliff. "Elijah!" I cry, my mind and body exploding in a glorious climax.

"Yeah, that's it. That's perfect. Fuck!"

Once he's milked every last second of pleasure from my orgasm, both hands go to my hips, and he holds me steady. "Baby, I'm going to enjoy this so much." He drives his cock into me hard, and I gasp at the power of it. Now that I've come and he knows I can take him, it's as though he gives himself permission to let go, and he rails into me like a demon. It's wild and scary and like nothing I've ever experienced. I love every heart-pounding moment of it. He comes, groaning and yelling my name as he empties himself inside me. After pulling out, he collapses, and I lie next to him, sore but so very satisfied. He turns onto his side to look at me, his pupils huge and his breathing reduced to ragged gasps.

He strokes my hair back from my face and kisses me gently. "I love you." It's such a sweet moment, especially in contrast to the animalistic way he was fucking me only seconds ago.

"I love you too," I murmur. "That was um … merry?"

He rolls onto his back and grins up at the branches of the giant tree. "Nothing says Christmas quite like a cock in the ass. Thank you. Thank you for sharing another first with me."

"You're very welcome. I liked it."

He stretches his arms over his head and yawns. "Fuck, I'm tired. Keeping up with you is exhausting. Shall we go to bed?"

His question makes me freeze. I'm tired too, but I cannot allow him to stay. What we just did was deeply intimate, but sleeping in his arms, waking up with him … I'm still too hurt by everything that has happened to go back to the way things were.

There was an innocence to Mr. and Mrs. Smith that no longer exists. Now, we're very much ourselves, and Mr. and Mrs. James are a couple in the process of getting a divorce. What the hell are we playing at?

I stand up and start to dress. He looks up at me, then follows suit. He's figured out from my silence that a sleep-over is not on the cards, and it's clear that he's both hurt and angry.

"I'm sorry, Elijah," I say once we're dressed. "I just don't think it's a good idea for you to stay overnight. Probably none of this was a good idea."

"You're undoubtedly right," he says, his tone clipped. "It

was a mistake. I'm good enough to fuck, but not good enough to share a bed with."

"That's not fair," I say, feeling my own anger stir. "I told you how I felt, Elijah. I told you, after you hurt me like you did, that I didn't trust you enough to try again."

"But you trusted me enough to let me fuck you like that?"

He's lashing out because he's upset, but I'm not willing to simply take it. "Yes. I trust you physically, Elijah, one hundred percent. But with my heart? With my feelings? Not so much. Also, I didn't ask you to come here tonight, did I? That was your decision. You invited yourself. I'm sorry I let you through the damn door."

How can I still have his cum inside me, still be wet from my own orgasm, while we stand here and shoot barbs at one another? The sex is the only damn thing that works between us, and it's not enough.

"I don't want this," I say quietly, looking into his stormy eyes. "I don't want to fight. We always end up fucking or fighting."

Tears flow down my cheeks, and he's starting to tear up also. "I know, Amber. I know. I don't want this either. I'll leave now. I'm sorry. Fuck, I don't even know what I'm sorry for. Both of us, I guess. We just can't seem to get it right."

He puts his Santa hat on my head, kisses me on the nose, and gives me a sad smile. "Take care, baby. See you around."

As he closes the door behind him, I tell myself that this is for the best, but the assurance falls flat.

CHAPTER

THIRTY-SIX

ELIJAH

We meet in Drake's office, which we have declared Switzerland. Amber and I sit across from each other, with my brother sitting across from Amelia while she takes notes.

We haven't spoken to each other since the night Amber kicked me out of her house. I have been on the verge of calling her so many times, but I've held back. She had every right to ask me to leave. As she pointed out, I was never invited in the first place. I understand why she wants to keep her distance—I fucked up big time. Just as we were starting to find our way back to each other, I hurt her badly.

But I have feelings too, and it sucked to go to her house, have that mind-blowing sex with her, and then be unceremoniously booted out the door. I don't know what I expected. That I'd seduce her and she'd forgive me? If only it were that simple.

We both need time. This is not a game I need to win—this is about the rest of our lives. It's about honestly looking at our relationship and acknowledging the damage we've done. The patterns we seem unable to break.

At the moment, she clearly doesn't think there's any coming back from that, and she's busy building her own life. A life I am not welcome in. I fucking hate it, but for now, I have no choice. Besides, there's that nagging voice in the back of my mind. The one that tells me she might be right— that no matter how much our bodies call to each other, we aren't a good fit and will never be happy together. I don't completely believe that voice, but it's there, always whispering.

So I've kept away from her, and she's kept away from me. Drake called this meeting to update us and to get us to sign more papers. The fucking legal system must be responsible for more deforestation than any other industry. We could have done this separately, but he insisted—I suspect it's his last-ditch attempt to make sure this is what we want.

He passes around the papers and Amelia distributes pens as he speaks. "It's been six weeks since you initially filed. There will be delays due to the time of year, and it can take anywhere between six and twelve weeks anyway. This is one of your last opportunities to change your minds." He glances from me to Amber and back again. She nods, smiles politely, and signs the damn paper without a second thought.

She looks fucking incredible, obviously. Skinny pants and a red blouse made of some kind of floaty material I don't know the name of. Heels, as usual, make her legs look sinfully long. I keep my face in neutral and remind myself we're only here to confirm our divorce arrangements. My libido needs to go fuck itself. Except, of course, it would rather go fuck her.

So far, we've both been completely courteous and perfectly civil, like good little robots. I want to scream and shout and shake her by the shoulders, to snap us both out of this fucking insanity and stop us from sleepwalking toward the end of our marriage. One look at her calm exterior tells me not to bother. This isn't easy for her either, and she's dealing with it in her traditional way—shutters well and truly down. Closing out the world, especially me. The familiar expression on her face fills my stomach with acid. It's like sitting next to a polite stranger, and I lived that way for too many years. Fuck that. I sign the papers and pass them up the table, ignoring my brother's frustration. He seems the most upset of all of us.

Drake shakes his head and goes on, running over the basic details of the settlement. Amber gets the Manhattan townhouse and a one-off payment of fifty million dollars. At her request, no additional spousal support will be offered. There are other points, but we've already agreed on all of them, and I'm barely listening. How can a marriage end like this? How can it be reduced so quickly to facts and figures, like it meant nothing at all?

"Are you both still happy with that?" Drake asks.

"No," Amber says, the first time she's spoken since a basic greeting when she arrived. "I would like an amendment. I don't want the townhouse."

"You don't have to live in it, Amber," I snap. "Just sell the damn place if you prefer."

She shakes her head, and her stubbornness pushes me over the edge. "What?" I ask, my voice low and angry-sounding to my own ears. "You want me to increase the settlement instead? Add an extra ten mil on top to make up for it? Is that what you're angling for?" I'm deliberately provoking her. She didn't even want the fifty million and only relented when Drake told her that she would hold up the entire process by insisting on a modest living allotment that would last until she found a full-time job. "What the hell do I need that much money for?" were her exact words.

Accusing her of being greedy makes me an asshole, but I'm on the asshole train and can't get off. The whole thing just makes me so fucking sad, and she's giving me nothing. No emotions at all. I always hated it when she shut down like this.

She glares at me, tears shining in her eyes. I seem to have that effect on her a lot these days. And I really am an asshole, because I'm glad to see them there. I want her to cry. I want her to feel as shitty as I do.

"No, Elijah, I don't want an extra ten mil. I don't want anything to do with the townhouse. All it represents is the miserable state our relationship ended up in. Keep it, sell it, blow the damn place up—I don't care. I don't even want the amount we agreed on. I don't need it. I might be useless in the real world, but I *will* find a way to support myself without you."

The pain in her voice is lined with steel. She means every word, and damn, I can't help but admire her. "We've agreed on the settlement, Amber, and we're sticking with it. Call it compensation for having to tolerate our *miserable* relationship for so long."

Eyes flashing, she opens her mouth, but then she takes a deep breath and maintains her calm tone. "I'm sorry I said that. It was not all miserable, and I apologize. But I do mean it about the cash, Elijah. I will happily walk away from this marriage with nothing."

She's trying to defuse the situation, trying to calm me down, but it's impossible. Everything suddenly feels like too fucking much. She left me, and although she's right—we were miserable a lot of the time—I still love her. I've messed up in so many damn ways, and it kills me that I can't fix it. But how can she sit there and talk like this? How can she be so damn *composed*? Doesn't she care at all?

"You're very mild-mannered today, Amber," I say, narrowing my eyes at her. "Almost serene. Is it the thought of escaping me, or my whole family? Are you excited to finally be free of us?"

Her nostrils flare and she shakes her head but remains infuriatingly silent. She's not even blinking. I lean closer. "And as for you walking away from this marriage with nothing, that's not possible. At the very least, you will walk away from this marriage with my fucking heart. Is that *nothing* to you?"

"Your heart?" she echoes, finally pushed far enough to raise her voice. "Your fucking *heart*? We all know that belongs to your family, Elijah—there was never enough left over for me, was there? I was always scampering around underneath the table, looking for scraps. Gratefully snatching up anything that Nathan or Mason or your dad didn't use first."

"That's bullshit," I cry, jumping to my feet. "Yes, I love my family. Is that a fucking crime? Don't blame me—you've been doing your best to alienate them for decades now." She stands too, and we glower at each like prizefighters.

"Stop!" Drake slams a leather-bound law book down on

the table, making us all flinch. Amelia looks distressed, her eyes going from my brother to us. Drake just looks pissed. "You two are behaving like fucking children," he says, slamming the book down again for good measure. "Children who still love each other. If you didn't, you wouldn't be reacting like this. From where I'm sitting, this marriage does not look over—so what the fuck are you playing at?"

Both Amber and I try to talk at once, and he shakes his head. "Sit down, right now, and shut the fuck up. I am sick to death of this stupidity. I have something I need to say."

I'm tempted to leap over the table and punch his lights out, but I recognize that urge as the impostor it is. I sit down and force myself to stay quiet. Amber does the same.

Drake runs his hands through his hair, and Amelia lays a calming hand on his shoulder. When he looks back up at us, sadness has replaced his anger. "Amber, you need to tell him," he says calmly. What the fuck is he talking about? "Tell him what happened that night."

My wife immediately pales, and her hands curl into fists. "No, Drake. It doesn't matter. It was so long ago. It's irrelevant now."

"I say it is relevant," he insists. "And if you don't tell him, then I will. Your choice. Amelia and I are going to leave now, because frankly, I need a fucking drink. Possibly I need several. Then I'm going home with my girlfriend, and I am going to tell her I love her all night long. You two, sort your shit out."

He grabs his coat from the back of the door and storms out. Amelia lingers behind, smiling awkwardly. "Help yourself to coffee. And he keeps a bottle of Scotch in his second desk drawer." With that, she leaves me alone with my wife.

I have no fucking clue what's going on, but Amber looks ready to run right after them. No fucking way. She's not going anywhere until I find out what Drake was talking about. I stride over to the desk, find the Scotch, and grab two cups from the coffee machine. I glug in generous amounts, and shove one in her direction. She sniffs it and makes a disgusted face but swallows some down anyway. I follow suit, and the familiar warmth of the Macallan helps calm me down.

"Amber, what the hell was Drake going on about? What do you need to tell me?"

She shakes her head and bites her lip so hard she leaves an indent of her teeth in her skin. "He had no right to say that. And it really isn't relevant."

"What isn't? You heard Drake—if you don't tell me, he will. Just spit it out."

She buries her face in her hands for a moment and emerges looking even paler. After downing the rest of her Scotch, she makes a "fill me up" gesture, and I oblige, pouring her half a cup. She picks it up and walks over to the window. It's not yet five, but darkness has fallen.

"Doesn't it look spectacular?" she says. "I mean, it always does, but with the Christmas lights ..."

"It does," I agree, joining her. I don't give a shit about the view, but she clearly needs a moment. "Beautiful."

She nods and sits on the big leather couch, staring past me at nothing in particular. "Drake is talking about something that happened years ago. I don't want to dredge it all up. There's nothing to be gained by that."

I sit next to her but don't touch her. I give her space. "Maybe that's for me to decide. Drake certainly seems to think so anyway. Fuck, baby—things can't get any worse, can they?"

She lets out a bitter laugh. "You shouldn't say that, because in my experience, they always can. Okay. I don't suppose your darling brother has left me with much choice. So, this happened at the end of October, fourteen years ago."

I frown and put the pieces together. "When my mom was sick?" She died on the first of November.

Amber nods and sips more Scotch. "It was late, and we were staying with your parents. I went to check on her. I loved your mom so much, Elijah. You know that, don't you?"

"I do know that," I say, confused. "And she felt the same about you."

Her smile is brittle. "I thought so too. You know how I grew up, what my childhood was like. What my parents were like. You know there was no love in that home. When I met you, and then your mom and your brothers, I felt like I was part of a real family for the first time ever. Like I'd finally found my place, you know? And then it all fell apart. It started that night."

"What do you mean? I have no clue what you're talking about."

"I know, honey," she says, gazing up at me with those huge, sad eyes. "That's because I hid it from you. That night, your mom told me some home truths. She was in so much pain, taking drugs that messed with her head, but I never totally believed that was all it was about. I suppose I've always thought, deep down, that she meant it."

"Meant what?" I prompt after she falls silent again.

"Meant it when she told me I never should have married

you. When she told me I was broken and barren. And that the whole family resented me for what I'd done to you."

I stare at her, seeing the tears spill down her cheeks, unable to comprehend the words she just spoke. "She said what?"

"That I was broken and shouldn't have married you. That you were pretending you didn't mind that I couldn't have children."

"No," I murmur, casting my mind back to that terrible time in our lives. "No, she wouldn't." The woman I knew wasn't capable of such cruelty.

Amber gazes up at me and stays quiet for a few moments.

"Right," she replies gently, a defeated look on her face. "Of course, you're right."

She stands up and gulps down the rest of her Scotch before leaning down and kissing me on the cheek. "I need to get going. I'm sorry Drake brought this up. Like I said, ancient history. I'm sure you're correct and I've simply misremembered. Look after yourself, honey, okay?"

Still too stunned by her revelation to speak, I simply stare at her until she's gone.

THIRTY-SEVEN

ELIJAH

"Where are you?" I say into my phone as I march along the busy Manhattan street. People get out of my way, jerking their Christmas shopping bags to one side to avoid me. "I need to see you."

"I'm out with Amelia," Drake answers. "I'm happy to talk this through with you, but I'm not in the mood for more melodrama, okay?"

I grit my teeth. I'd still quite like to punch his lights out. However, he isn't wrong. Typically, I am not a man prone to theatrics, but I can't deny the part I played in what happened in his office.

The address he texts me is only a few blocks away, and I bump into Amelia leaving as I step inside the quiet bar. "You don't have to go on my account," I say, feeling guilty.

She smiles and pats my arm. "This is between the two of you, Elijah. Just go easy on him, okay?"

Before I can respond, she leaves me standing there, confused. Go easy on him? What the fuck does that mean?

I find Drake in a corner booth, a bottle of Scotch and two

glasses in front of him. Fuck. It's going to be that kind of conversation. I slide into the booth, and he wordlessly pours me a drink. He rubs the bridge of his nose and looks upset, like he might have been crying. I can count on one finger the number of times I've seen Drake cry in adulthood, and I'm reminded of Amelia's warning.

"She told you?" he asks, glancing up at me.

I nod. "Yeah. But I don't fucking understand it. Why the hell would Mom say those things to her? If it were anyone other than Amber telling me, I wouldn't believe it."

"Believe it, Elijah," Drake replies firmly. "I was there—I heard everything."

I tilt my head to one side, studying him. He's a few drinks in already, and this is clearly tough for him. "What do you mean, you were there?"

"It was a few days before she died. You guys were staying over. I'd gone to get a beer and walked past her room on the way back. She was laying into Amber. I couldn't fucking believe it either, to start with. But she wasn't herself—you remember how fucked up she was? The way she didn't even recognize us by the end?"

The way she changed will always haunt me. I've worked hard over the years to banish those images from my mind —to not let her last few days overshadow everything else. She was a loving mother, a caring wife, a passionate and fun-loving woman who never forgot her Spanish roots. She was all of that and more. I refuse to remember her as the pain-addled animal who suffered so much before she passed. Her death was a mercy after seeing what she went through.

"I do remember. But I still don't get it. Mom could be a

firecracker, and sure, she had a temper—but she was never cruel."

"I know this is hard to wrap your head around, but I promise you I heard every single word, Elijah. She called her barren. Told her she was broken. I think her exact words were 'he'll resent you for what he had to give up.' She even said that the rest of the family all felt the same—sad for poor Elijah. Fuck, it was awful. Amber was crying her eyes out. She was damn well *apologizing* for not being able to give her grandkids."

His hand trembles as he picks up his glass. I don't think I've seen him this unstable since our mom actually died. Despite his obvious distress, I'm pissed as hell at him, struggling with what he's saying. I can almost understand why Amber kept this from me, but him? My own fucking brother. That, I don't get.

"Why am I just hearing about this? How could you have kept this from me?"

My calm tone doesn't fool him. Drake is as good as Nathan at reading people. "You're pissed," he says. "I get it. I'll do my best to explain, but if at the end of this, you want to take a swing at me, I won't try to stop you. I owe you that."

"We're not kids anymore, Drake. I'm not going to fight you. Just ... Talk to me, please."

He nods and runs his hands through his hair. "Amber ... To start with, she made me promise not to tell you that night. She knew how much you were suffering and didn't want to make it worse. She wanted you to be able to focus on Mom and Dad, and hell, I suppose us too—you always did take your big brother duties seriously. You were trying to hold us together, and she knew you were struggling. Maybe she thought she'd talk it over with you at some point, but then after Mom died, it's not like things got any easier. The funeral, the aftermath. Dad was a mess. We all were. You were grieving, then Maddox went off the rails. It was one thing after another, and I guess she never thought the time was right."

I gulp down my Scotch. Fuck. I was wrong. I do want to take a swing at him. I'd like to punch him square in the face for keeping something so important from me. Something that ultimately destroyed my marriage. Amber didn't tell me because she didn't want to hurt me, and she carried that weight all alone while also grieving for my mom—and for the babies she would never have.

And minutes ago, after she finally did tell me, I looked her in the face and ... Fuck, what did I even say? I was in shock. Did I make her think I didn't believe her? The way she looked at me before she walked out of Drake's office flashes in my mind's eye, and my stomach drops. I may not remember what I said, but I know I let her down. Again. I close my eyes and wish I could turn back time. What the fuck is wrong with me?

"I still don't understand why you didn't ever tell me." I try to keep a lid on my temper, but it bleeds into my tone regardless.

"That's complicated. For a start, she kept making me promise. But I had my own selfish reason. I hated myself for the way I spoke to Mom that night. I didn't think, I just reacted, you know? Amber was sobbing, and Mom loved Amber. She was just ... She was confused. And she didn't remember saying anything. She ..." He gulps, and another tear drips onto the table. "She accused me of making it up. Of saying it to hurt her. The last lucid thing she ever said to me was to go away and leave her in peace. And the last memory she had of me was that I caused her pain. She was never really with it again after that night. Never really herself. I've ... Fuck, Elijah, I've always hated myself for that."

He drains his glass and slams it down. I stare at him, beyond shocked. My last real conversation with my mother was about my pop and how she wanted him to live and love again when she was gone. She made me promise to look out for him, to make sure he found someone else when the time was right. She talked about my brothers and asked me to keep an eye on them. Finally, she talked about me. She held my hand to her dry lips and kissed it. "Te amo, Elijah," she murmured. "My firstborn. My beautiful baby boy. Always so strong. Te amo."

I have treasured that memory. Have taken it out and examined it over the years, allowed it to console me. Used it to paint over the awful picture of those last days near the end. I didn't realize how lucky I was until I heard Drake's story and saw his anguish.

I pour him another drink and push it toward him. "I get it, Drake. I understand. I'm so fucking sorry. But you know she loved you, right? And she felt loved by you. None of that gets wiped out by one fucked-up conversation when she was out of her head on pain meds."

"I know, yeah, logically at least. That's what Amelia said. But it's been hard. And you and Amber ... Fuck, I should have said something earlier. I think it broke something in her, you know? After the funeral, she started to pull away from us. Stopped being as involved."

I remember it all too well. It started small, her withdrawal from the family. From me. Little things like being too busy to come to Sunday brunch. She was there for me when I needed her, a shoulder to cry on, but I sensed she was holding back. She never talked about her own day, her own problems, her own concerns. She retreated, not only from me, but from everyone. That's when the rot started to set in. When my dad launched his anti-love campaign. She was slipping away from me, and I had no idea what had caused it. Months later—maybe even as much as a year—I broached the issue of children with her. I asked her if she was interested in pursuing IVF or looking for a surrogate, and she dismissed me. "I'm sorry, Elijah," she said. "I know this isn't what you signed up for. It was supposed to be simple, wasn't it? But I don't see the point in prolonging our agony. Neither of those options are guaranteed to work, and really, doesn't the world have enough babies in it already?"

At the time I was hurt, confused. When had she decided this? But she was already shutting down by then, and truthfully, I was still grieving. Still trying to hold my fractured family together. Things had gone sideways with Maddox, and my dad was losing his grip at Jamestech, and I felt like I was carrying the weight of the world on my shoulders. Maybe part of me was relieved at not having to go down the fertility path, and that's why I never pushed it. Of course, now I understand so much better—by that stage, she had started to convince herself that I resented her and that my family despised her. Fuck. What a god-awful mess.

"I'm sorry, Elijah," he says, his apology heartfelt. "I'm sorry if I made things worse. I was in my own hell, and then I ran away to Chicago. I always thought you two would work it out."

I'd be lying if I say I'm not pissed and frustrated. It's possible we could have avoided a lot of pain and suffering. But my wife is a force of nature—she could convince a cat to bark. Convincing a grieving young man to hoard harmful information from his grieving older brother would have been a walk in the park. As angry and disappointed as I feel, I can't let him blame himself.

"You're right, you should have told me," I say, nodding. "But I forgive you, Drake. There's no telling whether it would have changed anything, and what has happened with my marriage is not your fault. Amber and I are grown-ass adults, and we made our own choices. I gave up too easily. Even now, even recently ... Fuck, even today. I acted like an ass. The look on her face ..." She looked so goddamn sad. Like I once again chose someone else over her. Once again didn't have her back. Fuck! I shake my head to clear it and refocus on my brother. "That's not on you, Drake. That's on me."

"Fuck. Okay." He nods and puffs out a breath.

We finish our drinks in heavy silence before he speaks again. "Well, bro, I suppose the only question that remains is this: How shit-faced are we going to get tonight?" Despite my hurt, I force out a laugh and clink glasses with him.

"Nah. You need to go home to Amelia. That is an incredible woman you have there. As for me ... I need to go find Amber." And somehow make her understand that not only was my mom wrong about everything she said that night, but that I will never give her cause to doubt me again.

THIRTY-EIGHT

AMBER

I 'm not scheduled to lead a class this evening, but I head to the center anyway. There will be company and warmth and far less temptation to drink until I hit oblivion. Sanjay drops me off a block away because I want to walk off some of my emotion. He's his usual chatty self, and I don't think he notices anything off about me at all, but then, I am a master at this. At hiding my pain. I'm so good I could give a damn TED Talk on the subject.

Listening to Drake go over the divorce details was hard enough, but what followed almost destroyed me. All these years, I've kept that night from Elijah. I needed to protect him from the awful things his mother said to me, no matter how dearly it cost me. The way he stared at me, rejecting what I was saying after he forced me to confide in him—it was a heavy blow. Part of me understands his disbelief, but I'm so sick of being second best. Sick of knowing that his instincts will always keep him loyal to his family and not to me—his wife.

Well, I won't be his wife for much longer, I remind myself

as I walk toward the community center. Tonight is the first time I've believed, without a doubt, that the divorce is the right choice, and the heaviness of that breaks my heart. Elijah and I still love each other, but we're doomed. It's time to accept that.

I blink back tears and tell myself to concentrate on the here and now. The inviting lights of LOJ welcome me. In this working-class neighborhood, I feel more alive than I ever did in Manhattan. There are threats and dangers, but at least you know what they are. You can see them coming.

I walk through the big metal gate at the entrance and immediately see a group of young men. That's not unusual or cause for concern. Sissie is quick to point out that a lot of young men in this area feel the need to look and act tougher than they are to survive. But something about this group sets off alarm bells in my admittedly inexperienced mind.

They're clumped together at the side of the building, out of line of sight of the street where kids sometimes go to sneak a cigarette. I'm sure many of them wish for something stronger but none are willing to break Sissie's zero-tolerance policy on drugs of any kind.

The gathering is maybe five or six strong, and they're circled around something—or someone. It's probably nothing, but I should get help. There are two big bikes parked in front, so a couple of Misfits are here, and Sissie herself keeps a baseball bat in her office. I don't even have to walk inside. I could just get out my phone and call. Yes. I should definitely do that.

I stare at the little group, see the way it moves, and hear someone crying. I don't want to get help—I want to *be* the help. I stride toward them, my heels clicking on the concrete.

"Hey!" I yell as I get close. They whirl around in surprise, and it takes them about two seconds to go from surprise to suspicion and all the way through to certainty that I'm no threat at all. Shawn, the talented dancer from my class, cowers in the middle of the circle.

His lip is bleeding, and he's holding his hands in front of his face. "I'm okay, Miss Amber," he says desperately. "These are my friends. Please don't get involved."

Oh, hell no—the kid is getting the snot beaten out of him, and he's trying to protect me? No fucking way.

I push my way into the circle, and they assemble around me like vultures. I must look like easy pickings. Maybe I am.

"They don't look very friendly, Shawn," I say, putting as much confidence into my voice as I can. The leader breaks rank and gets right in my face. "What the fuck you know, lady? Shawn here is one of us."

"No, he's not, you asshole. Now get out of my way. I am not in the mood for this bullshit. I've had a very bad day, and you don't want to mess with me."

His eyes widen, and I realize how big of a mistake I've made by calling him out in front of his group. Now he looks weak, and the only way he can stop looking weak is by showing them who's boss. "Shawn," I say quickly. "Leave now. I'm fine."

I'm not fine, I know, but all of this will be for nothing if Shawn is hurt even more. I meet his frightened eyes, see how brave he is trying to be. "Now, Shawn—get inside."

One of them tries to grab him on his way past, but those dance skills of his come in handy. Shawn ducks and dodges and scurries away between his legs. Quick as a flash, he runs toward the community center.

I gulp down air and swallow my fear along with it. I am not prey, and I will not show fear.

"You got some balls, bitch. Who the fuck you think you are?"

"I'm nobody special, but I'm not going to let you touch that boy, you hear me?"

He shoves me against the wall, and his pals snigger as he tugs at the strap of my purse. "You want that?" I ask. "Take it. There's cash in there, and a Tom Ford lipstick that I think is your exact shade."

His friends make guffaw, and one of them wolf whistles at him. He, however, doesn't look like he's finding any of this remotely amusing. From the corner of my eye, I see Shawn disappear through the door of the center.

"Maybe I'll take your purse, and maybe I'll take you too," the leader says menacingly. "You look pretty good for an old lady."

"I'm not old, I'm forty," I snap back. "And don't you dare touch me."

I can take the verbal abuse, and I don't care if he steals my purse to save face. But he will not be laying a hand on me, no matter how big he is. And he is big. I have had it with men who think it's fine to touch women like they're property, and my fear is overshadowed by my determination not to let it happen to me again.

He reaches out and grabs my shoulder, and I start to very obviously raise my knee—a trick Rafael taught me. If a man suspects you're going for his crown jewels, his focus will go straight to protecting his dick. Sure enough, my harasser immediately glances down and starts to swerve. At that exact moment, I slam the heel of my palm right up into his nose. A sickening crunch is followed by spurting blood, and he screams, "Fuck! You fucking bitch! You broke my nose."

Tears are streaming from his eyes, and his baseball cap has fallen off in the struggle. The guys standing behind him look shocked, and I realize they're younger than I initially thought—not a single one of them is a day over twenty.

"Leave Shawn alone," I say sternly. "In fact, leave all these kids alone. And get a belt, for fuck's sake. You're going to trip over your pants walking around dressed like that."

I step around the group, adrenaline surging and the reality of what just happened catching up with me. I force myself not to look back, not to show weakness, but I realize how crazy that whole incident was. How badly it could have gone. Any one of those men could have hurt me.

I stride briskly, wanting to run, and I'm flooded with relief when I see Erik and Rafael heading in my direction. Erik stops briefly, asks if I'm all right, then continues on to deal with the group of kids, which quickly disperses. As Sissie said, they're all a bit scared of the bikers. Rafael looks at the guy with the busted nose as he walks past, then looks at me. "You do that?" he asks.

"I did," I reply, suddenly feeling shaky.

"Nice hit. Stupid, though—why didn't you come get us?"

"I don't know. I was in a bad mood, and I may have had a couple of whiskeys too many," I answer honestly. "They just pissed me off. Is Shawn okay?"

"He is. His mama is on her way in. You still in a bad mood?"

"I feel a bit better after that. My husband—soon-to-be-ex—is a boxer. He loves punching things. I get it now."

Rafael nods but stays silent, as usual. From this close, I

notice that one of his many tattoos is a king cobra, the hood at the front of his throat, the body of the snake wrapping around his neck then disappearing off under his tank top. I wonder idly what the rest of his tats look like. It's not a sex thing, it's a curiosity thing. He is hot, but for the time being, men hold no appeal for me. Apart from one, and he is off-limits.

"You got time for a lesson?" I ask.

"Why? You still need to punch things?"

I nod. "I do. It'll make me feel better. Plus, I have some ideas about Shawn and his situation, and I need to clear my head."

Erik overhears and says, "Nothing clears the head like punching things. Come on, Miss Amber. Do your worst." He grins and gestures me toward the large rec room.

"Why, thank you, kind sir." I smile back, grateful. For the next hour, I will be too busy throwing and blocking punches to even think about the James family.

THIRTY-NINE

ELIJAH

A s soon as I discover she's not home, I consider calling Sanjay to ask if he's taken her to the community center, but the man still doesn't like me, and I'm happy to leave it that way. Fuck knows she needs an ally.

I've been fielding calls from Luisa and Mason about work, and Nathan is worried I need company after signing the final paperwork today and wants to know if I want to grab a drink or dinner or to come stay the night at his place. And Dad left a voicemail asking if I'll bring my "new lady friend" to brunch at the house soon.

Christ. I love my family with all my heart, but right now I wish they'd all back the fuck off. I need to find a way to press a mute button so I can concentrate. Shit, I should have figured out a way to do that years ago.

After telling Gretchen where we're heading next, I deal with the rest from the back seat. I answer the work queries about the South Korean deal, tell Nathan I'll call him tomorrow, and send Dad a message telling him there is no new lady friend despite what he may have heard through the family grapevine. Hell, I'll be lucky if the woman I've loved for over half my life will still agree to be my friend at all.

Jesus fuck, what a mess. I rub my hands over my beard and try to let go of some tension. For her sake, maybe I should let her go. But I'm not that good of a man—and damn it, I need her in my life. The way she behaved earlier, so calm as we swung a wrecking ball through our marriage, drove me mad. I still think of her as mine and can't bear the thought of that changing.

So what now? I can't force her to feel differently. It's not like I've done a good job of persuading her. Why the fuck would she want to belong to me after the way I've treated her?

By the time we arrive at the community center, I'm no closer to clarity. I am a jumble of nerve endings and energy. "We're here, Mr. J," Gretchen says, meeting my eyes in the rearview mirror. "I'll wait for you, okay?"

It makes me smile. My five-foot-nothing driver is worried for my safety. "Sure. Thanks, Gretch."

Light spills from the windows of the sprawling building, and I catch a glimpse of a garden, walls covered in spectacular graffiti art. It's bright and welcoming, and I'm met by a familiar face at the reception desk. "Mr. James," Vicky says as I stride toward her. "Welcome to LOJ—it's great to see you here. This is Alfie. Alfie, this is Miss Amber's hubby."

The adolescent boy smiles at me. "I like Miss Amber. She's real nice."

"She is," I agree, smiling back. "That's actually why I'm here. Where would I find her, Vicky?"

She checks the screen in front of her and tilts her head.

"Uh, I'm not sure Mr. J. She's here, I've seen her, but she's not down to lead a class. Here, take this." She hands me a clip-on name badge that labels me a visitor. "You can go on in and look for her."

The building smells of cleaning products and baking, and the walls are covered in more graffiti art, along with a variety of posters and flyers. I take in the signs for cooking classes, exercise clubs, bingo nights. Music and children's laughter drift from behind closed doors along the hallway. I can see why Amber likes this vibrant, friendly hub of activity. There's more genuine warmth in this center than all of her society functions put together.

I pop my head into a room where a boxing lesson is taking place and watch with interest. The kid in the ring is young and slightly built, but powerful and clearly talented. A lot of great fighters come out of local community centers like this.

I look out of place in my suit and designer shoes, but people still nod and say hi as I wander the halls. Eventually, I start to wonder if she's even here. One room remains, and I peer through the small glass panel to check what's going on inside. With a roar, I burst into the room.

My wife is lying pinned to the floor, her arms held above her head, some massive Viking motherfucker lying on top of her. I vaguely register there's someone else in the room and know I should slow down and assess the threat, but I can't. Amber is in danger. Someone is hurting my wife.

I crouch low and barrel into him, slamming him off her and onto the ground before he has time to react. I straddle him and punch him in the side of the head, white noise filling my ears and red mist filling my vision. I pummel the guy, vaguely aware of Amber screaming, "Stop!" in the background. I pause and look around in case the second guy has her, and the Viking makes the most of it. He takes a swing at my jaw and knocks me backward onto my ass. I get right back to my feet and am about to dive in again when I'm grabbed from behind. Strong arms pull me backward, and my feet lose their grip on the floor. I struggle and pull one arm free, snarling.

I've never felt so wild—I will fucking kill them. The Viking stays on the ground and stares at me, shaking his head and holding his hands up in a gesture of surrender. Amber walks toward me and places her palms on my heaving chest. "I'm okay, Elijah. I'm okay."

Her hands on my body and the placating tone of her voice take hold, and I suck in a breath. "What the fuck is going on?" I demand, shaking myself free of the man behind me. He lets me go, and when I turn to glare at him, I see that he has blood coming out of his nose. I must have headbutted him, and I can't say that I regret it.

"This is Erik." Amber gestures at the blond giant scrambling to his feet. "And that is Rafael. They're teaching me how to defend myself."

My anger is still bubbling away beneath the surface, but I force myself to calm down. She's wearing gym clothes, her hair is tied up for exercise, and she is totally unhurt. I place my hands over hers on my chest and gaze into her eyes, and only then do I finally start to relax. And then I feel like an asshole.

"This must be the husband," Erik says, laughing and offering me a big paw to shake. Blood dribbles from a cut above his eye, but it doesn't seem to bother him. "Nice moves, man—though I almost had you."

I raise an eyebrow. "I don't think so, Erik. But fuck. I guess I'm sorry?"

Rafael, equally large and covered in tattoos, wipes the blood from his face. "No need. We'll let that go. Must have looked bad." His voice is low and quiet. "But she's doing great."

"She's a natural." Erik laughs again. "Took out a baby gang banger all by herself."

"She did *what*?" I repeat, narrowing my eyes at my wife.

She shrugs. "I did no such thing. I merely … spoke to him sternly."

"You broke his fucking nose," Erik says.

Amber grins devilishly, a glint in her eyes. "Yes. I suppose I did, didn't I?"

I shake my head, letting this new reality settle in. My wife, the ass-kicker. "Amber, can we go somewhere and talk?"

Both of the big men look at her, waiting for her response. I tense, because they won't get in my way, no matter how big they are.

She nods. "Okay. There's a pub two blocks over called O'Shaughnessy's. Let me get changed, and I'll meet you there."

O'-fucking-Shaughnessy's? Since when did Amber start hanging out at Irish dive bars? Over the summer, before any of this divorce stuff, I took Drake to a real spit-and-sawdust joint in the East Village. I said I loved it because she would hate it. God, I was such a dick. But it really does drive home how much she's changed in such a short time. She hasn't only shed her fucking skin—she swapped out every cell of her DNA.

With a nod toward Erik and Rafael, I head out and let Gretchen know where I'm going. I'm not surprised that she knows the place—her brother's a cop in Queens, and she spends time here. Turns out it is Irish, but it's not so much of a dive. In fact, it's pretty nice. I order a Guinness and a Bushmills for myself and a pinot for Amber and settle down at a table to wait for her. Fifteen minutes later, she walks in. She's obviously had a quick shower and is dressed in yoga pants and a tank. Her hair is shaggy and damp, and she's not wearing a scrap of makeup. She looks like a complete stranger—a gorgeous, intoxicating stranger. She nods at me, sits down, and gulps a mouthful of wine. Some things, at least, haven't changed. Thank god.

"I'm sorry," I say, determined to start this off the way I should. "For what happened back there. I just saw you on the ground, and ..."

"It's okay. I get it. They get it. If I saw you in that position, I'd have done the same."

I smile at her. "Yeah, I think you would. You're full of surprises, Amber."

"Most of them," she says, smiling back, "are surprises to me too. Now, what are you actually doing here, Elijah? If you've come to discuss the thing about your mom, please don't. I think we both said everything we need to."

There's a hint of steel to her voice, but I also spot the slight tremor in her hand as she lifts her glass. As usual, she's trying to appear less human than she actually is. For years, she hid her vulnerability underneath a cold exterior. I might be the right guy for steaming into a room and attacking

Vikings, but I haven't protected her in other ways. The ways that matter. And that realization continues to come like a punch to the gut.

"No, I don't think we have," I reply. "And I don't think there are enough words in the English language for me to apologize with. I might have to start with Spanish."

She quirks an eyebrow at me. "What do you mean?"

"I mean that I'm more sorry than I can ever fucking say. I'm sorry that I didn't immediately take you into my arms and apologize for the things my mom said to you. I never doubted that you were telling the truth, Amber, I hate that she said those things. Even more, I hate that you felt like you had to protect me from it when you were hurting yourself. I let you down, and I'm all out of excuses."

She pales a little and shakes her head. "No. Like I've said before, we both made mistakes. I hid things from you. I shut you out. I played a very big part in all of this."

"Maybe, in the past, yeah—we both made mistakes. But the thing with Freddie? The thing today? That's all on me, Amber. I love you. I've always loved you. And I want you back, more than anything in the whole world. It's taken all of this for me to understand how much. That being said, I think we needed time apart. I needed to do some serious thinking and sort my shit out. You needed to ... Fuck, baby, you need to keep on doing what you're doing, because it suits you. You're fucking radiant. I can see you growing and changing and lighting up from the inside. I don't want to get in the way of that. I don't want to hold you back. But you need to know that my love for you has never faded. And it never will."

She bites her lip, and stares at the tabletop. The old

Amber would have simply given me the evil eye and said something pointed and sharp that shredded me to pieces. The new Amber? I have no fucking clue.

"What do you want from me, Elijah?" she says quietly, finally looking up with tears in her tawny eyes.

"Everything," I reply. "And nothing. I think we're worth fighting for, but I also know that this isn't the right time to push you. I understand that you still need time."

She laughs and wipes away the tears. "You think?" The challenge in her eyes is the perfect combination of the old Amber and this new one. "After everything that's happened, I don't know if there ever will be a right time to push me. I love you, but I'm also wary of you. You hold so much power over me. I see you, and I want you. I can't stop thinking about you. I want to fight for us as well, but I think ... I think for now, I need to fight for myself instead. Does that make any sense?"

"It does," I answer, knowing she's right but hating every second of this. "I understand. And for now, I accept it. But Amber? This is not me giving up on us. This is me giving us space to breathe. I need to sort things out with my family and to look at the way work has taken over my life. How about we press pause? Really press pause, until next year?"

"Elijah, it's already December 21." She smirks. "That's a lot to fix in ten days."

"I know, and it's not a deadline. It's just ... Amber, we've loved each other for more than two decades. Surely it's worth another few days at least. Or longer, if that's what it takes. Let's see how we feel in the new year."

I see the indecision in her eyes, the mix of hope and fear. I put the fear there, and now all I can do is pray that hope wins out. "And you promise you'll leave me alone until then? No turning up at the door, no suggestive texts, no ...uh ..."

"Spectacularly hot sex? No tying you up and fucking you? No blindfolds, no torturing those sweet nipples of yours? No orgasms, no spanking ..."

She goes bright red, and my cock responds in a predictable fashion. "Elijah! Stop it."

I grin at her. I could talk her into bed right now. But a deal is a deal, and I fight back the urge. "I promise."

Her nod is small but firm. "Okay. I agree." She drags her chair back quickly—she wants to touch me as much as I want to touch her. She was right that night. Fighting and fucking—we're awesome at both, but we need more than that if we're going to make it.

She leaves in a cloud of coconut shampoo, and I stay and finish my whiskey. Fuck. I have no clue what's going to happen between us, but at least it's not the end.

FORTY

AMBER

I meet Martha for brunch the day after Elijah and I decide to take a real break. She looks sheepish as she waves me over to her table, and neither of us attempts our usual air kiss.

I raise my eyebrows at the coffee mug in her hands. "I know," she says, grimacing. "There's not even any vodka in it. Look ... I wanted to say I'm sorry. For setting you up like that. I was an asshole, and I regret it."

I nod and order my own coffee. She looks and sounds genuinely remorseful, and I wonder how much she knows. "What did he tell you about it?" I ask after the waiter leaves.

"That he pitched to you, and you weren't interested."

Huh. Well, that is certainly one way to describe it. "And you knew that he was going to, ah, pitch to me?"

"Yes. As soon as the news broke about you and Elijah, he was ... God, Amber, he was enraged. He was so angry with me."

"With you?" I ask, confused.

"Yes, with me. Because we're friends, and I didn't warn

397

him that the biggest divorce of the decade was about to hit the headlines. I tried telling him I didn't know, but that only made it worse. He was ... I've never seen him so mad. It was like he thought it was his god-given right to represent you, you know? Because we've known each other for so long. He was furious and told me I had to make it up to him by arranging that meeting. It sucked, but I was scared, Amber, and as usual, I did what he wanted. I'm sorry."

My cappuccino arrives, and I buy time blowing on its frothy surface. "Why were you scared, Martha? Truth now. If you lie or give me some fake bullshit, I'm out of here. I have a busy day."

"Truth? I'm not sure I remember what that tastes like, darling. Oh, what the fuck, why not?" She meets my eyes and lets out a sigh. "I'm scared because he made me sign the world's worst prenup. You know Freddie—he's brilliant at his job. He has me completely under his thumb. I get literally nothing, and more importantly, neither do the girls."

"What? Why would he do that? They're his own flesh and blood."

"They are, and I have no clue if he'd go through with it. But the last time I threatened to leave, he ... Well, he told me to go. But he warned me I wouldn't get a penny, and that he would see me and the girls homeless before he'd budge on that. His face, Amber ... His fucking face. I believed him. I still believe him. Personally, I suppose I'd find a way to cope, but the girls—I couldn't do that to them. It's been like this for years. He's in charge of all our finances. I don't have my own account, my own money. He pays all the bills, the school fees, the house is in his name. It's like I don't exist. To start with, I thought he was just old-fashioned, you know? But it's not that. It's ..."

"A form of control. I see that. Is there anything else, Martha? We all know about the affairs, but is there anything else?"

She gulps down coffee and avoids my gaze for a few moments. "He can be ... uh ... controlling in other ways too. Let's just say he has a high sex drive."

"No, sweetie, let's not just say that—let's call it what it is. He abuses you physically, emotionally, and sexually. He controls you through your love for your daughters and your lack of financial independence. Is there anything else?" I place my hand over hers, feel her fingers trembling beneath mine.

She looks at me, tears shining in her eyes, and gives me a halfhearted smile. "He always leaves the toilet seat up?"

I smile back. This is overwhelming for her, I know. Facing reality often is. "Martha, your husband is an abusive asshole. He tried it with me, that day in his office."

I watch her closely, and her shock is genuine. "Oh god. Oh my god, no. Amber, I didn't know—I swear I didn't know."

"It's okay, honey, I believe you. And I'm fine. But what we need to do now is find a way out for you. I'm not going to go into too much detail here, but Elijah has some leverage over Freddie. I'm guessing he's been pretty quiet on the subject of the James divorce recently?"

She nods and swipes tears away from her cheeks. "He has, yes. He's been in a foul mood and hell to live with, but he hasn't mentioned you or Elijah. What ... What is the leverage?"

I consider telling her, but it's not my story to share. I won't expose other women without their permission. "I'm not going to discuss that, Martha. But we can help if you want us to. What would a happy ending look like for you right now?"

She thinks about it, and as she does, she nibbles at her so-far untouched food. It's the first time I've seen solids pass her lips in years. "He fell down the stairs a while ago and busted his face up. I enjoyed that. But … No, at the end of the day, he's still the father of my children, so I wouldn't wish for him to die in a freak accident. I think I'd just like some freedom. I want to be able to live my life in peace and keep my girls in the same house and at the same school and have plenty for their college funds. And I'd like to … Fuck, I want to feel safe. To know that he wouldn't try and take some kind of revenge on me. I've been living scared for so damn long I don't remember what safe feels like."

I turn it over in my mind. That sounds eminently possible, and I'm sure Elijah would be more than happy to help facilitate that kind of arrangement. He'll be glad of any excuse to turn the screws on Freddie—and it couldn't happen to a nicer guy. The little turd deserves everything he gets. He will not be touching any more women, and if Elijah has his way, his business reputation will also be taking a dive. It's not an arrest, but for someone like Freddie, stripping away his power and his status is just as bad. We merely need to make sure Martha and the girls are secure beforehand. "Okay. Leave it with me. Are you all right if Elijah contacts you directly?"

She nods but looks confused. "You'd do that? You'd help me like that, after everything?"

"Of course I would. In fact, it will give me a great amount of pleasure. Just stay quiet for now. Avoid him whenever possible and fake it when you can't."

She laughs. "Well, that really won't be a problem. I've been faking everything from smiles to orgasms for the last twenty years. But ... you and Elijah. I was shocked—really shocked. You two always seemed so right for each other. That night at Elodie's wedding, I remember thinking how sweet ... and hot it was. The way you two couldn't keep your eyes off each other."

That night feels like a lifetime ago now. And she's right, we couldn't keep our eyes off each other, but not necessarily for the right reasons.

I'm still so confused about all of it. It feels like as soon as I make a decision, something else happens. I want out, he persuades me back in. I want back in, we fall out. I'm building a life without him, but it would be so much richer with him in it. I love him, and I yearn for him—even if I know he isn't always good for me. Nothing is clear, and the physical pull I feel toward him doesn't help. It's been exhausting, and I need the respite that he promised. Tonight, I'm headed to Charleston to spend Christmas and New Year's with Granny Lucille, and I can only hope that will help uncloud my mind.

"Well, Martha, you don't need me to tell you this, but you cannot possibly know what's going on in a marriage from the outside looking in."

Or what's going on in a divorce.

"I know, but ... Are you sure?" she persists. "Even now, the way you talk about him—he's still obviously part of you. I'm not judging, and like you said, I know better than most how good we are at pretending. But I have genuinely been miserable with my husband for most of our marriage. I'm not sure I ever really loved him. I certainly never enjoyed sleeping with him—well, that's not true. I used to, before the affairs started, but they started early. You and Elijah, though—you can't fake what you two have. Are you sure that's all dead in the water?"

That, of course, is the $64,000 question. And that is what I will be trying to figure out.

"Well, we seem to be getting divorced," I reply, keeping my tone light. "That's not exactly a classic sign of a healthy marriage. But who knows? I'm damn sure I don't."

She pulls a sympathetic face and raises her coffee mug. I clink mine against it, and we both smile. We're having a real conversation, and we aren't even drunk. Wonders will never cease.

FORTY-ONE

AMBER

The time away from him, from my New York life, does me a world of good. Granny Lucille is her usual delightful self, and the weather is a hell of a lot nicer in Charleston. The physical distance gives me the break I need, and the feeling that I'm living in a pressure cooker starts to fade.

Elijah has stayed in touch but has been true to his word and behaved like a gentleman. We have talked and messaged and shared stories about our days, but we have not flirted. I kind of miss it. Perhaps he's playing a very canny game. By being the perfect gentleman, he has made me wish for the deliciously dirty-mouthed monster I know he can be. Still, it has been nice to take sex out of the equation. To simply talk and allow ourselves to take a beat.

Today is New Year's Eve, and Lucille is hosting a party. Her house is crammed full of interesting people—musicians, writers, academics, artists. They come in all shapes, sizes, and ages. Someone is playing a fiddle, and an impromptu dance floor has been created in the middle of the living room.

I've just finished up a jig myself and head outside to cool down. I sit in one of the wicker chairs on the veranda and enjoy the sounds of revelry coming from the house. Lucille has invited all the neighbors, so at least nobody minds the noise.

Within a few minutes, she joins me, fanning her face with a paper plate. She takes a seat and gulps down the rest of her punch, and when I raise my eyebrows, she says, "What? I don't want to dehydrate. Besides, I'm a million years old—whatever I've been doing, it seems to work."

I smile and sip my own wine. "Well, I can't argue with that."

She points at the cell phone on my lap. "Keeping that handy so you can speak to Elijah?"

She's right, but I'm embarrassed about it. Is it so wrong to want to hear his voice? And anyway, isn't she the one who told me I should care less about what other people think?

"What's with the face, Bam-Bam?"

"Oh, I don't know, Granny—it's just all so complicated. My poor little mind can't keep up."

"Pah! Don't give me that hooey. Your mind is more than capable. Anyway, it's not that complicated. I've watched you since you got here. I've listened. I've been paying attention."

"Okay," I reply, narrowing my eyes at her. "Out with it then, Jessica Fletcher. You clearly have something to say."

"I do. You light up when you talk about him, you smile when he sends you a message, and you practically squeal with joy when he calls."

"I do not!"

"Do so. Anyway, it's obvious you still love him, and he still loves you. Treat this as what it is—a wake-up call. Sort your crap out and get back together. I know this all must feel like it's lasted a month of Sundays to you, but it hasn't. It's been the blink of an eye, and look how much you've changed. How much you've achieved. What's that awful phrase people use on TV shows? Being the best version of yourself? Well, that's what I see you becoming, darling—but I still don't think you're happy without him. You're a lot better than the last time I saw you, but it's like there's still a piece missing. An Elijah-shaped piece."

She's right, of course. That's exactly how I feel. The last time I stayed with her, I was a mess. This time? Well, I'm still a mess—but at least I'm working on it. And what she doesn't know is that in the time since she saw me last, I have had a heart-stopping affair with my own husband. Maybe she does ... I wouldn't put anything past her.

"Possibly," I say. "But there's a lot of history, and we've hurt each other badly. I don't know if it's possible to come back from all that."

"Sounds like nonsense to me. He wants to try again, and deep down, I think you do too. I'd be the last person to tell you that you need a man to be complete, child, but in your case, I think this specific man could make you happy. If you were willing to let him try."

I wish it were that simple. "I don't trust him, Granny. I don't trust him not to hurt me again."

She must hear the pain in my voice, because for once she doesn't go for the jugular with the pep talk. She reaches out and lays her gnarled fingers over mine. "Trust is a tricky beast, Bam-Bam, I know. But it can be rebuilt over time. Whatever you decide, I'm here for you, you know that. You can always move in with your Granny, and I can look after you when you're old and frail."

She cackles at herself and climbs to her feet. "Right. Well. It's almost time. You coming in?"

I shake my head. "No. It's too wild in there for the likes of me."

She kisses the top of my head and disappears back inside, and I glance at my phone and find a message from Elijah. I break out into a big smile—damn, she's right.

He'll be at his dad's house, about to ring in the new year. In the beginning, I never missed a James family New Year's Eve bash, but I didn't feel comfortable going after Verona died. They were such a tight unit, the James boys and their father. After the incident with his mom especially, I felt like I was intruding. If they did all secretly resent me like she suggested, then the last thing I wanted to do was spend New Year's with them. It's been so long now that we've created our own tradition—being apart at midnight.

The message is simple and makes me smile even more.

> I wish you were here.

I'm not sure I totally agree with him. Sure, I'd like to see Drake and Amelia, maybe even Melanie and the baby. But that still leaves the rest of his family.

> I wish you were here too. You're missing a crazy party.

He starts typing a response immediately.

> I can be there in a few hours if that's what you want. I'll tell them where I'm going. I'll tell them I love you and can't live without you. Just say the word, baby.

I pull in a surprised breath. Would he really do that? Would he leave his family behind and head here to be with me? As for telling them ... I don't underestimate what a big deal that would be. He has a trip to Seoul planned for next week, so work will also be playing on his mind as usual. I struggle with the idea that he would disrupt his life so completely just to see me.

> Really? You'd do that?

> Of course I would. You want me to come?

Oh god. Do I? Part of me does, for sure. But how much of that part only wants to say yes to test him? To push him and see where his boundaries lie. If we're going to rebuild, that's not a healthy way to begin.

> No, stay in New York. But I appreciate the offer. I'll see you when I'm back and we can talk.

> I can't wait to see you. I love you.

After replying that I love him too, I lean back in the chair and gaze up at the star-filled sky. There are already a few premature fireworks lighting up the night, and they make me grin. Or maybe it's Elijah that makes me grin. It means a lot that he wants to tell his family about us.

For now, though, I don't want to analyze anything too

deeply. I don't want to dismantle it all and examine it—I just want to enjoy the way I feel in this moment.

I hear the countdown from inside the house and laugh as explosions of color erupt in all directions. Under that rainbow shimmer, I am filled with hope. Granny Lucille is right, as usual. He is my missing piece—and I want to rebuild.

FORTY-TWO

S he loves me. She fucking loves me. And she wishes I were there. And ... Shit, should I just go? What's the point in having a private plane if not to do crap like this? If I left now, I could be in Charleston by three. In her bed by half past ...

I'm still turning it over in my mind when Mason nudges me so hard I almost drop my phone.

"Bro," he whispers, nodding toward the balcony. "Look."

I'm annoyed at being dragged out of my fantasy of being in Amber's bed, but I follow his gaze. Drake and Amelia are out there alone. "So?" I ask.

Maddox sidles over, drinking orange juice out of a cut-crystal champagne flute, and grins at me. "Drake's been shifty all day. I think this is it."

I realize how wrapped up in my own drama I've been. I worked late, catching up on the Kim deal, and by the time I arrived, the party was in full swing. I chatted with my brothers, caught up with Ashley and Tyler, and checked in with my dad—but if I'm honest, none of them had the whole of my attention. I've been waiting all night to message Amber. To catch her near midnight and let her know that although we're apart, I'm still thinking of her. I remember all the New Year's Eves I spent here without her and wish I could take them back. All I can do is try to move forward, and I meant every word when I offered to join her in South Carolina.

Now, my focus is drawn back to my family—and to that balcony.

"Oh man, I hope he's going to," says Mason, glancing at his watch. "She's perfect for him. Come on, come on, Drake. It's almost midnight."

Luz and Dad start the countdown, and the place erupts into cheers as the clock turns. As soon as that dies down, we all turn our eyes back to the balcony, where Drake is down on one knee. Fuck, he's actually doing it. None of us can hear what he's saying, but her hands are on her face, and he's holding out a small black box.

"Put the ring on her finger before she changes her mind, bro," yells Mason, making us all laugh. We whistle and holler and look on as Drake does exactly that. I feel tears brimming in my eyes. Fuck, this is a great start to the new year. My baby brother, finding his happy ending. I couldn't be more pleased.

It doesn't take long for everyone to storm the balcony like fans at the end of a football game. We smother them both with hugs and kisses and congratulations. Maddox and Mason hoist Drake up on their shoulders and parade him around, and as soon as Nathan joins, we do the same. He clings to us, laughing and telling us to put him the fuck down so he can get back to his fiancée.

We eventually do, but we don't let him go without another round of hugs and handshakes.

Now, as I watch my family celebrate together, my heart filled with warmth and love, I know it's time to leave. It's time to find my own happy ending, and the only person in the world who can give me that is Amber James.

FINDING a pilot willing and able to fly me to Charleston after midnight on New Year's Day isn't easy, but this is one of those occasions when having vast wealth is extremely useful. Our usual guy suggests some colleagues, and eventually I find someone who is both sober and happy to work—at inflated rates, of course. I don't care. This will be worth it.

I've been to Lucille's charming home a few times before, but it's been several years. Little has changed in her historic neighborhood, and I smile as I'm driven through the pretty streets. It's almost five, and only a few of the buildings are lit up and active. Lucille's is one of them.

I climb out of the cab and stretch my legs. Is this a crazy fucking idea? It definitely is. But Amber and I have been cold and civilized for way too long. The passion of Mr. and Mrs. Smith unlocked something in us, and it feels right to act on impulse like this. I know I told her I'd give her space, but I'm going to start my year the way I intend to finish it—with my wife by my side. I think deep down she wants that too.

The front door is open, and inside, I find the remains of what was clearly a legendary party. The house is quirky at the best of times, and now it looks like the aftermath of a Halloween frat party. Slumbering guests are sprawled on the couches covered in crocheted blankets, and one is sleeping upright beneath the broad green leaves of a monstera plant. Goblets, glasses, and paper cups cover every surface, and the huge punch bowl is completely empty. Low music is playing in the next room, and I find Granny Lucille curled up on a large bean bag with a woman with long gray hair. Lucille looks up at me and smiles, not looking remotely surprised to see me.

"About damn time," she says. "Upstairs, third door down. She's been in bed for hours—the youth of today have no stamina. And Elijah?" I nod for her to continue. "Two things—one, happy New Year. And two, if you hurt that girl again, I will find you, and I will kill you. Capisce?" She says the last word like a Mafia don.

I hold my hands up in surrender. "Capisce, Lucille. I have no intention of hurting her."

I climb the stairs, stepping over a fat black cat that glares at me with vivid green eyes, and find the right door. She's asleep on her side, only half covered by the sheets. The light from the hallway shows me she's wearing a silky pink slip, and her hair is spread over the white pillows. After closing the door, I quickly take off my clothes and climb into bed next to her. Careful not to startle her too much, I curl myself around her and stroke her hair back from her ears. Fuck, she is so beautiful.

"Baby," I whisper, "it's me. Happy New Year."

She mumbles and smiles, then her eyes flutter open. She looks adorable, her eyes widening with surprise. "Elijah ... What are you doing here?"

I cuddle into her and kiss her cheek. "I wanted to be with you. Is this okay?"

She pulls my arm more firmly around her. My fingers gently explore her, and she sighs as I caress her breasts. Her nipples are immediately taut under the silk of her slip. She wriggles her backside against my already-stiff cock. "Yes. This is okay," she murmurs, her voice still sleepy. "It's more than okay."

She stretches languidly against me, and I kiss her slender neck as she makes contented little noises. I push up her slip and let my hands wander. Her skin is soft and warm, and she angles herself perfectly to take me. "Oh baby, you're already soaked."

"I know. I was dreaming about you. It was a very naughty dream."

I groan and slide my cock deeper. She feels like heaven. She gasps, leaning her head back against me. Her pussy is tight and wet, and it takes all my resolve not to rail into her. Instead, the moment is sweet. Our bodies work as one, perfectly timing each thrust, both of us moaning at the simple pleasure of being together again. I reach around to stroke her clit as we make love, and it doesn't take long for me to get my reward. Her perfect pussy squeezes around me, and she lets out the most divine little cries as the ecstasy takes her. We ride it out together, and I build up my rhythm. Her coming is enough to push me toward my own release.

"I love you, Amber," I whisper as I shudder against her.

We stay like that for several minutes, her lean body snuggled into mine, my arms wrapped around her. She strokes my hands and kisses my fingers, and it's pretty much one of the most perfect moments of my entire fucking life.

Eventually, she rolls over to face me, and her whiskey-brown eyes are sparkling. She places her palm on my cheekbone and smiles. "We don't seem able to stay away from each other, do we?"

"No, we don't—and why the fuck should we? You're mine, Amber, and I'm yours. We can't give up on us. I won't give up on us. Not ever."

"Did you tell them where you were going?" She doesn't need to explain what she means by that.

I shake my head and hope like hell she understands. "I didn't, but not because I didn't want to. It was because it wasn't my night. Drake proposed to Amelia."

She looks delighted and laughs, and the tension eases out of me at the sound. "Let me guess—at the stroke of midnight, on the balcony?"

"Yeah, how'd you know? Did he tell you what he was planning?"

"No, it's just ... Well, it's classy. It's romantic, and since he met Amelia, so is he. I'm thrilled for them, and I completely understand that you didn't want to step on their toes. Was your dad pleased?"

I examine her words for any traces of pain, any evidence that she's faking this, but I find none. "He was, yeah. Everyone was, including me—but all I could think about was this. You. Being here by your side. And if you're willing to give us another chance, I will tell them, I promise."

She looks solemn, and my heart sinks. "I think I am, Elijah. Willing, I mean. But I'm still ... I don't know, scared?"

"Of course you are." I drop a kiss on her forehead and pull her closer. "So am I, truth be told. But I believe in us. We can do this."

CHAPTER
FORTY-THREE
AMBER

E lijah had to leave the night after he arrived to get back to work, and I bid a fond farewell to Granny Lucille a few days later. She was smug about being right, and I was too happy to mind. The fact that he left his family and flew all the way to see me proved he wants to rebuild our relationship from the ground up. This time last year, he never would have done that.

Like Lucille said, this has all been a wake-up call. No matter how difficult the road ahead might be, I believe Elijah and I are better off together.

I'm both excited and nervous about what the future holds. There are a lot of challenges ahead. When I first ran to Charleston back when all of this began, Granny told me I needed to be brave and bold. I had no idea then that being brave and bold would mean agreeing to a fresh start with my own husband.

Now here I am in Queens, where I've just finished leading my first dance class of the new year. It was for the younger age group, and as ever, it was a blast, and I was surprised and pleased by our special guests, Melanie and baby Luke.

Luke loved every second, slamming his chubby fists down onto the mat with the music and struggling up onto wobbly legs to join in. He's a joy to be around, and Mel and I are laughing at his playful antics as we chat.

Mel looks a little tired and seems grateful for the chance to sit and let Luke enjoy himself with the other kids. He's big and active for his age and is sitting in a circle with some other toddlers, bashing the floor with a large Duplo until it's abandoned in favor of the rice cake he's gnawing on. Guess it's so good it requires all his attention.

Mel and I keep our conversation surface-level, and I feel rotten for not being able to open up to her. Despite her dubious taste in men, my sister-in-law seems like a lovely woman, and I'm hoping that we'll become friends. For now, though, she avoids the subject of Elijah and me with admirable diplomacy. Instead, we talk about Drake and Amelia's engagement, which is safe and pleasant ground.

"Sorry. I'm not sleeping well," she says after a big yawn, looking embarrassed. "It's great here, isn't it?" She gestures at the bright, cheerful room.

"It is, yes. I really enjoy it. You know my history, I'm sure. It's taken a while for me to feel comfortable around children. Now it seems like they're everywhere I look."

She pulls a sympathetic face. "I ... I had miscarriages. One before Luke, and two when I was younger. It's not something I talk about much, but for a while, I wasn't sure if children would ever happen for me. And now, I'm ... Well, here I am." She clearly stops herself from saying more, and I suspect I know what it is. The tired eyes, the yawning. The decaf coffee. I won't put her on the spot—she'll tell people when she's ready—but it seems the James clan is about to get even bigger.

I do a quick emotional triage to see if that upsets me and find that it doesn't. It appears that I no longer feel these things so deeply or personally. "That sounds terrible, Mel. That kind of loss must be devastating. I'm so happy you ended up with this little tank at the end of it all."

We both glance at Luke and notice at the same time that his color is off. Mel immediately goes to him and checks his mouth, then pats his back firmly. She talks soothingly to him, but he isn't breathing, and his face is turning darker, tears dripping from his eyes.

"Luke!" she cries. Other parents start to notice, and other children begin to wail. Mel pats him again and looks around the room. "What should I do?" she begs. "He's choking. Call 911!"

Without pausing to think, I grab Luke and place him face down on my legs, then slap him sharply with the heel of my hand, right between his shoulder blades. Mel hovers at my side, shaking and crying. On the fourth blow, a big blob of half-chewed rice cake flies out of his mouth and goes splat on the floor. He immediately sucks in air and starts screaming, slamming his fists into my thighs. Mel grabs him up, strokes away his tears, and does that mom thing where she checks him over for damage.

"Is he okay?" one of the other mothers asks, clearly on the phone to 911. "They're asking if he's conscious."

"Well, he's yelling his head off, so I'd guess that's a yes," another quips in response. This information is relayed, along with a few details about if he stopped breathing completely

417

and for how long. We're told he's probably fine now, and that because it only lasted a matter of seconds, his brain was not deprived of oxygen long enough to do any damage. The parent relays that we should take him to the ER if we have any concerns.

There's a communal sigh of relief as Luke continues to demonstrate how powerful his lungs are, and one of the parents comes over to pat me on the back—a lot more gently than I did to poor Luke. "Well done, Miss Amber. That coulda got real nasty."

Once she is sure her boy is okay, Melanie comes to me. My adrenaline levels are still high, and I barely notice as she takes hold of my hand and squeezes it. Her green eyes are shiny with tears. "Thank you, so much. You might have just saved his life. How did you know how to do that?"

"Um, this is kinda embarrassing, but I think I saw it on an episode of *Grey's Anatomy* … What can I say? I watch a lot of late-night television."

She laughs and kisses the now much-calmer baby on his round cheeks. "Well, thank God you do, Amber. I can't tell you how much I appreciate what you did. Some use I was, huh?"

"Seeing your own child choking would be enough to send anyone into a blind panic, Mel. But you're very welcome."

Seeing her snuggle her baby and close her eyes as she takes deep, relieved breaths, I feel a little glow of pride, and then a far less noble emotion takes its place. *Try to hate me now, Nathan James.*

FORTY-FOUR

AMBER

Mel ends up taking Luke to get checked out for peace of mind, and he's given a clean bill of health. And wonder of wonders, about an hour after her update, I received a phone call from the Ice Man himself.

I almost didn't answer when I saw his name. Something about Nathan always triggers me, makes me feel sick and anxious. Naturally, I cover that up by acting frostier than usual, and I am concerned that as Elijah and I try to navigate our new normal, I won't be able to change that pattern of behavior.

"Nathan" was all I said when I answered. I hoped he didn't hear the silent "go fuck yourself."

"Amber," he replied, equally cold. I definitely hear the silent "I hate you with every fiber of my being." There was a pause, and cartoons played in the background. Either Nathan has become a fan of *Bluey*, or he was at home with Luke. That softened me up a little.

"Is he all right?" I asked.

419

"Yeah, he's great. Mel told me what happened, and I guess I just wanted to call and, uh, thank you?"

"Is that a question?"

"No. No it's not. Thank you, Amber. Mel was a mess, and you looked after her too, in addition to Luke. I appreciate that. I know we've had our differences, and, well, thank you."

I rolled my eyes. It was like pulling teeth.

"You're welcome. The fact that we've 'had our differences' does not mean that I'd watch your child choke to death, Nathan." I made a big effort to keep my tone calm. "Even I'm not that much of a monster."

"I know you're not a monster," he said. "I just don't think ... Fuck, I've said what I wanted to say. Thank you again."

"That's okay. And, uh, thank you for calling."

It was torture for both of us, and I was relieved when he hung up. I stared at the phone, shaking my head.

I have no idea if things between us will ever improve. I am the Ice Queen, and he is the Ice Man, and somehow we never seem able to play anything other than those roles when we're around each other. I'm nervous about him finding out Elijah and I are reconciling. He still hasn't told his family, and I'm making a valiant effort not to let that derail me. There's been a lot going on what with Drake's engagement, the Seoul deal, and Dalton going in for a series of tests on his heart. So far he's been given the all-clear, but it's a worrying time for them all. It wouldn't help our long-term marital harmony if his dad dropped dead of shock because I was back on the scene.

That all happened this morning, and in the afternoon, I led a class for the older kids once school let out. I stayed a little longer to do a one-on-one session with Shawn, and now I'm home. At a dangerously loose end. My hands are idle, and I suspect the devil might be about to make use of them.

I'm supposed to be seeing Elijah tomorrow, but I don't want to wait. He's working at home in Manhattan, and I'm here in Brooklyn, and I want to be with him. Everything feels better when we're together, and imagining the surprise on his face makes me smile. He'll be leaving for Seoul soon, and I want to make the most of every minute we have together before then.

After getting dressed in a very special outfit that he'll love, I add a little makeup and perfume, then that long tasseled necklace he's so fond of. I top the whole thing off with a deep blue trench coat. Sanjay is here within a few minutes, happy to see me as usual, and by the time he drops me outside the Manhattan house, I'm grinning ear to ear.

I haven't been back here since I left for Brooklyn, and I thought it would feel stranger than it does. But now it's the building where Elijah is, and Elijah is my beating heart. It's so odd how splitting up has resulted in us being closer than ever. I now get to be playful in a way I haven't been since I was in my twenties.

I'm wearing spiky heels that are high even by my standards, and I climb the steps to the door carefully and ring the doorbell, knowing I look perfectly normal and respectable from the outside. I hear footsteps approaching and bite down on a giggle—he is going to freak!

I time it absolutely perfectly, waiting until the very last second, when the big wooden door is swung back and he appears. "Surprise!" I exclaim, pulling open the trench coat.

Underneath it, I'm wearing my sluttiest black bra and matching panties set, complete with black stockings and a lacy garter belt.

"Fuck!" says Maddox, jumping back and shielding his eyes like a flash bang just went off.

"Fuck!" I parrot, hastily pulling my coat closed and belting it firmly. "I'm sorry, I'm so sorry. I didn't expect you."

Maddox dares to peek through two of his fingers to check whether I'm decent. He might be the baby of the family, but he is very much a grown-ass man these days. The blush on his cheeks is endearing, and I suspect mine is spreading over my whole damn body.

"I assumed that," Maddox says, gesturing me inside. He's wearing an apron that belongs to Dionne. "Uh, I was cooking. The rest of them are drinking, and I was making snacks."

"The rest of them?" I ask, freezing in terror and tugging that belt tighter around my waist. He nods apologetically, and I register the raised voices coming from the living room. Shit. Talk about bad timing. "Elijah said he had something to tell us. I'm thinking I can pretty much guess what that is now. You two are back together?"

I look up at his handsome face and nod. He pats my arm and gives me a reassuring smile. "Good. Whatever makes you guys happy. You want to come down to the kitchen? Or, uh, go upstairs and put some actual clothes on?"

I can tell he's eager to move me anywhere but here. Anywhere that is safe from the clearly escalating argument taking place in the next room. I shake my head and head back toward the door. Nathan and Mason are so predictable, I could write the script myself, and I have no desire to hear what Dalton's first reaction will be. I have far too much self-respect to stand here and listen to any of them bad-mouth me. And if Elijah and I are going to make this work, then I'll have to build some kind of relationship with all of them. And once something is heard, it can't be unheard. A lesson I learned a long time ago.

Maddox shoots me a worried look. "Don't go, Amber. Stay and eat."

"I really must go, but thank you. Please don't tell Elijah I was here." He'll only worry I got upset about hearing them arguing.

"No way, Amber," he replies, following me down the steps and into the street. "You seem upset. I'm going to get Elijah."

He doesn't quite understand why I'm leaving. "I really am all right, Maddox, I promise. I just didn't expect them to be here."

He inspects me cautiously, as if trying to figure out whether I'm lying. "It was a last-minute thing," he explains. "He was supposed to be working, but then Nathan told him what happened with the baby, and Elijah invited everyone around." That makes sense. Elijah would have seen my dubious heroism as a stepping off point into his news. In his mind, it probably went something like "Hey guys, you know Amber, the woman who stopped Luke from choking to death today? Well, we're getting back together. Isn't that great?" My husband has always seen the best in people.

"I see. Look, this was bad timing on my part, and I'm sorry I flashed you. I'm going to leave him to it and go home. Please, pretend I was never here. I'm so embarrassed." I manage a blush and hold my hands to my face.

He frowns, and I'm not sure he's totally buying it.

"You didn't, uh, really *see* anything did you?" I ask, sounding horrified. "I'd be mortified."

That's enough to reel him in, and he shakes his head quickly. "No. I promise you. It was a blur—I didn't see a thing." He obviously did, and I almost feel sorry for him. He's clearly as embarrassed as I'm pretending to be, and in the end I think that's what swings it.

"Let me sneak away." I lay a hand on his arm and give him the big eyes. "Honestly, I'm really not upset. I'm just a little humiliated to have turned up like this, and I'd feel worse if they all knew. I'll catch up with Elijah later, it'll all be fine. Hey, at least it wasn't your dad who answered the door."

We both share a grin at that, and I can see the tension leave him. "Okay. If you want to go, at least let me walk you to a cab. It's late, and you're dressed in, uh ..."

"Very little?" I supply, smiling.

"Exactly," he replies as he takes my elbow and guides me down the street. I take the opportunity to ask him about how things have been going since he came home, and within a few minutes, he manages to hail me a taxi.

Alone in the back seat, I allow myself a satisfied smile, proud of how I handled that. I could have stayed and listened to Mason's and Nathan's objections. Could have gone in there and torn the pair of them a new one. But I chose to trust that Elijah would handle it. That he would defend our relationship and tell them all to go to hell if necessary.

I realize that I don't feel like going home. I'm nostalgic for old times when things were full of promise and hope for the future. Just as they are now. And I know just where to go.

FORTY-FIVE

ELIJAH

"Bro, no. Come on, for fuck's sake, man, you can't be serious. You've only just escaped from her," Mason says. And predictably so. I expected this reaction from him when I told them all about me and Amber.

"I am serious," I reply, my voice strained but calm.

Drake congratulates me, and I thank him, but now my eyes are fixed on Nathan as I await his objections. "I spoke to Amber this morning. As you know, she saved my kid's life, and for that I will be eternally grateful. But Elijah, this is fucked up. She made your life a living hell for years. You're better off without her."

From the corner of my eye, I see my dad gripping the arms of his chair tightly. "Dad? Dad, are you okay?" I'm at his side in a second. He's pale and appears to be in pain. The fight I was about to embark on with my brothers is temporarily forgotten.

"Of course I am," he snaps, his nostrils flaring. "I'm just … Goddamn it, where are those snacks Maddox promised us? I haven't eaten since lunch."

My brothers move closer, all of us expressing our concern. He slaps us away and stands up tall, puffing out his chest as though to remind us boys that he is still the boss around here. "I. Am. Fine. I do not need you all to behave like my nanny. I appreciate your concern, but I'm not about to keel over. If you must know, I'm on a new medication, and if I don't eat regularly, I get a little faint. That's all this is."

Nathan reaches into his jacket pocket and passes over a packet containing a biscuit in the shape of a bunny, and we all stare at him. He shrugs. "They're Luke's, but I kinda like 'em."

Dad quickly chews it down, and almost instantly, his color is back, and he sits back down. "Fucking delicious," he says, making us all laugh.

Dad's right; we are acting like his nanny. Crisis averted, once I am one hundred percent sure that he's actually okay, I get back to the business at hand. I love my siblings dearly, but I have had enough of their bullshit. My father, at least, was respectful enough to simply ask if I was sure rather than lecturing me.

"Mason, Nathan," I say, glaring at them both. "You are both full of shit. You don't know what the fuck you're talking about, and you don't really know her."

Nathan opens his mouth to object, and I hold up a hand to silence him. Every now and then, big brother power pays off, and he stays quiet for once.

"No. I will not stand here and listen to another goddamn word about the woman I love. If you have any respect for me, you will shut the fuck up, and you will listen. I am in love with Amber, and I always have been. I'm devoted to my wife, and I should have shown her a hell of a lot more respect than

I have the past several years. I stopped making her my priority, and even worse, I let her believe that she wasn't enough for me.

"I am going to spend the rest of my fucking life with her. If you can't live with that, if you can't find a way to deal with my choices, then you'll have to steer clear of me. Because I will live without all of you if I have to, but I sure as fuck won't spend one more day without her. From this day forward, we come as a package deal. Do you fucking understand?"

I glare at both of them like they're naughty schoolboys in the principal's office. Mason is desperate to make some kind of snappy retort, and Nathan would quite like to take a swing at me. "Well?" I snap.

"Okay, bro, we understand," Mason finally says, shaking his head. Nathan nods once, which is as close to approval as I'm going to get. Drake simply gets up and slaps me on the back. "Congrats, bro," he says, beaming at me with as much force as Nathan's glower.

Dad gets up and shakes my hand. "Seems to me like you're sure, son," he says, grinning. "Now, who wants a club soda to celebrate?" He's cutting back on the Scotch, and we all laugh at the sheer horror in his voice as he utters the words "club soda."

At that moment, Maddox walks back into the room. And he has no damn snacks. I didn't mean to break the news without him here, but Nathan started talking about Luke and what happened in Queens, and one thing kind of led to another. "Hey, asswipe," says Mason, shoving Maddox playfully. "Where the hell have you been? You missed the big announcement."

Maddox looks around the room, frowning. Eventually, he blows out a big breath. "I think I can guess what it was," he says, jerking his chin at me. "Amber was just here."

"What?" I reply, confused. We were supposed to be meeting up tomorrow, and I was looking forward to telling her about all of this. I'm booked on a flight to Seoul the day after and wanted to make our reunion official before I left. "Amber was here? Where is she now?"

"She left. She was wearing ... Uh, well, that doesn't matter. She came in briefly and heard you guys arguing."

"What did she hear?" I ask. "The whole conversation?"

"How the fuck do I know? I have no idea what the whole conversation was. She heard raised voices, and then she left. I walked her to a cab, and she asked me not to tell you she was here."

Double fuck and shit! Classic Amber move—hide the pain and pretend it doesn't hurt. I'm grateful Maddox was somehow immune to her epic powers of persuasion and told me.

I replay the scene from earlier in my mind, a sinking feeling in my stomach. What the hell did she hear? If she was only here briefly, that means she likely heard the absolute worst of it and didn't hear me say a word in her defense. For fuck's sake.

I don't bother explaining. I just leave, intending to get to Brooklyn as fast as I can. I try calling her from the car and leave a voicemail telling her I'm on my way. I'm halfway across the bridge when her message lands.

> I'm not at home. Still in Manhattan. I felt like a walk. Meet you at the Moonlight Diner.

The cabbie barely reacts when I tell him I need to go back. The Moonlight Diner is off Broadway and is somewhere we used to go when we were younger. It's a fun place that pulls in an eclectic mix of customers, everyone from firefighters to thespians. I haven't walked through its doors in years, but it hasn't changed at all. I find her in a corner booth, nursing a mug of coffee and dressed in a dark-colored trench coat. She doesn't look like she's been crying, but that's no guarantee she's not upset—or pissed.

"Damn Maddox," she murmurs lightly as I slide into the seat opposite her. "I thought I had him."

"Looks like your Jedi mind tricks don't work on my baby brother. Amber, what you heard—"

"No. Let me stop you there. It doesn't matter what they said."

I guess it only matters what she didn't hear me say. Before I can respond, the waitress brings over a mug and a coffee pot and pours without a word. I take a sip, scalding my lips and wait to speak until we're alone again. "I told them. They didn't react well—but we expected that, didn't we?"

She remains silent, sipping her coffee. My heart is cracking wide open here. If she heard what they said, if she heard me asking if my dad was okay instead of laying into them ... Fuck, I know what that must have sounded like and how much it must have hurt her.

I rush to explain about Dad looking pale and his new meds, and the look of concern on her face has me trailing off.

"Is he all right?" she asks.

"Yeah, it was nothing, but that's why you didn't hear me jump in and tell them to go fuck themselves."

"And you did?" she asks, tilting her head. "Tell them to go fuck themselves?"

"Basically, yeah. I told them that from now on, we're a package deal. That you don't get one of us without the other, and if they have a problem with that, then they don't get to be a part of my life, because you are the most important person in the entire world to me. You are the only person in this entire goddamn universe who I'm unwilling to live without, and I am so fucking sorry it took us getting divorced to make me realize that."

She turns the new information around as she drinks, and damn, she has the world's best poker face. "Do you believe me?" I ask.

She stares at me over the coffee steam, and I genuinely have no idea which way she's going to jump. "Baby," I say, my voice low. "I love you, and I will turn my world upside down to make this thing between us work. But I need to hear your words."

Her tongue darts out, and she licks her lips. Then she places a twenty-dollar bill on the table, more than enough to cover our coffees, and steps out of the booth, pulling the belt of her coat tighter around her waist.

This is it. I've fucked up one too many times, and it doesn't matter that I stuck up for her—for us—tonight, because all of those times that I didn't can't be undone. I was a shitty husband, and this is the price I am paying for it.

"Where are you going?"

Her eyes are full of emotion as she pins me with her gaze. "Home."

My heart shatters into a million pieces.

Then she holds out her hand to me, and for a few

seconds, I simply stare at it. Is she inviting me to join her, or this a final goodbye handshake? Her gentle laugh snaps me out of my stupor. "Aren't you coming?"

Am I coming? Home? With her? Hell the fuck yes I am. I slide out of the booth and take her hand in mine, and we walk out of the diner together.

Standing at the corner, waiting for a cab, I wrap my arms around her waist.

"I didn't hang around to hear you telling your brothers about us, honey," she says, resting her hands on my shoulders. "I didn't want to hear their objections, and I trusted you to stand up for us."

Relief washes over me. "You couldn't have told me that ten minutes ago, before I convinced myself you left because you heard all the bad stuff and none of the good?"

She looks up at me, grinning mischievously. "Did Maddox also tell you what I was wearing when he opened the door?" Her voice has been dipped in sin.

I flick the end of the belt on her trench coat. "No, but given this sexy little number, please tell me it's nothing but underwear, mi amor."

"I guess you'll find out soon enough." She gives me a wink.

I hail a passing cab and practically shove her into it, making her laugh again.

I am desperate to get my wife alone—not only to find out what's going on beneath that coat, but so I can tell her and show her all the ways I cannot live without her.

FORTY-SIX

AMBER

As soon as my eyes flutter open the next morning, I see him staring down at me, propped up on one elbow. Our bodies are flush, my leg draped over him and his arms around me. My muscles throb with a delicious ache, and I don't think I've ever felt so happy. After Elijah discovered what I was wearing under my trench coat, he tore every scrap from my body and fucked me on the stairs. And then again in bed. In *our* bed. Twice.

"You do know it's creepy to watch someone sleep, right? Like serial killer creepy?"

His lips twitch into a smirk. "You do know how much I love your smart mouth?" He presses a soft kiss on my lips. "But I would very much enjoy spanking a little of that sass out of you."

I run my hands through his thick hair and tug him back for another kiss. I know from experience how much we would both enjoy that. His tongue slides against mine as he deepens the kiss and rolls on top of me, and all we do for the next however long is make out like a pair of teenagers. He's always been an incredible kisser, and I forgot how much pleasure could be found in this simple act.

The sound of Elijah's cell phone vibrating on the bedside table interrupts us. At least it interrupts me, and I pull back. "You should probably take that."

He shakes his head and goes back to kissing me, and for a few blissful seconds, I let him before pushing him away again. "You can answer your phone. Your work and your family are important to you, Elijah. I don't expect you to change who you are."

He frowns. "You *should* expect me to change. I've spent most of our life together prioritizing the wrong things and neglecting the most important thing—no, the most important *person* in my world, and that absolutely has to fucking change, baby. It's nonnegotiable."

I rest my hand on his cheek. He's right, we both needed to make some changes to be right for one another. "I love you."

He drops a tender kiss on my forehead and then rolls onto his back, pulling me with him so my head rests on his shoulder. "I've really fucking missed this." His tone is so sad that it makes my heart ache. "Just lying here with you is the best thing in the whole fucking world."

"Surely not the *best* thing?"

That gets a laugh from him. "As much as I love the incredible sex, baby—and believe me, I really fucking do— nothing beats this."

I hum contentedly. The man has a point.

He rests his lips on my hair. "I didn't realize how much I missed how close we used to be. I had no clue that it was

433

possible to miss a person when they were right there next to you."

I press my body closer to his, recalling how many times during the later years of our marriage that I wanted to reach out and touch him. To feel a connection to the man I never stopped loving. But there came a point when I was too afraid of his rejection. Not that he would have rejected me at that exact moment in time, but later when he'd leave for work or for some family issue that required his attention, I'd have felt the sting of his leaving. Of him choosing them over me. "I know exactly what you mean."

ELIJAH IS on a call with Mason when my cell phone vibrates, Drake's name flashing on the screen.

"Hey, how are you?" he asks, his voice filled with concern.

"I'm good. Really good."

"Please tell me Elijah's with you."

I assure him that he is.

"Oh, thank fuck. I thought you heard what my idiot brothers said and left before he tore them a new one."

"Well, I didn't hear any of it, but Elijah told me what happened. He also said your dad looked unwell."

"Yeah. We thought he was having some kind of turn, but he seems fine. Thank God."

I didn't need confirmation of what Elijah told me because he is not a liar and I believed what he said, but it's still nice to hear it from Drake. "He tore them a new one, huh?"

Drake laughs. "Yeah, he went full big brother on their

asses. I wish you could have seen their faces. But seriously, Amber, he gave it to them with both barrels, and they deserved it." Imagining the looks on their arrogant faces, I laugh too. "I'm glad you've worked it out. You have worked it out, right? You're still back together? He's not cuffed in the basement or anything?"

"Not right now. Had you called a few hours ago ..." I laugh. "Kidding. We had nothing to work out. At least not yesterday. We are very much together."

"That's good to hear." His tone is serious now. "I'm happy for you both."

"I'm happy for us too."

"Now, how would you both like to come to our place for dinner tonight? It will just be Amelia and me. Oh, and Maddox. And Dad. And Luke because we're watching him for the night while Nathan and Mel go to some animal charity thing."

"No Mason?"

"Nope. Hot date, apparently. What do you say? Dad and Maddox are looking forward to seeing you both. It will be fun. Promise."

I roll my eyes. Fun isn't the first word that comes to mind when considering an evening with the James family, but this could be the perfect way to ease myself back into that world. I love Drake, Amelia, and Luke. Dalton has never been actively unpleasant to me, and Maddox—well, I don't think he has a mean bone in his body. "Let me talk to Elijah, but I think we should be able to make it."

"Great. Be here at six for canapés and champagne."

I promise him I'll try, and we end the call right as Elijah

ends his with Mason. He wraps me up in his arms like he can't bear to not be touching me for long.

"Drake invited us for dinner at his place tonight. Your dad and Maddox will be there too. And baby Luke."

He slides his hands down to rest on my ass. "I fly to Seoul tomorrow. I'd much prefer to have you all to myself until then."

Snaking my arms around his neck, I step into him. My body molds to his, another reminder of how well we fit together. How well we've always fit, even when we couldn't see it. "I think it might be good for us. Your family is important to you, Elijah, and that means I want them to be important to me too. This could be a great first step. Drake and Amelia, and obviously baby Luke, are on our side. And your dad and Maddox are much less hostile than Nathan and Mason."

His eyes narrow. "You don't have to do this. Yes, they are important to me, but not half as important as you are."

I rest my head on his shoulder. My lips brush his neck. "I love you for saying that and meaning it. But I really do want to have dinner with them. It will give me chance to speak to Maddox with all my clothes on, and then ..." I run my fingernail down the buttons of his shirt. "As soon as we get home, you can show me how much you're going to miss me while you're in Seoul."

He scoops me up into his arms bridal style, making me giggle like a teenager. "Why wait until tonight when I can show you that right now?"

≈

ELIJAH'S HAND rests on the small of my back as we ride the private elevator to Drake and Amelia's loft. "You okay, baby?"

Only six months ago, that question would have been met with ice-cold hostility—I would have snapped at him, telling him that of course I'm fine. That I've dealt with far more intimidating men than Dalton and Maddox. Now, I take a deep breath and admit my true feelings. "I feel a little nervous. Like when you brought me home for the very first time."

He pulls me into his arms, pushes a lock of hair behind my ear, and smiles. "I'd already told my mom you were the woman I was going to marry. Did I ever tell you that?"

I comb through my memories. "No, you never did. Is that why she made her famous paella and had me sit next to her at dinner?" They were all so warm and welcoming that day, even Nathan. Well, as much warmth as he could muster for anyone back then.

"No." He smiles down at me. "She did that because she loved you from the minute she met you."

My heart splinters a little. Before that awful day, Verona and I were close. That's why I was so hurt by what she said. And yes, she was sick and not entirely herself, but she tapped into my deepest, darkest fears. "I'm sorry she hurt you, baby." His voice is low and sincere. It cost him a lot to come to terms with the fact that the woman he idolized hurt me so badly, even if she didn't intend to. Now, with the benefit of distance and hindsight, I know that she didn't do as much damage as I did. One conversation can't undo all the wonderful memories we made before then. And I'm disappointed that I spent so much time using her words as a tool to deconstruct our marriage because I didn't know how else to deal with my pain.

"I'm sorry too, honey. But this is a new start, right? That's probably why it feels like I'm meeting them for the first time."

He nods. "Thank you for giving them all another chance too. And whatever happens, whatever's said or not said, know that I will do anything to make you happy. You are always the most important person in any room as far as I'm concerned. You want to leave for whatever reason, all you have to do is give me a signal and we're gone."

I curl the thick hair at the nape of his neck between my fingers. "And what would such a signal be, sir?"

He grins, but the elevator doors slide open before he can answer.

"Jeez, put her down, bro," Maddox says.

Elijah coughs, and I step out of his embrace and into the loft. "It's nice to see you again, Maddox," I say politely. "Especially when I'm fully clothed."

He blushes adorably. "Hey, I saw nothing." And then he does something unexpected and sweeps me into a giant bear hug, murmuring into my ear, "It's really great to see you, Amber."

I'm overcome with a rush of affection for him that catches me off guard. He's dealt with so much heartache in his life, yet he still has the capacity for so much kindness. Instead of trying to hide my feelings, I embrace them, letting a tear fall. "Thanks, Maddox. It's great to see you too."

"Amber, it's been far too long." Dalton holds out his arms when Maddox lets me go, and I steel myself and walk right into them, deciding to embrace this new start with my whole heart. Being hugged by Dalton James feels warm and familiar. He's worn the same cologne for over twenty years, but it's more than that. It feels exactly like it did the first time I met him.

THE BUZZER in the kitchen signals someone has arrived in the lobby and makes Amelia squeak excitedly. "That will be Mel with Luke. I'll go help her with the baby bag."

Drake winks at her, his hands covered in raw chicken, and nods toward the bubbling saucepan on the stove. "Not unless you want to serve your signature sauce with a fork, mi rosa."

She flutters her eyelashes at him. "I'm sure it will still taste delicious." They're staring at each other now, sexual energy crackling between them, and I suddenly feel like a voyeur. Especially as I'm the only other person in the room while the other James men set the table.

I set my champagne flute on the counter, happy for a chance to leave the two lovebirds alone for a moment. "I'll go help her." My heels click on the marble as I hurry for the door, excited to see Mel and Luke. Except when the doors open, it's Nathan who steps out, his sleeping son in his arms.

With an inward groan, I roll back my shoulders, preparing for battle. Our eyes meet, and a shudder runs down my spine. Sarcastic remarks are right there on the tip of my tongue, but I bite them back. If Elijah and I are going to make this work, I need to at least try to be civil.

Nathan speaks before I do. "Before you say anything, I want to apologize for whatever you may have overheard yesterday. Elijah is a grown man, and I know that it takes two people to make a marriage work—or not. If you two are happy together, then I have no right to get in the middle of any of that."

I can imagine how hard that was for him to say, but I can't resist making him squirm. "Is that your idea of an apology, Nathan James?" I make sure to follow the question up with a wicked grin.

He screws his eyes closed like he's in agony. "You have no idea how much that fucking hurt."

"Oh, I think I do."

Luke's eyelids flutter open, and he looks around, trying to identify where he is. As soon as he realizes he's in his dad's arms, he gleefully shouts, "Dada!"

Nathan's entire being softens, and he kisses his son on the head. I've never seen him interact with Luke before. It makes him look ... Well, almost human. Then Luke spots me, and his sweet brown eyes sparkle with delight. "Bam!" he yells, holding his chubby little arms toward me.

Nathan quirks an eyebrow as I take the baby from him. "Looks like your son kind of loves me."

He hums, running a hand over his beard. "My brother too. And my wife apparently."

I suppress a satisfied smirk. "Guess that means we'll have to see more of each other, huh?"

He rolls his eyes. "As long as there's a good bottle of Scotch available, I may find it tolerable. And obviously, I'm only ever calling you Bam from here on out."

I shrug. "Better than what you usually call me, I wager."

His lips twitch, and he tries to suppress his grin but fails miserably. "Since I'm here apologizing, I guess I should also apologize for that day I saw you in Freddie Kemp's office."

I school my face into neutral, but I feel the color drain from my cheeks. Not even Luke's adorable gurgling is enough to banish the memory of that day.

"Elijah never told me what happened, but ..." He sucks on his top lip. "But whatever it was, given the people he asked me to put him in touch with after, and reflecting on the state you were in ... Well, I can imagine." His throat works as he swallows.

I'll be damned. Confronted with his uncharacteristic unease, I feel a little less anxious.

"I made an assumption that I now know was erroneous. I'm sorry that I wasn't a safe space for you, Amber. If it were Mel, and she bumped into any one of my brothers in that state, I would expect them to take care of her and to kick Freddie's ass. No matter what's happened between us, I'm ashamed that I wasn't that for you. I should have been."

I'm about to tell him that he doesn't need to apologize, that he couldn't have known what had happened, but I stop myself. I was sexually assaulted and I ran into my brother-in-law immediately afterward. He's absolutely right—I should have been able to at least ask him for help.

So I force myself to recognize the role I've played in our antagonistic relationship and nod, holding onto Luke's chubby fist to stop him from shoving it into my mouth, which he appears intent on doing. "I appreciate that, Nathan. Thank you."

Obviously sensing my unease with this conversation, he clicks his tongue against the roof of his mouth. "Did we just have a civil conversation?"

I gasp, feigning surprise. "You know, I believe we did."

Nathan looks behind me and gives a nod in greeting to

someone. "Everything okay here?" Elijah's smooth, deep voice fills the entryway, and a second later, his reassuring hands are sliding around my waist as he pulls me against him. I can't deny how good it feels. Like we're on the same side. A united front.

"Everything's good," I assure him.

He leans over me to give his nephew a kiss that makes Luke giggle and squirm in my arms, then Elijah directs his attention to his brother. "I didn't expect to see you. I thought Mel was dropping Luke off."

"I wanted to apologize to your wife for what I said yesterday. For some other shit too." I can only imagine the look of disbelief on my husband's face when Nathan adds, "And she accepted gracefully."

Elijah kisses the top of my head. "That's because she is both gracious and accepting."

I can practically feel Nathan struggling not to roll his eyes, but he manages it, and I can't help but smile.

This doesn't mean we're besties, Nathan and I. We're not going to call each other up to discuss the latest episode of *Drag Race* or go for drinks after a tough day. But we're no longer enemies, and that is definitely progress.

FORTY-SEVEN

AMBER

F our days after I accidentally flashed Maddox, I received an email from Drake. It wasn't a surprise, but it still made my heart sink and my stomach churn. The words held a power over me that I didn't expect.

The divorce is final. Elijah and I are no longer married. I glance at the wedding band and engagement ring still adorning my left hand. It never felt right to take them off, and it feels especially wrong now.

The paperwork will follow, but as of yesterday afternoon, I'm not Mrs. Amber James anymore. It feels so odd after all this time. I was a child when I met him, only nineteen years old. Married at twenty-two, which seems almost Shakespearean by modern standards. I was always happy with that, though. I'd had boyfriends before, and they paled into insignificance next to Elijah. The way I fell for that man ... It was like my heart took a plunge down the Tower of Terror.

Now, here I am. In my forties, unmarried, and a completely different human being. Heck, I'm a different woman than I was mere months ago. The sheer amount of time I save by not doing a full face and hair every day is astounding, and I don't miss my huge wardrobe or my fake society friends in the slightest. Instead of persuading other rich people to donate to charities that support faceless victims, I'm now hands-on, providing the help myself. My residence is a tiny house in Brooklyn, I hang out with bikers, and I swear whenever I damn well please. And I absolutely love it.

As Granny Lucille would tell me, we live many lives—we are constantly changing and evolving. The Amber looking back at me from the bathroom mirror today is not the same as the Amber who made her vows to Elijah all those years ago. She's older and wiser, in some ways stronger, in others more fragile. But she is most definitely still in love with Elijah James.

I get ready to head to the center for my evening class, wishing he were here. He's finalizing the Kim deal in Seoul, and I haven't heard from him since the email arrived. Korea is thirteen hours ahead of New York, so while I saw that email at two in the afternoon, it was three a.m there. I hoped he might be in touch by now, but he's busy with nonstop meetings, which I understand. Work is important to him. It's not about money—lord knows he has enough of that. It's about his family and his ethics and his whole identity. And those are all things I'm proud of.

Still, I wish he were here. Reading those words chilled me to the bone.

I leave my little house in Brooklyn and climb into the back of Sanjay's cab in a bit of a blur. He chats, I chat back, but a cloud of melancholy hangs above my head the whole time.

Nobody can predict what the future holds. Nobody can ever know if a relationship is going to work or not, and Elijah and I have a lot of rebuilding to do. But the divorce feels so final, so brutal. It's evidence of all the ways we hurt each other and all the time we wasted. We're not old, and we have a lot to look forward to, but for the first time in nearly twenty years, I'm no longer his wife, and that makes me feel unsettled.

During my meeting with Sissie to discuss fundraising for LOJ, I come up with many suggestions and take on several tasks. This is something I can do with ease. I might have slipped out of my old world, but those skills remain. If all else fails, I am now a rich woman. Sissie wants to raise money for a pool at the center—not only for swimming, but also for therapy for disabled residents and training for some of the local schools' sports teams. It sounds like a grand idea, and I make it my next goal to see it happen.

Between the meeting and the class I'm leading, I check my phone and have to bite down my disappointment when there's nothing from Elijah. More than a day has passed since Drake's email. Time difference be damned—he must have seen it by now. He must know that he's no longer my husband, and I am desperate to know how he feels about it.

Yes, we've both committed to trying again, but this is a big moment. A tiny, paranoid corner of my mind worries that he's relieved. That now that he knows, he's thinking about all the benefits freedom may bring. Perhaps that's why he hasn't been in touch.

Enough! I'm tying myself in knots over this, and there's no point. If Elijah decides that, then he does. And anyway, I have important things to do—the room is starting to fill, and

I have twenty kids between the ages of four and twelve to deal with. The noise level rises as they talk and laugh, some of them waiting quietly, a few of them pushing and shoving. My admittedly limited experience has already taught me that if I don't take control soon, I'll lose them. I clap my hands together sharply, and they all look up. The chatter cuts out instantly.

"Welcome, my friends," I say. "Who here has heard of *Swan Lake*?"

"Is that in Central Park, Miss Amber?" one of them asks.

"No, stupid, it's in Canada," another retorts.

I hold my hands up to silence them. "Nobody is stupid, so let's add that to our list of banned words, all right? *Swan Lake* isn't a place. It's a ballet. And before you ask, yes, it's another one by an old white dude."

We've been learning about various types of dance, including contemporary styles from all over the world to represent all their cultures. And while ballet has changed some since my day, the most famous pieces are still by old white dudes.

I play a video clip on the TV in the corner and show them the famous Dance of the Little Swans. I talk very briefly about it, and then we do some swan-inspired warm-ups.

Obviously, we're not going to reenact the complex choreography in a community center in Queens, but we can have a little fun and learn a few things. I've already decided to use part of my settlement to gift the center with an annual budget to fund cultural trips. These kids only live a few miles away from much of the most famous art, theater, and dance in the whole world, but most of them have never sampled it. I'll get Sanjay to drive a bus. It'll be fun.

After teaching them a few simple variations, we break for water. Shawn continues to practice alone, and I smile, impressed by his dedication. By ballet standards, he's way too old to start at eleven—but he has the raw talent few people can boast.

While the kids are otherwise occupied, I do something that they're all banned from doing—I check my phone. There's still nothing from Elijah, and I'm starting to run out of excuses for him. Time differences, meetings ... None of it is making me feel any better now. I messaged him this morning, and still, there's no reply. It's a niggle of doubt that taps into previous hurts, and I'm so glad to be here with these kids. Glad to feel useful and have the distraction.

After five minutes, I clap to get their attention, and we resume our class. Or at least we try to—we're interrupted by the arrival of an unscheduled visitor.

He walks into the room and looks as out of place as it's possible to look. His suit is rumpled, but it's still a suit, and his height and build mark him as a giant in a room full of kids. He strides toward me, smiling confidently, his intense gray eyes on my face. The classical music fades thanks to Shawn at the sound desk and becomes a gentle background murmur, competing with the excited chatter of the children. They point and stare and giggle, obviously intrigued by the new arrival.

His hair is mussed up and his tie is loose, but good lord, he looks delicious. It's the eyes—stormy gray, peering at me as though nobody else in the world exists. "What are you doing here? Shouldn't you be in Korea?"

"Yeah, I should," he responds, grinning. "But I left Luisa and Mason to handle things. Mr. Kim is a family man. He'll understand that sometimes, you have to put work second." This is quite a revelation for Elijah. "Sometimes," he continues, "you have to put the most important thing in your life first. That's you, baby. You are my world. You are my number one, now and always. As soon as I saw that email from Drake, I jumped on the jet and headed straight back here. I left in such a hurry, I forgot my cell phone. It took me a while, but I'm here, and I promise you I will never leave your side again."

Tears sting the backs of my eyes. Those are beautiful words. Words I never thought I'd hear come from his lips. He drops to one knee, and all the children start to whoop and holler. They might not have seen it in real life before, but they all know what dropping to one knee means. So do I, and it leaves me breathless with excitement. He pulls a box from his jacket pocket and opens it up. It's perfect. "Is that … Amber?"

"What else would it be, baby, but the most precious stone in the entire world? Nothing shines quite like Amber. And nothing else makes me a happier or allows me to be a better version of myself …" He swallows. "Than you."

The orange-yellow stone shimmers in the overhead light, and I'm overcome with so much joy and so much love for him that it takes me a moment to catch my breath. "It's beautiful, Elijah."

The jewel is stunning, and it represents so much more than the insanely expensive diamond he bought me for our first engagement. But it's the look on his face that melts me. The look in his eyes that tells me he means this. That I am his, and he is mine.

"Amber, I love you. I can't live without you. Will you do me the honor of marrying me?"

"Again?" I ask, smiling down at him.

He grins. "Again. But this time, forever. This time, we do it the right way."

I nod and let the tears flow as he slides the perfect ring onto my finger—there's quite the collection building up there now, and it makes us giggle.

He climbs to his feet and pulls me into his arms. I lean into him, feeling his heart thud in his chest, his warm breath on my skin. Safe, happy, loved. It's been a long, winding road, but it's led us right here, and there is nowhere on earth I'd rather be. All of our missing pieces are now together.

The kids are going wild around us. Shawn puts on a new song—"Celebration" by Kool and the Gang. I wonder briefly how a kid his age knows a song that old, but I guess it's a classic for a reason.

A party erupts around us, and although it's not a slow song, Elijah keeps me in his arms and sways, his lips pressed against my ear. "I'm never letting you go again, baby," he whispers.

I feel exactly the same. Together, we dance in the middle of the room, surrounded by the energetic joy of youth. Surrounded by life and love.

We are in each other's arms, exactly where we belong.

EPILOGUE
AMBER—SPRING

The warm waves of the Mediterranean Sea wash against my legs, and my toes sink deeper into the sand. I sigh and look up at the perfect blue sky above me. Not a cloud in sight, only the gentle heat of the early evening sun.

This place is perfect—almost. I smile as I hear him behind me, splashing through the shallow water. Now it's perfect. He slides his hands around my waist, holding me tight against him. His firm chest, those terrific thighs ... The familiar and always-welcome touch of his hard cock. He's not wearing trunks, which I suppose is fine as this is our private beach. I lean back into him, loving the heat of both the weather and my husband. My brand-new but also pre-loved husband. The only man I have ever truly loved.

"Are you happy, mi amor?" he asks, kissing my shoulder. We're here on our honeymoon on the coast of Spain, close to his mother's hometown of Valencia. This is the place the James brothers used to come on vacation as kids, and it holds precious memories for him. I resisted coming here before, but now, I'm at peace. I'm at peace with what happened with his mom, and I'm at peace with his brothers. The past remains there where it belongs, and our focus is locked on the future we are building. This man is one hundred percent mine, just as I am undeniably his, and nothing and nobody will get in our way because we have learned from our past mistakes.

"So happy," I reply. "The happiest I've ever been. Thank you for bringing me here. It truly is a special place."

I feel him smile against my skin. "It always felt magical when I was a kid. Thank you for agreeing to this, Mrs. James."

"There's no need to thank me. It's beautiful, Mr. James. The perfect spot for us to celebrate our fresh start."

Elijah and I remarried quickly. It was a small affair in his family home, attended by only his family plus Granny Lucille and Vivienne. I didn't invite my parents, because they would have brought toxic energy with them.

I was worried that the same might be true for Nathan and Mason, but they were both on their best behavior. I even got a hug from each of them. We'll probably never be best friends, but we don't need to be—we just need to let things rest. We all love Elijah, and for his sake, we're capable of calling a truce.

I know Elijah loved it—especially the small party afterward, with all his loved ones in the same place for the first time in so many years. Luz cooked a feast for us, and a few friends joined us later—including Martha.

As I predicted, Elijah was more than happy to help her out. I haven't asked too many questions, but Martha seems happy with the divorce settlement that freed her from Freddie's control. And a funny thing happened not long after she was secure and set up—a large quantity of cocaine was discovered in Freddie's car. He swears up and down it wasn't his, and from the smirk on Elijah's face when the news broke, I suspect he was telling the truth. But it's no more than the slimy turd deserved.

After the wedding party, we went back to the little house in Brooklyn, and Elijah carried me over the threshold. It was corny but sweet, and I couldn't have been happier. The Manhattan mansion will never be right for us, not after everything that happened there. We've talked about finding something new, but neither of us is any hurry to leave the house that ushered us into this new chapter.

And now, we're here in the beautiful Spanish sunshine after a day filled with fine food, swimming, and simply enjoying each other's company. Plus the sex. Oh my. There has been so much sex. It feels like we've only just discovered it despite the two plus decades that have passed since we first made love.

His big hands roam my body, and I gasp as he slides them under my bikini top. His fingers play with my nipples, and the kisses on my neck drive me crazy.

"We haven't made love in the sea yet," he murmurs, pressing his rock-hard length into me.

I giggle. "I think that's probably the only place we haven't."

He hums his agreement, his lips never leaving my skin. "The balcony. The kitchen island. The sofa. The shower. The Jacuzzi tub. On the sand." He presses a kiss on my neck after each place he lists. "But not the sea."

"Well, maybe now's the time for that. Unless you're too tired?"

He spins me around and rapidly hoists my legs up and around his waist. "Tired? I'll show you tired, you cheeky minx."

I laugh and hold onto his shoulders, loving the way the droplets of salty water glisten on his muscular body. I lean down to kiss him, and he shoves aside the flimsy fabric of my bikini panties. One finger slips inside me, and his thumb is on my clit. He knows exactly how to work my body. He knows all my secrets. But I know his as well. I reach between us and grip the thick base of his shaft. "I want you inside me."

He twists his finger. "I am inside you, mi amor." Despite his teasing, he knows exactly what I want, and a few seconds later, he's sliding me onto his thick cock, filling me so completely that I call out his name. Before long, we're both crying out in pleasure, the waves gently lapping around us. He buries his head against my neck, and I hold him there. A perfect moment, frozen in time.

"I love you so much," he murmurs. "Can we stay here forever?"

"No. But we'll be together forever, and that's even better."

We stay entwined and watch the spectacular sunset turn the sky pink. It's breathtaking. But as long as I'm with Elijah, it doesn't matter where we are. Brooklyn, Queens, Timbuktu.

Wherever we are, that is home.

EPILOGUE TWO
ELIJAH—DECEMBER

The look on my wife's face is priceless. My eyes should be on stage, but for me, the greatest show on earth is sitting right by my side.

We're in the crowded auditorium of one of the most prestigious dance schools in Manhattan. They're putting on their Christmas show, and it has been magnificent—a mix of different styles of choreography and music, with kids ages four to fifteen showcasing their remarkable talents. We're here to see Shawn, who started his scholarship at the school in September. Our whole row is packed with his cheerleaders —Sissie, the bikers, his mom and siblings. And in the middle of it all, Amber. The woman who made it all happen.

She has her hands clasped together in front of her and is gazing up at the boy she's become so fond of as he dances on the stage, her tawny eyes alight with joy. Her plump lips are parted, and she looks fucking gorgeous. Yeah, even here, I want her. More than that, though, I admire her.

My wife has become a force of nature in a whole new way, a woman on a mission. She used her settlement money to start a foundation, and Shawn was the first recipient. She made the most of her contacts to get him an audition here, and the rest was down to him. Nobody was surprised when he was admitted and given the largest scholarship the dance school has ever given. The Intrepid Young Voices Foundation pays the remainder of his tuition in addition to all the "extras" required by a school like this.

Sanjay was the first driver employed by the foundation, and more have been added since, so kids aren't limited by a lack of transportation. Basically, she's helping kids get where they need to go in so many different ways—there's a talented young boxer who's now receiving top-level coaching, a superstar math student who's taking college-level math courses, and a teenager from the Bronx funded in her quest to become an architect. It's not only the Leslie Odom Jr. Community Center that has benefited, either, but young people from all over New York. She's taken all those skills from her years as a charity fundraiser and combined them with her passion to make a difference. I couldn't be prouder of my clever, kind, and yeah, jaw-droppingly beautiful wife.

The show draws to a close, and she's the first to her feet, applauding and yelling and shocking the hell out of me when she puts two fingers in her mouth and whistles as Shawn takes his bow. Even after all this time, I am learning new things about the woman I love.

Shawn's mom has tears streaming down her face, and the way she gazes at my wife really brings it home to me— Amber has completely changed this young man's destiny. His whole family's future could now look very different.

I cheer along with the best of them, then wait with my wife as everyone files out of the auditorium, headed for the champagne and canapé reception in the foyer. I hold her back in the darkened auditorium and pull her into my arms as soon as we're alone.

She lets out a delicious little squeal, and I smooth her hair back from her face. I kiss her cheekbones, her neck, and finally her lips. Her arms wind around me, her fingers twining in my hair.

She laughs as we part. "I see that ballet now makes you horny as well, Mr. James."

I run my hand down her back and rest it on her perfect ass. "No, that's all you, Mrs. James. I'm always horny for you. And proud. So fucking proud. What you've done ... It's amazing."

She blushes and waves the comment away. "No, it's not —Shawn is amazing. And all those other kids. But I'd be lying if I said it wasn't satisfying. I love watching them blossom, you know. Watching them grow. It's so exciting to see what they might become in life."

I realize as she says it that in some ways, these young people are like her own children now. She's invested in their futures, working with their families to give them the best possible outcome. I wonder if that's enough for her. We're not too old for surrogacy or to adopt, but so far, neither of us has mentioned it. Partly because we've been too busy enjoying each other. We've moved into a new home together, a smaller place where we can build new memories, and although there's room for children, that's not something we've discussed.

"I just talked about them like they're my own kids, didn't I?" she says, her thoughts clearly mirroring mine.

"Yes, but there's nothing wrong with that. You can be

mom-like without being a mom."

She runs her hand down the side of my face, and I turn to kiss her palm. Her eyes are on mine, and I can feel the strength of our connection. We have vowed to always be honest with each other, to always communicate. Hitting rock bottom was a starting point for us to rise back up, together. Now nothing and nobody will ever separate me and my wife again—including us. "I'm happy with this, Elijah. With the life we've built and with being an aunt. How about you? Because if not, we can sit down and talk about our options."

Nathan and Melanie have a new baby, Henry, and Amelia is due soon. The James clan is expanding, and we're playing an active role in that. We're on-call babysitters, and Amber has helped Amelia prepare the nursery for their new addition in the Tribeca loft she shares with Drake. Being around mothers and babies no longer seems to hurt her the way it used to. I think she's made her peace with it, and so have I.

Besides, spending more time with kids has taught me one thing—they're fucking exhausting. I love having them around, but I also love giving them back. Life with Amber is perfect. We're like a pair of head-over-heels teenagers who can't get enough of each other. It might be selfish of me, but I want to keep it that way.

"I'm happy with what we have too," I say, putting my arm around her shoulders and reluctantly walking with her toward the party on the other side of the auditorium doors. She looks up at me, and I can't resist sneaking in one last kiss. "You, baby, are enough for me. You always were, and you always will be. I love you so much, exactly as you are. Exactly as we are."

She slips her arm around my waist and gives me a

radiant smile, and we walk together into a room full of friends and happy faces. A lot has changed over the last few months, but one thing remains the same—I cannot keep my eyes or my hands off her. We walked through hell to get where we are today, and I wouldn't change a single second of it. Because our love is stronger than it has ever been, and there is nothing in the world that can stand in our way.

Not quite ready to say goodbye to Elijah and Amber? Want to find out what happens next for them? You can find out in the bonus epilogue, and if you're reading this in paperback, you can get the link from Sadie's Facebook reader group - Sadie Kincaid's ladies and Sizzling Alphas.

Have you read Nathan and Mel, or Drake and Amelia's story yet? If not you can find out all about them in Broken and Promise Me Forever

The rest of the James brothers' stories are available for preorder now

Mason

Maddox

ALSO BY SADIE KINCAID

If you'd like to know more about the famous Ryans and their wife, Jessie, you can find out all about them in the full New York Ruthless series. Available on Amazon and Kindle Unlimited

Ryan Rule

Ryan Redemption

Ryan Retribution

Ryan Reign

Ryan Renewed

And the complete short stories and novellas attached to this series are available in one collection

A Ryan Recollection

Have you tried Sadie's bestselling paranormal/ fantasy series yet? If you love possessive broody vampires, witches, wolves and all things magic, then try the Broken Bloodlines series here

Forged in Blood

Promised in Blood

Bound in Blood

The complete, bestselling Chicago Ruthless is available now. Following the lives of the notoriously ruthless Moretti siblings - this series will take you on a rollercoaster of emotions. Packed with angst, action and plenty of steam.

Dante

Joey

Lorenzo

Keres

If you'd prefer to head to LA to meet Alejandro and Alana, and Jackson and Lucia, you can find out all about them in Sadie's internationally bestselling LA Ruthless series. Available on Amazon and FREE in Kindle Unlimited.

Fierce King

Fierce Queen

Fierce Betrayal

Fierce Obsession

If you'd like to read about London's hottest couple. Gabriel and Samantha, then check out Sadie's London Ruthless series on Amazon. FREE in Kindle Unlimited.

Dark Angel

Fallen Angel

Dark/ Fallen Angel Duet

If you enjoy super spicy short stories, Sadie also writes the Bound series feat Mack and Jenna, Books 1, 2, 3 and 4 are available now.

Bound and Tamed

Bound and Shared

Bound and Dominated

Bound and Deceived

About the Author

Sadie Kincaid is a dark contemporary and paranormal romance author who loves to read and write about hot alpha males and strong, feisty females.

Sadie loves to connect with readers so why not get in touch via social media?

Join Sadie's reader group for the latest news, book recommendations and plenty of fun. Sadie's ladies and Sizzling Alphas

Acknowledgments

As always I would love to thank all of my incredible readers, and especially the members of Sadie's Ladies and Sizzling Alphas. You are all superstars. And thank you to my group mods, Connie and Sydney for helping keep that amazing group running smoothly.

To my amazing beta readers, Kate and Dani, who helped shape Elijah into the man he is today. (Jaime also says thank you, Kate, for making her job so much easier—ykwim).

And for all of the readers who have bought any of my books, everything I write is for you and you all make my dreams come true.

As always, I couldn't do this without my editor, Jaime. I know without a doubt these books would not be what they are without you. Thank you from the bottom of my heart.

To my author friends who help make this journey all that more special.

To my lovely PA's Kate and Andrea, for their support and everything they do to make my life easier.

And my eternal gratitude to Bobby Kim. Thank you for continuing to push me to be better and for making each book release even better than the last.

To my incredible boys who inspire me to be better every single day. And last, but no means least, a huge thank you to

Mr. Kincaid—all my book boyfriends rolled into one. I truly couldn't do this without you!

Made in United States
North Haven, CT
17 May 2025

68942130R00275